THE HOMECOMING

'This most readable novel has its own
authenticity'   *Homes and Gardens*

'A lively plot amid the troubled rural scene of
fifteenth century England'   *Daily Telegraph*

'A fascinating family chronicle. The
characters are vividly alive; strongly drawn.
Her unsentimental picture of life in an
isolated mediaeval village is sharp with
telling detail'   *Eastern Daily Press*

'A richly textured novel ... Gives the sordid
side of life in the Middle Ages most
impressively'   *Liverpool Daily Post*

Also by the same author,
and available in Coronet Books:

The Homecoming

Norah Lofts

CORONET BOOKS
Hodder and Stoughton

First published in Great Britain 1975 by
Hodder and Stoughton Limited

Coronet Edition 1977

Printed and bound in Great Britain for
Hodder and Stoughton Paperbacks, a
division of Hodder and Stoughton Ltd.,
Mill Road, Dunton Green, Sevenoaks,
Kent (Editorial Office: 47 Bedford Square,
London, WC1 3DP) by
Cox & Wyman Ltd, London, Reading and Fakenham

ISBN 0 340 21803 7

CHAPTER ONE

Sir Godfrey Tallboys and Sybilla, his wife, lay together in Knight's Acre's second-best bed. They had been separated for almost eight years.

The first dizzying ecstasy over, she felt, under her fingertips the ridged scars on his back, and said, 'Dearest, what did they do to you?'

He decided not to mention the dreaded *khurbash*, or the two floggings. Why permit the memory of past humiliation and pain to intrude upon this joy?

'For much of the time I carried slabs of marble on my back,' he said. It was true.

'And she — that girl — saved you from that?'

'Yes. She saved me from that.'

'I'm glad that I gave her the best bed,' Sybilla said.

She already knew — it had been said at the moment of meeting — that Godfrey owed his freedom to that girl, so beautiful in a dark, foreign way, but from exactly what conditions she had freed him Sybilla could not imagine in any great detail. There were no slaves in England. A few serfs, rapidly diminishing in number, but no slaves.

Now, with her man miraculously restored to her, the man to whom she had been, except for one incredible moment, strictly faithful, she saw in the eye of her mind, Godfrey being used like a pack-pony. The furrowed back was more eloquent than words.

Sir Godfrey wished that Tana had not been mentioned just then. He had put himself into a position with which his honest, single-minded nature was ill-equipped to deal. All through the years he had thought about Sybilla, loved Sybilla, made doomed, abortive attempts to escape and return to her, his first love. Yet, on a bleak mountainside between Moorish Zagela and Christian Spain, faced by imminent death by starvation, in company with the girl who had saved him, and loved him, he had experienced something new.

He was not innocent or unworldly; in fact until he went to

Spain on that ill-fated expedition, he had moved in the most sophisticated society. He knew that adultery was anything but rare; there were men who acknowledged their bastards without shame, but he had never suffered even the temptation to infidelity. This he regarded, not as virtue but as good fortune. He had married the woman he loved and loved the woman to whom he was married. Even at the height of his passion for Tana his singularly uncomplicated mind found it difficult to admit that a man could be in love with two women, and in two very differing ways. Now he was forced to face another contradiction. His homecoming would have been happier, had he come alone; and even to think thus was proof of the blackest ingratitude, since without Tana there would have been no homecoming at all.

In the next room, in the best bed which seemed to her anything but luxurious — she had spent some time in the royal harem of Zagela — Tana lay thinking long thoughts, backwards to the moment when she had fallen in love with Godfree, the scheming and the plotting that had led to their freedom; forwards to the time when she would come into her own. As she must, she must. She knew what was taking place on the other side of the wall and was not actively jealous because she had always lived in a polygamous society. In the tribe into which she had been born, a man had as many wives, or concubines as he could support and divided his favours between them. Certain courtesies were due to the first wife whose position was reinforced if she bore a son. That old woman, now in Godfree's bed, certainly scored there. One tall boy called Henry, the image of his father; another, younger, John, and yet another, Richard about whom Godfree had asked as soon as he had embraced the other boys and the girl, called Margaret whom Tana's keen eye had instantly assessed — very pretty, probably resembling her mother when young and definitely simple-minded.

She is his wife, Tana thought, and I saluted her with respect. She accepted me; and in accepting me, the child I shall bear. I flung open my cloak, and she saw.

I shall accept her, too. But she is old, and lame, and poor. Poor in fact past belief. A servant to servants . . .

It was true, when the miracle happened, and Godfrey came

home, Sybilla had been drawing water at the well in the yard. The last unkindly glimmer of the winter sunset had struck, revealing the three to one another with merciless clarity. Then they had all gone into the kitchen, where the only fire in the house was burning on this cold afternoon. There was a bare scrubbed table, exactly like those in cheap hostelries, plates and drinking vessels that did not match and a meal which though plentiful, was lacking in all refinement — boiled pork with beans, and bread. They drank water. Henry and John and an older youth called Tom came in from work in the fields, and they were all dressed much alike — as ploughmen; only a certain clarity of feature, a likeness to Godfree distinguished the sons of the house from the hireling.

There was a great deal of talk, largely incomprehensible to Tana. Once he had made his decision to bring her to England Sir Godfrey had begun to teach her English and she had learned quickly, anxious to please him, but confronted by six people all speaking English — and to her ear, very rapid English — she was unable to make out more than a few isolated words. Although it was an exciting occasion, a family reunion which animated everyone except the girl Margaret, Tana was not allowed to feel excluded. From time to time Godfree had turned towards her and spoken in Arabic. That pleased her because it excluded everybody else. Right here, in the very heart of his family, he and she had something that nobody else could share. Her shrewd, cunning mind took note of this and she decided that however quickly she learned to understand English, she would speak it as little as possible. While he spoke to her in Arabic she could command his full attention.

CHAPTER TWO

Not, outside his knightly business, the most observant of men, Godfrey Tallboys could not be blind to the circumstances in which he had found Sybilla. It grieved him to think that had things in Spain gone otherwise, he would have come home with money in his hand.

'Sweeting, it seems to be my fate — ever since I had a house to come back to – to come back to it a pauper. I went to that Welsh war to get money; to the Winchester Tournament for the prize; and then to Spain. And again I return penniless and find you in worse case than I ever imagined. What happened to Walter?'

'He died,' Sybilla said shortly, not wishing to say what had happened to Walter in any detail. 'But that was long ago. Until the plague struck I had a good serving maid. Her name was Madge. She died in the plague. And the village was so stricken that women are at plough.'

He had already enquired about his elder brother, Sir James at Moyidan and learned that the plague had not touched that place.

'James could have helped you. William would have . . .' William, the good Bishop of Bywater had succumbed to the plague.

Sybilla said, 'It was my fault. I annoyed them both. When . . . when it was understood that you were dead, my dearest, both William and James offered me and the children a home. I chose to stay here. Later I annoyed them again. Security — as they saw it — was offered from another source — and I refused that also.'

'Marriage?' Deep in the marble quarry, tending the palace garden in which the ladies of the royal harem walked in the cool of the day, scrambling and starving on the mountains, riding helter-skelter across Spain, he had often visualised Sybilla as re-married.

'Yes. But there is no need to consider that — except to remember him as kindly and honest and charming. He is dead now.' She no more wanted to think about Sir Simon than she did about Walter, so she added hastily, 'I think you should let James know that you are home. Darling, at the worst, in the most desperate hour when we here had no medicine and little food, Emma was generous. Very generous.'

'I will go tomorrow.'

'That would be well. But I think . . .' For a moment Sybilla reverted to what she had been before Sir Godfrey had rescued her — the pupil, the novice whom the cunning old Abbess of Lamarsh had been training to succeed her. 'I think some rather ordinary explanation of *her* presence would be desirable.'

'She saved me,' he said simply.

'That I know, and am truly grateful — as I have endeavoured to show. But ... Godfrey, so far as I can see she is neither wife nor widow and by summer will be a mother ...'

'God!' he said. 'God!'

So many things now fell into place. Tana's determination to drown herself rather than be left behind in Spain; her scrupulous observation of her promise to behave well — never once on the ship had she attempted to lure him; the buying of the cloak and the refusal to remove it — 'Godfree, it is so cold.' And how slowly she had run, once they were on English soil and he was hurrying towards the place where he expected William to be; how sedately she — such a wild rider — had ridden from Bywater to Intake. It all fitted.

'I hoped you need never know,' he said in a voice of the utmost misery. 'I cannot exonerate myself. I will try to explain ...'

She put her hand, once soft and white, now coarsened and hardened, over his mouth. 'Love, there is no need. I understand. She had saved you. You were alone together. You did not know whether I was alive or dead — or remarried. There is no blame. I shall look upon her child as my own, the child of my middle years. My Benjamin.'

This magnanimous, this truly noble statement served only to emphasise his feeling of guilt. How could a man with such a wife ...? And although she had summed up the situation almost exactly so far as external things went, speaking indeed almost the very words he would have used had he attempted to explain, there was much that she did not know. That upsurge of joy, so overwhelming that he had thought — perhaps even said — that after this he was willing to die.

'But we must be practical,' Sybilla said, and he recognised, even in his misery, the manner of his oldest sister, the Abbess of Lamarsh. 'She is young. When — when this is over, she will need a husband. She must have a name, some status. In that language you speak together, that Spanish, what is the equivalent of *lady*?'

'I do not know. We were only a few days in Spain — I mean before the disaster — and we saw no ladies. After the Moors took me I was a slave, consorting with slaves. And it is not Spanish that we speak, it is Arabic.'

'And have *they* no ladies?'

9

Abruptly, disconcertingly, Sir Godfrey thought of Arcol, his wonderful but arbitrary warhorse — now happily siring foals in the pastures beside the Loja River. Of Arcol somebody in the stableyard at Zagela had used the Arabic word for noble — *serriff*.

Humbly he offered the word.

'It will do well,' Sybilla said. 'Not unlike our own word, Sheriff. Lady Serriff. Yes, that comes easily. Can you explain to her?'

CHAPTER THREE

Sybilla knelt in the cold church where years ago she had knelt and prayed for Godfrey's safe return, and then, believing him dead, prayed for his soul. Now, with tears of joy and gratitude pouring down her face she thanked God and the Blessed Virgin for bringing him back to her.

She wished she could have brought something, a thank-offering some white lilies and roses for the altar and the little niche in which Our Lady's image stood, its once bright colours fading and peeling from age and exposure to damp. Sir Godfrey's great-grandmother had built the little church and endowed it with what, in her day, had seemed an adequate income. But the value of money had changed since then, and though old Father Ambrose put the needs of God's house before his own and lived more meagrely than any peasant, he could not keep the church in repair.

He met Sybilla at the door and asked the inevitable question. 'Any news of Sir Godfrey, my lady?' He must have asked it a thousand times since Sir Godfrey, mounted on Arcol, had ridden away on a crisp autumn morning in the year 1452. At first she had replied, 'No, not yet, Father.' The old man had said, 'I will remember him in my prayers.' Then there had been one letter, written by somebody else, but signed by Sir Godfrey, and saying that the worst was now over. Informed of this, Father Ambrose said, 'I am glad, my lady. I will pray for his safe homecoming.' Then the blow fell. She was obliged to say. 'He died in Spain.' Father Ambrose made the right answer. 'I am sorry. I will say a Mass for his soul.' But his mind had never absorbed that piece of information. It could take in nothing new and he went on and on asking the question, making the same reply. Yet when the plague struck, Father Ambrose had understood, had behaved admirably, his mind stepping backwards to former outbreaks and knowing exactly what actions to dictate.

Now the lady said, 'Father, he is home. Home! He came home yesterday. Safe and well. Is it not wonderful? After all these years.'

The rooted, trained mind produced the right response. 'I am happy for you, my lady.' But the ability to grasp anything really new had deserted him. He recognised Sir Godfrey when he saw him, but any chance encounter with Sybilla alone would provoke the same anxious question.

On this winter morning Tana made her ritual obeisance to the brightening East. It was all that remained of the old Sun Worship which her remote ancestors had brought with them from Persia when Alexander's empire collapsed. Settled in North Africa her small tribe had held its own, having the best horses and the best swords, the strongest will to survive. The great wave of Arabic people which swept over the north of Africa and from there into Spain, into France, in the ninth century had affected her tribe in some ways, made them adopt the Arabic language, methods of weighing and measuring, but they had not become followers of Mahomet. They had lived too long without any rules to take kindly to those which Allah, through his Prophet, had laid down. No alcohol; no pig-meat; women relegated to the status of beasts of burden for the poor, segregated toys for the rich. Until the final disaster, the battle in which she had fought alongside her father and her brothers, Tana had lived a life of almost unlimited freedom; un-trammelled by religious obligations apart from the ritual bow to the Sun, the begetter and the giver of all things. What moral content had ever been involved had been forgotten, centuries before she was born. There were rules of course, you never forgave an enemy, or betrayed a friend — a friend being one whose salt you had eaten. Tana had most scrupulously avoided Sybilla's salt, offered in the plain wooden bowl.

Sir Godfrey's welcome at his brother's manor of Moyidan was hearty and unfeigned. Sir James and the Lady Emma his wife, had always been fond of him — while thinking him a fool. A fool to have married a penniless orphan; that most of all. And then to allow her to spoil her great quarrelsome boys to such an extent that they were intolerable. Indeed, in their view, the only sensible thing he had ever done was to build a house of his own so that his unruly brood need never again trouble their relatives.

Dead, as they thought, they had mourned him; alive they welcomed him back with joy. A miracle, no less.

Sir James's winter gout, which differed in some ways from his summer gout, was in full spate, but he forgot the pain in his feet as he listened to Sir Godfrey's account of what had happened to him in the past eight years and four months. Not that the story was well told; Godfrey lacked the ability to describe, to tell a coherent story, just as he lacked the ability to manage monetary matters. But bit by bit, prompted by a question here and there, the gist of the story was told. And James and Emma intercepted now and then to show that they had not been completely neglectful of the woman left alone in a remote place. Godfrey must know that when he was deemed dead they had offered Sybilla and the children a home. So had poor William. That established, James and his wife exchanged a look, a marital signal. Better not mention that infatuated young man, Sir Simon Randle who had offered more than a home.

'Yes,' Sir Godfrey said, 'Sybilla said that you had been very kind and very generous.'

'Well,' Lady Emma said, 'due to most careful precautions, we were spared the plague. It was our duty to help the less fortunate.'

In this household money was very highly regarded and mention of it was never long absent from even dinner-table talk. It was painfully plain that Godfrey had returned as poor as he went away. Also it was more than eight years since he went away; his high reputation was forgotten, his skill possibly impaired; he would not be in such demand. Admittedly he carried his forty-four years well, the silver streaks in his fawn coloured hair were not unbecoming; there were new lines in his face; but hard physical labour had kept him slim and lithe and his blue eyes had retained their astonishingly candid look.

Over the meal Sir James pondered for some way in which he could help his impoverished young brother without dipping into his own purse; and presently said, 'After dinner, Godfrey, I will show you what I have done at Moyidan, to make the place more profitable. You could do the same at Intake.'

'And more easily,' Lady Emma said. 'So many of your tenants being dead.'

Gouty as he was, Sir James made shift to climb to the top of the old castle keep. He wrapped his head in a woollen shawl lest the cold wind should bring on another attack of gout in his eyes.

From the castle ramparts the whole of the manor of Moyidan and far more was visible; the road from Bywater, the course of the river. The castle had been built to overlook and to defend this vulnerable, flat hinterland.

'See any difference?' Sir James asked.

Where terrain was concerned Sir Godfrey had the trained soldier's eye.

'Changed completely.'

Changed indeed. Moyidan had once been a typical manor; three great fields divided into strips, of ploughland, divided from one another by unploughed banks called baulks; and one of the three lying fallow in turn. There had been a number of low humble houses, huddled together, and an open common with geese and goats, oxen.

There was still the huddle of houses, and the church, but everything else had changed.

'I enclosed,' James said. 'Turned everything I could into a sheep run. Fellows with inalienable rights I accommodated with the equivalent . . .' He pointed with his puffy hand at a patchwork of small fields, hedged or bordered by bits of fencing, even by stones. 'They much prefer it. They say they fare better and certainly there are fewer quarrels about boundaries and about which day ploughing, or seeding or harvesting should start. So they are happy and so am I. With my sheep run. Look a little farther, Godfrey.' Sir Godfrey looked and saw a vast open space, reaching to the horizon, some sheep, a man and a dog.

'Land that it took thirty men to till,' Sir James said, pulling the shawl closer, 'turned over to sheep, needs only one.'

'And what happened to the others. The ones with no in⸗ alienable rights?'

'Some are employed here, either by me or by the small farmers. Some sought work elsewhere. A number of likely young men went to sea. Oh, and of course, there is always seasonal work. Shearing, for instance.'

'And the common land?'

'Ah! There again, a few had rights, and were compensated by an extra half acre on their holdings. But most, although they had enjoyed common rights for many years, had no legal claim. The common land became part of my sheep run. With wool rising steadily in price, this is the most profitable move I ever made.'

Sir Godfrey had no quarrel with that; a man had a right to do what he liked with his own.

'I thought I would show you,' Sir James said, turning away towards the worn stone stairs, 'because you could do the same. And far more easily. In a manner of speaking, Intake is already enclosed. It was never a manor.'

That was true. Intake — as its name implied — was land clawed from the forest by twelve men, malcontent serfs, of whom Sir Godfrey's great-grandfather had been happy to be rid. He'd given them permission to take what land they could, the right to call themselves free, five years rent free and after that a rent which yearly became more absurd. This unusual village had been left by Sir Godfrey's father to his youngest son who had thought himself lucky to have anything at all. The rent, fixed, 'in perpetuity', was now all but worthless; but the land had enabled him to build his house on a space once cleared, then deserted as a result of an earlier plague. And Walter, the most wonderful, most faithful servant — and the most resourceful, had got one field under cultivation by the time Sir Godfrey left for Spain. Now there were three, looked after by Henry, Tom Robinson and John.

A natural transference of thought. Following James down the stairs Sir Godfrey said,

'I was sorry to hear about Walter. Often while I was ... away, I sought comfort in the thought that Walter had charge of things.'

Typical, typical, Sir James thought. Never an eye for the real issue. Here am I trying to tell him how to make a little

14

money in this difficult world and he talks about that rogue! This feeling lent a certain sourness to his voice as he said, reaching, thank God, the last stairs,

'It was disgraceful. Mark you, no more than could have been expected. I never liked him. Nor did Emma.'

Deaf?

'I spoke of Walter, James.'

'So did I. Whom else? Running off like that. No notice given. Leaving Sybilla stranded, after the way she had favoured and spoiled him!'.

'But he died. Sybilla said so.'

'She may have had information. Since. At the time we were given to understand that he had simply walked away. No matter, come to the fire. It is a bitter wind.' In the warm room, over the mulled wine — Emma was a good provider — Sir James spread out the parchment, the original deed of gift that concerned Intake.

'Twelve men,' he said, 'all named. Hodge, Martin, Robin, Wade, Fisher, Smith, Archer, Alan, Edmund, Egbert, Eldred, Alfred. This grant to them, and to heirs of their body, in perpetuity. How many, Godfrey, do you think can claim to be direct heirs?'

'How could I know, James? It is different for you, you have always lived here, on your manor. I have never lived at Intake, in the real sense. Granted I was there for a while before I went to Spain, but lame as a three-legged donkey. Then I was exercising Arcol, getting my armour into trim. I do not even know their faces; far less their rights.'

'That is what I am advising. How many direct heirs? I take it that the priests have kept a Kin Book, to prevent incest.'

'I suppose so,' Sir Godfrey said vaguely.

'Then it should be easy. And remember, daughters and illegitimate sons have no rights.'

Sybilla, explaining why she had no servants, had mentioned that since the plague women had been at plough. How many of them, Sir Godfrey wondered, working on land to which they had no right?

He made a remark which was characteristically unworldly — and in view of what Sir James had just told him, extremely tactless.

'I should be loth to turn anybody out. They might be homesick. I know I was when I first left Moyidan, and in captivity I was homesick all the time.'

Useless to argue, Sir James knew. Godfrey could be stubborn as rock. He said briskly,

'Time enough to think about *that* when we know where we stand. At least it would be interesting to know how many of these,' he tapped the parchment, 'have direct heirs still alive.'

Godfrey would pursue the enquiry half-heartedly, or make a muddle of it, or be put off with lies.

'I'll lend you my man, Jocelyn. He managed the change here. But the common is unquestionably yours — there is here no mention of common land or rights to it. I'll start you off with a nucleus to your flock. A young ram and six ewes. And a boy who understands sheep.'

'That is most generous, James. And now, I need help in another matter. Could Moyidan provide us with a cook woman and a serving boy? Sybilla is doing it all. And now we have a guest.'

Emma who had entered the room during the conversation, said, 'A guest?' Her tone expressed astonishment and disapproval. How could that poor house possibly entertain anybody? But how like Sybilla and Godfrey to attempt it!

'Yes.' Explaining things never came easily to Sir Godfrey, and now he was aware of trying out Tana's new identity for the first time. 'It is a Spanish lady. She is a widow. I told you I was helped to escape. She is the one. I had to bring her with me, because, in helping me, she put herself at risk.' He hoped that sounded convincing. He need not have bothered. The eyes exchanged another signal.

'Of what age?' Lady Emma asked.

'Oh. Young. Sixteen or so.'

'And a widow?'

'She was married young.'

Into both minds the thought shafted — A possible bride for Richard!

For the last two years they had been searching and without success. Curiously enough, the fathers of marriageable daughters found themselves able to overlook Moyidan Richard's poor physique and mental backwardness. They looked to the wide acres, the wealth to which the boy would be heir. Mothers were the difficulty. One had even gone so far as to say that she did not wish to be grandmother to a pack of idiots!

A Spanish woman, without relatives, and probably herself knowing English imperfectly and unlikely to notice that Richard, when he spoke, sounded simple, and when silent, looked witless, might be the answer to some really heart-felt prayers.

Tentatively they put forward the suggestion and Sir Godfrey found himself unaccountably in violent opposition, although from the moment when he knew that Tana had organised not only his escape, but her own, he had planned a suitable marriage for her — to some man who would not marry her simply for all that wealth that she carried.

In his heart he knew very well that Tana was fully able to look after herself; but he also knew that Emma and James should not be rebuffed too sharply, because they had been kind.

He said, 'At the moment she is pregnant. Better leave it for a while.'

'I can find you servants,' Lady Emma said. There might in some places — where the proper precautions had not been taken — be a shortage of labour. Moyidan, untouched by the plague, but touched very much by the enclosure had labour to spare. Some families, during the upheaval, had split up, others had clung together, the man with the inalienable rights supporting, however unwillingly, dependent relatives . . .

CHAPTER FOUR

Sybilla was glad of the servants. Freed from kitchen duty she could rest the lame leg which had bothered her ever since her fall, during the plague time; she could give Margaret a little more attention; more attention, too, to her own hair and hands. But the fact remained that Knight's Acre was now supporting five more people than it had done in the immediate past; all mouths to be fed; Godfrey, Tana, Jill and Eddy, the servants sent from Moyidan, and Young Shep who had come with the seven sheep.

She was not, by nature, mercenary, but she was practical.

Knight's Acre, thanks to Henry who had shouldered the burden of it, had just survived, just managed to be self-supporting. Now it was over-loaded.

'I must look about,' Sir Godfrey said. 'I may have lost skill. I have no destrier, no armour, but in some minor tourney, if Astallon can fit me out, I might win something. In the old days even the smallest prize he offered was a silver gilt cup.'

It sounded terrible, even to think that a man, so lately home after so long an absence, must be off again. But Sybilla knew that Lord Astallon's tourneys at Beauclaire were relatively mild affairs and that Alyson, Lady Astallon, Godfrey's sister, would give him a hearty welcome.

'There is also,' he said, 'the matter of Tana's jewels.'

'That pearl-studded hair net?'

'Oh, no. She brought away with her a king's ransom, in rubies, emeralds, diamonds and pearls. Nowhere, except in London,' he said, 'would such things find a market. And Alyson would know how to go about it.'

'That is very true.'

CHAPTER FIVE

'I abandoned tournaments,' Lord Astallon said. 'In this quarrel between Lancaster and York, I have tried to remain neutral. But what we live in now is not peace. A truce, frail as egg-shell. Take Bowdegrave, at Abhurst. He held his usual tourney and some silly girl flung a rose — a red rose — to the knight she favoured. He put it in his helm and the civil war broke out again, there, with servants sent to strip the garden of flowers and the tourney ground becoming a battlefield.'

'If many feel as you do, the outlook for me is gloomy,' Sir Godfrey said.

'From what I hear, genuine warfare is likely to break out again at any minute.'

'Of that I have had a bellyful.'

So far, a disappointing visit. He had hoped to see Richard, his second son. Sybilla had told him how Henry and Richard had quarrelled and actually fought so often and so fiercely that it was impossible for one house to contain them; and how Henry had refused so absolutely to be sent to Beauclaire to become a page, squire and eventually a knight, that Richard had gone instead. Sir Godfrey had not spent much time with his children even in the days before he went to Spain, but he was attached to them all, and actually had a sneaking feeling of sympathy for Richard who had never accepted his place as second son.

Lady Astallon, Sir Godfrey's beautiful sister, Alyson, explained in her remote, languid way why Richard was no longer at Beauclaire.

'He was so clever, Godfrey. Within a week he had learned all a page should know. Then he learned to read and write and cypher. He acquired Latin from our chaplain and French from one of my ladies. The Bishop of Winchester came here and was much impressed. He begged to be allowed to take Richard away with him.'

'To become a clerk!' The natural scorn of the man of action for the scribe rang loud and clear.

'It offered the more promising future,' Lord Astallon said.

Well, one son lost to the plough-handle; and one to the pen. And no tournaments. I have come back to a strange world.

There was, however, one area in which his visit to Beauclaire might yet be satisfactory. He produced the jewels with which Tana had entrusted him; only a fraction of her loot from the palace of Zagela; one string of pearls, and a necklace, five sizeable rubies suspended from a golden chain.

'The Spanish lady, Lady Serriff — I told you, she saved me — asked me to dispose of these for her. I thought perhaps you could tell me how to set about it.'

His beautiful sister — in youth all white and gold, and still, growing old, beautiful, white and gold — snatched at the pearls.

'Humphrey, I want them.'

'Then they are yours,' her husband said. He had always been a rich man, well able to indulge his beautiful wife's whims, and the abandonment of the tournaments had saved him considerable sums of money. 'What is the price, Godfrey?'

'That I do not know. I hoped that you . . .'

Typical! A fool, likeable — they were both glad to see him back, safe and sound, but a fool. Offering for sale something that even Lord Astallon could see was practically priceless, and without any idea of its value.

'There is a man I have had dealings with,' Lady Astallon said, and for a moment Sir Godfrey saw the resemblance between his elder, plain sister, Abbess of Lamarsh and his younger, pretty one, mistress of Beauclaire. 'I will send for him. He shall value both,' she glanced from the necklet which she did not covet, to the pearls which she did — and were almost hers already.

The man for whom Lady Astallon sent first thing next morning, was a Jew, and strictly speaking no Jew had set foot on English soil since Edward the First had banished them all, bowing to popular opinion. But a few, here and there, practising Christians so far as anyone could see, and with names subtly changed by the addition, or omission of a letter or two, had come back and established themselves, and flourished.

The Jew came and within minutes understood the situation. Lady Astallon, always a good customer, wanted him to put a low value on the pearls, which she proposed to buy, and to make a good offer for the rubies.

The pearls, one experienced glance told him, were exceptionally fine — dredged up from eastern seas by men who dived and dived until their lungs burst. They were well-matched, and unlike many that came upon the market, not sick from having been locked away in darkness. He could see no actual flaw which would account for a low estimate: his subtle, supple mind could, however, produce a reason.

'My lady, they are superb. But were they offered to me, I should hesitate a little. Few people could afford such a rope, yet to divide them would be a shame, they are so perfectly matched.'

'Too good to be readily marketable,' said the lady who in the ordinary way appeared to drift through life in a dream. 'What of the rubies?'

He cupped the necklet in his hand, estimating the weight; held each stone to the light, revelling in the deep, rich colour.

'Of these the same might be said, but here division is possible, perhaps even desirable. With five, each detracts from the other. Re-set they would be marketable.' Any one of them would make a hat ornament, a pendant, a splendid thumb-ring. He wondered idly how such things had come into the lady's possession; the gold work of the necklet had not been wrought west of Damascus.

Over the price they haggled a little, but amicably. Then Lady Astallon said, with seeming aimlessness.

'These belong to a lady of my acquaintance, recently widowed and suddenly poor. She has others . . .'

The Jew understood that, too. The others, in due time would be offered to him, if he made a good offer now.

Sir Godfrey was astonished and delighted by the sum thus raised, and, ingenuous man that he was, allowed astonishment and delight to be seen.

'You have done well, Alyson! Tana — Lady Serriff — will be pleased.' The name slipped out because part of his mind was recalling that night in the mountains when Tana had tumbled what she called 'loot' out on to a flat-topped rock, and the last rays of light shone on the jewels, while over them she bent with three ropes of pearls falling from her neck into the valley between her firm young breasts. He had felt then, with relief, that she would be well provided for. How well he had no notion.

Lord Astallon was also pleased. He was not — and actually never had been — in love with his wife in the ordinary, earthy way. She had never seemed quite real to him, though she had, amazingly, given him an heir and a daughter. His devotion to her had an almost mystical quality and when he gave her things he was not unlike a peasant making an offering at the foot of Mary's image.

In all other departments of his life he was a hard-headed man and in thinking over his brother-in-law's predicament, had arrived at what he considered a possible solution.

Over the wine-cups Godfrey had spoken, in his unenlightening way, all halts and diversions and gaps, of what had happened to him during his long absence. And of what had happened to those who had gone with him to Escalona in Spain and then to Zagela in Moorish territory.

One name stood out. Lord Robert Barbury, son of the Earl of Thorsdale, said to be the richest lord in England.

'I think,' Lord Astallon said, 'that you should go to Yorkshire, and inform Lord Thorsdale.'

'Impossible. The truth was so horrible. It haunts me still. Even to you, who never saw Lord Robert, I could not give the full story. After all, Humphrey, I am seasoned, but I never saw a death like that.'

'I am not proposing that you should carry a harrowing tale. In fact the contrary. You said yourself that once in Spain, supposedly for a tournament, you — and those with you — became involved with what was virtually a *crusade*. Would that not comfort his parents?'

And would not Lord Thorsdale *do* something for the man who brought such news? An obviously poor man who had gone out of his way to bring comfort. Some kind of appointment.

It was well within Lord Astallon's power to have offered a place in *his* household to his brother-in-law, but that would have involved bringing in Sybilla who managed her children so badly. The fact that Sybilla was to blame for their misbehaviour was proved — was it not? — by the way Richard had conducted himself, once removed from her influence.

Blind, as usual, to all material advantage, Sir Godfrey said, 'I suppose it might comfort all the bereaved. It *was* a crusade, in a way. And they took part — except Sir Ralph Overton. He refused. I gave him a letter for Sybilla. She never received it, so I am afraid . . . Strange,' he said, 'some names I do not even remember. Sir Stephen Flowerdew, the best of company; Sir Thomas Drury, with his great dog . . .'

It was all long ago and far away. His great horse, Arcol, had saved him from death, and Tana had, in the end saved him from slavery. The clearest memory that had stayed with him, even through his own afflictions, was the way in which Lord Robert had died. Roasted within his red-hot armour.

With seeming irrelevance he said, 'I did my utmost,' and looked down at his hands. Thanks to the Moorish way of treating burns, they had healed well, were flexible and in no way unsightly; but they lacked the padding on palm and inside the fingers that they had once had; taut skin over hard bone.

'I should not propose,' Lord Astallon said, 'a visit to all. You would ride for a year — even could you recall names and where the men came from. But I do think that Thorsdale should be informed.'

'I will think about it. But first I must go home and take all this money to Lady Serriff.'

CHAPTER SIX

'And now,' Tana said, 'can I have my own pavilion? A place of my own?'

In her father's great mountain fortress each wife had had her own apartments, her own courtyard, her own servants. When her father went out on a peaceable errand, collecting his dues from the oases that studded the Spice Road from the East, the Gold Road from the South, he took women with him; and each had her pavilion. In places where fuel was scarce food might be cooked on a communal fire fed by camel thorn, but always there was privacy.

And here at Knight's Acre there was none.

With the arrival of two servants, the family had moved into the hall. The old, white-haired, lop-sided first wife no longer cooked or served food as she had done at first, but she spent some time in the kitchen overlooking things there; when she sat in the hall she was always busy with some kind of needlework. With smiles and gestures she invited Tana to join in this despicable pastime, slaves' work! Tana refused to learn. The weather was horrible, cold and dull, day after day; the hall was chilly and uncomfortable, only one settle and some backless stools; nothing of colour or brightness anywhere. And with Godfree gone nobody to talk to. The lanky boy called Henry stared and stared; and sometimes addressed the girl whom he had regarded from the first moment as the most beautiful creature he had ever seen. He told her the names of things — some of which she already knew. 'Fog' however was new to her, both in name and actuality; and detestable it was.

All through Sir Godfrey's absence Tana cheered herself with the thought of her own pavilion, silk-lined, carpet spread, furnished with many cushioned divans upon which one could sit or recline, warmed by braziers upon whose glowing charcoal sweet-smelling substances had been scattered.

Answering her question Sir Godfrey said, 'Yes. You can now build or buy yourself a house.'

His mind made a comment — how strange that two women as different as women could be, had used the same phrase. 'A place of my own'. Sybilla had said it in English — and Knight's Acre was the result; Tana said it in Arabic, and he visualised for her the establishment which he had once, in the days of innocence, planned for her; a snug, comfortable house in Baildon; near enough for him to keep a brotherly eye on her, see that she wasn't cheated or seized upon by some mercenary fellow attracted solely by her wealth.

'I want a pavilion, Godfree.'

'It wouldn't do here, Tana.' He knew what he was talking about; in his time he had lived under canvas and more than once plodded through mud to his bed, or wakened to find his bed almost afloat. And he had seen splendid pavilions, erected to accommodate knights at magnificent tourneys, flattened, uprooted, tattered by wind. 'The English climate,' he said, 'is not suitable for temporary structures. You must have a *house*.'

'About that you know best,' she agreed. 'But I want it here. With you, Godfree.'

That had always been her plea — or rather her demand. And it was her right. She had by resolute will and exploitation of her physical charm, reached a position in the royal harem of Zagela from which she could organise his release from the marble quarry at Andara, that nightmare place, and into the relatively mild enslavement of the palace garden at Zagela; and from there, at imminent risk of her life, she had organised his escape and her own. On one shoulder he bore the debt of gratitude, on the other the burden of guilt. Shuffle both off and think in practical terms.

'It could be arranged,' he said. 'There is ample room. I will see to it.'

He explained to Sybilla — to whom no explanation was actually necessary. Tana was here, she was going to bear a child, naturally she desired what every woman desired — her own place. But when Godfrey said that so far as he could see the best place for Tana's house would be the site on which Walter's little place had stood, Sybilla said, 'Oh no!' in a voice so sharp and positive that he was astounded.

'Why not? It was burnt, I know. But not to the ground. I had a look, the foundations are still there, sound and good . . .'

Yes, and go digging under that bit of charred, tumbled wall, and you will — or the builders will, come across Walter's bones! She remembered all too well, that hasty interment, by lantern light. Walter, the best servant anybody ever had, shot dead by Henry with the weapon that Walter had made for him, and taught him to use. By mistake, a very natural mistake. The servant, so good and faithful, had wished to become lover. And she had screamed . . .

No need to mention Walter now, Sybilla thought. Walter had his memorial, because in his moment of madness he had taught her something, something which had enabled her to understand the relationship between Godfrey and Tana. Only a moment, but it sufficed.

'It is not a good place,' she said. 'In fact it is a charnel house. I told you about the raiders . . . They set the place on fire. A few came out and danced in the yard, but most stayed within, roasting a pig, and were themselves roasted, when the roof fell in . . . Darling, let us not disturb the dead. Let us think of the living. That Tana should wish for a place of her own is understandable, but not *there*. Could we not build out on the other side of the yard? Beyond the still-room? Truth to tell I have never used it, having so little to preserve and so little time.'

Sir Godfrey, in planning his house, drawing lines with a stick in the dust under the old oak, had been ambitious, wanting the best for Sybilla who had so long waited for a place of her own. He had ordered a solar — a room which a lady could retire from the hurly-burly of the hall, and a still-room where she could deal with stuff too delicate for kitchens. He had, in fact grossly overestimated.

'She could, in fact have the still-room for her kitchen. It has a hearth, and shelves.'

He thought, rather sadly, that Sybilla's willingness to sacrifice her still-room reflected upon their hopeless financial position. Short of a miracle, he would never now be able to afford all the costly things that went into still-rooms. Still, he was determined to go on trying to find some kind of knightly employment, however modest; something that would bring in a little money so that the family was not entirely dependent upon Henry's farm. Surely every great lord in England had not adapted Astallon's and Bowdegrave's attitude towards tournaments. Perhaps in the North, further from the storm-centre of London, there were still cups to be won, and hastily sold for cash, as every trophy he had ever won had been.

He would set Master Hobson to work on Tana's apartments,

and then ride for Yorkshire, keeping a sharp ear and a sharp eye open as he went.

Nine years earlier, when Master Hobson undertook the building of Knight's Acre, he had ridden a poor looking horse lest any of his clients should suspect him of being unduly prosperous; now he had no choice in the matter for substantial jobs were rare. There had been a time when men whose businesses had prospered were moving out of towns like Baildon and building houses — often more grand than Knight's Acre — in the countryside. Unsettled times had changed all that; in times of danger people tended to huddle together and ever since the first battle in the civil war Master Hobson's work had consisted mainly of patching, or extending old houses within the town walls. And plain work at that, for he had never managed to replace his disagreeable but gifted son-in-law who had done such beautiful pargetting — and at Knight's Acre died in the doing. Young men these days didn't take to a trade that demanded such skill, such long training.

Master Hobson still said 'Ah', as a sign that he understood, and 'Aaah' long-drawn out to give him time to think before answering a question. He understood what was wanted. Two additional rooms, both on the ground floor; one of fair size, one smaller, with a communicating door between them. There were to be no windows looking out on to the yard; only one in each room giving upon the garden. The larder room was to have a door from the garden, too.

The foreign lady for whom these rooms were to be built stood by Sir Godfrey as he explained things, and somehow Master Hobson got the idea that although she never said a word of English, she understood it. When Sir Godfrey explained that the still-room of the main house was to be the kitchen of the extension, Master Hobson said, 'Aaah. Then that'll mean knocking a door in that wall.' He was thinking of serving food.

Instantly the lady broke into her outlandish talk and Sir Godfrey answered her in the same. She did not wish for a communicating door. The still-room already had a door which gave access to the yard.

'Aaah. But Sir Godfrey, sir, that'll mean every bit of food'll have to be carried right round, if you see what I mean; out of

26

what'll be the kitchen, into the yard, round the house and in at the door facing the garden. Inconvenient to say the least.'

But that was what Tana intended. Her privacy was going to be very private indeed. No servants spying and gossiping.

'That is how Lady Serriff wishes it to be,' Sir Godfrey said, when he and the lady had had another consultation.

Now, as to cost?'

'Aaah. Let's say a hundred and fifty pounds, give or take a bit.'

'God's eyeballs,' Sir Godfrey said, shocked. 'You built *my* house for a hundred! Two rooms, no stairs . . .'

'Sir, things have changed. Excuse me — you've been away a long time. You might think that with so many men idle — through no fault of their own — labour'd be plentiful and cheap. Sir, that ain't so. The Guilds closed in. Even apprentices. Meat once a day, and river fish, even salmon, they don't count as meat. Aaah, and there's another thing to remember, if I may remind you, sir. In *your* house there was that oak, the trunk as king-pin, the two main lower branches as beams. I took that into consideration. Here we start from the bare ground.'

'And when could you start?'

'Aaah. Next week, if the weather holds.'

It held, in fact an exceptionally early and clement spring.

CHAPTER SEVEN

Lies had never come easily to him and faced with Lord Robert's parents, both elderly — Robert being their much youngest son, Godfrey, to his own dismay, found himself breaking down and telling the truth, the appalling truth about how Lord Robert had died in that narrow, balconied street.

He did not realise that the mere telling, in all the horrible detail, too horrible to be explained even at Beauclaire, he found relief, the kind of purging that came from confession and absolution. He told the simple truth — linked to the comforting statement about the crusade.

'It was a crusade,' he said. 'We were fighting the Infidel. And of us all there was not a man more gallant, cheerful, noble than Lord Robert. At the first setting out I had ill-feeling — that summer at Winchester he had unhorsed me, the first knight to do so for many years. I did not care to be reminded. But long before we reached Spain. I knew his worth. I loved him as a son ... What was thrown, I shall never know. A terrible weapon, ten times as fierce as the fiercest fire. And his armour was new-fangled. I did my utmost, to no avail ... Afterwards I knelt there and committed his soul, so far as I could, to the mercy of God.'

(Deep in that marble quarry he had also done his best to commit another good Englishman's soul to God. But he did not think of John Hawkes now.)

He said what everyone would wish to hear of the dead.

'He died very bravely, and in a good cause. And his suffering was short.'

Lady Thorsdale said, 'He is an honest man. Can nothing be done for him? When he spoke of Robert he looked at his hands. I looked, too. And they *had* been burnt.'

'I could, of course, give him money. But there is his pride to be considered. When Robert unhorsed him, all those years ago, at Winchester, Sir Godfrey was the premier knight in England.'

They were able to speak of Lord Robert quite calmly because their grief was old; they were now long accustomed to thinking of Robert as dead. And they were both old, too. Lady Thorsdale had borne Robert at the unlikely age of forty-four and had he lived he would now have been nearing thirty. In all but one thing — a firm and dedicated devotion to the Yorkist cause — they had almost finished with this world. Lord Thorsdale, even older than his wife, was indeed becoming forgetful; but always, at his elbow was his chaplain and man-of-affairs.

To that shrewd and lively-minded young man Lord Thorsdale presently said, 'I wish to do something for this good knight. He has a house and some small portion of land in ...' he tapped the side of his head to set his memory to work, 'in Suffolk. Do I own anything there?'

The chaplain and man-of-affairs, a young man who had climbed up the ladder which education offered, and was at heart almost a revolutionary, almost at one with Wat Tyler,

John Ball and Jack Cade — but with this difference; he was a churchman and knew that any attack on entrenched authority meant an attack on the Church, the most entrenched authority of all, thought — How *wrong* that one man should own so much that he cannot even keep count of it!

His answer gave no sound of grievance.

'There is Bywater, my lord. There the river runs, one bank in Suffolk, the other in Essex. And the jetty. Yes,' he shuffled papers. 'That is on the Suffolk side. If I may remind your lordship . . .'

Quite an ordinary story. The coal-carrying ships, called cobs, labouring down from the mouth of the Humber to the mouth of the Thames, sometimes needed a half-way stop, somewhere to shelter, somewhere to take on supplies, somewhere, now that coal was more and more in demand, to unload. The cobs had not been welcomed at Bywater's busy established jetty, so Lord Thorsdale's father had built his own. The coal-cobs had priority at its moorings, but in slack times other ships used it, paying a small fee to Lord Thorsdale's overseer. There had been a succession of men in this post, and not all were honest.

Bit by bit subsidiary interests had added, a small repair dock, some storage sheds, strings of pack-ponies, a few wagons; and naturally houses for all those directly employed upon Thorsdale business. One quite sizeable house had for years been occupied by couples, or widows of good reputation who paid no rent but earned their house room by taking in and caring for men who worked on the cobs and had sustained injuries or fallen sick.

This small, self-contained world was a mere fragment of the Thorsdale estate and its present owner had never set eyes on it. But it offered an opportunity now.

'I wish,' Lord Thorsdale said — and apart from the difficult area of political activity, his wish had been law ever since he could speak — 'to appoint Sir Godfrey my agent there. How much, do you think, I should offer as salary:'

A chance here for a young, able and ambitious man to strike a blow! Keeping accounts, Lord Thorsdale's man of affairs had not failed to see that of late those who worked with their hands were out-racing those who used their heads. Masons, carpenters, smiths all had their Guilds, sitting in solemn conclave and saying what wages should be. Outside the Guilds was a vast reservoir of hand-power, head-power, but it could never be channelled unless the Guild opened the ever-narrowing gate. The men like himself, who could read, write and reckon, had no Guild, except the Church, where, in fact, preferment meant far more than merit. A topsy-turvy world.

'I would suggest, my lord, a hundred and fifty pounds a year. If he is as honest as he seems, he will save you far more.'

And on the horizon, no bigger than the cloud, the size of man's hand which had brought such abundant rain, was the thought — When the time comes, I shall be able to say, in all honesty, If Sir Godfrey Tallboys was worth a hundred and fifty pounds a year, what am I worth?

Astounded by his good fortune, riding home to tell Sybilla, Sir Godfrey nevertheless, turned aside. In that horrible place, the marble quarry at Andara, he and the man called John Hawke — the man who had warned him to beware of the whip — had finally come together and talked as much as possible, in fits and snatches. The Moorish guards had distrusted talk and discouraged it by the free use of the whippy canes, but Sir Godfrey had learned that John Hawke had been born at a place called Tadcaster where his father was a saddler — a man with a heavy hand. A hand so heavy, in fact that it had driven the boy to run away and go to sea — and be captured by the Barbary pirates, sold as a slave, and die, as the result of the prevalent cough, deep, deep inside that quarry.

So Sir Godfrey turned aside, wishful to bring as much comfort to John Hawke's parents, as he had to Lord Robert's.

And that was a wasted errand. John Hawke's parents were hardly remembered and the saddler's business had changed hands three times.

So, home to Knight's Acre; to tell Sybilla the good news that he now had an appointment. To see that Master Hobson was going ahead with the building which Tana insisted upon calling her pavilion and to take up his new duty as Lord Thorsdale's agent.

CHAPTER EIGHT

At the foot of the stairs Sybilla called, 'Margaret! Margaret! Supper.'

Until very lately Margaret's whereabouts had always been easily ascertainable; at twelve years old she was as dependent, as clinging as a child of three. Quite useless; in the worst days of her single-handedness, Sybilla had never been able to rely upon her daughter to set a table, wash a dish, sweep a floor; but not troublesome, except over the matter of eating. Margaret still had to be encouraged to eat, urged to get on, not to keep everybody waiting. She had always been very pretty in an ethereal way, and seemed to grow prettier as she grew older. In fact she closely resembled her beautiful aunt, Lady Astallon, but who would marry her, Sybilla often wondered, as the years brought physical maturity and no flowering of intelligence. A pretty simpleton with a dowry might just be acceptable, a penniless half-wit had no future outside a convent and even in convents some kind of endowment, if only the ability to work, was desirable.

'She was in the yard when we came in,' Henry said. And that was some while ago, for since the order of their lives had been changed, the boys no longer simply washed their hands before coming to table — a rule upon which Sybilla had always insisted — but put on their better clothes. Henry infatuated by Tana, willingly made this small extra effort, wishing to appear well in the eyes of their guest. John saw no purpose in the performance but was now accustomed to doing whatever Henry did. So here they were, clean, neatly clad and hungry.

Tana sat in the place assigned her from the first; the warm place on the bench nearest the fire. Eddy, the serving boy from Moyidan, brought in the pigeon-pie which Jill — also from Moyidan — had cooked.

Sybilla said, 'Henry, you serve. Look after Lady Serriff. I shall not be long.'

At the back of her mind a thought, not yet firm enough to be suspicion, had formed. Margaret, with no capacity for doing anything herself, found entertainment in watching the activities of others, and ever since the foundations of Tana's house were being dug, had spent much time simply staring. She had been known to eat — quite willingly, a portion of one man's noon piece, a very hard piece of bread, some cheese and a raw onion. The man had probably attributed her wistful stare to hunger.

On that occasion Sybilla said, 'You must not allow my daughter to be a nuisance to you.' The man had replied, good-naturedly, 'She don't bother me none, my lady. I got little girls of my own.'

The workmen ate lightly at mid-day — not wasting the precious daylight hours — but well at night, and Margaret must have drifted away with them to the 'lodge' which they had built for themselves, making use of the biggest bit of wall left standing of Walter's little house, some struts and some well-tarred canvas. Margaret would be sharing their supper. They'd feed her, much as they would a stray dog, and then go away and say that up at Knight's Acre Lady Tallboys' little girl didn't get enough to eat — a statement borne out by the child's appearance.

Hurrying towards the makeshift shelter Sybilla reflected that exhortation and explanation were wasted upon Margaret; she could not understand. She recognised a scolding tone of voice, and scolded, would cry, but the tears were as meaningless as all else about her.

The men had made a bright fire, above which salt herrings were suspended.

Margaret was not there. Nor was the man — a carpenter — who had little girls of his own! The gravest suspicion now, and alarm; but both controlled, subject to common-sense and swift thinking. First to explain this visit, an unprecedented thing.

'I had a message for the carpenter — the one with red hair.'

'That'd be Joe, my lady, just stepped outside for a minute.'

'Ask him to have a word with me before he starts work in the morning.'

'I will that, my lady.'

Outside in the moonlit yard again. She had no doubt in her mind now that the idiot — but recently nubile — girl and the man who could occasionally make her laugh, were together somewhere, and up to no good, though Margaret must be held blameless. Where?

Behind the house Layer Wood stretched away. But the night

was cold. The man, at least, would have had sense enough to seek a sheltered place. The stable, with its store of hay on a kind of low platform which Walter had built to keep the hay from the muck of the stable floor.

Sybilla saw and heard simultaneously; moonlight streaming in from the opened door showed her just what she feared; and there was hard-breathing, small whimpers — of pleasure, not fright — the hay rustling.

Now, not at all controlled, impelled by red fury, Sybilla sprang. She had the strength of ten. With her left hand she seized the man by the hair and pulled, with her right, clenched into a fist, small but hard, she struck him again and again, on the nose, the mouth, the eyes. And at the same time she noticed that although his clothes were in disarray Margaret's were not — yet. At least, not below the waist.

Self-possession returned. To the man, caught in the most vulnerable situation, surprised, guilty, afraid, Sybilla said fiercely, 'One word of this and I'll see you hanged!' She then reached down and jerked Margaret to her feet. Abusive terms came to mind, slut, hussy, bitch, but to utter them was a waste of breathe. Think in practical terms. The girl's bodice was open, there was probably hay in her hair.

Go in through the kitchen and there would be Jill, and Eddy and Tom Robinson and Young Shep, all eyes. All country-born too; knowing the word for it — a roll in the hay. God be thanked the front door opened very near the foot of the stairs; Tana and the boys would be intent upon their supper, and the only candles would be on the table, the rest of the hall in gloom. So they went in by that door. Margaret was whimpering in another way now; the pleasure cut short, the hard hand on her arm pulling and jerking.

John did spare a glance, a second's interest. 'So you found her, Mother.'

'She'd lost her way,' Sybilla said, hustling Margaret up the stairs.

No *real* harm done, the brief distasteful examination proved. But what of the future? You couldn't keep a girl locked up, or under constant surveillance. You couldn't make this girl understand. A convent seemed to be the only answer, and there was now some hope of finding the necessary dowry.

Sir James had wasted no time. Jocelyn, his man of affairs had been sent to make strict investigations, comparing the original deed of grant with the Kin Book. A state of affairs very promising for Sir Godfrey had been revealed; of the twelve men who had made Intake, only five had founded families whose descent could be clearly traced. Holdings had been divided, and sub-divided; illegitimate sons had inherited, so had daughters; widows had assumed rights — and sometimes remarried. Out of an intricate maze, Joycelyn emerged triumphant; only five men could claim those inalienable rights; all the rest must pay a reasonable rent or be evicted. And even the five whom the ancient document protected could claim no rights to the common land of which there was no mention on the parchment.

'Oh, yes, my lady, I assure you, it is perfectly legal. It is indeed the letter of the law. The common land is Sir Godfrey's property, absolutely. In fact, had anyone been so rash as to build on it — as fortunately is not the case — any such building could be destroyed.'

'Well done,' Sir James said. 'Now the thing to do is to get it fenced, no matter how roughly, before my brother returns. He is prone to sentiment . . . Order Young Shep to begin fencing immediately; he has nothing else to do at the moment.' And out of the increased rents Godfrey could buy more sheep, get a proper flock which under Young Shep's care would flourish.

The villagers watched, impotent and resentful. This was a blow even to those who — with inalienable rights — had felt superior to those without. It was *their* common; their forefathers had made it. They were not grateful to Sybilla who, acting for Godfrey and knowing his mind, ordered that a path should be left on the edge of what was to be the sheep run — a means of access between the village and the church. Why be grateful for what they regarded as something of their own? Why be glad that the young man from Moyidan, sparing of his labour, left rather more than a path, left indeed enough of the common to accommodate a few geese, some goats, a donkey or two? A seething grudge towards Knight's Acre took the place of indifference; a grudge that was nourished, revived, reinforced every time any Intake man looked out and saw what had been the common, and was now known as Grabber's Green.

CHAPTER NINE

Sir Godfrey came home, this time jubilant. He had obtained a post involving responsibility and authority, and he had, for the first time in his life, a settled income of a hundred and fifty pounds a year. Not great wealth by some standards, but riches by his and comfortable by any.

He was so happy that Sybilla forebore to tell him the truth about Margaret, contenting herself by saying that she thought the time had come for the girl's future to be considered and that given the promise of five pounds a year, the convent at Lamarsh would probably take her — not as a novice, since Margaret could never understand what was required of her — but as a permanent guest.

He made one small protest. 'You were not happy there, Sweeting.'

'Only because the Abbess, your sister, was always trying to force the veil upon me. Before she conceived the idea of making me her successor I was very happy. And later I greatly envied the guests, with their pretty clothes and little pet dogs. At Lamarsh she would have company — here she has none. Also to be considered, is the future, Godfrey. Nobody will marry her, and you and I shall not live for ever.'

Sybilla was, in truth, tired of keeping guard over a girl who, once sexually aroused and feeble-minded, was a problem, demanding constant vigilance.

'I will see to it,' Sir Godfrey said. 'I must ride down to Bywater and see that all is in order there. That is my first duty. After that, Lamarsh.'

Something intervened, however. Tana wanted divans, and he was at first a little uncertain as to what they were. He had never been in a well-furnished Eastern household. Escalona, his destination when he left England for the tournament that had turned out to be a crusade, had been Spanish-furnished with ordinary tables and chairs. Of the Moorish customs of Zagela he had seen nothing; cast into slavery, seated on the floor, bedded on straw pallets. But as Tana explained, faint and far away the memory rang. In that vital interview when he, the

35

last surviving knight, the last outpost of Christendom had refused the easy way, Selim, King of Zagela had sat upon a kind
of bed, eight inches from the floor, many-cushioned.

Yes, he knew what a divan was.

'A sort of bed, sir,' the old carpenter-turned-cabinet-maker
said. 'A truckle bed?' He had made many in his time, beds with
no head-pieces, no foot-piece, capable of being pushed under
an ordinary bed and brought out only when guests overflowed
the available accommodation, or a child was ill and needed
attention by night.

'Not exactly,' Sir Godfrey said; he had occupied many a
truckle bed in his time. 'Wider, softer . . .'

Whether the thing, when finished, held a mattress stuffed
with horsehair, with wool or with feathers was no concern of
the man who made the frame, so that could be disregarded.
How long, how wide, how high on its legs? The more Sir Godfrey tried to explain the more the old man thought — but that
is what I said in the first place, a truckle bed!

A vast quantity of silk was needed too. Far more than the
one mercer who also stocked woollen stuff and linen, had in
store. The average woman, lucky enough to have a successful
father or husband, looked to have one silk gown and make it
last a lifetime. What silk was to be had was in modest colouring, black, blue, buff, grey. Scarlet and crimson, purple and
ochre could be ordered, of course, from London where young
popinjays went for their clothes. Sir Godfrey ordered. He happened to mention that the silk was needed to cover walls and
the mercer thought that either his ears were failing him, or Sir
Godfrey had come home, after a long absence, not quite right
in the head. Still it was a good order.

On the whole Sir Godfrey's shopping expeditions went well.
He was able to buy, for Sybilla a length of silk in a soft, pretty
colour, not unlike a dove's neck feathers, and it delighted him
to be able to pay for it.

Bywater was under control; Tana's pavilion well under way;
Intake, little knowing the threat that had hung over it for a
while had settled down to the loss of half its common; and now
he could give his full attention to Margaret, his only daughter.

About her he had observed — unobservant as he was in general — something that Sybilla, thank God, had not observed. At least, it was more a matter of feeling than of sight. Young as the girl was, slight as she was, and stupid as she was, she was ripe, perhaps even over-ripe for marriage. Man-hungry. He knew by the way she flung herself into his arms greeting him, after the briefest absence with kisses and clutchings which eight, nine years ago, he would have welcomed as proofs of affection. Then they had not been forthcoming, in fact Margaret had hardly recognised his existence until lately and now her recognition of him was not as a father, but as a man.

He rode to Lamarsh willingly. And there was rebuffed. The first battle in the Civil War, followed the peace which Lord Astallon had called a truce, frail as egg-shell, had had repercussions on convents — reputable places, like Lamarsh. Widows, young women whose putative husbands were dead, crowded its walls.

'I could,' Sir Godfrey said, desperately, 'manage even twenty pounds a year.'

The calm-faced woman who had succeeded his sister as Abbess here, said, sweetly, 'I am sorry, Sir Godfrey. Money cannot buy space — unless in such quantity as to allow us to build. We are overcrowded now, and a long list of names waiting. I hesitate,' she said, 'to suggest Clevely; it is a decayed house. But five pounds a year might mean much there.'

So he rode on to Clevely. A decayed house indeed. A place so tumbled down, inhabited by a few old nuns, deaf, blind, toothless, that the idea of consigning Margaret to it was unthinkable. In fact as soon as the place was in full view — it stood the width of two fields from the road — he would have turned and ridden away, but one of the nuns came screeching out, gabbling about a pig. She was under the misapprehension that he had come to buy a pig. Times were so hard, she explained, and flour an absolute necessity, so they must sell the pig. It was young, and this was the wrong time of year, but it was a good little pig, and if allowed to live until autumn, would be double its present size. She spoke loudly, being stone deaf, and at the sound of her voice speaking to somebody, other old women came out; visitors were an event in this forgotten place; even the good old Bishop seemed to desert them. Two of the old nuns made a pathetic sight, one very lame supported by

37

another whose eyes were opaque with the sightlessness of ex‑ treme age. In the hope that somebody here had the use of her ears, Sir Godfrey explained that he had not come to buy the pig. He was prepared to say that he had lost his way and was asking direction. However, as soon as he spoke of not buying the pig, the blind woman said,

'Holy Mother of God! Then we shall starve!' She began to cry, and seeing her tears the others began to shed theirs. Fumbling in his pouch, and gratified to be able to do so, Sir Godfrey brought out three nobles and handed them to the deaf woman who happened to be nearest.

'Three,' she exclaimed, passing from misery to jubilation. 'I did not expect . . . It is a lot for one pig.'

The lame woman said, very loudly indeed, 'the gentleman does not want the pig, Dame Martha.'

Unhearing or unheeding she said, 'When will you send for it?'

The blind nun said, 'It is a gift from God. An answer to prayer.'

Addressing those who could hear, Sir Godfrey said, 'Buy flour; and eat the pig yourselves.' They had, as well as old age in common, the wan, frail look of long under-feeding.

He bowed for the benefit of those who could see, replaced his hat and re-mounted. Blessings followed him as he rode away.

CHAPTER TEN

Sybilla stitched diligently, now on the beautiful silk that was her own, and now on the crimson velvet which Godfrey had managed to procure in Bywater for Tana.

The problem of Margaret she had set aside for a while. Tana's apartments, needing no stairs and granted no par‑ getting, were almost ready; the workmen would go away, vigil‑ ance could be relaxed, presently. As to the far future, a convent the only answer, it could wait a little. There were other re‑ ligious houses. One — though a terrible scandal was attached to it, at Bury St Edmunds. But that could wait; the clothes could not; and the clothes presented a very delicate problem.

Tana's measurements — until about June — were predictable; the gradual enlargement allowed for by a complicated system of tucks and gussets.

What of my own? Have I come to the second great watershed of a woman's life or am I pregnant? Has that remark, about Tana's child being my Benjamin, rebounded upon me? Shall I in this silk, the colour of a dove's neck, make deep seams and tucks to allow for letting out as the year ages? Shall I ripen with the harvest and bear another child in September? Not so old yet; pushed, in fact into premature age by uncertainty, worry, bereavement by predicaments which few women had faced; Henry's refusal to conform; the raid which Walter had managed so well; Walter's death; the plague, and the long, grinding process of being poor, of having no time ... not to think of the fall, on that terrible day which had inflicted a hurt which had left her lame for ever. A rest *then* could well have been effective, but she had had no time. Alone with three plague victims to be tended, how could I rest a mere lame leg. Give my hair, my hands attention?

Now, stitching away here, I am I; but also she, that lonely woman, bent on survival and little more. Now, blessed as few women could have been, the husband restored to her, a mind sufficiently expanded to accept Tana, and the faint, but day-by-day growing hope that the disturbance of regular cycle might mean not an end but a beginning. Presently she was sure, and hoped for a daughter, one with her wits about her; a girl to whom could be passed on all the things which Sybilla had acquired; the arts of reading and writing, fine needlework and embroidery, still-room work, and even — since nobody knew what life might bring, the down to earth household skills, baking bread, making butter and cheese, preserving meat.

Spring came to this cold northern country. The dark woods became speckled with green, Henry, at the far end of the farthest field saw a bank all starred over with primroses and gathered a few; fair-minded — loyal to his old love though infatuated by his new one — he laid a small posy by Sybilla's plate as well as Tana's. Pale, frail, insipid, Tana thought them; just like the sun which occasionally gleamed from behind the greyness, only to retire again, but which made everybody say,

'Oh, what a wonderful day!' She now understood English very well, but concealed her knowledge because the Arabic which only she and Godfree could understand was the one thing that was their own.

Now and again, on his way to and from Bywater as the days lengthened, Sir Godfrey turned off and went to Moyidan. It was curious — and he recognised the fact — that of the thing he had been trained to, reared for, become expert at, he had never for a moment been proud. The fighting man that was Sir Godfrey Tallboys, Godfrey Tallboys took for granted. Of his suddenly acquired and quite unforeseen ability as agent and administrator, he was proud. He had enjoyed telling James and Emma about his appointment; they were suitably impressed. He enjoyed taking them little presents, things had fallen into his hand by virtue of his new office. Bribes he would not accept, and one or two ship's captains who had thought that a timely gift might gain priority at the coal jetty had suffered crushing rebuffs. On the other hand a man who was *there*, unbribable and incorruptible, but with money in his hand, often hit upon a bargain, and it delighted him to be able to give things to Emma and James who had given him and his family hospitality in the past.

That year Sir James enjoyed no intermission between his two gouty seasons and although he often declared that next week he must surely be better and able to ride to Knight's Acre to meet Lady Serriff, he had not in fact been able to do so. He and Emma had not, however, abandoned their intention to make a match of this — if a match could be made. Emma had never ridden except as a pillion passenger, and she felt that to make the errand alone, either behind Sir Godfrey, or a servant, would show that she was losing hope for James. So they dallied and privately thought Godfrey was unhelpful in not offering to bring the girl to them.

'Many women,' Lady Emma said to her husband, 'take journeys while in her condition and no harm done. I do not wish to sound suspicious of Godfrey, but he said the girl was sixteen, which is just Henry's age.'

'That is true.' Sir James brooded and then gave orders that his lightest wagon should be fitted with a padded seat at the back. 'I will make this last effort, for the boy's sake. Once the girl has shed her load ... And Henry is big and strong ...'

Godfrey proved obstructive again.

'The lady will be in no condition to receive you. Sybilla reckons that she will be having her baby towards the end of June.'

'Midsummer Day is not the end of June,' Emma said firmly. 'And first babies are invariably late. We shall make our visit as arranged. On Midsummer Day.'

He felt sorry for them. Moyidan Richard could only appeal to a poor woman, past her prime. And all other considerations apart had Tana intended to marry would she have built and furnished her pavilion? When he left after that visit Lady Emma came with him, beyond the outer door and said quietly, 'I fear it is the last visit James will ever make. When gout reaches the eyes there is little hope.'

Sir Godfrey repeated this to Sybilla when she exclaimed, 'Of all the ill-chosen times!'

Henry said, 'Must John and I come in that day? *What* a waste of time! Washing and changing clothes in the middle of a hay-making day!'

The arrangement was irksome to him because it was part of a general feeling of having been reduced to second place. Ever since Walter's death Henry had been the man of the house; the prop; the stay; the provider. When the plague struck he had not sickened but stood by his mother's side, staunch tough weary — and had worked the farm, too. Then Father had come back, taken his rightful place as head of the household, and soon, without soiling his hands or shedding a drop of sweat, was bringing home money which made Henry's income, so hard earned, seem pitiable. In addition to this there was jealousy — not consciously sexual because to Henry his father seemed old. What Henry envied was his father's ability to talk to the beautiful lady, and to make her laugh. Once Henry had conceived the idea of learning this strange, clicking language himself, but his father had discouraged that, saying that the best thing Henry could do was to speak in English, very slowly and distinctly, so that Tana might learn. This Henry had conscientiously attempted, to the point of sounding as though he

himself were learning English. 'It — is — a — sunny — day.'
The beautiful eyes looked at him blankly.

Knight's Acre, in fact no longer revolved about Henry and
this asking for guests to dinner on a hay-making day was proof
of the change.

On the bright sunny day of the visit it was plain that Sir
James was pitiable indeed. His feet were so swollen that he
could not wear even slippers, but had his feet tied, like
puddings, in velvet bags, and he wore, not only a hat but a
black scarf over his eyes to shield them from the sun. The
driver of the wagon, helped and admonished by Lady Emma,
hauled him out on to the ground.

'Is Richard here? Where is Richard? We will enter together,'
Sir James said. Richard had learned to ride, and mounted on a
meek horse, looked well. He arrived while his father was asking
about him.

'He is here,' Emma said.

'Are we watched from the windows?'

The fond yet shrewd old mind had reckoned on their being
looked for. He wished the arrival to make a good impression.
Richard, in tawny slashed with yellow, and on horseback, was
looking his best.

'Something moved,' Emma said. And then the door was
flung open and there was Godfrey extending a hearty welcome.
Once out of the sun Emma whisked off the scarf and blinking a
little through the slits which his puffy lids had formed, Sir
James advanced towards the settle upon which Tana sat, looking pretty and not — in the cunningly fashioned crimson velvet
gown — as pregnant as Godfrey had implied.

Introductions were made. Sybilla, in the purple-grey silk
rustled in from the kitchen where she had been seeing to a few
last things, and instructing Eddy: and really Richard did not
look at all bad until Henry, followed by John, came clattering
down the stairs. Then the contrast was as sharp as it had been
when the boys were young; Henry lean and brown, upright
and alert; his cousin wilting, drooping and vague.

It was disconcerting, too, to find that the lady, after six
months in England was so completely ignorant of the land-
guage as to be impervious to hints. This is my son; my only
son; my heir. Richard will inherit Moyidan. Meaningless!

Tana had perfected that blank stare. Lady Emma had never before encountered a person of foreign birth and fell back on insular instinct. Shout loud enough and something would get through. It must! She shouted to Tana about Richard being heir to such a prosperous estate; so many tenants, all paying regular rents, so many sheep.

Finally Tana turned to Godfrey and asked, in Arabic, 'Is this woman angry with me that she speaks so loudly?' Assured, in that same barbaric tongue that this was not so, she said, 'I am glad. I wished to ask everybody to see my pavilion and to drink wine with me.'

The visit had coincided with the completion of the pavilion. It was now ready for occupation. Godfree had found her a waiting woman called Ursula who could cook and clean and look after babies. (Ursula was a middle-aged woman, thrown out of work by the running down of the Foundlings' Home at Bywater) Sir Godfrey translated the invitation which was accepted eagerly. Only Henry was irate. He'd had a glimpse or two of the beautiful place while it was in the making and would have loved to go in now that it was finished and sit on one of the divans — as near Tana as possible. But he had been trained by Walter, to whom work had always come first, and who had used such old country sayings as, 'Make hay while the sun shines'.

Grumpily, Henry said, 'Come on John. Back to work.'

John was by disposition idle, and only ten years old. For his youth Henry made no allowance, having gone to work himself at the age of six.

John said, 'Oh, must I?'

'You'd better!' John took swift stock of the situation; here with the family assembled, he might successfully rebel, but there would be tomorrow, and tomorrow. Better go.

Tana led the way; out at the main door, passing Sybilla's roses and round to the side, to her own door. Sir Godfrey gave his brother a helping arm, Sybilla and Emma came behind.

'I thought a pavilion was a tent,' Emma said. 'This is an ordinary house.'

'Godfrey used the word without thinking,' Sybilla said. 'Inside it is far from ordinary ... I am sorry to see James so much afflicted.'

'Yes. He is failing in other ways, too; and he does so long to see Richard settled . . .' Sybilla made sympathetic noises. What could one *say*?

With malice and amusement Tana had realised the purpose of this visit. The procedure was not so different from that followed by her own tribe, a display of elegibility. She had understood every hint, every shouted word, and had issued her invitation in order that they might see how rich she was, how immensely far from needing to marry a boy, not without a certain girlish prettiness of face, but weakly built, mumbling, senseless. A male version of his cousin Margaret.

The ceiling of the pavilion was lined entirely with sky-blue silk, stretched taut. The walls were draped with pleated silk, crimson, white, yellow, green. The two divans which when bare much resembled truckle beds were covered with silk and piled with cushions of varied colours. In the angle where they met stood a low table upon which Ursula soon placed silver cups and jugs. Under the window another table bore candlesticks and a silver bowl of red roses. In the whole of their lives Sir James and Lady Emma had not seen so much silk and even Moyidan could not show more silver. James, blinking, could hardly believe his eyes; Emma believed hers and understood.

Tana's wine was excellent; sweet and red — the colour of her gown. But the divans made uncomfortable seating for people accustomed to chairs, benches, stools; they were so soft and so low that to sit on them in the ordinary way brought the knees very near the chin. Only Tana was fully at ease.

Due to give birth almost any day now, Sybilla thought, but so young, so taut of figure that she is more graceful and active than I am, with three months more to go . . . And that made her think of children. She realised suddenly that Moyidan Richard and Margaret, bringing up the rear of the procession, had not entered the pavilion. They might, in their aimless way have followed Henry and John into the hayfield; they might have lingered among the roses. Instinct told her otherwise.

'The children,' she said, heaving herself with difficulty, to her feet, gathering up her skirt, making swift if clumsy progress round the out-jutting wing of the house and into the yard. To the hay.

This time, too late. On the new hay, still sweet-smelling, the half-witted boy and the girl with no wits at all were locked in ecstasy; doing the one thing that needed no sense at all.

Emma's son; Sybilla's daughter. Hands which had tended, patted, soothed, now tore the two apart. Interrupted from a boyous mating neither of the semi-idiots showed shame; simply resentment. Margaret clawed Sybilla's face, Richard pushed his mother with such force that she almost fell.

Father's arrived, late because Sir Godfrey had been obliged to heave his brother to his feet, and then in the dazzling afternoon sunshine, guide him.

Sybilla, still holding Margaret by the arm, ashamed before Emma, just as Emma was ashamed before her, barely felt the nails' raking. Another, more familiar pain lanced her, low down in her body. A warning pain. She bent over it and said, 'Emma . . . I think . . .'

Emma took charge, issuing crisp, purposeful orders.

'Godfrey, carry Sybilla to bed.' 'Wat, Wat, where are you? Get the wagon ready. Take Sir James home.'

'James, take Richard home. Richard go home with your father.'

'And what about you, my dear?' Sir James asked. He had not seen anything and was bewildered.

'I am needed here — at least until tomorrow. Send the wagon then and if I can I will come home.'

She seized Margaret's arm in a clasp that left marks visible a fortnight later and hustled her into the house. She thanked God that James seemed not to have seen that shameful sight; she prayed God that Richard would not be able to explain. She did not speak until they were on the stairs and then she said, 'You wicked, wicked girl,' and administered a sound shaking before bundling her into the nearest room, which happened to be the right one and locking her inside. Then she went into the room where Sir Godfrey, having laid Sybilla on the bed, was loosening her clothes.

It could not be even a premature birth; Godfrey had been home less than seven months. A miscarriage so late could be lethal. And all that wicked girl's fault! She did not blame Richard at all; he had never shown before the slightest interest in sex.

She sent Godfrey running to the kitchen for what was needed — none of the items that anticipated the birth of a living child, just provision against the inevitable mess.

'Send your kitchen woman up with them. And then, Godfrey, ride after James. I forgot his scarf in the confusion. It is in the hall.'

Racked with pain Sybilla said, 'I am sorry that this should have fallen to you, Emma.'

'Be thankful that I am here. Between Margery and Richard I had two miscarriages myself. I know what to do.'

Presently it was clear that this was no miscarriage. It was a birth. A boy, no bigger than, and much resembling, a skinned rabbit, but alive. Lady Emma applied common-sense. Ejected so abruptly from the womb the little creature would need a makeshift one; must be kept warm, handled as little as possible. If it could be saved Lady Emma was the woman to do it, even though she thought with some bitterness — This is Sybilla's *fourth* boy!

Tana had not joined the rush to the yard. The children — by which she understood the idiot girl and boy — were no concern of hers. She reclined upon her divan and finished her wine, and then Godfrey's; it pleased her to drink from his cup. She was nearing her time, but the thought did not perturb her; she came of a tribe resistant to pain and from living so much among women, she knew what to expect. In both her lives, the one in North Africa, the one in Zagela, women had rallied around a birth. The old wife would see to all the necessary business, just as she had seen to the making of tiny garments.

She heard nothing of the bustle in the yard, for Master Hobson built well and she herself had decreed that her pavilion should not even have a window on that side. Everything was very quiet. When the first pain struck she thought I will wait a little, then call Ursula, who will call Sybilla; a baby takes a long time to be born. Ursula should have been in Tana's kitchen which had once been Sybilla's still-room, and which had a window on the garden side, quite close to the door of the pavilion. When, eventually, Tana did call, the sound should have carried and brought Ursula running by the inconvenient way which Tana herself had insisted upon, through the kitchen door, into the yard, round the out-jutting wing and so to the door. But Ursula had been drawn by the drama going on in the main house. The heating of blankets, the heating of bricks to be wrapped in flannel to be laid alongside the little rabbit-like

46

baby in the plain wooden cradle which Sybilla had ordered for Tana's baby and which had not yet been carried into the pavilion. The second cradle, not expected to be needed for three months was still in the making. Lady Emma was fully occupied with Sybilla who, having suffered something that was not quite a birth or quite a miscarriage, was in a very poor way.

When silence answered her calls, Tana pressing her hands on either side of the yielding mattress of the divan, heaved herself up and staggered to the door of her pavilion. It was late afternoon now and roses and lilies swooned, heavy-scented. In the doorway she realised that some births did not take long. It was happening now, she could no longer walk. Crawl perhaps. She crawled towards the front of the house and then screamed, at a fortunate spot, just under the window of the room where Lady Emma was beginning to be hopeful that Sybilla would not bleed to death, and at the same time being worried because the child having come so untimely, there was no milk for him.

She said, crossly, 'And what is to do now?' And went down to deal, competently, with whatever was to do. The second task was far easier, a full time baby, a girl, and curiously, girls were tougher than boys; and Lady Serriff had, thank God, enough milk for two. And Emma thought — We must not go jogging that poor little thing up and down stairs. So the two babies lay, side by side in the cradle.

Few women, Lady Emma thought had managed two deliveries in so short a time. And that after a shock.

She did not forget Margaret as everybody else had done. She opened the door, took the idiot by the arm to the stool-room, locked her in again with a hunk of bread and a cup of water. 'That'll cool your blood, you little bitch.'

Next day, as instructed, James sent the wagon which went back empty. It was impossible for Lady Emma to leave Knight's Acre while Sybilla was still so helpless and her baby in need of such diligent care. The foreign woman could, at a pinch, have taken control — peasant women often gave birth and cooked a meal on the same day — but she understood nothing and only Sir Godfrey understood her. And neither of the hired women was fully to be trusted. Men were useless at such times, hanging about and asking, 'How is she?' twenty times a day; so Emma devised an errand for Godfrey.

'Ride over to Moyidan and explain to James why I shall be

here for at least two days more. Take your dinner with him, and for my sake make sure that it is a good one. And see that his shutters are closed.'

'*Two* babies on the same day,' Sir James said. 'Poor Emma! Still they could not be in better hands. One is yours, Godfrey.'

Both are mine, God forgive me.

'Yes, the boy, born untimely is mine.' The girl, twice the size and twice as lusty, he must not claim.

Behind the swollen watering eyes there was an active mind at work. Richard, hustled out of Knight's Acre in summary fashion had said something which had struck home and Sir James feared that shortly he would need his foolish young brother's consent and connivance.

'Then you need two cradles, Godfrey.'

'They are managing. Sybilla had ordered one for Tana's, that is Lady Serriff's baby — and that was delivered in good time. The other is still in the making.'

'No need for that! Somewhere ... I think in the old castle, near the stairs when I last saw it, under a bit of sailcloth, is the one we were all rocked in. Take it. Make use of it for your son.'

The head-piece of that cradle was carved with the family emblem, the timid hare rampant in defence of its young. It had been painted once, but like all painted things, it had faded and in places flaked. But the lending of it was a gesture, brotherly, imbued with family feeling, and awkwardly as it balanced across the pommel of his saddle, Sir Godfrey carried it home with pride.

CHAPTER ELEVEN

It took Margaret's slow wits two days to realise that the way of escape lay open to her. From her window to the roof of the new building was not much of a drop; from that roof to the garden was a bigger one, but she did not flinch from it. No definite purpose drove her, she was following an animal instinct to escape, to be free of the deadly routine, bedroom, stool-room, bedroom again, to be away from that hostile eye.

She had no sense of direction, but that did not matter; there was only one way out of Intake, and that was the lane. Its verges were white with the big daisies that Mother had said was her name flower — the marguerite — and Henry called bull-daisies. Of the smaller kind of daisy Sybilla had once shown Margaret how to make a daisy chain. The instruction, seemingly not much regarded at the time, had made an impression and as she walked Margaret made herself two. One for her neck, one for her head.

Halfway along its length the lane was crossed by a little stream, a casual, nameless tributary to the river, it was unbridged because even in winter rains it was still shallow, merely a water-splash. Its banks were thick with wild strawberries, so many and so ripe that they scented the air. Margaret did not notice this immediately. What she saw was a man.

He was a carter. Somebody called Wade, of Wade's Acre at Intake had commissioned him to bring — with all his belongings — an extremely old man from Nettleton. The enquiry, earlier in the year, though nothing had come of it, had shaken Wade whose claim to Wade's Acre was shown to be poor. But old Uncle Arthur's claim was good and valid, and Wade of Wade's Acre was not the man to miss an opportunity.

Having delivered the ancient man and his belongings, the carter, offered no hospitality, had turned about and was making for Baildon. He had no settled home there, he was in fact a homeless man, sleeping, eating where he could, but he frequented markets because there were to be found a good number of men with goods to be carried — things that could not be transported on a donkey.

The carter was mindful of his horse; not in a sentimental way, but because it earned him his livelihood. So he halted by the stream to let the horse drink and graze a bit, to drink himself and eat his bread and cheese. As an addition to this fare he had gathered a big dockleaf full of the wild strawberries.

'Margaret likes them,' a sweet voice said.

The carter turned and stared, his eyes bulging and, despite the heat of the day, a shiver between his shoulder blades. Strange tales were told of Layer Wood. The Little People were said to live there. And here was one! Never in his life had the carter seen anything so beautiful. The fall of yellow hair, the blue eyes, fair skin and a mouth the colour of a hedge-rose. She was a child in height, but with a woman's breasts. She wore a crown and a garland of flowers.

If he could have run then, he would have done so, but fear held him captive. Then, gradually fear receded, for the fairy was looking at him kindly. She sat down, close to him, and ate a few of his strawberries. He had never seen anybody eat so delicately before. Sybilla had instilled table manners into all her children, and Margaret had never eaten with heartiness.

'Margaret likes you,' she said, and began to give proof of this liking, kissing him, taking his coarse brown hand and pressing it to her cheek, to her breast. With awe, with astonishment, with delight he discovered that a fairy woman was much like any other — except that she was so different. His traffic with women had been confined to hirelings, bored and indifferent, doing what they did for pay.

It was an experience that he would never forget, never speak of, something out of this world.

At the end of an afternoon of the sweetest dalliance, the real world made sharp impact again. He had thought that she would vanish as suddenly as she had appeared, but she said, 'Take Margaret with you.'

'I wish I could, my pretty, but I ain't got no home. Mostly I sleep in the wagon.'

'Margaret sleep in wagon. With you.'

Abruptly into his mind came the memory of another old story.

Long, long ago, a Bywater man, fishing for herring, had dredged up a mermaid in his net, fallen in love with her and taken her home and lived unhappily ever after.

'No,' he said, 'that wouldn't do. That wouldn't do at all. You must go back where you belong. And I gotta get to Baildon.'

When she saw that he meant it, she began to cry, and that again she did differently. No snuffling or blubbering. Tears filling the eyes and spilling.

Now he was anxious only to get away, for fear he might weaken. Lucky he hadn't unharnessed. He ran to his wagon and jumped to its seat, with shouts and blows rousing the drowsing horse.

For a while she followed, calling piteously, 'Take Margaret with you. Take Margaret . . .' When he reached the end of the lane, the place where it joined the road which led in one direction to Baildon, in the other to Moyidan and eventually to Bywater, he ventured to look back. She had crossed the water-splash and was still in pursuit. He turned the horse into the Baildon road and hurried it along.

When Margaret reached the fork she turned towards Baildon too, and the light wagon from Moyidan missed her only by a minute or two.

Sir James' man of business had written at his dictation.

My dearest Emma, I am sending the wagon for you. You must come home at once. My eyes are much worse and Richard will not eat anything. He has not taken a crumb since that dinner at Knight's Acre, and swears never to break his fast until he can marry that idiot cousin. Please come. Whatever their need it is less than mine . . .

This was heavy news. Whenever Richard's will was crossed, which was not often, his parents being so doting, he had refused to eat. And worry of this sort was the very worst thing for poor James. Lady Emma took a look at the situation here. Sybilla lay upstairs, still very weak, but mending. Lady Serriff, young and strong was feeding both babies, and eating heartily herself. The two babies were with her, the cradles side by side, so that the poor little boy should not suffer the handling, the jolting which being carried up and downstairs would entail. Lady Serriff's new maid, Ursula, had her experience in the Foundlings' Home behind her, and Sybilla's maid, Jill, now understood how to make good chicken broth and how to infuse lovage, that herbal specific for female pains.

Yes, I am free to go. I have done my best. Then she remembered Margaret. Well, presumably she had now learnt her lesson and could be allowed to rejoin the family. Mounting the stairs Lady Emma decided to speak strictly to Godfrey, handing over to him the responsibility of looking after his wicked daughter. Sybilla must not be bothered. Oh, and she intended to tell him another thing, too. It would be most unwise for Sybilla to risk child-birth again. She was so crooked. Emma had not realised how crooked Sybilla was. If that baby had gone full-time Sybilla would have had a very difficult — possibly fatal — delivery.

Godfrey had gone to Bywater that day, but he had said he

would be home for supper. Emma proposed to delay her departure until he arrived, say her say and then go about her own business.

Thinking thus she unlocked the door of the empty room. The open window told its own tale.

From experience with her own son — though compared with Margaret he was almost sound — Lady Emma knew that what those defective in sense lacked they often made up for with cunning. That sly little bitch had clambered out and made for Moyidan. Pray God she hadn't reached it. Two stupid creatures, impervious to reason, acknowledging no rules but their own, and James, so afflicted . . . And so worried.

She kept her head. Wat who drove the wagon, had just come from Moyidan.

'No, my lady. Nobody extra was there when I left and I didn't see nobody along the road.' So the idiot girl had not gone in that direction. There remained the woods — the river. If she wandered, lost and starving in the one, drowned dead in the other, what a blessing!

But Sir Godfrey, arriving just then, repudiated either idea.

'Oh no, Emma. Margaret was always frightened of the woods. Sybilla told me — Margaret liked flowers, but she would never venture far in unless Sybilla held her hand. And to get to the river she would have to go through the village, and she was frightened of that, too. Frightened of the boys and the dogs.'

'Then where can she be?'

'I can go and look.'

With a jolt of his heart he remembered that this was the week of the Midsummer Fair in Baildon. Margaret's understanding was limited, but who knew where the limits ran? Somebody might have said something which had attracted her vagrant attention . . . A pretty girl among that riff-raff!

At the lane's end he turned in the direction of Baildon and rather more than a mile along, found her, walking in the middle of the road, looking about from side to side in a frightened way and crying, quietly, but with infinite desolation. Dusk was thickening here because two spurs of Layer Wood almost met, branches linking across the road. It was getting dark, and she was afraid of the dark, when she was alone.

He called her name, and she turned.

She said, 'Da-da,' her name for him when she was very young. He scooped her up and set her across the saddle in front of him. She smelt of wild strawberries and crushed grass and wilting daisies. The garland had been broken but a few flowers still clung to her hair. He felt relief and exasperation in equal measure. And also a slight repulsion. He had not seen her since he had caught one horrified glimpse of her, skirts tossed up, legs asprawl, face set in ecstasy, changing to sullenness. It seemed to him suddenly that some faint odour of that encounter still hung about her . . .

In the shuttered room, Sir James said testily, 'Don't keep saying "Cousins, cousins," Godfrey. We know that as well as you do. It's *our* boy who won't eat! Do you realise that it is almost a week? If it could be arranged, would you consent?'

'Of course. A girl like that would be far happier here — and married, than she would in a nunnery. But the marriage of first cousins needs a dispensation.'

'It needs a little cunning. And a very old priest with poor sight. That you have on your doorstep. Sybilla was telling me that day how almost blind, how astray in his wits your Father Ambrose is. He *still* asks for news of you. Did you know that? I've worked it out. So far as I know Father Ambrose has never set eyes on Richard in his life. That they — my boy and your girl — share a surname means nothing. Richard Tallboys could well be a brother of that Eustace you once had as your squire. Very distant relative.' Sir James wiped his eyes, shifted his painful feet. 'If any,' he said. 'Now what do you say?'

'I am agreeable. Sybilla might have scruples about the deceit.'

'You must talk her out of them. God's teeth, Godfrey, can we see the boy *die*?'

Lady Emma said, succinctly, 'The fact that Sybilla and her baby are alive today, is due to me, Godfrey. I think you owe us a small accommodation.'

This small accommodation Sir Godfrey was willing to make. He had never been very pious and he had spent a long time in a place where the rules of the Church, of Rome, did not apply. Emma and James had sent for him in sheer desperation, and he understood, indeed shared their point of view.

'I will try,' he said.

Ramming her point home, Emma said, 'It is astounding what you can do if you set your mind to it. If anyone had told me that I should deliver two women in one afternoon . . .' For her the most immediate thing was to get some food into Richard. She went away and told him that so soon as arrangements could be made, he should marry Margaret.

As Sir Godfrey had predicted, Sybilla had scruples. Such a marriage, unless by dispensation, was against Church law and it was a shame to take advantage of Father Ambrose. She told Godfrey how heroically the old man had behaved during the time of the plague, how he denied himself in order to keep the church in some kind of repair. 'We should be doubly breaking the law to play such a trick on him, at the altar he has served so long.'

She was right, of course; and added to that it was difficult to pursue an argument which caused distress to a woman still far from well. He could only say mildly that Richard's health — perhaps even his life was at stake, that the worry was hastening James into the grave and that the investigation of the Kin Book, ill-kept as it had been until Father Ambrose's coming, had revealed marriages between first cousins which seemed to have been attended by no ill results. Sybilla held firm and Sir Godfrey was obliged to ride to Moyidan and report failure.

'Then you must try again, and harder,' Emma said. 'I have already told Richard that he can marry Margaret — and he ate a whole piegeon pie! And it seemed to me that his understanding has improved, too. He asked some quite sensible questions, about how soon, and where. You must assert your authority, Godfrey.'

'Sybilla looks so frail,' he said.

Relentlessly, Emma said, 'But for me she would probably be dead! And you probably exaggerate her ill looks by comparing them with those of Lady Serriff who gave birth as easily as a cow.'

There might be truth in that.

For Sir Godfrey this was a miserable time. And then, with no word of warning, Sybilla capitulated. She gave no reason except that she had given the matter more thought and come to the conclusion that this was, after all, the best way.

What had made her change her mind was the matter of the

monthly cloths, regularly used, soaked, scoured, put out to bleach in air and sun, stored in the clothes chest. Margaret should have needed some a day, or at most two or three after her misbehaviour with her cousin. The need had not arisen, and added to all Godfrey's arguments about Richard's health, Sir James' happiness in his last days, and their unquestionable debt to Emma, was the fact that a pregnant girl needed a husband, and a baby a father.

Once, halfway through the ceremony, it struck Father Ambrose that the young couple he was uniting in holy matrimony looked curiously *alike*. But his eyes were failing, he knew only too well, and perhaps they looked alike because they both looked so happy. God keep them happy always.

After the wedding was to be a double christening, and about the baptism of the foreign lady's baby, Father Ambrose had entertained some qualms. She had lived in his parish for quite some time — he could not remember exactly how long — and had never once set foot in his church. Admittedly, most of the people of Intake were irregular in attendance, but they came at Easter and at Christmas. Still, he had faith in Lady Tallboys who certainly would not have offered to be a god-mother to the child of a heathen, or to have her own baby baptised from the same font, at the same time.

Sybilla had wanted the baby to be named Geoffrey, a name not unlike Godfrey while unlike enough to avoid confusion, but Godfrey had wanted him to be named Robert, in memory of Lord Robert Barbury upon whom he had come to look as a son.

Tana — the daughter a disappointment, for although within her tribe women were allowed an unusual freedom, sons were actually valued more, and the woman who bore them had power — had suggested the name Jamil, meaning in Arabic, beautiful for the little girl's name. But Sir Godfrey had reminded her that she was supposed to be Spanish and the child could have, if not an English name, a Spanish one. In their helter-skelter ride across Spain — neither knowing any Spanish — they had heard several women called Juana. So they settled upon that. However, at the end of a day with so many ceremonies, Juana was more than Father Ambrose could manage so he said, 'I name thee, Joanna.'

CHAPTER TWELVE

Through all this troublous time, Sir Godfrey had been mindful of Lord Thorsdale and of his duties towards the patron. He would perhaps have denied that it was relief for him to get away from Knight's Acre where two women were tending children both sired by him, but that was the truth of it. Get down to Bywater, see that no ordinary ship put in at the coal jetty without paying his dues, that the coal cobs from the North were unloaded, quickly, sheltered, repaired, sent on their way properly provisioned. He was an honest steward and he enjoyed his work. In the communal house, kept by a woman of good reputation, he made himself a little office with a clerk, named Harold, to keep meticulous accounts, a narrow, hard bed upon which, when winter brought short days and bad weather, he could sleep if necessary. He thought he was prepared for everything. What he was not prepared for was a ghost.

But it came, and announced itself. 'Sir Godfrey? I am Sir William Barbury. Lord Thorsdale's nephew. At your service, sir.'

Like Father Ambrose at the altar, Sir Godfrey saw the cousinly resemblance. A spitting image of Lord Robert who had died in that narrow, balconied street, long ago and far away. Even to the way his hair grew, and the certainty, allied with grace, of manner.

Sir Godfrey welcomed the boy, and steadying himself under what had been quite a shock — though ridiculous, waited to hear what his errand was.

It was simple, and yet not simple. War had broken out again and there had been a battle at Northampton, a victory for the Yorkists.

'But my uncle,' the boy said, 'does not think the Queen will be content to leave it there. He is reasonably certain that she will now appeal to the French — her kindred. He wants Bywater held against any French who might come to help the Lancastrian cause. But not so openly as to invite retaliation. I am to be your aid; and cost does not matter. So he said.'

'Not openly. That is wise. People here are not concerned

with the quarrel. Sir William, I doubt whether you could go into the town, the inn or any place within thirty miles and find a man committed to red rose or white.'

'Sir Godfrey, are *you* committed?'

He thought for a bit and then said, 'No. Not in my heart. I was absent from England when this festering boil broke. To be frank I don't understand what it is all about. Two claimants to the throne. And who am I to say? I am not a political man, Sir William.'

'You owe my uncle some allegiance, Sir Godfrey.'

'That I could not deny. In fact I willingly admit it.'

Now that he came to think about it, Sir Godfrey saw that free as he had always seemed to be, he had almost always owed somebody some allegiance — even that mad man in Spain. And a conversation with Henry flashed back into his mind. He had suggested to Henry that now that they were not so poor there was no need for Henry to work so hard; they could hire hands. Henry had retorted that *hands* was an apt word, you could hire hands but not heads and that he had no intention of leaving his harvest to mere hands. Sir Godfrey had then suggested that Henry should come down with him to Bywater and learn, prepare himself to take over the stewardship, and that also Henry had despised, his voice polite, his eyes scornful, 'Sir, I prefer to tend my own fields.'

Exasperated, Sir Godfrey had said, 'Oh, get back to your hay!' and Henry, with an unusually merry look, had said, 'Sir, the hay is safely in. Today we start on the oats.'

Now, not on his own field, not truly his own man, Sir Godfrey said, 'What does Lord Thorsdale wish of me?'

'That Bywater should be prepared — secretly — to repel any French forces who might come to the aid of the Lancastrian cause.'

The trained mind sprang into action. Even the need to make preparations in secret was in attune with experience.

'We need a look-out tower, for early warning,' Sir Godfrey said. 'And that need cause no stir. This is my Lord Thorsdale's jetty, and on it he might wish to have a tower to keep watch for the cobs from the North. There is also a device of which I have heard though I never saw it put to use — the fire ship. We could place one on either side of the harbour. What about men?'

'They are on their way; twenty archers and twenty pikemen, all trained, hired men, and loyal to the white rose and to their lord. My uncle judged that to be sufficient force because the townspeople themselves will rise against the French. Even un-committed men, like yourself, Sir Godfrey. Four knights are also coming — the greatest number that can be spared. With you and myself that makes six.' He smiled with his dead cousin's charming, confident smile.

'The presence of so many men can hardly be concealed,' Sir Godfrey said.

'We hope so, with Master Johnson's aid.'

Christopher Johnson was the most prosperous wool mer-chant in Suffolk, possibly in all East Anglia. He bought wool from as far away as Yorkshire and a good deal of that wool was Lord Thorsdale's. Johnson was a shrewd enough man to take advantage of Bywater's exemption from the Staple — a favour granted it long ago in return for some singular favour the town had rendered the king of the day.

'Master Johnson,' Sir William said, smiling again, 'is about to employ some singularly ablebodied pack-drivers, wool-pickers, general handy-men. Sir Wilfred, Sir Giles and Sir Martin, my brother Philip and myself propose to buy or hire a house and set up a disreputable, merry knights' lodgings of our own.'

'It would have given me great pleasure to offer hospitality,' Sir Godfrey said, truthfully. 'But my house is twenty miles inland.' And small, and bare — and ruled by a lady not yet fully recovered in health.

However, the word hospitality, reminded him of what he could offer, wine and food at the Welcome to Mariners.

Over the wine Sir William explained a little more about the political situation, and Lord Thorsdale's attitude. Lord Thors-dale was a Yorkist, everybody knew that. The Battle of Northampton had been a Yorkist victory — but not decisive enough to end the war and put Richard of York on the throne. So there was certain to be another battle which the Lan-castrians would lose, unless help came from the French; and there were still enough Lancastrians alert and alive to take note of any sudden defence measures taken in such a place as By-water.

'Frankly, I think that if they come, they will make for the

Cinque ports, nearer to France, nearer to London. And indeed, they may not come at all. The King of France has other things to think about, and would stand to gain nothing. Nonetheless, my uncle said, "Prepare" and prepare we will. Enjoying ourselves along the way.'

It could have been Lord Robert speaking.

Through all that fine summer Sir Godfrey did enjoy himself in a way he had not known since his old tournament days. Of the five knights three were young, boisterously merry; two older and completely responsible, but never dull. The young were respectful, too, and when Sir Godfrey, Sir Martin or Sir Wilfred reminisced they were all attention. And of course nobody had such a tale as Sir Godfrey had to tell. Nobody else had been to Spain, taken part in an assault seemingly insane, won and lost a city, been a slave, escaped by the most romantic means. He was a bad story-teller and perhaps for that very reason, never boring. He had to be prompted, asked, 'What then, sir?' There were things that he still could not bring himself to speak of, and perhaps they sensed that, prey, as all men were to curiosity.

He had found for them an old spacious house, empty since the plague, and tradesmen in Bywater, butchers, bakers, dairywomen, fishmongers, revelled in an increase of custom and never questioned the origin of it. Carpenters did not question the purpose of their work, which was to erect a tall tower of no great substance, really no more than a skeleton. Trusted men from the contingent ostensibly lodged and employed with Johnson, took turns to man the watchtower. Out in the harbour two old ships crammed with straw and tallow and dry wood, rocked. They were also manned, turn and turn about — and for a perfectly good reason which everybody in Bywater understood, left unguarded they would have been stripped down to the water-line.

Sir Godfrey went home as often as he could. The two elder knights — Sir Martin and Sir Wilfred — were able and experienced men, and it had been proved by experiment that should the man at the top of the tower sight a conglomeration of vessels which might hint at invasion, and set fire to the combustible materials always ready in an iron pan, the blaze and the smoke could be seen at Knight's Acre. Lord Thorsdale had said that cost did not matter, so Sir Godfrey always had one fresh, swift horse in reserve, so that should the beacon flare just as he had arrived home he had only to remount on a horse ready to run twenty miles at top speed.

The French did not come in July, in August or September; it began to look as though the Queen's appeal to her country-men had been in vain. Tension relaxed. October was the month of westerly gales. November brought fog. As for December, singularly few wars broke out, or were renewed in that month.

When he went home Sir Godfrey passed abruptly from the carefree masculine society which was his true element — one he would never have deserted had he not met Sybilla — into one heavily charged with femininity. By October Sybilla was strong again and Tana's supply of milk had ceased; and where simply looking after babies was concerned, Sybilla had come into her own. After all, she had reared four with little help, never having been able to afford what she considered a proper nursemaid. Tana completely lacked the maternal instinct and was happy to leave the care of the babies to Sybilla.

Joanna gave little trouble, anything she could swallow she could digest; Robert was more frail and prone to coughs and colds and stomach troubles. Presently Joanna cut her teeth almost unnoticed while Robert was miserable, flushed, feverish and peevish. When in good health however, he was lively and merry and Sybilla's great fear — that one of these children could turn out like Margaret or Moyidan Richard — soon re-ceded. Robert and Joanna greatly resembled one another, both being blue-eyed and fair-haired, when they were asleep, with only their faces exposed they might well have been twins. Now and again, when Sir Godfrey saw them thus he felt a pang. His daughter had no real name; was in fact a bastard.

Sybilla's behaviour over the whole affair, the equality with which she treated the two, evoked his sincerest admiration; she was a woman in a million and although the ultimate intimacy between them was now forbidden, he loved her, if anything, more dearly than ever. That thought always brought him back to the problem of Tana.

So far she had kept her promise to be good, but now his animal instinct informed him that he was being hunted.

Dozens of times Ursula would come and say, 'Sir, please will you come? My mistress cannot make me understand.'

It was always some trivial thing, often something that could have been demonstrated if not explained in words. One could not expect a middle-aged serving woman from Bywater to acquire a working knowledge of Arabic, but Tana could have, should have, by now picked up enough English to enable her to give simple orders. She had once been eager to learn, had learned. All this nonsense was simply an excuse. Yet how could he express even the mildest irritation when, but for her he would still have been labouring away in the marble quarry at Andara — or dead of the cough that had claimed so many?

The nonsense disposed of, Tana always said, 'Now that you *are* here, take a glass of wine with me.' Everything in her pavilion had been planned to be seductive, and Tana herself, her figure restored, was seduction personified. He had never before seen her against the background that suited her so well; the silken scented background; he had trudged with her over the mountains, ridden across Spain with her, seen her in mean inns, on shipboard, and then in his own hall, with its one half-comfortable settle.

Sometimes she said, 'When will you be home again? Good. Ursula by then should have mastered the kebab. Come and take supper with me.'

Then he would mention that one of the knights had been invited to Knight's Acre for that evening, and she would say, with a most recognisable air of one retreating only to remuster and fight another day, 'He, too, will be welcome.'

One by one he brought them, and one by one they all — even the older men — succumbed to the charm of which he was so well aware, but to which he must not, must not succumb. She resolutely refused to speak any English, outside a few formal phrases, but the grace with which she served them, her smiles, her poses, the seemingly innocent way in which, seeing them laugh, she would join in, were all designed for a single purpose.

Sybilla never once evinced a sign of jealousy. The old Abbess had trained her to logical thought; it worked now, informing her that if Godfrey had been completely enamoured with this girl, so pretty, and as it had transpired, so rich, he would have gone off with her somewhere, not brought her back here, to his home. At the same time she was not blind; she saw through all the tricks and sometimes felt a faintly complacent pity for the girl who had almost everything except the one thing she wanted. Such an *empty* life. She did not even care for her own child.

October came, at first with gales from the west which would deter any fleet setting out from France, and then passing on to sunny days, invigoratingly chill at dawn and dusk, summer-warm at mid-day. Layer Wood was a riot of colour.

This year they could afford to eat fresh beef from the steer they had raised, and when, in the second week of the month Tana issued one of her invitations — having seen Sir Godfrey come home alone — he was able to say that this was one occasion when she must take supper with them, since they had a fine joint on the spit.

Towards the end of the meal, Tana turned to Sir Godfrey and asked when he would go back to Bywater. He told her, next morning. Although he came home whenever he could he was scrupulous about taking his turn of duty. She said, 'I wish to go with you. There are things I need to buy.' Hitherto he had made her purchases and offered to do so tomorrow but she smiled and said that there were things that only she could buy. He then made another objection; it would mean upsetting his careful shuttle service of mounts with one horse always fresh, crammed with corn, at Knight's Acre. But she was insistent; just this once. And he, like Sybilla, had thought what a dull life she led; no friends, nothing to do all day. He said, rather grudgingly, 'Very well.'

'It is like old times,' Tana said, as they rode through the coloured woods. She had never seen an English autumn before; she had not been on a horse for nine months; nor, so cunningly he had managed it, had she been alone with him, for more than a little while, for, failing other support, on a few rare occasions, he had brought Henry, the staring, infatuated boy with him. Now, so stubborn he was, he refused to admit that this was merely a continuation of their ride through Spain; he said, 'This is England, Tana.' England, a place where a man had one wife and no concubines. A state of things which Tana intended to change before this day died. And Sir Godfrey, exhilarated by the morning air, the colour, the leaves, lemon yellow, scarlet, crimson, bronze, dropping gently down, making a path for them, thought — but for her I should never have looked on this again . . .

With an eye as keen as his for terrain, Tana marked the spot. An ancient tree with low branches, suitable for the tethering of horses.

They clattered into Bywater and stabled at the inn. They arranged their meeting time.

When she failed to appear, he was not immediately anxious. She could hardly be lost. All the main streets in Bywater led down to the quay, and the side lanes from which the sea was not visible did not contain the kind of shop that Tana would be likely to patronise. He went into the inn and ordered wine. The delay was probably because at the mercer's she could not decide between two colours; or perhaps she was being measured for new shoes. There was also a possibility that being a stranger she had mistaken the bells which marked the day's divisions.

Presently, however, he began to worry. He remembered her method of shopping when they were in Spain, point to what she wanted and display money. Had she been a little careless in her display of money, been noticed, followed, dragged into one of those squalid narrow lanes and robbed? Had her beauty attracted some undesirable attention? There were always disreputable characters hanging about a port.

People came and went. The landlady who knew and liked him, hovered and then approached to tell him that the fresh pork was almost gone; unless he ordered now there would be nothing but salt beef. 'No matter,' he said, 'I will wait.' The landlady turned the hour glass and by that simple action reminded him that he had been waiting for more than an hour. Something must have happened to her, he must take action, alert the knights and ask them to help him to comb the town. He must also take precautions against Tana arriving here and finding him gone.

'If a lady comes, tell her to wait. I shall not be long.'

'What lady, sir?'

'You will know her. Young, very pretty. She is wearing tawny velvet. With fur, and a little cap of the same colour. And she has . . .' He was about to mention the black hair, most unusual in this district, when there was a clatter of hoofs outside and the landlady who was facing the window said, 'That looks like her now.'

He ran to the door, and there was Tana mounted — could a man believe his eyes? — on one of Tom Thoroughgood's horses — a stallion!

She must have stolen it. There was no other explanation. No Thoroughgood stallion was ever sold; only mares and geldings. England was riddled with monopolies but none was more strict than that exercised by successive Tom Thoroughgoods over this particular breed. Even their stallions' services were restricted either to Thoroughgood mares in the Nettleton pastures or to strange mares with no strain of the original blood. Because of their rarity, and their beauty — they were all pale cream with manes and tails a shade darker — they were in great demand and very costly. Queens and other ladies of high rank were proud to own a Thoroughgood.

'I am late,' Tana said. 'I am sorry. But that is a stubborn man. And the other horse delayed us.' The horse which she had ridden in the morning was on a long leading rein. Sir Godfrey had considered it an excellent horse, but comparison diminished it.

He had not missed the remark about the stubborn man. He could just imagine Tana pointing to the horse she wanted and Tom Thoroughgood refusing to sell. Then she'd hung about and stolen it — saddle and bridle, too! Terrible! There was nothing for it but to ride to Nettleton at once and explain that she was a foreigner and did not understand. He glanced at the sky; the West was already brightening and he'd told Sybilla they would be home early.

'We must take it back at once,' he said.

'But why? He is mine.'

'No Thoroughgood ever sells an entire.'

She laughed.

'So the stubborn man said. And he did not *sell*. I won him in a wager. I will tell you as you go.' She had lost or discarded the little cap and her hair flowed free. 'He does not like to wait.'

Sir Godfrey called for his horse and when it was brought round Tana said, 'You lead the other. It makes Jamil restive. Now I will tell you ... Last night you said, Godfree, that to lend me a horse would upset your arrangements; so I thought to myself — I will have a horse of my own! And I asked, where are good horses? The boy in the yard said at Nettleton and told me a short way to reach this place. And it was true, many,

many beautiful horses, but this the most beautiful of all. The man said he never sold a stallion. I showed him money. I promised more. Much more. But it was useless. He offered me others. He said stallions were not for ladies. This one, he said, was scarcely broken to the saddle yet and even he could hardly ride him. I said I could. Then he laughed and said that if I could ride this one once round the field he would give him to me but more likely I would get a broken neck. I said, "Saddle him." While he was being saddled I let him smell me, and I talked. I told him his name was Jamil and that he belonged to me. Then I rode round the field three times. The man called upon his God to strike him dead, but that did not happen. Instead he *cried*. That big strong man, he wept. Then he made me promise never to mate Jamil to any mare except one of his own, at that place. I swore by the sun. And I left all my money on the gatepost.'

'No wonder Tom Thoroughgood cried. He was breaking a rule that his family has kept for longer than man can remember,' Sir Godfrey said. Then a thought struck him. 'Did you speak in English to the stable boy and to Thoroughgood?'

'How else would they understand?' She made this admission without shame. 'I know what you think, Godfree. But the Arabic we speak together is all that we can share. It is precious to me.'

'Well, in future you can speak English to Ursula.'

'Then I should only see you when you come to supper with me. And to do that too often would not look well.'

To herself she thought that if her plan worked this evening he would come of his own accord.

'You are always welcome at my table,' he said.

'Thank you. I think that now I shall give Jamil his head a little.' Horse and rider disappeared around a bend in the lane. He followed as fast as he could, but both the Knight's Acre horses had covered ground already that day and he did not sight Tana again until he was through the water splash and entering the tunnel of trees where it was almost twilight. Then he saw the pale horse standing, without a rider on the verge of the lane and Tana huddled on a heap of beechleaves at the wood's edge. The brute had thrown her! Tom Thoroughgood had spoken of breaking her neck.

He dropped the leading rein and kicked his horse to a gallop.

Then, throwing himself out of the saddle he ran to her, 'Tana! Are you hurt?'

'Only tired,' she said in a soft, languorous voice. 'I have not ridden for so long. Now in one day, to Bywater and to Nettleton, and three times round that field . . . I must rest a little.'

'It's no distance now. We'll walk.' What with one thing and another they'd be late, not early as he had promised.

'I am so stiff. Help me up,' she said and held out her left hand. He took it. Her right arm went round his neck and pulled him close.

A man being tempted — and aware of the temptation — but determined to resist, does not cut an admirable figure. Among a medley of feelings he was aware of seeming ridiculous, longing for what he must repulse. Her kisses, the murmured endearments, the very scent of her hair stirred memories of the joy they had once known, even as he grappled to reach and control her caressing hands. The Devil whispered that Sybilla would never know; that he had lived like a monk since June . . . He said, short of breath, 'Tana . . . no. You promised . . . to behave . . . We must behave . . .'

'You promised that I should be *with* you. For me there is only one way to be with. It is this, heart of my heart.'

He had her hands now and could free himself, get to his feet. He jerked her to hers and still holding her at arms' length said,

'You must understand. I will *not*. Never, never do this to me again.'

'Then how can I live? And who would be hurt?' There was no real answer to that, unless he spoke stark truth and said — I should; in my own eyes; Sybilla and I made mutual vows; she held to hers for more than eight years, lonely years. I broke mine, but she understood and forgave me and treats our bastard exactly as she treats her own.

'And you do love me, Godfree. I could tell by your voice when you thought Jamil had thrown me. It was like that time in Seville . . .'

'I love you, but in a different way. Come, we must get along.'

Final touch to a ridiculous situation, was to find both his horses gone. They were within easy reach of their own stable, their own manger and at an easy pace had set out for home, the one which had carried Tana that morning, now and again tripping over the long leading rein.

'God in Heaven,' Sir Godfrey said, 'if they get home before us . . .'

He started to run.

Tana untethered Jamil and stood for a moment leaning against him, her face buried in his silky mane. 'At least I have you, my beautiful one.' But the resignation was not real. She had just suffered another defeat, but not, she felt, the final one. She had underestimated the strength of Sybilla's hold on him. She would not make that mistake again.

CHAPTER THIRTEEN

Sir William Barbury, having read his uncle's letter, gave them the gist of it. Bywater was no longer of any importance; the French were not coming, had never intended to come. The final confrontation between York and Lancaster would be in the North. The Queen's forces were mustering and Lord Thorsdale wanted every fighting man who owed him any allegiance to move immediately.

Only one man failed to respond. An archer, sweating and raving in one of Master Johnson's outlying barns. Genuinely ill, Sir Godfrey saw with his experienced eye. The others were rounded up and sent on their way and Sir Godfrey went hastily to his home to take leave of Sybilla who said, 'My love, I thought we were done with all this . . . And you not yet home a year.' But she was trained; a knight owed his allegiance to his lord. So she put on a resolutely cheerful face, hastily gathered a change of clothing and some food that would be edible for a month, kissed him, said as she had said so many times before, 'God keep you and bring you back to me, my dearest dear.'

Afterwards he could not remember where exactly he began to feel ill and had no appetite for supper, but forced it down and then went out to be sick. In the morning he mounted and rode alongside the others; and then his throat became so sore that even bread sopped in broth was hard to swallow, yet he must eat in order to be strong and keep up with the others. He was not conscious of the fact that he talked what sounded like nonsense — 'What happened to that donkey? But for it Arcol would never have gone aboard ... Oh yes, I can swim. It was the new armour, everything in the wrong place ... And I will not do it. Every sworn knight in Christendom is my blood brother. Tell him no ...'

They left him at an inn at a crossroad. A miserable place, but they had no choice; in the saddle he sagged, on ground he reeled about, calling Sir William Sir Robert. Useless. The landlady, Sir William noted had a mean face, eyes like pebbles, a mouth like a trap, but she was susceptible to money. Sir William had noticed that Sir Godfrey's pouch was thin. As usual when he went on campaign, Sir Godfrey had left almost all that he had with Sybilla, taking only just enough for bare necessities. Sir William therefore dived into his own purse and pressed into the hand a sum sufficient to keep a man for six months, and said, 'Good dame, tend him well.'

'He shall have the best that this poor house can offer, sir.'

She was afraid of infection, and left the work of caring for the sick man to the young maid of all work whose position was practically that of a slave. Upon her Sir Godfrey made a strange impression. At first she thought that he resembled a stone man who lay in the near-by church with his legs crossed and a little dog by his side. Then, as his illness ravaged him, he came more to resemble Christ, just taken down from the Cross, in a wall-picture in the same church. Also he had a beautiful voice, and although much of his talk was disorderly raving, he never said anything offensive.

There was nothing even remotely sexual in Griselda's attitude; she disliked men. She had been raped in a ditch when she was six. Shortly after that she had been taken into a convent orphanage, and from there thrust into the hurly-burly of life in a low-class inn; and there, despite her tangled hair and poor clothing, some men had used her. It was a case of comply or be beaten. She would have run away, but she had nowhere to go and she had vivid, painful memories of life on the roads as a beggar-girl.

On the third day the landlady was sure that Sir Godfrey would not recover; and his room was needed, for a steady stream of men, knights, archers, pikemen, were going through to the north. So she said to the man who was her only other

68

assistant, and to Griselda. 'Put him in the barn. He will die in any case.'

After that Griselda's behaviour was dictated partly by her almost mystical feeling towards the sick man, and partly by a hatred of her mistress. He shouldn't die if she could prevent it.

She was supposed to look in on him twice a day, to see whether he were alive or dead. She went far more often, usually under cover of darkness. She smuggled out broth, and milk, and propping him against her bony little shoulder, spooned the stuff into him. Once when a customer left wine in a jug, she took that, too. Now and again, mannerliness, ground into him from childhood, broke through the haze of delirium and he would say, 'Thank you'. Sometimes he called her Sybilla, and sometimes, Tana.

When the frost clenched down she took him an extra blanket, snatched from the bed of a customer whose face she did not like. Keeping him clean was easier here than it had been in the proper bed. He lay upon straw and all that was needed was to pull away that which was soiled and push clean under him.

Sir Godfrey became fully conscious, after what seemed like years of wandering in strange places, to find himself in a real, but equally strange place. The barn at The Swan was a rickety building with gaps in its walls, and the light that came through the gaps was the curiously chill light of sunlight on snow.

No pain; just an overwhelming weakness which prevented him from getting up and investigating. He could remember nothing and lying there could only conclude that he had gone to do battle and been hit on the head. And reached, or been carried to, the sanctuary of a barn. Yet he had no wound.

One of the chinks widened, admitting so much of the bleak light that he was obliged to close his eyes. Then, opening them, he saw a tatterdemalion figure, rough edged against the light. A lot of hair, skirt. Female. She carried a jug in her hand. He asked the natural question — 'Where am I?'

She said, 'Ah, you are back in yourself. But nobody must know. Drink this and then lie still. I will come when I can. We're busy.'

Busier even than they had been with the surge to the north. The tide had turned, now the move was to the south, or to the east. Not the gay, free-spending men of the wave which had landed Sir Godfrey at the cross-road inn, but desperate, defeated men, fleeing. Staying just long enough to snatch a bite of bread and cheese, to water and bait their horses. But of this Sir Godfrey knew nothing. All he knew was that he seemed somehow to have survived whatever it was that had stricken him down, that he was weak as a new-born kitten and that lying still would only further weaken him. What the young woman, whoever she was, had brought him in the jug, tasted of beef and onion and barley. Oxtail soup? Fortified by it he set himself to crawl, like a baby to the nearest wall and there, pulling himself up by its struts and beams, try his legs. The broth-bringer had said nobody must know that he was back in himself and as he stumbled, legs, arms, hands as flaccid as half-melted candles, his mind was alert and he was ready at any moment to drop down, to pretend to be asleep.

Before the last blue-white light faded he had made the circuit of the barn three times and was glad to lie still, in the straw, as she had told him to do.

Then it was dark and when, at last, she did come, she carried a lantern and in the crook of her arm some bread, some cheese. Welcome, for he was hungry now.

Wolfing down the first solid food he had had for a long while, regarding her as a friend, he asked, 'How did the day go?'

'What day?'

'The battle.'

About that she was informed. 'Badly for the White Rose. The Queen, or so they say, is terrible spiteful. She put the Duke of York's head on the city walls. With a paper crown on it.'

Then, click, click, click, things began to fall into place. He had come north, rallying to Lord Thorsdale's call to arms for all good men and true.

The girl said, 'If you was for the White Rose, sir, you was lucky not to be there. And you should move as soon as you can. Where do you come from?'

'Suffolk.'

'Is it far?' He tried to think back, but the last stages of his journey were still hard to recall.

'Several days' ride.'

'You'd want a horse, then.'

'Did I not arrive on a horse?'

'Yes. She sold that to a gentleman whose own went lame.'

'Who did?'

'My mistress. The landlady. You're at The Swan, at the crossroads, near Tadminster.'

'In the barn, why?'

'So's you should die and not know about the horse and your money. She took that, too. And you would of been dead, 'cept for me. I been looking after you as well as I could.'

'I am deeply grateful.' He finished the bread and cheese and lay back. Badly for the White Rose, the girl had said; a defeat always meant heavy casualties, so the chances were that Sir William and the others were dead. God rest their souls in peace.

The girl gnawed on her thumb, meditatively.

'If I got you a horse, could you ride?'

'I'd make shift to.'

'And take me with you? Find me a place? I'm a good worker and I don't eat much.'

'I owe you my life,' he said. 'While I have a roof and bread on my table, you shall share them.'

'That'll do for me,' she said. 'I'll fetch the horse while you dress. I brought your clothes to make you a pillow. I'll leave you the lantern. It's a moonlight night.'

He found his outer clothes and fumbled his way into them. The effort was exhausting and when the girl led the horse — its hoof-falls muted by snow, to the barn entry, he thought, weakly, 'What a tall horse!' And nothing, nobody to help him to mount, with his shaky, tremulous legs, he, whose pride it had once been to get astride Arcol with a single, smooth movement. The girl crouched, offering her shoulder. She said in a low voice, 'Heave on me, sir. I'm strong as a donkey.' Agile, too. She had no sooner thrust him into the saddle than she was up herself, her skinny little arms clasped around him, less to suport herself than to support him.

They rode through a night, sharply black and white. Now and again waves of weakness washed over him and the black and white mingled into a grey blur. He would not yield to it. Nor would he think about the ethics of his situation; riding a stolen horse, absconding with a girl. Presently, after endless years the sun came up, unfriendly, a pale lemon yellow. But it was to his left, the East, so he was riding South. Sheer luck since he'd been too weak and confused to consider his road.

A village of grey stone, such as he remembered from his first ride to Yorkshire.

'Go straight through,' the girl said. 'The Queen's men may be looking for people like you. I'll look out for a haystack.'

When she sighted one she thought suitable she said, 'Go to its far side,' and jumped down, ready to help him to alight. As soon as he was on his feet he stumbled and she said, 'I'll have a bed for you in a minute.' She dragged hay from the base of the stack, making a slight hollow. He was asleep, or unconscious as soon as he was prone. She stood for a moment looking at him dubiously. He wasn't fit to travel, but she hadn't dared delay. She'd always been aware of the risk that the landlady might think he was taking too long to die and order the yardman to pull enough straw over his face to suffocate him. That danger, at least was over, but he seemed to be a White Rose man; and between them they'd stolen a horse! Griselda turned her attention to that animal, placidly eating hay. When it had had its fill who could guarantee that it wouldn't wander off while she took a little nap? She made herself a little niche in the hay, higher up the stack, level with the horse's head, so that she could keep her arm through the rein. It was not very comfortable, but she slept. She had been awake and busy since dawn on the previous day.

A jerk on the rein woke her and looking down she saw a large shaggy dog sniffing suspiciously at the horse's heels. Then, on the farthest rim of the white expanse there was movement; a man, some sheep, coming this way. The little haystack had in fact been pitched in this isolated spot so that sheep could be fed when the ground was snow-covered.

She was down on a flash, shaking Sir Godfrey with rough urgency. Not knowing his name she could not use it, but she shouted, 'Wake up. Get up. We must go. Somebody's coming.'

Weak as he was, he still had the old soldier's trick of being instantly awake and active. The dog was trained to work silently with sheep, to bark only in emergencies. Satisfied that this was one, it gave tongue. It followed them, barking, as far as the road which was outside its territory. Its master who had intended to give it a good hiding for running off ahead, gave it

a pat instead. Plainly somebody had been at the hay. Would
have done more damage except for Old Rough.

'Do you feel better, sir?'

'Vastly better,' he said, though he had not taken stock of his
state. He had noted the place of the sun however. It was west-
ering, its cold lemon-yellow mellowed to pale gold and pink.
He must have slept for hours.

'What we need now is something to eat. Presently I'll do a
bit of begging. I used to be good at it.'

She was not in fact very hungry, having learned early in life
to do with little. She had, as she said, been good at begging, a
stick-thin little girl, but usually one of the adult members of
her band had taken the biggest share. Then there had been the
convent where the meals, though regular, had been sparse,
unless you were a favourite. After that The Swan where everything depended upon whether the place were busy or not, and
even at the busiest times she'd lived largely on what people left
on their plates. In slack times she had subsisted mainly on
Tinker's Broth; bread crusts and crumbs soused with hot
water and if you were lucky a little salt, if very lucky
a sprinkling of pepper. But he was different. He was a man,
accustomed to eating well: and for days he had had nothing
but slops.

It was almost sunset when a cluster of houses and a church
tower came in sight.

'This'll do,' she said. 'Set me down here. I mustn't be seen on
a horse. You ride straight through and wait for me, well on the
other side.'

Despite his sleep he was exhausted again, glad to halt the
horse and lean forward sagging, half-dozing. Yet it seemed a
long wait. Once when he roused himelf it was deep dusk; next
time the moon was bright. He tried to make allowance for the
fact that she had had to approach the village on foot, and had
perhaps been turned away from several doors. He had a vague
idea that some places had rules about begging and punished it
as a crime. Of that level of life he had no experience at all. He'd
always been rather poor and from time to time hungry, but the
net of privilege had always been there. And no doubt, not so
far away from this place there was some house where Sir Godfrey Tallboys would be welcomed. Unless the owner were a Red

Rose man. But he did not know where he was; on his ride North he had ceased to be observant. This might be Yorkshire, or Lincolnshire . . . All he could do was sit and wait for a good-hearted little kitchen slut to bring him food that she had begged — that is if anybody had given.

She came at last, pattering along over the snow. She was breathless and vociferous. 'Mean old bitch,' she said. 'Made me work for it. But I got it. Enough for a day. *And* found a place for the night. No, not worth getting up. It ain't far. Back this way. Follow me.'

She led the way on the road back to the village and stopped by a broken wall. 'In here,' she said, and there was a derelict house, its roof sagged, one wall was gone, but it offered shelter of a kind. And to its side a pond, greyly glimmering under a thin covering of ice.

'Ah yes,' Sir Godfrey said. 'The horse needs water.'

They had eased their thirst by scooping up snow and sucking it. The horse, offered a handful, had turned his head disdainfully.

'I'll see to him later. I want you settled first. I got a loaf and a pie. But I had to scrub out a bakehouse. Funny thing, soon as anybody sees me they think about scrubbing! I tried the priest first. Sometimes they're good. This one wasn't but he sent me along to what he called a good charitable woman and she said scrub the place out and she'd give me a loaf.'

'And a pie.'

'No. I took that.' This confession she regretted immediately as she remembered her company. Not like the old days when such an act would have been applauded. 'I earned it,' she said, defensively. 'I shouldn't think that floor had been swept, leave alone scrubbed, for about a year.'

She insisted upon his eating the pie while she contented herself with a small portion of bread.

'You have been ill,' she said, when he protested. 'You gotta build up your strength.'

There was much in this escapade — the makeshift food, the makeshift shelter, that recalled those days in the mountains with Tana. Curious, he thought; this makes the second time I have been saved by a woman. Their attitudes were very different, nothing seductive here, simply a brisk, businesslike motherliness.

'Now you lay and rest, and I'll have a look round for some-thing that'll hold water.'

He fell asleep immediately and woke to faint morning light. The girl was not in sight, but she came in almost immediately, holding her raggy skirt in a pouch.

'We're in luck,' she said with a grin that completely altered her sombre little face. 'Look what I found.' She displayed her treasure, a lapful of bright red apples. 'Nobody's been this way for a year I should think. These was still on the tree. Some on the ground, too. I gave them to the horse.'

Munching the cold, crisp fruit he said, 'I don't even know your name.'

'They called me Griselda at the covent.'

'It's a pretty name.'

'Is it? I almost forgot the sound of it. At The Swan it was always *girl*, or *you there*. What's your name?'

'Sir Godfrey Tallboys.'

'I reckoned you was somebody important.' Cracking the last pip of her apple between sound white teeth, she went on. 'We'll stow these about us and be on our way. That woman may have missed the pie. You'd hardly believe what a fuss people'll make about nearly nothing. I have watered the horse.'

'Did you find a bucket.'

'No. Nothing. So I took him to the pond and jumped on the ice.'

The horse was still bridled and saddled and Sir Godfrey thought — tonight I must do better, not go straight to sleep, neglectful.

He felt better this morning, clearer in his mind, stronger on his legs. They were still moving south, the snow covering grew thinner; here and there dark patches of earth and winter-bleached grass could be seen. Griselda did no begging that day; they finished the loaf and the apples, dismounting only to per-form natural functions, about which Griselda showed a sur-prising delicacy — until one remembered that she had spoken of a convent. From one of her modest errands she returned with an armful of hay. And after all, Sir Godfrey thought, such petty thieving, except that it was so petty, was no different from the process known to all fighting men — living off the country, gathering loot.

There was very little traffic on the road, and they attracted no attention; why should they? A man with a half-grown beard taking a girl to a new situation. Towards evening that day he recognised the inn where he had forced his dinner down and been sick — the onset of his illness. So now he knew where he was, and was back — so he thought — in a place where his credit would be good. The net of privilege tautened beneath him, and turning his head slightly, he said to Griselda, 'We may find a welcome here. And proper beds.'

He was disappointed. The first wave of refugees, fleeing to the coast to take ship to the Netherlands, had carried news of the terrible vengeance that Queen Margaret was taking upon all the supporters of the White Rose. Innkeepers had never been able to afford partisan sympathies, but they could at least be careful. And this one was. Yes, indeed, he remembered Sir Godfrey Tallboys, even though this gaunt unshaven man bore only a slight resemblance to the man who had been one of a number who took their dinner here on their way to Thorsdale — and to defeat at the Battle of Wakefield, fought while Sir Godfrey lay raving in the straw. 'But, sir, I can do nothing. The Queen's men ...' And it was strange, Sir Godfrey thought, that the King, Henry VI should now be so utterly discounted — not savage enough; he, the gentle scholar would never have ordered that mockery of a severed head, crowned with paper.

'They are widening their search. If you were found here ... But on the other hand, if I did not *know* ... If you rested in one of my outbuildings and your horse took what he could find. In the pasture. That is all I can do. I am sorry, Sir Godfrey.'

The horse, free of saddle and bridle after so many hours, cast himself down and rolled in the bit of pasture, easing his hide. Sir Godfrey and Griselda slept warmly, in hay again. And woke hungry.

But at least he now knew where he was.

And next day, hour by hour, the countryside became more familiar ...

Unlike Sybilla who had thought Knight's Acre too large and unwelcoming; unlike Tana who had thought it mean and small, to Griselda the house looked wonderful. Just the solid, sturdy kind of place which in her dreams had always meant home. Some image, imprinted upon an infant mind, too young to have conscious memory, had been with her, through the beggar days, through the convent days. She had a distinct feeling that at last she was coming home. She had in fact spent her first two years in such a house. Then the owner — an oldish man had died and his heir had made what he called a clean sweep ... The impression had remained, however.

CHAPTER FOURTEEN

Once again Sybilla said, 'Darling, darling,' and flung herself, weeping into his arms. 'I have been so worried. Not about the battle, I knew you were not there, but about your sickness.'

He said, after endearments and embracings, 'How did *you* hear about the battle, sweeting?' It was a reasonable question, for as he and Griselda had moved south knowledge of the great Lancastrian victory at Wakefield had faded away. Nobody knew; nobody cared.

Sybilla said, 'Sir William Barbury is here. He escaped. He needs help, more than I could give.'

'Here?'

'Here. In our hall. He was hurt, but not seriously.'

All the jauntiness and confidence had leached out of Sir William together with the blood he had lost. He made light of his wound, which was in his shoulder, a well-directed arrow having pierced the joint in his armour, but he was grave about his predicament.

'The Queen is rooting out all known Yorkists, Sir Godfrey. I am the last of the Barbury family. My uncle, my cousin who was his heir, and my brother died at Wakefield. I am Lord Thorsdale now and I am safe nowhere in England.'

'We must get you out,' Sir Godfrey said. Something in his mind said — Tomorrow! In the eyes of the Queen, in the eyes of every Lancastrian, all Yorkists were rebels, and to harbour a rebel was as bad as being one. He thought — and was not proud of the thought — that apart from harbouring Sir William, his own record was fairly clear. All the preparations for holding Bywater against the French had been, as Lord Thorsdale had ordered, secret; he himself had not been within miles of the battle; neither he nor his brother James had ever taken a stand for Red Rose or White.

Money! The essential thing which for many years he had taken so lightly.

'You will need money, Sir William.'

'I know. That is why I came. I have none. One does not ride to battle with a pouchful of money. All my friends in the north were dead or in flight. I could only hope that you had recovered and reached home. And would help me.'

'And so I will. To the utmost,' Sir Godfrey said staunchly, though the thought occurred that now there would be no more regular payments.

'It will not be for long,' the new Lord Thorsdale said. 'Edward of York will avenge his father.'

'I will arrange money, and a passage for you. Rest easy now.' Suddenly he remembered Griselda. 'My love, I brought a girl home with me. She saved my life.'

'You make a habit of it,' Sybilla said, laughing rather shakily. 'Does this one plan a pavilion?'

The most obvious person to make a loan was the wool-merchant, Master Johnson who had had so many dealings with Lord Thorsdale in the past. But he was a cautious man and without sentiment. He had been accommodating over the secret defence of Bywater — but he had been paid for it. He was willing to make a loan, but he must have some security.

'I have a small flock,' Sir Godfrey said. 'I'll pledge them, hoof and hide.'

'Unreliable,' Master Johnson said. 'The bloody flux or the liver rot can wipe out a flock in no time at all.'

Sir Godfrey thought of his brother James and of Tana and quickly dismissed them both. James was not only careful with his money, but with his politics as well; and to borrow from Tana would commit him further.

'I have a good house,' he said, 'and three fields.' And even as he spoke he thought — the house is Sybilla's, and the fields are Henry's. However, in the eyes of the law they were his, and he pledged them at a crippling rate of interest. About that he dared hardly think. Instead he thought that Sir William — so like Sir Robert — need not beg or starve in Amsterdam, to which city there was, most fortunately, a ship about to sail.

Sybilla took charge of Griselda in whom she saw the possibilities of the kind of nursemaid she had never been able to find when the other children were young. Griselda's hair, well-washed, proved to be the colour of straw and naturally curly. It was her best feature; her eyes were greenish, but small and seemed lashless, the lashes were so fair; her nose was snub, her mouth thin-lipped. Not pretty, but in one of Sybilla's made-over dresses, she was a neat trim figure. She was anxious to please, and in the convent orphanage had learned something about the care of children. She began to model herself, voice, manner, posture upon Sybilla who, for her, was compact of every virtue, every grace.

Jill and Eddy and Ursula across the yard who had seen her when she first arrived and thought that here was somebody to be put upon, given all the unpleasant tasks, were envious of her status, cruelly mocking about what they called her fine airs. Generally she ignored them but occasionally she would show them something of her other side. She had a vicious tongue and where abuse was concerned a vocabulary that vastly exceeded theirs.

For the first time in her memory she was consciously happy; pleasant easy work in a clean, orderly house, a kind mistress to be copied and adored. Her feeling of homecoming at the sight of the house had been fully justified.

In the shuttered room where Sir James now spent most of his time, Sir Godfrey said, 'I'm sorry James, that I did not take your advice a year ago. I've come to it now. My employment has ceased — and I have incurred a debt.'

Sir James' wits were still sharp enough to enable him not to ask about the debt. Godfrey, apart from the one period of prosperity which had had so short a run, had always been more or less in a financial muddle. And over the eviction of tenants with no unalienable rights at Intake he had been definitely wilful.

'You mean you are about to tidy up your estate?'

'Short of causing any great hardship, yes. It was never an estate, James. The rents fixed by that old parchment were ridiculous, even in Father's day. I cannot exactly remember how many of the people are protected by it.'

'Less than half, if I remember rightly,' Sir James said. 'But

Joycelyn will know. He looked into the matter for you and he remembers everything. Poor fellow he grows very stiff.'

Curious the pleasure ageing and afflicted people took in the ageing and affliction of those who were their contemporaries. Sir Godfrey had seen it before without reflecting upon it much. Now he did, thinking it not unlike a game of cards; one man slapping down his stiff joints, another his gout, a third his failing sight. Pray God, he should not end in such decrepitude, suffering infirmities and taking comfort in the infirmities of others. God, let me die in battle, my spirit high, my blood hot, my end sudden.

Yet Sir James had his comfort. Richard's wife was pregnant and Richard was happy. He and his wife walked about hand in hand; a pair of turtle doves. And Emma — choking back her doubts and fears, spoke cheerfully, admitting that Richard was not quite what one could have wished, but that could be explained by the fact that he was so late born. Margaret was, in her opinion, just a silly girl, made sillier by Sybilla's mismanagement. 'She spoiled all her boys until they were intolerable. She spoiled Margaret until she was stupid. There is *no* reason why the child should not have all his wits about him.' If prayers were answered, he would, for Lady Emma constantly added to her ordinary prayers an urgent plea that the child should be all right and that James should live to handle his grandchild.

At Intake there were no evictions, for most of the vulnerable tenants, warned by the inquisition in the previous year had money ready for the increased rents. There was a good deal of grumbling, many sullen looks, but at least Sir Godfrey was able to pay the interest on Master Johnson's loan, due on Lady Day.

At Moyidan, on that same day, Margaret, who had no clear idea about her state, said, 'Margaret has a pain.' Within an hour Margaret had a baby, in such a state of profound indifference as not to bother to ask, girl or boy? Richard seemed almost equally unconcerned. Lady Emma was cautiously delighted. It was a boy, a good compact child with a lot of black hair. That meant nothing; birth hair almost always wore off and grew again. It was too early to tell whether the baby's wits were in good order; it would take six months. Lady

Emma remembered the moment when she realised that Richard, at six months — the son so long awaited, so much desired — had seemed so inert and un-noticing compared with what his sister had been. But then Richard had been frail from the first. This was a lusty child; and Margaret, however stupid and indifferent should feed him, Emma decided, even if she had to take her by the neck and force her to it.

The family cradle had been brought back from Knight's Acre and thoroughly refurbished. The family emblem had been reprinted by a good craftsman; the hare brown, the leveret buff, the grass green. Lady Emma had seen to the stuffing of the little mattress and the pillow with the finest goosedown, and with her own hand had quilted the cover. The carter's son lay soft and warm.

'Of course I wish to see him,' Sybilla said when the message came. 'And of course I can still ride . . .' It seemed a long time since she had threatened, if Sir Godfrey couldn't rouse himself to do it, to exercise the great warhorse, Arcol. 'I am not so nimble as I was, but I shall manage.' The years reduced one's nimbleness; and her fall had left her lame and slightly lopsided and then Robert's birth had taken toll. Also just lately, she had been subject to sudden attacks, about which the less said the better. Quite disgusting. She thanked God for Griselda, so capable, so reliable, and so understanding. 'Griselda, say that it is just a head-ache. No need to mention . . . the rest. My head does ache.'

During the attacks she ached everywhere and was sick, forced to the stool-room five times in an hour, afflicted with pins and needles in her hands and feet. But the attacks always passed and she was well again — until next time. It was her age; she accepted it. Some women grew grossly fat or violently ill-tempered . . . She had seen it happen to others and thought that on the whole she was getting off lightly. On the day of the visit of Moyidan she felt very well and was able to say to Emma, on the other side of the cradle, 'Well, here we are, Emma. Grandmothers. God send that his wits are as sound as his limbs.'

'God send it should be so. We can only wait . . . Sybilla, what have you been putting on your face? Allow me to say that it does not become you at all.'

In the old days, before Knight's Acre was built, when she had no home of her own and was forced to accept the increasingly grudging hospitality of Moyidan, Sybilla had become accustomed to criticism. She had always done her best with re-made, even re-turned dresses and the latest hair style, and she could make a fashionable head-dress out of almost nothing. All the little secrets and the little tricks she had been most willing to share with Emma who had very seldom accepted the humble offering in the right spirit. But this accusation of putting something on her face was quite unjustified.

'What do you mean, Emma: Nothing but water has touched my face today. As you should know, such frivolity I gave up years ago.'

'That may be. But come to the light. Yes, I am not mistaken. Your skin is a most peculiar colour. Less yellow than jaundice . . . Not sun tan — not that there has been much sun so far. Did you wash in muddy water?'

'No. Our well, even in high summer gives good clear water.'

'Well, all I can say is that you have a dusky look. Almost bronze. And you had such a pretty complexion . . .'

'We grow old, Emma.'

'That is true.' But, turning from the window to the cradle, Emma thought — I must not! My son is a fool, his wife is a fool, James is failing; there is something wrong with Sybilla and Godfrey, if a bugle blew ten miles away would ride off on one of his fruitless errands. On me and me alone this child depends.

Gallant to the end Sybilla said, 'No. I do not want a doctor. He would only bleed me and give me calomel. The one thing I do *not* need. I will try the Lamarsh cure. Dame Agnes there, when I was going through my training in the infirmary always said "Give them nothing to be sick *with*". It often worked.'

It worked — or seemed to for her illness receded when she took nothing but water and a bite or two of bread. Not a diet, Sir Godfrey pointed out, upon which one could live for ever. 'There never was much of you, darling, and now you seem to be wasting away.' It pained him that he could no longer afford the good red wine which was so heartening — however, Tana was generous with hers, and also with various dainty dishes which Ursula had at last been taught to make.

Without telling Sybilla Sir Godfrey fetched the physician

from Baildon. He spoke portentously about a bilious humour, bled her from the third finger of the left hand, advised a light diet and prescribed, not calomel, but opium pills which did something to alleviate the stomach cramps.

Henry worried, too. Their manner of life during his father's absence had bonded mother and son very closely not only because of the raid, Walter's death, and the plague, but in the shared work and the business of making ends meet. The cure for worry was hard labour, and of that the boy had sufficient to keep his mind occupied during the day; it was in the evening, coming into the house — perhaps to find Mother in her place at the supper table, assuring them all that she was better, but eating almost nothing and looking ghastly; perhaps to be told that she was having another attack, then misery smote. On one such evening he remembered her flowers, and went around to the garden and gathered a few of the first rosebuds and a stem or two of the lilies on which the flowers were just breaking. There was something infinitely touching in the way his big, toil-worn hands carried the fragrant, fragile offering. And he was so like his father . . . though Godfrey had been some years older when she saw him first. She was obliged to force back the tears. She thanked him for the flowers, and for the thought and then turned to practical things. 'You started the hay today, did you not? Is the crop good?'

She was ten times more conversant with the farm work than Father, who, now that his wonderful appointment had ended, did his best to help about the place, but so ignorantly and clumsily that it made Henry impatient to watch him. And suppose he'd been fool enough to heed Father's suggestion about leaving the farm!

They talked for a little. John had been Idle Jack, as usual; Tom Robinson had had to lie down for a bit; they'd caught two rabbits. 'Not as big as harvest ones, but they'll make a meal,' Henry said. He was again the provider — this time for more mouths.

'I must wash,' he said, and gave her one of his rare, but singularly sweet smiles, as though sharing a joke. She had always been so insistent upon the washing of hands before meals and upon other small niceties. She'd said, 'Poor we certainly are, but good behaviour costs nothing.'

'I hope you will feel better tomorrow.'

'I am sure I shall.' Dame Agnes' stringent cure had been again effective, and although she felt weak, she was better. But as Henry turned towards the door, Sybilla wondered for the first time, about the certainty of that betterment. Fasting did cure, but it also weakened. She said, 'Henry I pray that you may be happy and successful all your life. Choose your wife with care. A good wife is the best thing a man can have.'

'Is Mother dying?' the brutal, brusque question brought Sir Godfrey's own hidden fear to the surface and he rebuffed it.

'No, of course not! The doctor did not take that view at all. What made you think that?'

'Something she said. It sounded as though . . . as though she were taking leave of me . . .'

'She did not speak so to me when I carried up her supper and lit the candle. But I will see . . .'

'When was that?'

'Just before supper. I took her a few flowers.'

'But I've seen her since then . . . She said she . . .'

Abandoning his supper Sir Godfrey rushed upstairs, two at a time, stood at the top and drew a steadying breath and then, forcing a casual manner, entered the sick room.

'That was a very short supper,' Sybilla said.

Yes, he thought, she sounded weaker, farther away. He sat on the bed and took her hand. It felt cold and clammy. So little time ago it had been hot.

'You feel worse, darling?'

'Weaker . . . I think, perhaps, Father Ambrose . . .'

It was as much as he could do to call from the stair head.

The old priest was now so blind that except in his house or in the church, where he could feel his way about, he needed guidance or made slow progress by sweeping a stick in front of him to make sure that his path was not obstructed. With mounting impatience Henry saw him collect his little basket, guided him into the church and out again. Then he said, 'Father, with your permission, I will carry you.' The age-withered body was not very heavy and Henry was able to break into a trot. Not, Father Ambrose thought, quite the proper dignified way for the Host to travel, but so long as they reached the poor lady in time . . .

They were too late.

CHAPTER FIFTEEN

It took Tana some little time to understand that in disposing of Sybilla she had cleared her way to nothing. She was hardy, ruthless and young. She thought it natural enough that in this strange country — one woman to one man — when that one woman died there should be a little time of mourning. A few months . . . during which she must be patient, tactful. She absolutely refused to see that Sybilla's death had been, in a way, Godfree's too.

There was the small matter of the place where Sybilla lay. Henry explained that. 'My father grieves that my mother lies under plain stone. He wished for marble.'

'And where, in this country, is marble to be found?'

'How can I know?' In fact Henry was not quite certain what marble really was. Some kind of stone, he supposed, having regard to its purpose — a floor over the dead. 'There is a stone-mason in Baildon. I could ask him.'

The stonemason in Baildon did not usually stock such costly stuff, but he had, in the early summer, laid a floor in an ornate little side chapel of the Abbey, and due to a slight mis-calculation, had a bit of black marble left over from that job. Four feet by two and a half. Henry found it, brought it home in the wagon. Tana paid for it.

It made no difference. Sybilla under marble was just as dead and lost as Sybilla under stone. Tana was not warned by that, not by something that happened late in November, momentous as it was. What had been taking place in the outer world had concerned this bit of Suffolk very little. But here was Lord Thorsdale, with three friends, apologising for delay in coming — he'd had to take possession of his Yorkshire estates, attend upon Edward IV who had indeed avenged his father.

Faced with this invasion of young, and very happy men, Sir Godfrey had asked Tana to come and preside at his table. But when assured of his re-appointment, and of the paying back, ten times over of the loan, that harassing debt, he had simply said, 'It is too late. Sybilla never had anything . . .' and hurried from the table to hide his tears.

Henry said, diffidently yet firmly, 'Father, you now have money . . .' That was the odd thing, the boy thought; work from dawn till dusk, contrive, make do, and all you had was a bare livelihood. Do nothing useful, make no plans, and money simply fell into your hand. In his heart the son resented his father's extremity of grief and the way in which he had given way to it. *He* was sorrowful, too, but he had no time to droop about and nurse his feelings.

'Yes,' Sir Godfrey said mildly. 'Lord Thorsdale repaid the sum I lent him, with a very generous gift. And he re-appointed me as his agent. But . . .' And Henry knew that he was about to hear yet again, the cry that prosperity had come too late. He forestalled it.

'I should like to clear some more land. Walter and I did what we could and the three fields kept us. The household has grown since then . . .'

'*And* diminished . . .'

'Mother is dead,' Henry said, harshly because pain stabbed. 'And we miss her good management. That is one reason why we must do better. Also, with due respect, sir, this see-saw between York and Lancaster is not ended. It may tip the other way. It has before. The best guard against disaster is a field yielding food, and a well-filled stockyard.'

'Do what you think best,' Sir Godfrey said. He thought, with a slight resentment: Yes, the young recover and forget the dead, make plans, think about money. He forgot that he had, with equal resilience, survived the death of both his parents.

Tree-fellers came, and after them the ox teams, straining and pulling away the trunks of the cut-down trees. Then came the grubbers, men and women and children who, with the most unlikely tools, and with their hands, grubbed out the tree roots, carried them away and cut them up to be hawked as firewood. Henry, helping them all, hurrying them all because he wanted the newly cleared land ploughed and seeded, gained himself an unenviable reputation as a slave-driver.

Late in November of that year he looked out over the newly

cleared land and said to Tom Robinson, 'It's more than we can manage, Tom. Is there nobody in the village to be hired?'

'I'll go down and see,' Tom said. His real roots in the village had been severed in the time of the plague when he had lain sick, almost to death at Knight's Acre, and been tended by the lady and by Master Henry. Since then his loyalty had been absolute and his reputation in the place of his birth very low. The people of Intake — rebels to begin with, had never looked on Knight's Acre with any great favour. Walter had been hated, with his scarred face and arrogant manner — and there was the Wade girl, who had fled because — she said — he had assaulted her . . . But Tom Robinson had, when he cared to exercise it, a glib and persuasive tongue. Nobody was asking, he said, that men should live in the house, as he did himself, and apparently quite comfortably, if you didn't mind the servility which living in implied. Day labour was different; set times, set wages. Two of the families who had none of those 'inalienable rights', and who were now paying extra rent, decided that they could spare a boy. To be paid by the week and given a mid-day meal.

Tom, walking back at the slow pace which since the plague he had found most suitable to his state, just missed Father Ambrose who, clearing the way with his stick made his way from the church to Knight's Acre. He knew, only too well that he was almost blind and often forgetful. He also knew that what he had just experienced was unusual, if not unique.

'I was,' he told Sir Godfrey, 'changing the candles. The good lady, as you must know, gave the church a supply of good candles as soon as she could afford. I took no light . . . I work well, in the dark . . . by touch. So I was in the dark. Then I smelt lilies. She always brought them you know . . . for the altar. I smelt them and forgetful of time, of everything, I turned to thank her . . . I forgot — old men do, you know — that it was winter and she in her grave. There was a faint light, visible even to me, over her tomb and a strong scent of lilies. I am not a man to make judgments . . . and about what awaits us all, after death, I must only believe what the Church teaches. But . . . Would it be too fanciful to think that she knew how grieved I was . . . not to be in time to administer . . . while she was conscious, and could respond . . . and perhaps asked, or was given, leave to return . . . To re-assure me that all was well and that she was happy, with the flowers she loved?'

Hitherto Sir Godfrey's religion had been almost a military exercise. There were orders and rules which must be obeyed; rites to be observed, or, if disregarded, done penance for. Now and again, in a desperate situation he had called upon God; God help me; God save me . . . but always as a man might call upon his liege lord. Of mysticism there was not a trace in his nature. Even when God had seemed to fail him — in that narrow, balconied street with his scorched fingers trying in vain to release Lord Robert; under the lash of the whip in the mine, and more lately when he prayed for Sybilla's recovery; a disciplined soldier did not query his overlord's decisions. Now, however, something hitherto unknown sparked in his mind and what Father Ambrose said about the possible reason for the manifestation was absolutely in accord. If Sybilla wished to re-assure the old man who had not failed in his duty but had simply been too late, how much more would she wish to assure him?

That night he knelt on the cold stone, just inside the church door, with Sybilla's grave between him and the altar. He had kept a similar vigil, in the chapel at Beauclaire on the night before he received his knighthood. He did not think of that now, he was concentrating too fiercely upon his petitions, partly to God, partly to Sybilla's spirit, for some sign of her presence, of her awareness of him. No infatuated young lover ever craved more avidly for some glance or gesture of favour. In the chilly, damp-smelling church on this winter's night he sweated with fervour.

He saw nothing, smelt no lilies.

In the reluctant dawn, the sense of failure and rejection heavy upon him, he examined the cause of failure. Then he remembered that other vigil so carefully prepared for; the ritual bath, the clean clothing, the confession and the absolution, so that the would-be knight came to the altar as clean and pure, both in body and soul as mortal man could be. For this one he had made no preparation at all.

Henry, if asked, within his own mind, would have said that his father was irresponsible, but in fact his own deep feeling of responsibility was inherited from Sir Godfrey; they merely moved in different worlds. Sir Godfrey, as the light crept in through the unglazed window, was prepared to acknowledge that the failure was due to fault in him.

Father Ambrose came as always to perform the morning office. Between his house and the church he had no need to bother with his stick; he could feel his way along the walls. So he walked into, and stumbled over Sir Godfrey, and they fell together, in an ungainly heap upon the floor. Sir Godfrey scrambled to his feet and lifted the old man, apologised, asked was any damage done.

'No. No. I fell upon you, Sir Godfrey . . .' He recognised the man by his voice. 'Are you hurt?'

'No.'

'Why are you here so early?'

Sir Godfrey, never good at explaining, tried to explain. The priest with long experience with inarticulate people in this rural and not very friendly parish understood. Then, abruptly assuming clerical authority, as a man might don a cloak, he said,

'My son, that was a very wrong thing to do. Such an experience cannot be demanded. It came to me — the *last* thing in my mind. I was thinking about the candles, pure wax, and so thick. Her gift.'

'I was ill-prepared,' Sir Godfrey said, and he spoke as though he had, in his own sphere, neglected his armour or his horse. 'Father, will you take my confession now?'

It was rambling and incoherent, and with one exception, not concerned with anything that the Church regarded as sin.

'I neglected her . . . Not wantonly. Not for other women. But I was careless with money . . . Had I been more careful . . . I once gave her a ring, with a blue stone. It was no sooner on her finger than it was off again, because I needed a new horse. She always wanted a house — and that I did at last provide. And I spoilt her joy in it, coming home as I did, in evil temper . . .'

'My son, these are not *sins*.'

'They are to me, now. I only realised . . . when she was dead.'

The old priest in his way as rigid and disciplined as Sir Godfrey thought — if every man who bore hard on his wife and gave way to temper, came to confess, the line would stretch from here to the water splash! And what possible penance could I order?

Sir Godfrey said, 'And I did sin. I . . . I committed adultery.'

So! Father Ambrose thought — now we come to the nub.

'Did you confess, at the time?'

'I did. To the first priest I could find.'

'And performed your penance?'

'Yes, Father.'

'Took notice of the order to avoid the occasion?'

'To the best of my ability.' Sir Godfrey looked back; how many times? All confessed, all absolved. There had been that moment in the lane, and that he realised was more than a year ago. He *had* avoided the occasion for further sin. But in his mind something still weighed heavy. He said, bringing the words out with difficulty. 'My wife knew . . . and forgave me. What she did not know and what I could not tell her was that it was not only the flesh — as she thought . . . There was a time when my mind, my heart were corrupted, too.'

'And would that knowledge have given her happiness?'

'No.'

The old priest had met this condition before. Bereavement bringing remorse. Even the most earthy people would say, 'And I spoke sharply to him on Wednesday for forgetting my new needle,' or 'Only the day before last I fetched her a clout, as my dinner wasn't ready.'

Father Ambrose brought to the forefront of his mind a thought which had been nibbling behind the attention he had been giving. He could not see what was taking place at Knight's Acre, but he could hear gossip. The flock of sheep enlarged, more land being cleared. Bert Edgar and Jem Watson hired as day labourers. It all smelt of prosperity.

He said, 'It is best to put such thoughts away. The Lady Sybilla was a good wooman, and is now in Heaven where there is neither marriage nor giving in marriage . . . I cannot claim to have had a vision, but there was something . . . It is possible that there was a purpose behind it all. She loved this church. She brought her flowers, always. She gave the candles. She deplored, with me, the state of decay into which it has fallen. I am sure that, given the means, she would have repaired the roof.' He let the hint fall gently upon the contrite heart. The effect was immediate. Once Sir Godfrey was enlisted to a cause he was with it, heart and soul.

'I will do it,' he said. And he meant not the roof only; the walls upon which the painted pictures were almost indecipherable; the Virgin in her little niche, all should be restored. And the altar properly furnished. A fitting memorial to Sybilla.

It did not bring the comfort which had been a fraction of Father Ambrose's intention. Considering how small a part of their married life had been spent together, he missed Sybilla disproportionately. They had not always been together, but she had always been in his mind, his mental lodestar and there were times when, seeing some progress in the work, or a hitch, he would think — I must tell Sybilla and then realise . . .

Henry thought the whole thing a sad waste of money that could have been far better employed. Certainly mend the roof, which had been thatched; thatch could be patched; no need to strip it all and cover it with stone slabs, brought down from the north at vast expense; no need for the window behind the altar to be filled in with coloured glass, little leaded panes which when assembled formed the letters, S and T and some flowers. Pretty, but Mother, Henry was sure, would have preferred to see the money spent on practical things.

Tana watched. This, she believed, was Godfree's final tribute to his first wife. Men did such things. About a day's journey from her father's fortress, southwards, into the desert there was an oasis, a whole flourishing village which one of her forebears had established as a memorial to a dead woman; Mahbuub, beloved.

Once this was over Godfree would be himself again.

The villagers of Intake, knowing nothing of the debt which Sir Godfrey had incurred and which had been paid back, grudged every penny, assuming that it was their money, the extra rents, being so recklessly squandered. They were interested none the less and curious and for several weeks Father Ambrose had the kind of congregation formerly only seen at Christmas and Easter.

The year pulled itself out of the slough of winter and advanced steadily towards summer.

CHAPTER SIXTEEN

Sir Godfrey was not as his son thought him, a mere idler, a fritterer away of money, nursing his grief. He had been re-appointed to his post at Bywater and went there regularly to oversee matters. But every visit darkened his mood. There was the jetty from which Arcol would not move unless preceded by the old donkey. He remembered the clatter and clamour of that day and must think — I am the only one left alive. Then there was the house in which the knights had lived, making merry while guarding against an invasion from the French. There, God forgave him, he had enjoyed a taste of bachelor life, away from women and babies. He was not the only one left of that merry company, for William Barbury was now Lord Thorsdale; he sent kind messages and gifts from time to time.

In Bywater he had nothing to *do*. His post was a sinecure and everybody treated him as though he were old. All very respectful — 'A keen wind this morning, Sir Godfrey. Don't stand about. Everything goes well.'

'All that is needed is your signature, sir.'

He loathed it, being treated like a dotard. He was forty-six and he knew that given a chance he could still outride, outfast any of these bustling, careful, kind little men, appointed by Lord Thorsdale to make his post a sinecure. Curiously, his inner breakdown, his hopeless misery had affected his outer appearance very little. He'd lost weight all to the good in a man of middle-age. The silvery streaks in his hair had multiplied, but he had been fair once, and the paler hairs, mingling with the fawn of his later years made him look, if anything more youthful.

He made regular visits to Moyidan, and they did little to cheer him; James was now bedridden, his legs swollen to im-mense size, the rest of his body shrunken. Emma still cared for him competently but it was plain that the focus of her at-tention and emotions had shifted to the child; in her opinion the most wonderful child ever born. Certainly little Richard seemed to have inherited none of the weakness of mind and body which had afflicted his parents. Nor was he at all like a normal Tallboys child; he was thick set, black-haired, dark-eyed, and to Sir Godfrey's eye lacked the charm which his own sons had had, even at their naughtiest moments. A man should take pleasure in his grandchildren, but watching little Richard or listening to Emma's infatuated account of his latest show of precocity, strength and intelligence, Sir Godfrey felt nothing except, now and again, a vague wonder that the child should seem so different. Emma accounted for his colouring by saying that he resembled her side of the family. She had always accused Sybilla of spoiling her children, but no child had ever been so spoiled as this one.

Visits to his own nursery — established in what should have been Sybilla's solar — brought him little joy, though both children there were charming, lovely to look at, and — firmly ruled by Griselda — well-behaved. The thought was unavoidable, Sybilla had never fully recovered from that premature birth, and until Griselda's arrival, had worn herself out caring for both children. Joanna in no way resembled her mother but to look at her was to be reminded of the infidelity which Father Ambrose had dismissed so lightly. Easy enough for an old man who had lived all his life in celibacy. Also there was something about Griselda herself at times which was disquieting until he spotted the reason for it — a vagrant likeness to Sybilla, a mocking likeness. He decided that it was the dress and asked if it was one from the chest upstairs.

'Yes, sir. But I didn't *take* it,' Griselda said, instantly defensive. 'My lady and I were patching it just before . . .'

She was perhaps the one person who, given the slightest encouragement, could have offered him genuine sympathy and understanding, for she shared his sense of loss. Sybilla had been, as well as mistress and mentor, a mother to her — the mother she had never known. Without her Griselda felt stranded, there was nobody at Knight's Acre whose advice she could ask — or would have taken; and it was sad that the lady could not see how Robert's health had improved and the difference between the two children was growing slighter. A pity, too, that the lady could not see how well Griselda was managing, remembering all the rules, the gentle hints. Of all this the girl showed nothing; life had early robbed her of the capacity to show the gentler emotions.

'If it is already patched you'll soon need a new one,' Sir Godfrey said. 'I will bring you some stuff.'

Another painful reminder came when John discovered Sybilla's lute and soon developed an ability to play it. The lute having a limited range it was inevitable that he should make some sounds that evoked memories. To some men the sight and sound of Sybilla's son playing Sybilla's lute might have brought some sentimental consolation, to Sir Godfrey it merely rasped a raw nerve and one evening he said, 'Go and play elsewhere.'

Henry, who regarded the lute-playing as effeminate, and a waste of time, grinned and said, 'That's right. Go play to Young Shep. He spends half his day making pipes.'

In all this time Tana had behaved impeccably. She had never obtruded on his grief; Sybilla had been dead a full three months before she issued a supper invitation and that included Henry and John. She looked in at the nursery from time to time and occasionally drifted into the kitchen to spur Jill and Eddy into some show of activity and to see that the larder was kept supplied. Jill was no manager and would use the last handful of salt or flour without asking Henry to bring some from Baildon, or Sir Godfrey to buy in Bywater. Nobody seemed to mark that with Sybilla's death the ability to speak fluent, rather prettily accented English, had come upon Tana suddenly.

Apart from an exchange of suppers, at which there was never a glance or word amiss, Sir Godfrey and Tana met most often in the stable, for, useless at other work about the farm, Sir Godfrey could care for horses and Jamil was just as arbitrary as Arcol had been. He *just* tolerated Sir Godfrey who was not afraid of him, but preferred Tana. Everybody else was scared to death of him — not without reason.

The stable had been enlarged with the resurgence of prosperity. The newly cleared field had provided the timber. Henry now had two proper plough-horses, sturdy beasts, who under Sir Godfrey's care were glossy as war-horses. There was a lighter, leggier animal which was suitable for riding, or pulling a not too heavily laden wagon. There was also the tall black horse upon which Sir Godfrey and Griselda had ridden from

Tadminster. About his ownership of that animal Sir Godfrey, scrupulous man, had no scruples at all. Because inn-keepers so often had surreptitious dealings with horse-thieves there was a law that inn-keepers were responsible for animals stolen from their premises; the landlady of The Swan had robbed him of a horse, of the money in his pouch, of the money which William Barbury had left with her. But for Griselda's intervention, she would have robbed him of his life. So he hoped that the owner of the black horse had claimed his legal right.

For stable work Tana wore a kind of smock, anything but seductive, and had her head — the hair about which she was always so careful, wrapped in a turban of linen. She never talked to Jamil in English; she claimed that he had understood Arabic from the moment that she had told him that he was beautiful; and often, as he groomed all the horses, Sir Godfrey heard Arabic terms of endearment coming from the far stall. Words she had used to him — now as empty as a nut-shell eaten out by maggots who having consumed what fed them, died.

In a farmer's year there was a space, just before haycutting began, when a man could take a little time for himself; or, if he were industrious and ambitious do things about his house and yard, chop wood for the winter, mend his roof, slap clay on cracks in the wall. Henry, this year, had leisure to go riding with Tana — at her invitation. 'To ride alone is lonely, Henree.' That she should actually seek his company he took as proof of his adulthood; they were roughly of an age but she had always treated him as though he were much younger, lumping him and John together. Her change of attitude changed his whole world. He had been in love with her from the moment of her arrival when he had thought her the loveliest thing he had ever seen, but there had for a long time been the barrier of language; she was rich, he was poor; she had been married and borne a child, he had never even kissed a girl. He'd been obliged to adore her from afar, without hope. Now she was noticing him at least!

He was anxious to impress. And he had one thing which she had not, or at least not in England, family.

'We'll go to Moyidan,' he said.

This was a breaking away from Walter's standards. Walter had been scornful about ancestry. He said that come to think of it we were all descended from Adam and John Ball was right with his jingle; When Adam delved and Eve span, who was then the gentleman? At other times, however, Walter would say that Henry's mother would have been a lady if she'd been a goose-girl.

Of Moyidan Castle Tana said, 'It is very big,' and it pleased Henry to be able to say that he was born there.

'At least, not there, the castle is no longer used. The house is to the rear.' And that was impressive, too; much in the style of Knight's Acre but larger and with more stone about it, the family emblem carved in a massive block over the main doorway.

Lady Emma was entertaining guests for dinner. She entertained more than usual nowadays and with good reason. She wanted to show off her wonderful grandson and any guest worth his salt would step upstairs and talk to poor James for a little while.

In no time at all Henry realised that he had chosen his day badly. His aunt welcomed him and Tana most genially, and the table was at its best, stiff white linen over scarlet cloth, all the silver gleaming, the waiting boys neat and nimble — very different from Eddy who since Sybilla's death had grown slovenly. But one of the three other guests was a man whom Henry's instinct immediately recognised as a rival. Not young, almost as old as Father; not handsome really, but a well-dressed man, with exaggeratedly good manners and a kind of *look*. Something sparked in his eyes as soon as Lady Emma made the introductions. Had he been a dog Henry would have raised his hackles, bared his teeth. As it was he could only sit rather glumly through the excellent meal and hear the man — Sir Francis Lassiter was his name — talking about himself; how he had recently inherited Muchanger from an old uncle, rather miserly who had let the place fall into disrepair, how much in the way of re-building and decorating there was to do; how in these affairs a woman's hand and eye mattered so much, and how he, being unmarried, must rely upon the Lady Emma who in some complicated way was a relative.

Lady Emma whose whole life had altered when little Richard proved to be strong and sensible, smiled and said, 'Francis, as you well know, I can be relied upon for nothing but advice these days. What with poor James and this little rogue . . .'

(The little rogue, fourteen months old, knew his power. He ate heartily, but choosily, demanding and getting the choicest bit of every dish.)

'Ah well,' Sir Francis said, with one of those eloquent glances at Tana, 'perhaps some other kind lady will take pity on me.'

To Henry's intense disgust Tana said that she knew little about English houses, but she had built herself a pavilion with which she was delighted; perhaps Sir Francis would care to view it one day.

Little Richard allowed his doting grandmother no time to sit and digest her meal peacefully.

'Ducks, Umma. Ducks!' he cried, pulling at her hand with astonishing strength. She rose at once, excusing herself and explaining that every day after dinner they went to feed the ducks on the moat. As she allowed herself to be tugged away she looked backward at Henry and said, 'You will have a few words with your Uncle James, Henry.'

Outside, on the bridge which had long ago replaced the old drawbridge, Lady Emma thought— I daresay they think I am an old fool to pander so, but let them think what they like! Nobody knew the pleasure she derived from this little boy, so unlike her own son. Watching him throw some of the meal's debris with an aim singularly purposeful and accurate for one so young, she prayed, as she often did; God, grant me length of days so that I may leave Moyidan in his charge.

Henry mounted the stairs unwillingly, meaning to stay with Sir James the minimum of time permitted by civility, but the old man, bedridden by the gross swelling of his legs, and obliged by his sore eyes to live in semi-darkness, was avid for company and asked questions which must be answered. What did Henry think of little Dick? Henry who had been too much preoccupied to notice his nephew much, except to think that he made a nuisance of himself, replied, 'He's a splendid fellow.'

'In this dusky room I cannot see him so well as I should like. When he was smaller your aunt would place him beside me and I judged him a good solid child. He is too big and active for that now. With my legs as they are. Is he tall enough, do you think?'

'He looks to me to be almost as tall as my brother Robert who is— what? — nine months older.'

'Good! Good! I know that our name does not mean tall, being a corruption of Taillebois; but we have always been tall and it would come hard on a squat fellow to be called Tallboys.'

No subject in the world could have interested Henry less at any time and now he was anxious to get back to Tana, to remove her from the company of that leering old goat.

'Nothing to worry about there, Uncle James,' he said heartily. 'Well, I . . .'

Sir James recognised the about-to-take-leave sound. Nobody stayed long. A greeting, an enquiry as to his health, an expression of good wishes, and gone.

'Tell me, how are your sheep doing?'

It was not a subject upon which Henry could expound much. He was not trained to sheep; Walter had been against them, holding that they needed more open country than Intake could offer.

'We have some new ones.'

'Yes. So your father told me. Black-faced, I believe.'

'Some have black faces.'

'Not a breed I favour. They don't yield the wool. Some people hold that they're sweeter eating, but I never thought so. How does the flock look? On the whole?'

'All right.'

'They should. Young Shep knows his job. He was practically born in a lambing pen himself.'

Henry, knowing nothing of the rhythm of a shepherd's year; the periods of immense activity interspersed with times when little but watchfulness was needed, privately thought that Young Shep was an idle fellow, but he did not pursue the subject. He said firmly that he must be going.

The dining hall was deserted so was the smaller room beyond it. From the window he could see Emma and little Richard on the bridge, still feeding the ducks. A horrid thought occurred. Tana had gone off with that abominable man, either to see his hateful house or to show him her pretty pavilion. He rushed out and said, 'What's happened to everybody?' The two other guests had left, she explained; Richard and Margaret

98

had wandered off — 'They make wreaths for one another all day long.' She could say such a thing without bitterness now. 'Your Lady Serriff took Sir Francis to the stable yard. She could not convince him that she rode a Thoroughbred stallion.

It was all right. They were not even standing close together; Jamil would not let Sir Francis near him. And they were not alone. From various points around the yard men with awed faces were watching the beautiful animal whom only this young lady could approach.

'All the same,' Sir Francis was saying, 'I would like to try him.' His face set in cruel lines. Tana, leaning against the horse whose silky mane, only a few shades darker than his cream hide, made a perfect background for her, laughed and said, in her pretty English.

'If ever I am wishing, Sir Francis, to see your neck broken, that day you shall try Jamil.'

'That,' he said, 'would be too high a price.' Then he laughed too.

It was the kind of exchange of words of which Henry was ignorant. In his world people said exactly what they meant, and a broken neck was nothing to joke about.

He was a little silent on the way home, answering when spoken to but offering nothing. His first venture into social life had been a dismal failure, and that part of him which Walter had shaped and tempered said — and serve you right! Trying to show off!

Where the road forked, one to Baildon, the other to Intake, Tana, well aware of what was happening, halted and said, 'Henree, would you like to try Jamil?'

'Do you wish to see *my* neck broken?'

'I will speak to him,' she said. She leaned forward and seemed to whisper. The horse's ears moved. Henry watched and wished, absurdly for a moment, that he were Jamil. Straightening up she said, 'He understands. You are his master. Until the stable.'

Up the lane, through the water-splash, past the priest's house and the church on the one side of the track and the sheeprun on the other, Henry rode not on one of the best horses in England, but on air. She had granted him a favour denied to Sir Francis. What she could do for one man she

99

could as easily have done for the other. But she had chosen to do it for *him*.

When feeding the ducks palled because they were so full fed that they no longer competed for a crust, little Dick was ready with another occupation. He said, 'Umma, swarbwerries!' It was too early. Strawberries came with the hay and the shearing in June. But on a well-tended bed, like that at Moyidan, sloping slightly to the south and with every plant upheld to the sun by a collar of straw, one or two berries reddened early. And the boy had sharp eyes and a strong stomach. Only two days before he had found a few pinkish on their upper sides, green underneath and gobbled them down with none of the sorry results which might have been expected. Anything that little Richard could swallow he could digest, Lady Emma thought, with joy and while he searched, she could sit down. Never, never would she admit that just occasionally she found little Richard slightly exhausting. Never, never would she hand him over to hirelings.

She had barely seated herself before she heard hoof-beats on the trail that led from Moyidan to the road. It was Godfrey whom she was always nowadays glad to see; he at least did not grudge poor James a half-hour's chat. Not that he could be called cheerful company, but perhaps for that reason his visits seemed to benefit his brother who had even been known to take his eye off his own affliction long enough to say, 'Poor Godfrey.'

From her seat on the wall she could watch Sir Godfrey approach. The bright May sunshine shone on his hair, now much more silver than fawn, on his slightly hollowed cheeks and the lines that ran from nostrils to mouth. He had always been the handsome one, she reflected, and even misery had not ruined his looks. He was still good-looking in a melancholy way; and only about forty-five or six — not old for a man.

He rode without looking about him and did not notice her until she called his name. Then he halted and dismounted. He made what was a visible effort to cast off gloom and be pleasant, asking after her health and James', glancing at little Richard and saying, 'No need to ask about *him*.'

The gift of this sturdy child with all his wits about him had sweetened the Lady Emma's disposition; happy herself, she wished others to be happy, and even in her brusque days she had had a soft spot for Godfrey, while regarding him as a fool. The thought she now entertained was not new to her, but now she had a peg for her argument.

'Your young people were here for dinner,' she began.

'What young people?'

'Henry and the lady from Spain.'

'Oh. Something new for Henry to give himself a holiday. I'm glad.'

'If I am not very much mistaken they intend to make a match of it.'

'Well, I suppose they are much of an age.' In years, he thought; but Henry is an untried boy and she is older than Eve.

'Have you ever considered, Godfrey, how that would affect *you*?'

He gave her that singularly candid, very blue stare and said, 'How could it affect me?'

'That young woman has a mind of her own, and for a time at least, Henry will be wax in her hands. You would be pushed aside. You'd have no say in the ordering of the household. You'd find yourself in the second-best bed.'

'Where I sleep is of no importance.' (I sleep alone. In the biggest bed, half of it empty and cold; sometimes I wake and forget for a moment, and reach out — to nothing.)

Some of Lady Emma's acerbity returned. She could have shaken him.

'It should,' she said. 'I have thought this before and now I say it. You should marry again.'

'Never.'

'Why not? Sybilla, God rest her, has been dead almost a year. Would she — ask yourself — wish you to go about for ever grieving. And your clothes as they are.'

In the irritating way he had of muddling the important with the non-important, he said, 'What is wrong with my clothes?'

Lady Emma could have said — everything, and not been far wrong. His doublet had fitted him once, before he grew thin; now it was too big, it was faded, its sleeves were frayed and spotted with tallow; one hole in his hose had been patched, another gaped. With a sharp eye and a pointing finger she detailed the faults.

Griselda is good,' he said, 'but the children keep her busy.'

'Exactly. What you need is a competent, comfortable wife whose first care would be for *you*. And I know . . .'

'Spare yourself!' he gave her another look, just as blue and just as straight, but with something fierce in it. 'Emma, if you ever mention this matter to me again, I shall not come here any more . . .'

Well, she had done her best, she thought, and turned back to the child.

CHAPTER SEVENTEEN

After May came June. Still carefully emulating Sybilla, Griselda carried roses and lilies to the church. The shearers came, and despite his apparent idleness, Young Shep had kept the fleeces free of maggots and when the wool merchant's agent came to inspect and to haggle, he rejected none. The hay crop was heavy and the harvest promised well. So why was Henry so glum?

Sir Godfrey knew the answer. From the pangs of unrequited love, either real or pretended, he had escaped entirely, but he had spent a good deal of his youth with young men who had suffered, or pretended to. He'd been fortunate; in the chill convent parlour he'd seen Sybilla and known — that is the woman for me; and when he and Sybilla had married, she had told him that at first sight of him she had felt the same, had known instantly why she had resisted all attempts to make her take vows, take the veil. Happiness long past, and in a way he was paying for it now, but he understood and felt pity for the boy.

One evening, at the risk of being thought interfering, he said, 'Son, what's wrong? Is it Tana?'

'Yes. She blows hot and cold. It is all very well for her to say that now I employ men. So I do. But that does not free me. Tom works whether I'm there or not, but he's frail and cannot command. Bert and Jem work while I am there, setting the pace . . . She does not understand. She says come riding and when I say not until evening, she goes off. And where? To

Muchanger. Or he is here. Francis Lassiter. Have you not noticed his grey horse? How often . . .?'

No, locked in his grief Sir Godfrey had noticed little. Now he could remember that in what seemed another life, when he had thought of bringing Tana back to England with him, he had thought of protecting her from fortune hunters. Sir Francis was not that. He was a rich man, well-connected, distantly related to Aunt Emma. Not young, and Sir Godfrey dimly remembered that he had a reputation as a womaniser. All the better. His wild oats were sown and he was probably prepared to settle down and become a model husband and father. An ideal match, in fact. Very different from the proposed one with poor Moyidan Richard which Sir Godfrey admitted he had been reluctant to encourage.

'And yet,' Henry said in a puzzled way, 'sometimes she is so amiable to me. She even allows me to ride Jamil.'

'You ride him?'

'Quite often.'

Surprising and disquieting. Sir Godfrey considered himself a good judge of horses and considered the beautiful animal to be dangerous; even to Tana who managed him so well. He had warned her more than once that stallions as they grew older became unreliable, especially when denied the natural outlet for their energy.

'That is what I mean by blowing hot and cold,' Henry said. 'I never know where I am. Sweet as pie one day, prickly as a nettle the next.'

'You love her?'

The dark tan on the boy's face deepened as he blushed. Almost defiantly, he said, 'Yes, I do. With all my heart. She's the only girl I ever cared for — or ever shall.'

Coming from one so young, so entirely inexperienced that was an extremely pathetic statement.

'It's early days for such a decision,' Sir Godfrey said, rather awkwardly. 'Young women are notoriously fickle.' Not that most of them had much chance to be, before marriage, since their parents chose for them; it was later on that the fickleness showed and they switched lovers as they might switch horses; but he had known a case or two where a girl in great demand, and with indulgent parents had kept as many as four suitors on a string. He could even remember wagers being laid.

He brooded over the business for a day or two and then decided to take action. After all, Henry was Sybilla's son, he must not be made miserable for lack of a hint or two. It occurred to him that Tana might be playing one of the oldest games in the world, deliberately provoking jealousy in order to bring one man — in this case almost certainly Sir Francis — to the sticking point.

Walking through the scent of roses from his own hall door to Tana's, Sir Godfrey gave no thought to the risk to which he was exposing himself. Grief had purged him. And just as he had told Lady Emma that where he slept had no importance, so people had become unimportant; shadowy figures. Henry had for a little time emerged from the shadows, a real person, with a real problem; but Tana existed now only because of Henry. Also, since he had rebuffed her in the lane, on the day when she bought Jamil, Tana had withdrawn herself. Certainly during Sybilla's illness she had been kind, sending wine and tempting little dishes. Afterwards she had made no attempt to obtrude herself, even to offer comfort.

So here he was, exactly as she had foreseen when she designed her pavilion; he came, uninvited, to her door.

Perhaps in this strange country where a man could have only one wife there was another rule — that the old one must be a year dead before a man could approach another woman.

She said, 'Godfree, you are most welcome.'

Ursula, gossiping with Jill had once said that Spanish clothes were funny, not much sewing and very little cover, either. On this warm summer evening Tana wore what Ursula believed to be Spanish clothes, and which were in fact the very reverse, all gauzy folds, half revealing, half concealing.

She busied herself pouring wine, offering the cup prettily; and Sir Godfrey accepted it. He could afford wine now and could have drunk to excess had he been so minded; but it dulled his grief, he had discovered and thus seemed in a way which his simple mind could not even explain to itself, a betrayal of Sybilla. So, unlike many sad men, he had not become a drunkard.

Tana arranged herself to best advantage on one of the divans; he sat on the other, politely raised his wine cup towards her, took a sip and set it down. He said, 'Tana, I want to talk to you about Henry.'

'Henree? What of Henree?'

Getting the order wrong, Sir Godfrey said, 'I don't want his neck broken. Or his heart.'

'His neck? Jamil? Hee is no danger, Godfree. Always I am telling him — behave well and always he does. His heart?' Abruptly she slipped into Arabic, so much easier, more intimate, more given to aphorisms. 'The heart is its own keeper.'

Sticking stolidly to English, Sir Godfrey said, 'That may be. But Henry is young, easily hurt. I came to ask you not to play with him. Not to encourage him unless ... unless you have some fondness for him.'

'Fondness,' she repeated the word in English. 'As for dogs or a food or a colour. What way to talk!' She slid into Arabic again. 'The heart once given is a slave for ever.'

Sudden and sinuous as a snake she was across the angle where the two divans met and he was enveloped in the gauze, the scent, the soft desirous flesh.

In the lane, tempted, and responsive, he had repelled her. Now it was different. He sat like a dead man. Harem trained, she knew every trick, every word and movement calculated to stimulate a satiated appetite. And he sat like a dead man, feeling nothing, not even pity for a girl so wrong-headed and so set in her ways.

She soon understood and stood off, gathering the gauze and the dignity about her. 'Better you had let me drown,' she said.

Out in the garden among Sybilla's flowers, he suffered feelings which his unhandiness with words prevented him from expressing, even to himself. There was shame, but he knew that had he acted otherwise he would have been more deeply shamed. His mind produced a phrase — impotent as a mule! And that, which he should have minded, he did not. He thought how little he was wanted. Useless here, un-needed at Bywater. Get away! Get away! Throw off this life which was no life.

Into his muddled mind some words slid, as gently and naturally as the lily scent came to his nose. *The Knights Hospitallers of the Order of St. John of Jerusalem.*

And where had he heard of them? Fighting his way back into the past, he remembered. Aboard the *Four Fleeces*, outward bound for Spain, all those years ago; Sir Ralph Overbury who had been everywhere and knew everything, discoursing about his Order, men who were monks but also knights, banded together in the first place to guard the path of pilgrims to the Holy Land, and now devoted to repelling the Turks on their inroads into Eastern and Southern Europe. He hadn't paid much attention at the time. Sir Ralph had been a great talker. And even now he was not sure about the Hospitallers' headquarters. Malta? Rhodes?

Nor was he sure about his eligibility. He had been married, had fathered children; but he did not expect to be accepted as a member in the full sense; he was a trained knight, he could train others; at the lowest level he could tend horses.

The idea slid into his mind at a vulnerable moment and he did not recognise it for what it was — a logical step in his life pattern. Always since he was knighted — except for those years of slavery — he had been on the move, always hoping for something.

He set about the business in his usual single-minded way. He spoke to Henry; 'I am useless here; I am too old to become a farmer.' And that even Henry, though wishing to be civil, could not contradict. He regarded it as a favourable sign that his father had sufficiently recovered as to be making plans.

His next step was to seek information about the Order, its rules and the conditions of enlistment; the most likely source was the Dominican Priory at Bywater, so he went there and ran into a fog of deliberate ignorance. The knightly Orders had never been well regarded by those purely religious, too rich, too powerful, too worldly and the Templars — very similar to the Hospitallers — had been forcibly disbanded in most scandalous circumstances; they had been accused of homosexuality, human sacrifice and Devil worship. Doubtless the Hospitallers were much the same. The Prior did not say these things openly, he simply denied all knowledge, except that the Hospitallers' headquarters were in Rhodes. He found a map and pointed out the position of that island. Bent on escape, Sir Godfrey noted with satisfaction how far distant the place was.

The next problem was money and that, except for the briefest periods, had beset him all his life and he soon saw a way of solving it without bothering anyone very much. He went to Moyidan and asked Lady Emma to be good enough to write a letter for him. She agreed willingly and then, learning what he wished written, expressed her strongest disapproval. 'This is the most hare-brained scheme I ever heard of,' she said. 'When you went to Spain you had some hope of remuneration and the expedition was properly organised. Of these knights you know nothing — not even that they still exist. A tale told on shipboard twelve years ago! If they exist what guarantee have you that they will accept you. Forty-six years old and out of training! And what about those poor children?'

'Griselda sees to them well. Joanna has her mother and Henry will see to Robert.'

'Henry will get married and have children of his own. How can you so shirk your responsibilities? You have a comfortable home — at least it could be, with a little money spent on it. You have a salaried post . . .'

She went on and on, until he said, 'Will you write the letter for me, or not?'

'If you ask me to write, how can I refuse? I warn you it will be useless. Lord Thorsdale will take the same view of this madcap notion as I, as any sensible person would do.'

'I think not. He is my friend. Also he owes me a favour.'

'Gratitude is a plant of short life.'

But he was stubborn; all Tallboys were stubborn, she thought. Then she remembered that he could not read, so dipping her pen into the ink she set herself to write a letter far less final than the one he had outlined to her. She did not write that he wished to *join* only that he wished to *visit*. She did not write that John Burgess, the overseer, was an honest man and capable of taking full charge of his lordship's Bywater affairs; she wrote *temporary charge during my absence*. Instead of requesting two years' salary as a gift, she asked for it as an advance to be deducted from future earnings.

Innocently, Sir Godfrey wrote his name and thanked her. She thought: You little know how much you have to thank me for; I have left a way of retreat open for you.

The letter despatched, all that was left to do was to make his will. He gave this matter deep consideration. Margaret needed nothing, but some provision must be made for John and Robert. A younger son himself he was sensitive to the position of younger sons and grateful to his own father to leaving him Intake.

Of the money which he had no doubt Lord Thorsdale would send, he intended to take just enough to keep him in the most meagre fashion on his journey. This time when he embarked he would take no armour, no great horse. Even if he could have afforded to do so he felt that to present himself fully accoutred and mounted would appear to be an assumption that he would be accepted. He intended to travel whenever possible as a pilgrim. Rhodes lay astride the pilgrims' route, and most pilgrims travelled humbly. Sir Ralph Overbury, who knew everything, had once said that ship-masters and inn-keepers did well out of pilgrims though they charged them less than ordinary people; it was the numbers which brought the profit; four to a bed in inns, crowded like cattle aboard ship. This prospect did not deter Sir Godfrey who was intent upon leaving all worldly things, including comfort behind him.

He had, he thought, every detail of his will clear-cut in his mind when he entered the ground floor room of the house in Cook's Row which Master Turnbull, the lawyer, kept as his office.

Master Turnbull was all in favour of people making proper wills; when a man died, murmuring — *All to Edmund,* he was robbing a lawyer of his livelihood.

On his table Master Turnbull had a pile of scraps of parchment, some clean, bits economically snipped off finished documents, some grey and grubby from having been used, well-scrubbed, and used again. On one of the latter kind, its surface almost fluffy from scrubbing, he began to jot down salient points.

'Henry must have his rights,' Sir Godfrey said. 'Intake is mine — as you know, having drawn my father's will . . .' Do I really, the lawyer wondered, look so old? It was my *father* who dealt with Sir Godfrey's. But the fact was not worth mention.

'You wish, Sir Godfrey, to leave Intake to Henry Tallboys. Your first-born son.'

'No. I mean, yes, Henry is my oldest son, but he cannot have all. I must consider the others.' He had remembered that his brother William had found the ladder of promotion eased by a legacy from that same just father. In the same way he must think of Richard — his son whom he would not have recognised had he met him in the road. Richard had taken to the Church, and to the Law, had done his time at Cambridge, was, by the latest bit of information, drifting through, through the new Bishop, through Moyidan, now on the staff of the Bishop of Winchester.

'Richard must have his portion. The house is mine, I built it. Henry made the fields, that is the Knight's Acre fields not those of Intake.'

'They are readily distinguishable, Sir Godfrey?'

'Oh yes. Intake was never a three field manor. There are twelve holdings, none large.'

'Rented?'

'Yes. Different rents.'

'And you wish these holdings to be left to your second son, Richard?'

'No, divided fairly between Richard and John.'

Master Turnbull's quill scratched as he made his jottings.

'Then there's my flock. I should like that divided between Richard and John and Robert. My youngest,' he explained.

'And the land?'

'What land?'

'A flock pre-supposes a sheep run, Sir Godfrey.'

'That had better be Henry's. Oh, and I think that to be fair to Henry, if the others wish to sell the sheep, he should have first offer.'

He fell silent, sweating slightly. What else? 'Oh, two other things. I am expecting to receive a sum of money. I'd like Robert . . .'

'Sir Godfrey, a man can only bequeath what he possesses. Shall we say that any money of which you die possessed?'

'That is what I meant. Then there's a lady . . .' He did his best to make the situation clear.

The lawyer thought, what a muddle-minded fellow! Having just bequeathed his house to his first born son he now wants to leave part of it to another person.

Clearing his quill of the fluff it had collected from the rough surface of the old parchment, Master Turnbull said, 'In such circumstances it is as well to be precise. These apartments are part of the main house?'

'Yes. At least, no. They're at the back, but separate.'

'They do not adjoin?'

'Oh yes. Up to a point.'

And what might that mean?

'They share a common roof?'

'No. At least, yes. Perhaps if I might borrow . . .'

Master Turnbull handed over the quill and the greyest of the grey scraps and pushed the ink-pot across the table.

Better at laying things out than at expressing himself, Sir Godfrey proceeded to draw a lawyer's nightmare. Master Turnbull could see that, even looking at it upside down.

'And there is access to these apartments?'

'Oh yes. Lady Serriff's main door is here — on the garden side. And her kitchen opens into the yard.'

'Both of which constitute part of Knight's Acre?'

'That is so. As you see,' Sir Godfrey handed across his diagram — curiously well and firmly drawn for a man whose talk was so contradictory. The lawyer saw that this was a right-of-way case. He'd been pestered with them since enclosures began. When people shuffled land about, a well, common to all, could end up in the centre of one man's fenced field; a path, used by everybody through the generations could be brought up short at a newly planted quickthorn hedge.

'It would appear that this lady occupies an island in the centre of your property.'

Glad that he had at last made himself clear, Sir Godfrey said, 'Yes, that's just it. I was thinking ahead. When she wanted to build I said, of course she could; but we didn't bother then with any deed of gift. It *is* her house; she built it, but it looks like part of the house. I thought I should mention it.'

'You were right, Sir Godfrey. We must now assure her right of way. Otherwise she might be denied access.'

'Henry would never do that.'

You would be surprised, Master Turnbull thought, at what people will do where property is concerned. A death seemed to change ordinary, decent people into a lot of carrion crows.

'We must indeed think ahead. This will, properly drawn up,

will apply to your heirs, and to the lady's. They might well be inimical.'

He took his ruler and drew two parallel lines from the yard entry to Tana's kitchen door, dog legging it so that it should include access to the well which Sir Godfrey had indicated by a circle, remembering as he did so, how Sybilla had stood there, drawing water, her white hair blowing, when he and Tana rode into the yard.

There seemed nothing more to be done — except perhaps to make a search into the relative values of the Intake land, small holdings, rented differently. But when he suggested that Sir Godfrey became impatient and said that that had all been gone into. Everybody knew where he stood.

'Write it out on one piece and I'll sign it,' he said.

'It will take a little time, Sir Godfrey,' Master Turnbull said, thinking of the new parchment; the formal opening, 'In the name of God, Amen! I, Godfrey Tallboys, Knight, of Intake in the Country of Suffolk . . .'

'I'll give you an hour,' Sir Godfrey said. And still in a society based on a code of chivalry, a lay lawyer, however clever, took lower place than a knight, however poor and muddle-minded.

'I have no wish to hurry you, Master Turnbull. But it is urgent. I may be away, perhaps even tomorrow.' He gave the lawyer his singularly sweet smile.

'It will be ready, Sir Godfrey.'

Turning back to the business, Master Turnbull reflected upon how much better off his one son would be. The boy was studying law at this moment, but he would never, if things went right, need to apply his knowledge except where his own property was concerned. Master Turnbull had invested very carefully; he owned several houses in Baildon, small but steady paying, some shares in several mercantile adventures, bits of land to the north of the town, dry and scrubby, but excellent for sheep when the time came; other bits to the south, splendid building ground when building began again as soon as things settled. Not yet; this tug-of-war between York and Lancaster wasn't over yet: London and the south was Yorkist completely. The north was different and Master Turnbull had a shrewd idea of where Sir Godfrey might be going, in such a hurry. He had never heard of the Knight's Hospitallers, and he did not know that there was an island called Rhodes.

Over the will he did his hurried best. And because Sir Godfrey seemed to have so little, to be divided between so many, charged the minimum price.

Now there was nothing to do except wait for the money from Yorkshire. It might come by land, through Master Johnson, or by one of the coal-cobs. In either case it would come to Bywater, so Sir Godfrey went there every day. And the days shortened relentlessly. August; September. Layer Wood began to blaze again. Evenings and mornings grew chilly. He began to think that Emma's cynical remark about gratitude was justified.

At last a coal-cob put in. Its master, explaining that he had been delayed by bad weather, handed over a paper, folded and sealed.

'And is this all?'

'All I was asked to carry, sir.'

The dismay and disappointment lasted only a minute. Sir Godfrey remembered the complicated way in which money changed hands. This might be a money order which Master Johnson would cash for him. He broke the seals and stared at the meaningless words. There were nine of them. His own name, which he could recognise, was not among them. And there were no figures.

John Burgess, whom he had nominated to take charge was able to read but Sir Godfrey hesitated to carry the paper to him. The very brevity seemed ominous. It might be a curt dismissal; in which case he preferred Burgess not to know. He would resign and thus save a little dignity.

Lady Emma seemed hardly to glance at the words.

'It says, "Come at once. I have work for you here." '

'Just that? No signature?'

'No signature.' She turned the paper about. 'Nor is your name between the seals, Godfrey. It seems,' she frowned at the message, 'as though should the message have miscarried there would be nothing to show who wrote it, or to whom it was sent.'

'It could only come from Lord Thorsdale. It came on a coal-cob. And that was belated! Thank you Emma. I must go at once.'

Well, she thought, it was better than haring off to the world's end. Later she was to think that it was fitting that a man who had gone on so many wild-goose chases, should have gone on this one in response to a summons so carefully anonymous.

Leave-taking was brief and painless. He was back at Knight's Acre in time for dinner. He looked in upon the nursery, kissed the children and pleased Griselda by saying that he left them in her care with all confidence. Only to Henry did he say some valedictory words.

'My plans have changed. I was thinking of a longer journey, a longer absence, Henry. You spoke once of Lancaster and York being at one another's throats again — I think it is about to happen and that Lord Thorsdale is mustering men, secretly.'

Henry remembered Walter saying about knights that they were like hunting hounds, blow a horn ten miles away and they'd all come at the gallop. But Sybilla, as well as Walter, had had a hand in Henry's upbringing and he said all the correct things, including that myth, so often proved wrong but still held — It would all be over by Christmas.

'If anything should happen to me, my will is lodged with Master Turnbull. I leave you in full charge. Look after them all.'

'I will do my best, sir,' Henry said, little knowing the weight of the load he was accepting. After all, what had Father ever done about looking after anybody. 'When do you leave?'

'Now.'

About saying goodbye to Tana he was of divided mind. Since that June evening they had sedulously avoided one another. Even their stable work had been re-timed. He hated the idea of facing her — their shared failure heavy between them — but he was still grateful and he knew that he was going away for ever. Even if he survived the coming battles, he would not come back here. Perhaps he should just say farewell . . .

It was not his to decide. Kitchen spoke to kitchen and while he was saddling the black horse — the stolen one, the best of the lot — she came around the end of her pavilion and into the yard. Nothing now seductive about her dress or her posture, or her speech.

'I am understanding,' she said, 'that you go a long journey. If you wish you may have Jamil.'

A noble, magnanimous offer indeed. Akin, in its way to Sybilla's in accepting Tana and her unborn child. My God, what have I ever done to deserve . . .?

'It wouldn't do,' he said. 'Much as I appreciate it. Jamil just tolerates me, but only just . . . In inns and such places, he would be . . . an embarrassment, biting stable-boys. And if you would take heed . . . You should take him back to Tom Thoroughgood and make an exchange before . . .'

'Yes, you have said it many times. I am not agreeing . . .' Her voice changed slightly, 'It is to war that you go?'

'I think so.'

'May your dead enemies equal the number of stars in the sky.'

Sybilla had always said, 'God go with you and bring you safely back to me.' He had never before left on any campaign without a change of clothing and some food of the long-lasting kind; smoked or salted meat that was practically imperishable, bread baked once, sliced and baked again so that it was impervious to mould.

Late as it was, on one of the rose trees there was a half-opened bud. A latecomer, slightly discouraged by the morning and evening chill. Still, it was a rose, one of those that Sybilla had loved. He broke it off, carried it into the church and laid it on the black slab under which she lay. Then he knelt and said to Sybilla in his mind. 'You never come to me, but I shall come to you. Soon.' He could hear the steady thud of his heart — every beat brings me nearer. God grant me clean swift death in battle.

CHAPTER EIGHTEEN

Manuring the land — known as muck-spreading — was routine in the farmer's year; an unpleasant but necessary job. John who was fastidious always tried to evade it and since the flock was installed had always had the excuse that he must help the shepherd.

Sir Godfrey had never actually interfered with the farm work, but now and again, when Henry said bitter things about idleness, he had said mildly that John was still young. Henry replied angrily that John was fourteen, just about the age that he had been himself when he assumed full responsibility. Sir Godfrey would then point out, still mildly, that Henry had always had a taste for general farmwork, whereas John tended more towards sheep.

Two or three days after Sir Godfrey's departure, Henry said, 'You come and shovel muck today. Young Shep needs no help, and we do.'

'He has a name, you know,' John said coldly. 'It is Nicholas. How would you like it if people called you Young Ploughman?'

Henry's astonishment was genuine. 'How could they? Everybody knows that I am Master Tallboys of Knight's Acre.' That was true. There was something about Henry which forbade any familiarity, even in the market. Never any hob-nobbing, or back-slapping. 'Anyway, if I say you shovel muck, you shovel it.'

'It is not a job I care for.'

There had never been between Henry and John the urgent rivalry that had existed between Henry and Richard, the differences in age had prevented that, but Henry had always thought John idle and frivolous; now insubordination threatened. In earlier days when John had shown any sign of defiance a good cuff had sufficed, but now the boy was too big. Like most of the Tallboys family, at fourteen he was practically full-grown.

'Very well,' Henry said. 'You tend the sheep and *Nicholas*,' he brought out the name with sardonic emphasis, 'can come and help with the muck-spreading.'

Henry was far too lacking in sophistication to see anything sinister in the relationship between the two boys — if Young Shep at eighteen or so, could be called a boy. The link between them he saw as a mutual liking for making musical noises, and their mutual wish to loll about and avoid what Henry considered as *real* work. He did not notice the look of sheer hatred which John shot at him as he delivered his edict; and he missed entirely the significance of John's reply.

'I'll do it. I'm stronger than he is.'

The self-sacrifice contained in that remark passed unnoticed.

On the surface it was true enough. Young Shep was not very sturdy, but he looked healthy, always a good colour in his cheeks ...

'Right enough,' Henry said, the incipient rebellion quelled.

Shovelling muck himself he gave thought to another matter with which he could deal in a similarly masterful manner, now that he was in full charge. Tana.

Sir Francis Lassiter's grey, though most often in the yard or stable, was not the only one. Tana, who towards Henry had blown hot and cold, was plainly playing fast and loose with other men.

Not that he cared. With Walter's death, and Sybilla's he had learned that hard work could cure almost anything. Give your whole mind to the job in hand and there was no time to think; go to bed tired out and you slept. Henry believed that he had done with Tana. His father had said something about women being fickle; very well, she could be fickle with others. Not with *him*, not with Henry Tallboys who now, left in full charge, had at least the right to say what horses should stand in his yard or stable. He sincerely believed that he had outgrown his boyish infatuation and was his own man again.

January; a clear frosty night, sparkling with stars and the moon bright. In the hall the fire was heaped high and John said, 'Eddy and Jill let the kitchen fire die as soon as supper is served. I am going to ask Nicholas to bring his pipe in here. We have a new song to try.'

'Not here,' Henry said. 'The hall is no place for hired hands.'

'This is my *home*,' John said stubbornly. 'Half the fireside is mine. I have a right to bring my friend to share it.'

'This is father's house. And you would never have dared make such a suggestion to him.'

'Father was not fond of music.'

'If you call that music! Squealing and scratching!'

'We make very beautiful songs. As you will realise one day.'

'In the meantime, I am in charge here and I want no argument.'

John flung out, slamming the door, and Henry settled down to work, re-lining a worn horse collar. The words, *I am in charge here,* went on echoing through his mind. He was in charge here; he was responsible; and about what he had to say to Tana there could be no argument.

He got up and went into the yard. There was no strange horse, grey, brown or bay here tonight. He regarded the sky with a countryman's eye and was glad that the muck was spread, for it served a dual purpose, it protected as well as nourished. He walked round to Tana's door, knocked once and entered.

It was the first time he had ever set foot in the pavilion in his working clothes. Standards had lowered a little since Sybilla's death; hands were still washed before meals, muddy or mucky footwear left at the kitchen door. Otherwise he was just as he had come from the field and in this luxurious, scented bower he made an incongruous figure.

She had begun to blow cold to him for the last time somewhere back in the summer. On the Eve of the Midsummer Fair to be exact. He had actually offered to take a day's holiday in order to show her the Fair. They must go in daylight for after dusk rowdiness prevailed, but the Fair began as an immense market to which people brought useful things and beautiful things from great distances, some even from overseas. The Hawk in Hand put out an awning in its forecourt, a guard against too much sun, or a shower, and under it served strawberries and cream all day long. Still poor by most standards, and very poor by those which he had set himself to attain, Henry was yet prepared to spend money in order to give Tana a treat. He would even — unless her fancy was taken by something quite impossible, like amber — buy her a fairing . . .

She had rejected his invitation with cold scorn. The tone of her voice, the look she gave him, cut to the quick. After that he had made no overtures; nor had she, and it was a long time since he had been close enough to her to observe that she had changed. After that last encounter with Sir Godfrey she had despaired and turned to the wine cup for comfort; and to other men, lechery being one of Despair's jackals.

The room was bright; there were two four-branched candlesticks; it was warm; two charcoal braziers which exuded not only warmth but sweet odours. Between the flicker and the glow Henry saw her plainly for the first time since summer and saw that her beauty had begun to fade and blur, like those paintings on the church wall, before they were restored. For months she had lived just on the border of intoxication. Only Francis Lassiter had really observed this and decided that attractive, seductive as she was, he would be a fool to marry a woman who had to be half-drunk before she was any good in bed.

As Henry entered, and rudely sat down before being invited to be seated, Tana said, 'Oh. Henree. You have news?'

What had existed between her and Sir Godfrey was dead and done with. But now and then she found herself caring.

'No; if you mean Father. But I have something to say to you.' He drew a breath, deeper than he realised. 'In my father's absence I am master here and I will not have the place turned into a brothel.'

It was surprising that he knew the word, living here, isolated, jogging into market once a month or so, to sell and to buy. Already — this would be a lonely evening — she was wine-flown.

'Do you know what you speak of, Henree? A brothel is a place open to all. And men pay.'

'We won't split hairs. What I came to say . . . I will not have Sir Francis's grey, or any other horse in *my* yard. If you must play the whore, do it elsewhere.'

The easy anger of the half tipsy flared in her. This clod, this loutish boy whom she had toyed with, in the hope of making his father jealous, to make him see that she was desirable. A boy upon whose innocence she had never trespassed . . . Saying such things. Sitting there, so self-righteous . . . A bubble formed in her head and burst. With the same swift, snake-like action with which, months ago, she had flung herself upon Godfree, she crossed the space between them and hit Henry twice across the face, forehand to one cheek, backhand to the other. He flung up an arm to restrain, to control, and for all her anger she was no more than a butterfly . . . When, defending himself, he grabbed her by the arms, she fell, half across the divan, half across his knees.

It was, for both of them, a new experience. Henry had never possessed a woman before and Tana in all her time had never had a virgin love. She had given herself to many men, working her way up to the position of first favourite in the Zagela harem, always with purpose, to free the man she loved, the man who had been hers for so little time . . . those wonderful nights in the mountains as they made their escape, never sure of what the next day might bring; a few times in Spain. Then nothing, even after the old wife, the first wife was poisoned and dead.

Henry she found herself hating because in shape and size, in the way his hair was so crisp to the touch, in his body odour — a thing only recognisable by lovers and enemies — he was so like his father. The likeness should have endeared him to her, but it did not. It infuriated her. When the moment of frenzy was spent she eased herself away and said, cruelly. 'You must go. Henree. Or there will be more talk.'

'There will not,' he said. 'First thing in the morning I shall go to Father Ambrose and tell him. Banns can be called on other days than Sunday if the priest is agreeable. Darling, my darling, we can be married within a week. He will do as I say.'

She looked down the reaches of the years — married to Henry, a constant reminder by night and by day. And cold sober! Because how and when could she do her drinking? He had caught her this evening about halfway; she would need much more wine before she could sleep.

'I cannot marry you,' she said.

He had his father's single-mindedness, his full share of the Tallboys' obstinacy, and all the egoism of youth. He took no notice; this was probably fresh evidence of fickleness.

'Of course you can. You must. After tonight. And my dearest dear . . .' He took her hands and kissed them, pressed them against his face and vowed to love and serve her and honour her to the end of his days. He poured out promises and all his hopes; he would not always be poor; he'd set himself to prosper, and he would. With more money and more leisure they could cultivate acquaintances, entertain: she mustn't judge by what he was now, but consider what he would be . . .

On and on, with every nerve in her body screaming for the only relief she knew; wine and more wine.

From kissing her hands and talking he proceeded to give signs of wishing to make love again. Just to be rid of him she said, 'You must go now, Henree. All this can be talked about tomorrow.'

'Yes, tomorrow,' he said. The beginning of a new life. Dazed with happiness, he stumbled away.

Left alone she poured wine and swallowed it without tasting. More, and still more. Tonight no merciful blunting of mind and memory. The whole of her past, as it related to Sir Godfrey, was lived again as she walked up and down. Two women dead, the favourite of the harem by intrigue and Sybilla by poison. No remorse about that, only bitterness that with all her striving and taking of risks the end had been nothing.

She twitched aside the curtain and saw the world, bright with frosty moonlight. A gallop, she thought, might calm her. She went swiftly to the stable where the work horses sagged and drowsed and Jamil welcomed her eagerly.

The cold air cleared her mind and she could think again. She knew what she must do. Get away from Knight's Acre and the pavilion with had never served the purpose for which it was built. Get away from Henree and the men in whose embraces she had sought, and failed to find, consolation. She would go to the north, where the fighting was. Not in pursuit of Sir Godfrey, to invite further shame. She would go to the side of the Red Rose. The fierce Lancastrian Queen, Margaret, a fighting woman herself, would welcome a woman who could ride and handle a sword. Another memory from the past! Fighting alongside her father and brothers in that last disastrous battle.

But for the fact that she was unsuitably clad, and that her treasure lay in the chest in her bedroom, she would have ridden on and never seen Knight's Acre again. She would have ridden straight through Baildon, Jamil's hoofs on the cobbles disturbing the respectable men, each in bed with his one wife! But she must go back, so on the outskirts of the town she turned the horse.

On one or two former occasions she had had difficulty with Jamil in two places, both near the house; one in front where the trail ran between the rose-trees before curving towards the rear of the house, the other at the entry to the yard. She had attributed his jibbing and prancing to his intelligence — he realised that the outing was over and was reluctant to return to his dull stable. She'd always steadied him and forced him on, telling him in Arabic, 'Do not be lunatic.' Tonight there was no trouble near the roses, but at the yard entry he was more lunatic than ever. He stopped abruptly and then tried to turn. She fought him, keeping his head towards the opening between the end of the house and the ruined cottage. It lay in shadow, but for a moment she seemed to see a wavering light such as a carried lantern might give. Unperturbed she spoke into Jamil's ear, 'Steady, my love.' Then she called sharply towards whoever carried the lantern. 'Out of my way!'

Jamil reared and turned, swivelling round on his hind legs. Tana's left arm and knee came into sharp contact with the house wall; she lost balance and control. Even as she fell, she kept her head, let go, get your feet out of the stirrups so as not to be dragged ... As she hit the ground she could smell lilies ...

Henry came, stretching and yawning, out into the frosty morning. He stood for a second and stared at Tana's pavilion which presented a blank, windowless wall to the yard. Sensuous thoughts moved through him as he imagined her sleeping, all scented and silken. He could still hardly believe that what had happened had happened and that he had at last attained his heart's desire. But work would not wait. Success and prosperity had always been his aim and now, after all the promises he had made, they were more important than ever. He kicked up a clod with his heel and was pleased to see that although the night had been frosty the frost had not penetrated below the surface. At least, not here in the yard, where it was sheltered; it might be different in the open field. Just as well to make sure before harnessing the plough-horses. As he walked — with Walter's gait — towards the yard entry he planned for the evening. He'd go straight from the field to the priest's house and arrange for the wedding; then he'd wash, most thoroughly, and don his best clothes. And then ...

With that thought he came upon her, broken and dead, her head at a curious angle and a faint rime of hoar-frost on her black hair.

The shock stunned him into something like insensibility. He was like a wounded man who at first feels no pain however mortal the blow. Somebody — not Henry Tallboys — went back into the yard where the others were awaiting his verdict, to plough or not to plough, and a voice — not his — said from a vast distance, 'Lady Serriff is dead. She has met with an accident. Carry her in.'

So now here he was in the priest's low room arranging not for a wedding, but for a funeral. And Father Ambrose was making difficulties.

'Young sir, at a burial the Christian soul is committed to God. There was never any sign that the dead lady was a Christian. She never once attended Mass, never knelt at the altar, never made a confession . . .'

Henry said harshly, 'How could she? She was Spanish. In what language could she have confessed to *you*? And how, unconfessed and unabsolved could she have taken Christ on her tongue?'

Father Ambrose said humbly, 'That is a question I never thought to ask. I have been rash in judgment, forgetting that she was a stranger within our gates.' He gave Henry a stricken look. 'I should have bestirred myself. In the Dominican Priory there are those with the gift of tongues . . . I have failed in my duty.' He did not excuse himself because he was old, frail, blind. There and then he set himself a penance — no meat for a month. 'Of course I will bury her,' he said.

Rest in peace, the woman who, before she was fully-grown, had conceived an inordinate passion for one man and to gratify it had stopped at nothing. Rest in peace, also, the promise of happiness for Henry Tallboys whose childhood had been cut short by the need to work like a man, whose youth had ended with a night of joy and a morning of sorrow.

Tana's pavilion stood deserted. It had never been part of the main house and of those now living at Knight's Acre, Henry was the only one upon whose consciousness it had impinged. Setting himself to forget Tana, as he had forgotten other griefs, meant ignoring the place in which she had lived, never even glancing towards the windowless wall which bordered the yard. On the side overlooking the garden, spiders wove their webs between curtains and glass at the windows; a rosemary bush by the side of the door grew large and encroached, honeysuckle and ivy threw out exploratory fingers. Soon the door was almost hidden and quite inaccessible. Not until the children were old enough to be curious was the pavilion ever noticed. To them it offered the fascination of mystery; a house where no one ever went, a house no one ever mentioned, a house without a door.

CHAPTER NINETEEN

News came, slowly but surely. The Lancastrians had met with success early in the campaign, and then been defeated — surely for the last time. Sir Godfrey Tallboys had been killed in the re-taking of Bamborough Castle and lay buried in York, near his friend and patron, Lord Thorsdale. When this report had been twice confirmed, Henry ordered and paid for six Masses to be said for his soul and then turned to practical things. He remembered his father's mention of a will and in leisurely fashion, not making a special errand of it, called upon the lawyer who said that in his opinion Richard should come home; the last will and testament of Sir Godfrey Tallboys — God rest him — being far more complicated than it seemed.

'I don't know exactly where my brother is,' Henry said. 'When my mother died, my aunt, Lady Emma of Moyidan, did write to inform him; but she had no reply.'

'Where was he when last heard of, Master Tallboys?'

Henry, who had never given Richard a thought for years, said, 'He'd finished his Cambridge studies — we did hear that, and was something, chaplain or secretary to the Bishop of Winchester.'

'He should not be difficult to find. It is your wish that I should write a letter?'

'I should be much obliged. I can write my name and no more.'

He said this without a trace of shame and the lawyer thought that the perfect, orderly world could never come about until everybody was literate. When he eventually met Richard Tallboys, he changed his opinion. With his Master's degree from Cambridge, his ordination — he was now a deacon — and entitled to the courtesy of Sir, the young man was obnoxious. He criticised the form of his father's will in terms that were fully legal, and even justified. 'Hurriedly and badly made,' he said. He denounced the division of the Intake farms, with their differing rents, their differing terms of tenure, as 'most ambivalent. Are we supposed to draw lots, Master Turnbull?'

'Your honoured father — God rest him — had no time, Sir Richard. I did in fact suggest ... but he over-ruled me. The whole thing was drafted, signed and witnessed, in a single afternoon.'

'That is quite obvious! Never mind, Master Turnbull. I have no doubt that my brother and I will come to some amicable arrangement.'

'Ah,' Richard said, 'here I perceive a flaw of which John and I can take advantage.'

He had gone to Moyidan and borrowed that old, crackling parchment, with its mention of inalienable rights. At ridiculous rents. No word about what happened should the land be sold. This was the kind of loophole which his training and present occupation rendered him capable of dealing with. He and John would have some ready money soon. But it was not enough for Richard who knew that profitable appointments could be bought.

'I propose,' he said, in a most amicable way, 'to sell my share of the flock immediately.'

Henry was not much interested in sheep, but his commonsense made him exclaim, 'The very worst time! The lambs are not all down yet, some of the ewes couldn't travel. Then you'd lose the wool money. People sell sheep in June, after shearing.'

'If you buy now, you'll get both lambs and wool.'

'I can't afford to buy.'

'How unfortunate. I am afraid that I cannot afford to wait until June.'

'I want to sell mine, too,' said John. He had a plan in mind; he also relished a chance of getting his own back on Henry whose treatment of Nicholas had rankled.

'I'm not sure that at your age you can make such decisions.'

John looked to Richard for support and found it. 'Father made no mention of guardianship. Strickly speaking, Henry, even you are not of full age. John has as much right to sell his sheep as you have to inherit Knight's Acre.'

'Maybe Robert would like a say too,' Henry said sourly.

Resolutely amiable — imperturbable good temper, outwardly, at least was one of the qualities he had cultivated, Richard said, 'I see no difficulty. You have security, Henry. You could borrow money and buy us out.'

'I'm not borrowing money,' Henry said. 'Father did that once and hung a loan round his neck. Very well, if you are set on this absurd behaviour, sell — if you can find a buyer. Meantime, remember, they are your sheep now, running on my land. I shall charge rent...'

As Master Turnbull knew, only too well, no will was ever settled amicably.

John at least was happy.

'Our hut' to which he and Nicholas had resorted when Henry had been so disobliging, was a straw structure in the corner of the sheep run, that one-time common, now known to the villagers as Grabber's Green. It differed from a lambing pen only in that it was thatched while lambing pens were open to the sky. It was built of closely bound bundles of straw, made into walls, about four feet high, with branches laid across them, and more straw as thatch. Such huts were intended for a shepherd to take refuge in bad weather, and to live in, day and night, during the lambing season. The one to which John sped, hot-foot, was snug and cosy, with only one disadvantage, one could not have a fire in it or even very near it; but a fire six feet away gave heat and light enough.

Tonight the fire burned brightly, for with lambing imminent, Young Shep had taken up permanent residence in the hut, and the iron tar-bucket, full of black, viscous liquid stood near-by. There were two seasons for tar, summer, when flies laid their eggs which unless promptly dealt with grew into maggots, and lambing time when about one lamb in ten developed navel trouble.

Crouching to pass the low entry, John seated himself on a bundle of straw and said, 'Nicky. We can do it now. I'm going to have some money. We can *go*.'

They'd talked about it often enough, fashioning their tunes, making their songs which the outer world had only to hear to acknowledge and admire, they had talked endlessly. One day they would make music in great halls, in castles, in palaces. But neither of them was prepared to starve or beg while awaiting the recognition to which their genius entitled them. Knight's Acre did not appreciate them, but it offered bread and beds. So they had stayed, scorning the present, looking to the future and saying always, 'One day,' without the slightest idea when that day would dawn.

Now it had come.

'They're going to sell the flock,' John said, 'and a third is mine.'

Young Shep said, 'Sell. Now? With the ewes in pod? That'd be bad business. That old black-face is there now ...' He jerked his head towards the nearest lambing pen. 'Grunting. By the size of her, it'll be twins. Maybe I should take a look.'

He was gone for quite a time and when he came back he said, rubbing hands on a bit of sheep's wool, 'She's all right. It was twins. Bit small, but lively.'

'You won't be bothered with such things in future, Nicky. We'll be on our way ... I'd reckon that selling the flock, and the farms will take a bit of time. But my brother Richard is clever — and impatient. I'd say that by May Day ...'

'Yes. All right in summer. But there's the winter to think of.'

'I'd have enough money ...' delicacy of feeling made John change the words, 'We'd have earned enough, Nicky, to see us through the winter, somewhere cosy.'

'It'd be all right, time we're young. But Johnny, you ain't always young.'

It occurred to John that Nicky had accepted this glittering future with less enthusiasm than it merited. He failed to make allowance for the differing strain of character and behaviour which their ancestors had bequeathed them. John's forebears had been riding, as Walter termed it, helter-skelter, all over the face of Christendom. Even to Jerusalem. Griselda's recognition of the resemblance between the man cast out to die in a barn and the crusader, with his legs crossed, had been no accident. Young Shep's forebears had lived and worked at Moyidan since the first field had been scratched there; Briton, Roman, Angle, Dane, Norman — all in turn had overrun the place, and Old Shep had always been there. Even the move from Moyidan to Intake had caused Young Shep pangs of homesickness which his association with John, their mutual interest in music, had done something to assuage, something, not all.

'Don't you *want* to get away, Nicky? We've talked about it often enough.'

'There's a difference between talking and doing. Thing like that should be thought over.'

'Thinking won't help much if they sell the flock. You'll have to move then.'

'Some might go to Moyidan. There'd be a job for me there if so. My father's got all he can handle. Getting stiff, too.'

'If that's what you meant by getting away, we weren't talking about the same thing. I shall go whether you come or not.'

It was their first dispute. The first time they had ever sat in a silence which neither found easy to break.

Young Shep said, at last, 'Made a new song today, Johnny. Like to hear it?'

John gave a grunt of assent.

'I'll tell you the words first, then you'll see how the tune fits.' A lute-player could sing and play at the same time; with a pipe this was impossible.

Young Shep began.

Pray God the summer cometh soon
That I no more must be alone . . .

John struck the bale of straw that served him as a seat and said, 'Another of your whines about love; with a tune like the bellyache! And I know who it is. That red-haired trollop who came with the shearers.'

Most shearing gangs had a woman with them — old enough not to be a cause of trouble, active enough to keep up with the swift pace at which the men moved between jobs. Such women did a bit of washing and mending, prepared food at irregular hours, tied up a nicked finger. Last year's gang had been accompanied by a girl thin as a thread, berry brown, with flaming hair. She'd pretended to like music, and Nicholas had made a pipe for her. The shearers had moved on to other flocks, but twice while they were still in the neighbourhood, within running distance, she'd come back on some excuse or another. John had thought nothing of it at the time, but now he realised that lately all Nicholas's songs had been about love — as indeed was the fashion, so he had not been warned by that. Now he said, 'I know what *you* meant about getting away! You want a live-out job in a clod cottage, with a wife and a baby every year! You're welcome. Think of me — playing before the King!'

Rather more than half of Young Shep did want exactly that — but in Moyidan, if possible, and perhaps not a baby *every* year. He did want the clod cottage and the son who would be Young Shep when he was Old Shep. The other, a smaller part of him knew that in such a life his music and his songs would be wasted, never finding the audience they deserved.

Pull Devil, pull Baker!

'Maybe you're right,' Young Shep said.

John walked back to the house knowing that he fitted nowhere, except in the world of his own imagination. A dream he had tried to share. From this time on, he decided everything he planned would be secret to himself. *Secret to myself, my secret, my secret* — a good song theme.

CHAPTER TWENTY

Henry now faced the need to make some economies. He had expanded while his father was receiving a regular income and was responsible for the household expenses; but he had been allowed no time to consolidate. He was short of money because it had seemed sensible to buy a portion of the flock. He felt bound to keep Robert's third of the sheep and husband them carefully — they were all the poor child had inherited. 'All money of which I die possessed' meant nothing. Father had had no money. Still ignorant about shepherd's work, Henry had decided that since Robert's sheep were there, and the sheep-run was there, he might as well have a few of his own and for them his brothers demanded instant payment. His own animals were distinguished by a cross of red ochre. Henry intended to hoard every penny gained by the sale of wool, or sheep from Robert's flock, so that by the time the boy needed money it would be there.

Looking around his household, Henry decided that Young Shep and Eddy were dispensable; he and Tom between them could look after the flock, and if he himself took his meals in the kitchen, as most farmers did, there would be nothing for Eddy to do. Young Shep did not make the move to Moyidan — as he had hoped — but to Clevely, which at least was a place served by the same gang of shearers, and where he did not live in. When the berry-brown girl, whose name was Beth — rhyming with nothing except breath and death — came back in June, and if she still wished to settle down, as she had told him she longed to, he would have something to offer. Eddy, making a venturesome move, found a job as pot-boy at The Hawk In Hand at Baildon.

Henry had overlooked the fact that in his muddly way, Eddy had also waited upon the nursery, a service which Jill was not prepared to undertake in her present dejected mood. She missed Eddy, who, idle as he had appeared to be in Henry's eyes, had been good company. She also missed Ursula. Ursula, shedding ten years for her mistress and a hundred for herself had left before Tana was committed to the grave. She could never, never, she declared, go into *that* part of the house again; even to think of it sent icicles down her back: and she thought that Sir Edmund, over at Nettleton might give her a place.

Ursula gone, Sir Richard gone, Master John gone, Eddy gone, and Young Shep who so often obliged with a merry tune on his pipe, or with a song. Four men, the master, Tom, Jem Watson, Bert Edgar to cook for every mid-day as well as that upstart, Griselda, and the two children. And then, in the evening, everything was so glum, Jem and Bert went stumping home to Intake, Griselda was with the children, Tom, hoarding his remnant of strength, went to bed early; so did the master. So there was nothing left for Jill to do except to go to bed, too. Very dismal.

One morning, Henry rather early or Griselda slightly late, they met in the kitchen where Griselda and Jill had just had a dispute about the apportioning of fat and lean. Robert, though no longer weakly, could not stomach much fat and though in her inmost heart Griselda had small patience with foibles, a sick child was a sick child, something to be cleared up after. So she had put up a fight for a bit more lean.

She had grown since coming to Knight's Acre, but she was

still small, and a meal for three on a tray appeared to be a load for her.

Henry opened the door into the hall for her and said, 'Surely there is no need for this. They are old enough now to come to where the food is.'

Next day they were all in place. Henry sat at the top of the white-scrubbed table, to his left the two children, brought to table level by cushions from the settle in the hall; between them, Griselda. On his right, back to the hearth for convenience in serving, Jill and beyond her Tom; and at the far end Jem and Bert, consuming the mid-day meal that was part of their wage.

Sybilla lay under the black marble slab, yet something of her hovered about this table at which she had once presided and there was a marked difference between those who had come under her influence and those who had not.

Children tended to copy.

'Slosh your food like that,' Griselda said, addressing Robert, but with her eye on Jem and Bert, 'and you can go eat with pigs.'

Robert was slightly afraid of pigs and ceased what Griselda denounced as sloshing.

'Ask, don't grab,' Griselda told Joanna. 'You can say, *Please, the bread.* Come along, let me hear you.'

Joanna was less easily subdued. 'Bert grabbed,' she said.

There was the matter of the salt. It was contained in a bowl of wood and it had a spoon, also of wood, its handle nicely carved — one of Walter's whittling jobs, not an apostle as so many spoon handles were made to represent, because Walter had not been pious, but an oak leaf and an acorn. Those at the table who had come under Sybilla's influence used the spoon. Jem and Bert, asserting their rights did as they did at home, dug their knives, dribbling in drops of grease and gravy. One day, catching a look of pain on Griselda's face, Tom said sharply, 'There is a spoon, Bert.'

'Why so there is!' Bert said with simulated, sardonic surprise. 'Such a little tiddly bit of a thing. Never noticed it. Did you, Jem?'

Tom was not allowed to forget that spoon. It came up with heavy-handed humour again and again. 'Try a *spoon*, Tom,' one or the other would say as Tom struggled doggedly with some job just beyond his strength. 'Old Granfer Robinson used to wet the bed. They cleaned him up with a *spoon*.' 'Ah, thass how Tom got so handy with a *spoon*.'

The rough teasing covered something deeper and darker. Tom belonged at Knight's Acre, had lived there ever since the plague time. Jem and Bert worked there but they belonged to Intake, a community which held a grudge against the big house and the Tallboys family. First Sir Godfrey had raised some people's rent — and frittered the money away on the church; and then Sir Richard had done worse, found some legal way to cheat them out of their rights so that he could say, 'Buy or get out.' The fact that by pooling their resources every family had managed to buy, did not lessen the ill-feeling; and when Tom behaved in a mannerly way, he was siding with Them and being a sort of traitor to Us.

Also to be held against Tom was the fact that when he had recruited them to work at Knight's Acre he had promised them a sound good dinner every day. That had held for a while; now the food grew steadily poorer and the sight of Henry eating the same stuff didn't deceive them for a minute. They were being fobbed off at mid-day, and then, when they had trudged home this same table was spread with very different stuff.

Tom, though he could not match Walter's carving, could whittle quite handily, and out of a bit of birch wood he made another salt bowl into which Jem and Bert could drop gravy or bits of meat if they wished.

Griselda said, 'That was thoughtful of you, Tom,' and gave him one of her rare smiles.

'Can't do with this, can we Bert bor? No *spoon*!'

Usually Henry took little notice either of the lack of manners or the conversation at the far end of the table. This was a way of life forced upon him — temporarily; just a set-back — and he must bear with it. But presently it was borne in upon his self-absorbed isolation that Tom was being teased in a not-altogether pleasant way, and from the head of the table he said, 'That'll do.'

It was enough. They didn't like him, but they heeded him. He never had been particularly good-humoured and of late had been positively surly. Also, not to be overlooked was the fact that slave-driver as he was he drove himself even harder.

Up and about in the morning when they arrived; at it all day, and often when it was time to knock off, doing that little bit extra; or saying, 'Leave it. I'll mend it after supper.' How this repair of tools or harness accorded with those vast suppers which they imagined, they did not bother to think.

Tom Robinson decided that Spring that he was in love with Griselda. He had always been aware of her, seen her tripping about, neat and *nice*-looking, if not actually pretty. But he had never had an opportunity to know her until the household was re-organised. Now, the more he saw of her, the more he liked and admired her and the more he felt that she was the girl for him. He knew that he could never be content with a village girl — a female counterpart of Jem or Bert; and there were many things about Griselda which reminded him of the Lady Sybilla.

Tom owned nothing, not an inch of land, no roof. Down in Intake there was a holding called Robin's Acre, but Tom, younger son of a younger son had no claim to it. And he wasn't very strong; ever since the plague he had been subject to fits of weakness and dizziness, quickly passed, though liable to strike at the most inconvenient moments. However, he had taken responsibility for the sheep and Master Henry valued him; had indeed once said, 'Tom, you worth two other men.' He was reasonably sure that if Griselda agreed to marry him, the master would make no objection.

Tom had his eye on a more or less separate establishment — there it was, just across the yard. He'd never been into Tana's pavilion, but he knew from Ursula that there were two rooms and a kitchen.

All such things must be done in orderly fashion. It was May, and Layer Wood was a lake of bluebells; the perfect place for that preliminary walking-out during which a girl could give indication of whether she liked you or not.

He asked her as nicely as he could; he said, 'It's a fine evening, Griselda. And the bluebells are a sight to see. How about taking a walk when you've settled the children?'

Nothing wrong about that, was there? To Tom's amazement Griselda looked offended. Her green eyes seemed to glitter; her lips clamped down together before she spoke. Then they parted and she said, 'No thank you, Tom Robinson,' and closed them again, in a formidable line.

Griselda knew what went on in woods, in bluebell season, or out: and she wanted nothing to do with it.

Like Tom she had been looking to the future and it did not include *him*! One day, and that not so distant, when Robert and Joanna were three years old, independent, she was going to propose to Master Henry that she should take over the cooking and the management of the household; she *knew* that she could do it better than Jill, that idler, that sloven.

Tom accepted the rebuff. If she didn't like him there was nothing he could do about it.

Before the last bluebell had faded in Layer Wood, there was an incident at Intake. At Edgar's Acre.

Bert's father, making ready for cutting hay, sharpening his scythe, nicked his thumb as he had done at least ten times before. He took no notice, but it went bad on him and presently, his jaws clamped together and, his body arched in convulsion, he died. Nobody mourned him; he'd been a heavy-handed man.

He left two sons, Peter, first-born, Bert the younger. But Bert had contributed all he had, all he had earned, first to the raised rent and then to the outright purchase of the little holding.

The two brothers had a furious quarrel, ending in a tragedy which Bert's mother, bereft of husband and son within a few days, convincingly explained. They'd both, both her boys, been hot and sweaty from haymaking, the one in his own field, the other up at Knight's Acre; so they'd gone to the river to take a splash, and Peter had drowned. Of the shouting and the blows, of Bert carrying Peter's body to the river she said nothing; she needed Bert now . . .

There were hired labourers who in Bert's position would still be under compulsion to work to the end of a stipulated period, but in his case there was no such contract and he was free to go.

'You see how it is, sir. I got my own hay to see to.'

Henry saw how it was. That big extra field; hay and harvest to be got in by himself, by Jem and Tom. It'd mean neglecting the sheep a bit.

'Is there anybody down there who'd come and take your place?'

'There ain't the spare men there used to be,' Bert said, a

nasty undertone in his voice. 'Buying the land all of a sudden
. . . lot of families had to put boys out to work. Girls, too.'

Henry had had nothing to do with that transaction but he
was not going to excuse himself to his hired man. Nor did he
bother to say that if Bert hoped to make a success of Edgar's
Acre he'd have to work a good bit harder than he had ever
done here.

'Very well,' he said.

'I'll have a word with Griselda 'fore I go.'

Griselda was in the garden, doing her best to make up for a
year's neglect. The lady had loved her plants and it was still
Griselda's wish to be as much like her as possible, but last year
the children had been too young to allow her to divert much
attention from them. Now, nearing their third birthday they
could play about and amuse each other while Griselda did
vigorous and ignorant things which would have made Lady
Randle who had supplied most of the plants, turn in her grave.

Bert came and stood in front of her.

'Want a word with you.'

'I'm listening.'

'How about us getting married?'

For several seconds surprise held her dumb. Then she said,
'No, thank you, Bert Edgar.' Her lips closed in a thin line.

'You ain't thought about it. You think. The place is mine
now. Don't you want to be missus in your own house?'

'Not in *yours*' Her green eyes sparkled even more frostily
than they had done when she refused to take a walk with Tom.

'Whass wrong with it then? 'S'tidy little house. Look to me
you'd be better off there, looking arter your own children . . .'

'Do you think I want to spend my life watching you gobble
like a pig? Blowing your nose on your fingers? Sneezing without
so much as a hand up? Spitting all over the floor?'

The stolid East Anglian stood his ground.

'You could do a lot worse. Lot of men in my position'd look
for a wife with a bit to bring him. Or pretty, which you ain't,
let me tell you.' He jerked his thumb at the two children, busily
disinterring lily bulbs and calling them onions. 'They'll grow
up. Who'll want you then?'

'Get out of my sight!'

'Shan't arst you agen.'

She turned and vented her wrath and disgust upon the children, scolding Robert and slapping Joanna. It was always safe to blame Joanna for any mischief that went on.

Busy as he was just then, Henry was aware of the bad housekeeping. Jill seemed to grow more lethargic, more careless. He thought of his mother, how well she had managed, making the best of even poorer materials than Jill had to hand.

Jem, now aware of his indispensability, complained audibly, 'Cold bacon agen! This ain't what I call a dinner. My owd mother could put me up something as good as this, in a poke.'

'I was expecting roast mutton myself,' Henry said. 'What happened to the meat?'

'I let the fire get low, master. Time I mended it, it was too late to start roasting. *Eddy allus used to see to the fire.*'

Jill had not taken on any of Eddy's work.

'I suppose Eddy used to scrub this table, too.'

It had been clean once, now it was disgusting.

What, in fact, did Jill do? Griselda looked after the children entirely, washed and mended for everybody. She now did the garden, flung scraps to the fowls, helped by the children, gathered eggs, and from the wood's fringe the twigs which served for the kindling of the fire. Once Henry had even seen her carrying the swill bucket from just outside the kitchen door and tipping it into the pig-trough, doing it daintily, holding her skirts clear.

One evening Henry said, 'There is no salt.'

Jill said, 'No master. We ain't got none. I forgot.'

'I asked you especially, before I went to market for the last time for maybe a month, to think ahead and tell me what was needed.'

'*Eddy allus used to remind me about such things.*'

'Maybe you should have gone with him,' Henry said. He was irritable. Angry with nature which had ordained that haymaking and sheep shearing should coincide. You had either to be a farmer or a sheep man and Walter had been right in recognising the distinction. As each sheep, shorn of the wool which in this warmer weather had been more of an encumbrance than a comfort, jumped up from the shearer's hand it had to be marked anew if it belonged to Henry. The stick which applied the blob of red ochre, the stick which dabbed tar on the little wounds made by the shears were both kept busy and there were times when Henry was prepared to admit that Young Shep had earned his keep.

As soon as the shearing was finished one of Master Johnson's buyers arrived with pack ponies and a pair of scales. Over the selling, as over the shearing, Henry was careful to distinguish between his own and Robert's, and on his next visit to Baildon he took Robert's share — the larger part of the money — to Master Turnbull.

'I want this to be legal and in good order,' he said. 'So if you'd lock it away.'

Master Turnbull counted the money and wrote a receipt. Then he said, 'Money locked away earns nothing, Master Tallboys. This is not a large sum, but carefully invested it could increase.'

'Loaned out?' Henry could remember his father had once borrowed money — and been hard put to it to find the interest. 'I should not like Robert's money to be at risk. Suppose the borrower could not pay back, or died.'

'In my experience money invested in property is seldom lost. A plot of land or a house cannot get up and run away. One may wait to see returns but the demand is certain to come.'

'That,' Henry said, nodding towards the money, 'wouldn't buy much in the property line.'

'Not in itself, but added to other, similar sums. I have organised many such transactions for people who have only small sums to invest.'

Henry thought for a moment and said, 'You know best. Anything that could profit the boy. He'll have little enough.'

'You may rely upon me.'

Master Turnbull thought it strange that two brothers, quite similar in appearance, should be so different; Henry so honest; Richard so almost shifty, within the strict letter of the law. Young Robert Tallboys was lucky to have been entrusted to Henry.

This act of providing, in however small a fashion, for Robert's future, seemed to set Henry thinking about his own.

He thought in a mercenary way. They'd done well with the wool this year, the hay-crop was good and once again a good harvest promised. He had survived the set-back of having to buy, cash on the nail, what sheep he had and should this year end on the right side of the balance. His ambition and his determination to succeed were two things which had not succumbed to the shock of the catastrophe which had killed so much else within him. And when Knight's Acre was what he intended to make of it, it would need an heir.

Therefore he needed a wife.

He thought of marriage in a cold-blooded way. He wanted a decent woman, amiable, capable of child-bearing, capable of running his house. He would not love her, or even be fond — all that was over.

He never nowadays thought of Tana in his waking moments, with his will in control. Very occasionally he dreamed, sometimes dreadfully, sometimes blissfully, but as soon as he had splashed his face with cold water, and put on his working clothes, the horror or the delight were banished.

In finding himself a likely wife he intended to enlist his Aunt Emma's aid; a woman should be the best judge of a woman, and she knew a lot of people. Where the road forked he actually hesitated, thinking that he might as well go to Moyidan while he was tidily dressed. Then he remembered that he had done some marketing in Baildon and that flour was among the necessities he had bought. Jill might be waiting for it; she was a hopeless manager who never had anything in reserve. And nowadays every visit to Moyidan meant having a word with his Uncle James whose one idea seemed to be to detain anyone who called upon him. The business of marriage was not urgent. So he swung his horse into the lane that led to Intake.

Tom held a head of oats in his hand and said, 'Smut!' in a doleful voice. Henry in all the years that he had been farming had never had a case of smut, or 'black blight' as it was sometimes called. But there it was, the field of oats, so pretty a few days ago, now looked as though soot had blown over it; just as it was ready for the scythe.

'What's to be done, Tom?'

'Nothing. Save keep it off the wheat. If we can. It's as catching as the plague.'

'We cut it?'

'Take too long. Burn it. Fire's the cleanser. God send we're in time. Otherwise it's ruination. I've seen this afore. When I

137

was a tiddler. Seeing a whole field aflame I hopped about. Excited. Till my father fetched me a clout . . .'

Between the fields there were no hedges, just the headlands of unploughed land, the space left for the turning of the ploughs, at this season all full of wild flowers. Weeds. Poppies, cornflowers, cranesbill. And this field was the one known as Middle Field. Every field had its name, bearing some relationship to the house. Near Field. Middle Field. Far Field.

Henry visualised Middle Field all ablaze, the flames and sparks crossing the banks into Near Field, growing barley, or Far Field, growing wheat.

'Tom, if we fire this, can we contain it?'

'Beat the bounds sharp enough, yes. We want branches. And they're handy. Cut three good branches. I'll go fetch the fire.'

Henry stood there, staring at the blackened crop, appalled. It was a cash crop. Oats were always marketable. Rich men fed oats to their horses, poor men ate oatmeal as a dish by itself, or used it to thicken broth.

Jem arrived and corroborated everything that Tom had said. The black blight had struck Wade's place yesterday and Wade had fired his oats and reckoned he'd saved his wheat and maybe his two bullocks.

'Bullocks?'

'They're all connected, Master Tallboys. Smut on oats, black blight on wheat and the murrain in cattle. A sickness and a curse.'

'Now, mark my words,' Griselda said. 'You stay on this side of the bank and watch, or do whatever you like. But if you set a foot over it, you'll get a good spanking.' She addressed herself to Joanna; Robert was not venturesome. He would never do anything unless Joanna led the way. Having disposed of the children, Griselda broke herself a branch and joined in the tricky operation. The blighted oats must burn just long enough for the blight to die with those nodding fern-like heads, but not long enough to set the neighbouring fields afire.

In the middle of this battle, Tom had one of his weak spells and was obliged to lie prone for a while, but he recovered quickly.

By mid-day the stricken field lay blackened and flat and they all went into the house where Jill had not even had foresight enough to realise that four people, fighting fire needed hot water for washing. Even the children, safe on the far side of the flowery bank, had been smuttied. And they all deserved a better dinner than that provided. Jill had spent most of the morning watching the fire from an upper window.

As usual, Jem was the one to make open complaint, and Henry who had been about to issue a reprimand himself, changed course and snapped.

'If things go on this way, we may think ourselves lucky to have bread and bacon by this time next year.'

Tom said with as much cheer as he could muster, 'We may have saved the wheat.'

Griselda sat and wished that she could cook. It was an art in which she had no experience; the orphans' food had been prepared in the convent kitchen and the landlady at The Swan had done the cooking, relegating the rougher, dirtier work to Griselda.

Towards the end of the disagreeable meal Henry jerked himself out of gloom long enough to say, 'Thanks for lending a hand, Griselda.' It sounded a bit brusque so he added, 'And the children were good, too.' She took that as a compliment on her handling of them, and thought to herself — There isn't much I can't do, if I set me mind to it; I'll learn to cook.

Jill, however, was unwilling to teach; unwilling even to be watched. 'You fidget me,' she said, or 'Hadn't you better see what they're up to?' When she cared to Jill could cook, liked to make a mystery of her art and was certain that in a household a cook ranked higher than a nursemaid — despite all her fancy airs — whose charges were rapidly outgrowing the need for her ministrations.

The wheat had been saved from the smut, but at least half of the barley was affected by another plague, the rust. Henry's hope of a good year, financially, receded and his general air exuded gloom.

It was with no lightening of the gloom that he said one evening, at the end of supper, 'Griselda, I have something to say to you. Will you come into the hall?'

Everything within her dropped to knee-level. In one flickering second she remembered Bert Edgar's words about the children not needing her for ever. And Henry's words on the day of the oat-burning, about the children having been good.

She was about to be dismissed, as Eddy had been — a useless mouth. Well, there were other children in the world! But she loved Knight's Acre, the first place where she had ever been happy. She loved the house, and the garden in which by hit-and-miss methods she was learning management; she liked the little church — and even the embracing woods.

That Henry held the door for her to pass into the hall, meant nothing to her. He was surly and short-spoken, but the lady, his mother had drilled him to mannerliness. Passing through the doorway, Griselda set her lips together. She would give no sign of dismay. He was a fool if he thought that in retaining Jill and dismissing *her*, he was doing himself a service.

With a gesture, Henry invited her to a seat on the settle. Then, standing at a distance, he pulled his fingers, so that the knuckles cracked. He was finding the words of dismissal hard to say. And so you should, you great fool, she thought angrily. I'm worth ten of Jill.

Awkwardly, because however one approached the business, there should be some trimmings to conceal the harsh reality, he said, 'Would you consider marrying me?'

Griselda, the tough survivor of various vicissitudes had never swooned in her life. Now suddenly the hall tilted and darkened. She put out a hand and grabbed the side of the settle, and by that movement steadied both herself and her surroundings. She was capable of thought, and her thoughts were rapid and concise.

It would mean what she always thought of as *that*. But he was clean, different from men in ditches, men half-drunk at The Swan. And she would have Knight's Acre, for the rest of her life. Well worth it!

'Oh yes,' she said. 'Most gladly.'

With the burning of the oats, the threat to the wheat, Henry had realised that he was no longer what his Aunt Emma would consider eligible, except perhaps for some woman, well past her prime, and he was thankful that he had not, in an optimistic moment, turned towards Moyidan. He might well have found himself landed with a woman who had every right to expect more than Griselda ever would.

He moved forward, kissed her — on the forehead — and said, 'I shall do my utmost to be a good husband, Griselda.'

On an upsurge of confidence, she said, 'I will be a good wife to you.'

Nothing more to be said. And after all this betrothal was different from the majority only because the two people directly involved had struck the bargain between themselves. No parents hovering about and doing the haggling.

'I'll go across and speak to Father Ambrose,' Henry said.

When he had gone Griselda walked about the house, soon to be hers. By the best bed, in the biggest chamber — the bed in which the lady had died, she stood still, thought of *that* and knew that she could bear it. She made a promise — half to herself, half to Sybilla whom she had truly loved. *I will look after them all.*

After that she went downstairs, just looking about, planning changes, thinking, 'All mine. Mine.'

Jill said, 'You looking for something, Griselda?'

'No.'

In three weeks' time you will be calling me *Mistress*. And mistress I shall be. I shall watch you cook. You will never drive me from this kitchen again. And when I can cook, you will go.

CHAPTER TWENTY-ONE

Tom Robinson, the person most nearly concerned because he loved Griselda, took the news calmly. It seemed to him natural enough that a girl should prefer the master to the man, the healthy to the sickly. He was still grateful for what Henry had done for him during the plague time. He was able to wish them well with all his heart.

Lady Emma, the person next most nearly concerned was furious. It was a disgrace to the family. And fearful waste! Henry — she could bring herslf to admit this now that she no longer had to deceive herself about her own son — was a good-looking, well-set-up young man who owned a good house and some land; he was a Tallboys, too. Had she been consulted, as she should have been, she could have found him a wife ten times over; some with a little money; all with breeding. And without a word to anybody he had gone and married a kitchen slut, whose children would be little Richard's cousins! How disgusting!

The third person concerned was Jill. It was bad enough to have a nursemaid elevated to mistress, more irritating was the standard of cleanliness imposed . . .

Griselda's own experience of cleanliness was chequered; as a beggar-child she had been filthy and lousy. In the convent orphanage the standard of cleanliness had been so high that the children's heads were shaven. The inn was filthy, and she had reverted; and then she had come to Knight's Acre and been reclaimed by Sybilla. Now in full control, she was for ever saying — Scrub this table, scour this pot, wash your hands before handling dough. There was also the constant watch-fulness — Let me see how that is done, Jill; and the questions — Why do you do that?

Jill was denied even the relief of a good grumble. Against Griselda Tom Robinson would hear no word of criticism, and she had little opportunity of seeing Jem alone. Once she did catch him and began to list all that she now had to put up with, he simply said the food was better nowadays. That was all he cared about.

One day Jem happened to mention that Bert Edgar's old mother had fretted herself to a skeleton and got so useless that Bert had sent her to his married sister in Nettleton.

'Who do for Bert, then,' Jill asked.

'He do for hisself mostly. Some days he get a dinner at Wade's. They're sorta related.'

Next day, as soon as dinner was over and the dishes washed — This plate is still very greasy; take some ashes to it! — Jill slipped away, washed herself with unusual thorough-ness and put on the better of her two summer dresses and went down to the village. It was almost the end of harvest and in some of the brown stubble fields women and children were gleaning. Bert Edgar, single-handed on a holding which had kept two men busy, was still scything. He stopped when he saw Jill and wiped his sweaty brow with his sweaty forearm.

'What you want?' he asked ungraciously. She had never en-deared herself to him, lazy fat cow.

'I hear you got nobody to do for you, Bert.'

'Thass right.'

'I'd come. I can't do with things up there any longer. Come

into the house all rags and filth and now lording it over all.'
Here she could at least air her grievances.

As she talked Bert looked her over. Lazy fat cow, but given a
bit of stick behind her, she could be made to move; one or two
bad dinners chucked at her head would learn her! She was
strong, and if not actually young, not old, not past bearing a
child. One. That was what he wanted. A boy.

'When could you come?'

'Any time. Eddy and me wasn't bonded. We was just sent
over from Moyidan.' Wives *were* bonded, for life! And she'd
soon learn not to talk about Eddy. A clout on the jaw worked
wonders!

'I'll marry you. That is if you start in right now.'

She was almost as overcome as Griselda had been, some
weeks earlier in the hall. By the rough and ready reckoning of a
peasant family she was thirty-five years old, and nobody had
ever shown the slightest desire to walk out with her, take her to
the Midsummer Fair, leave alone marry her. She'd been fond
of Eddy, but he was years too young and he'd always be poor.
Married to Bert she'd be mistress of Edgar's Acre; the equal of
that upstart little bitch.

'All right,' she said. 'What'll I start on?'

'Making sheaves and stooking them,' Bert said. 'Then,
back at the house there's a rabbit I clumped. We could hev a
pie. . .'

He dealt fairly gently with her until they were actually married; it wouldn't do to frighten her off before she had committed herself. And in fact Jill, during that time exerted herself
to please. It wouldn't do to frighten him off until she was
legally his wife. Mistress of Edgar's Acre. After that she'd
show him.

Two loveless marriages, made for convenience, as most
were. The one at Knight's Acre was, apparently, the more successful. Henry and Griselda remained civil, mannerly and of
one mind. But the spark which bed-intimacy so often kindled,
even in loveless marriages, remained dead for them, two people
rippled by experience; the one in a ditch, the other in a silk-
hung pavilion. Griselda still, in a marital embrace, set her teeth
and endured and Henry thought that he must not compare;
this was something that he had let himself in for, something he

had deliberately undertaken. It suited him. Griselda made no demands, was capable, energetic and thrifty.

Thrift was of importance, because although the penury of the early part of that year had passed — never, Henry hoped, to be repeated — and the price of wool remained steady and the harvest not a complete disaster; taxes had risen out of all proportion. There was even a new one, grotesquely called 'a Benevolence' the proceeds of which were supposed to go to renewing the war with France. This form of direct taxation could not be evaded — tax on wines and other luxuries could be; you simply didn't buy. But by whatever standard the tax-assessors used — number of rooms, or windows, or hearths, or acres, Knight's Acre was a substantial property, to be taxed accordingly. Unless you paid, and paid promptly, an order for distraint was issued, and you lost your stock or any other movable.

To make matters even more difficult for a man just struggling to his feet, was the tinkering about with the coinage. Edward IV, ruling without a Parliament, which meant that he was out of touch with ordinary country people, while still in close contact with London, that centre of commerce, decided to abolish the noble and issued a new coin, the ryal, of greater face value, but less purchasing power. The result was raging inflation. And the result of that was cautious buying. Families who had eaten meat twice or even three times a week, now ate it once; those who had eaten white bread — priding themselves upon it — reverted to the dark brown bread of the poor. The market sagged.

Knight's Acre, so largely self-supporting, benefited in a way; it still had food, good food, and thanks to Griselda, well-cooked, but Henry's dream of prosperity, like the rainbow's end, receded and the silver, the hangings for walls and all the other things which he had promised, first to his mother, and then to Tana were as far out of reach as ever. He had never promised Griselda anything and she seemed to be happy and content with what she had. Good manager. Good wife.

They had been married rather less than two years when on a Saturday afternoon, Griselda went to the church with an armful of flowers. Robert and Joanna went with her. She was bringing them up to be useful and they could now be trusted

144

with such small duties as filling the altar vases from a bucket of water which Father Ambrose's housekeeper kept ready just inside the door. Less for flowers than against an accident. Fumbling about with candles the old man might well set fire to something. To himself.

Father Ambrose knelt by the altar and Griselda, putting a finger to her lips, hushed the children's chatter. Then she whispered, 'We will wait a minute. We must not disturb him.'

They waited for what seemed a long time, both to the restive children, and to the woman who had left a ham simmering in a pot over a fire which would die unless attended.

Presently Joanna said in something louder than a whisper, 'He's gone to sleep!' She giggled and so did Robert; to go to sleep in the afternoon, and in such a position, seemed comic to them. Griselda took a step or two into the church and looked more attentively. His posture was strange, she now saw, his head on the altar's edge and his arms stretched out on either side. She went forward and placed her hand lightly on his shoulder, and said, 'Father Ambrose.' At the touch he lurched sideways and she saw that he was dead.

Some women would have sent the five-year-olds away, told them to go and play. But death was death, they'd come up against it sooner or later.

'Father Ambrose is dead. God rest him,' she said, and crossed herself. The children solemnly copied her action. Griselda dropped the flowers alongside the body and said, 'We must tell Henry.'

Outside in the sunshine, solemnity fell away and Joanna shouted, 'I'll tell him,' and began to run to the hayfield.

'Me too,' Robert shouted and followed her. She could still outpace and outjump him, so she reached the field first, calling, in a kind of rhythm, 'Father *Am*brose is *dead*! Father *Am*brose is *dead*,' as though announcing glad tidings.

'I suppose it was only to be expected,' Henry said when Griselda joined them. 'But he'd lasted so long somehow it seemed as though he'd go on for ever. Well, that'll be the end of work for today. I'd hoped to get this finished. Tom. Jem. You heard? Go and take him up and put him on his bed. I'll have to go to Moyidan.'

'Why?' Griselda asked. So far as she could remember he had

been to Moyidan only once since their marriage — and that was for his uncle's funeral.

'Well, for one thing Father Ambrose must be buried. Also, because my great-grandmother built and endowed the church, Moyidan has some say in appointing the priest. Thank God for Aunt Emma. Richard would have sent us a deaf mute!'

Lady Emma received him more amiably than their last parting warranted. When Sir James died Henry had behaved correctly and offered his help with any affairs which the widow did not wish to deal with herself. She had replied sharply that she needed no help, and if she did, would not look to him who had so mismanaged his own. That was not only ungrateful but rude, and misguided for within his own limited sphere Henry managed well and had the reputation for being a shrewd though honest bargainer.

'I don't see that I've managed so badly,' he said.

'I am referring to your marriage. Most ill-advised. And a disgrace to the family!'

Had he married for love and been infatuated with his wife, Henry could hardly have been more deeply offended.

Now he stated his business bluntly and she dealt with it in her usual efficient way. 'I will inform Father Thomas today and he will see to everything. As for the future — I believe he has a nephew, recently ordained who would be quite suitable. I believe one should consult the Bishop, but how can one, when he is so seldom in residence? You can leave it all to me, Henry.'

He would have left then, but she urged him to take some cool wine. When he hesitated, she did a thing most unusual with her; she apologised.

'At our last meeting I believe that I offended you, Henry. You must not bear me a grudge. I was not myself that day.'

Actually she had been very much herself; her grief merely a bow to convention. Poor James had been dying by such gradual stages for so long a time, and had suffered so much that his death had roused little emotion but relief.

'We'll leave it at that,' Henry said.

The wine came with a dish of little saffron cakes. Hard after came little Richard.

Without greeting Henry, he said, 'I thought something was going on.' He snatched two of the cakes, and stuffing one into his mouth, spoke through it. 'Umma, you said pony as soon as it was cooler.'

'Yes, darling. Go tell Jacky to saddle him and then *walk* — mind what I say — walk to the bridge and wait for me. I have something to discuss with your Uncle Henry.'

She had decided when he was four years old — and big for his age — that he must have a pony and that no one should teach him to ride but herself. She was not a horse-woman, but she knew the rules and was willing to trot alongside, issuing instructions. The exercise exacerbated the stitch in her side, but it did not cause it. It was always there and sometimes kept her awake at night.

'I'm worried to death about that boy,' she said, when little Richard, with yet a third cake, had stumped away.

'There's nothing wrong with him that a good smack on the behind wouldn't cure.' Lady Emma had always accused Sybilla of spoiling her boys and had once administered to Henry the correction which he now mentioned. He thought — Mother would never allow us to behave in that oafish way!

'I mean his *future*. When ... if ... anything should happen to me. Two parents with not a ha'p'orth of sense between them. They think of nothing but themselves. Two good meals a day and a bed to sprawl on. Once I'm gone the nearest unscrupulous person who offers them that much could rule Moy-idan and ruin it. And I want it kept intact for him.'

She was not acting upon what might appear to be a sudden decision but which was in fact the result of long cogitation in the night hours when her mind would go round and round the circle of relatives and friends, suggesting and rejecting, and always coming back to Henry; honest, solid, and apart from his stupid marriage, sensible.

Sometimes her night thoughts would end with the idea of approaching Henry and making a proposition to him. But she had offended him, and would have to apologise, and night thoughts were unreliable, everyone knew. There was no hurry. A stitch in the side never killed anyone; she might have many years yet. So she had never moved in the matter.

To her the death of old Father Ambrose seemed opportune and here was Henry, looking exactly as he sometimes appeared to her in the night; honest, solid and sensible.

'What I need,' she said, 'is somebody reliable to assume control of everything. Naturally, in the eyes of the law, Richard will be heir, but I strongly doubt if he would even realise the fact. He would certainly never oppose any arrangement that kept him comfortable. I have thought about this very carefully, Henry and I know that there are provisions, in law, for the administration of the estates of those who are incompetent — but as I see it, that would be like hiring a pack of wolves to guard a sheep-fold. What I want is somebody honest and reliable — preferably a relative — to take charge and hold the place together until little Richard is old enough to take over.'

Henry sat there looking honest and solid, and sensible and reliable — but quite unhelpful. Had her apology not been humble enough?

'Would you do it, Henry? You shouldn't lose by it, I assure you. I have a little property of my own. I would leave it to you in return for your promise to look after Moyidan and keep it intact for the boy.'

'I couldn't do it. I couldn't spare the time. My own place keeps me busy from dawn to dusk. And I haven't the learning . . .'

'Clerks are ten a penny.'

'Maybe. But they need overlooking. No, I am sorry, but I could not undertake it. I have all I can handle.'

The stitch in her side tightened and she put her hand to it with a gesture that was now almost a habit.

'Would Richard?'

'How could I say? I know nothing about him — except that he went off with enough money to buy himself a bishopric, and took John with him.'

'Is he still in Winchester?'

'Even that I do not know.' Richard's behaviour and John's was still a matter of rancourous thought. If Richard, if John, encouraged by Richard, had not insisted on the break up of the flock . . . 'No,' Henry said, 'I know nothing. But surely there are people nearer. On *your* side of the family.'

They had all been sorted through during those wakeful nights.

'The old are too old; the young, too frivolous . . .'

From the bridge beyond the window Little Richard called imperiously, 'Umma. I'm ready! Umma!'

Lady Emma rose with a good pretence of her old briskness.

Naughty little boy! He had not heeded her order to walk; there he was, mounted.

She took short leave of Henry and went out. Impossible to scold this child who was so exactly what she had hoped her own son to be. Bold and able. She used the word *naughty*, almost as a caress, and then said that they must go into the village because she must talk to Father Thomas.

'I wanted to go the other way.'

Indomitable, she said, 'There is time for both.'

Time to go to the priest's house, along a path where, what with geese, dogs, goats and children all asprawl, Little Richard could have no real ride. His pleasure, she thought, must not be curtailed simply because another old man, due for death, had died. So, all arranged and the daylight lasting, they came out into the other way, the long straight way that led from Mo-yidan to the highway.

'You may go on your own,' Lady Emma said. 'As far as that big tree. Turn there and come back. We will then gather strawberries for supper.' She gave in to weakness and having shot out a few last instructions about the position of elbows and heels, and not making the jerks that hardened a pony's mouth, she sat down and once more placed her hand against the pain in her side, and for the first time felt the lump. Incredible! It had not been there earlier in the day. She remembered that her mother had suffered from what was called a growth, never complained of until it was too large to be concealed. Was it possible that for years her mother had suffered in silence? If so, how many years? There was no answer to that. No means of knowing how long . . . Dear God and the boy only four!

Obedient for once, he turned at the big tree she had indicated and came back at the fastest pace the pony could manage. As he neared her he called, 'Up, Umma! Up.' She rose, put her hand to her side. Nothing! Imagination, pure and simple. In any case, when her mother had died the growth was as large as a blown-up pig's bladder. What *she* had imagined . . . No, carefully probing, she found it again, no bigger than a walnut. So there was time. No need to write hastily to Knight's Acre Richard. Give Henry time to think it over. Not that she considered it likely that he would change his mind. Looking back she could hardly find an instance of a Tallboys changing his mind, once it was made up.

CHAPTER TWENTY TWO

When, at last, warned by a symptom even more sinister than the growing lump, Lady Emma wrote to her nephew Richard, the time was exactly right. The longed for, the schemed for, the *paid* for promotion had never come. Always promises that were never kept. Disappointment and disillusion, time after time.

Of the real barrier across his path he knew nothing. The truth was that His Grace of Winchester found Richard too good a servant to be spared. He never said so; even a hint to that effect would soon have reached the ears of the young man who had quite sufficient self-esteem. But in such a closed community as the Church no positive statement was needed; a silence, a shrug, the suggestion of another candidate ... Time after time Richard had had the embittering experience of seeing lucrative and authoritative posts go to men of less ability. He had just suffered another disappointment when his aunt's letter reached him. He gave himself leave of absence and rode to Moyidan to spy out the land.

Had he been capable of pity he would have felt sorry for Emma, aged so much since the last time he saw her, when he was in this neighbourhood to help settle his father's will. But why be sorry for her? She'd had her life; more years than most people, more power than most women, ever knew.

Weak as she was, she insisted upon showing him the land which was indubitably hers. And she explained.

'There was a time, Richard, when I feared that your uncle might die and my Richard might marry a strong-minded woman who would rule him and oust me. So I asked for this piece of land. I had then some intention of building a house, but it was never needed.'

Richard stared about him. The land was a sheep-run, and even at that, not very valuable. Too difficult of access. But that meant little; the real pickings would be at Moyidan; an old sick woman, two idiots and a boy of five.

'Well?' she asked anxiously.

If he accepted this job he would never become a Bishop — but he could live like one! He'd be done with dancing attendance on ungrateful men and be not only his own master but the master of others.

He asked a few cautious questions. Suppose Moyidan Richard and Margaret had no more children, and something unforeseen happened to little Dick, who would then be the heir?

'Your brother Henry.'

'And when would you wish me to take over?'

'As soon as possible. Not . . .' she said, and put her hand to her side, to the lump which her unfashionable loose gown concealed, 'that I am in imminent danger of death. I think you should come while I am still active and able to show you how an estate like this is administered.'

A comic statement since his work, ever since he left Cambridge, had been concerned with the administration of estates. Thinking of that work all done for other people, and no pickings, jerked him to a decision.

His Grace of Winchester was dismayed when Richard tendered his resignation because he had inherited a small property in Suffolk.

'But my dear fellow, that is a barbarous place. Only the other day the Bishop of Bywater was telling me that two months at a time is as long as he can stay there and remain sane. Hardly a literate person within miles. That would not suit *you*! No, you must appoint a steward and stay here and pursue your career.'

What career?

'I am sorry, Your Grace. It is not so simple. Family responsibilities are involved. *My* property adjoins that of some relatives — an elderly aunt and her grandson, a boy of five. I shall be able to care for all.'

'It is a thousand pities. I was planning to take you in my entourage on my next visit to Court.'

That might or might not be true; but no matter. Any man of sense, given sufficient resources, could hold Court on his own; and that was what he would do at Moyidan.

Within a week of his arrival — high summer of the year 1466, Lady Emma was giving thanks to God that Henry had refused her offer. Richard was charming to her, listened with attention and apparent respect as she instructed him, entertaining her with gossip, not only from Baildon and Bywater, but from the wider world in which he had moved. He did not criticise little Richard's behaviour — as Henry by implication had done. He constantly re-assured her that nothing should be changed; Richard and Margaret could be certain of comfort to the end of their aimless, useless days, and Moyidan should be most carefully preserved, handed over intact to little Richard when the time came.

She need no longer be busy or bothered. All was in good hands. Hitherto she had avoided as far as possible, the medicines which eased the pain, but dulled the mind. Now she could make free with them because all was in Richard's capable hands. She drifted towards death in a haze of opium, self-satisfaction at having managed so well, and gratitude towards God and Richard.

It was fitting to anyone who knew her well that the last clearly articulated word she spoke should have been 'Money'.

On the last day of September when Richard came in to wish her goodnight — she had taken to rising late and retiring early — she said, her voice muted and blurred, 'Richard . . . the money . . .' She and James had always lived well, but at the same time had been thrifty, sparing where they could, never thinking in Master Turnbull's terms that money laid away was unprofitable. They had, in fact, not wanted their gold to be earning, they wanted it to be safe; safe from robbers, and from the tax collectors. And from the ups and downs of a war which was no concern of theirs. They had lived in a time when a gold coin was worth its weight in gold — unless it had been clipped, and there was *no* clipped coin in their hoard.

'What money, Aunt Emma?'

She gave him no answer. Weakness and peace flooded in like the tide. She moved in the bed and arranged herself in the exact posture which, years ago, she had occupied in her mother's womb; knees drawn up, head tucked down. And so, in the night, died.

In the days immediately following, Richard sometimes wondered whether, on the threshold of death she had wanted to tell him something about money, stored and hoarded. For in the iron-bound strong boxes there was less, far less than might have been expected. Moyidan had always been well ordered, prosperous. When rigorous search revealed nothing more, Richard decided that enough was enough and that his plans should not be interfered with, he sent for Master Hobson and gave him such a job as came only once in a lifetime. Not merely an expensive job, but all indoor work, a consideration with winter at hand. And not merely that, but the kind of job to give a man prestige in the eyes of his fellows. Some of the work involved was a kind outside Master Hobson's experience, but he had his Guild to fall back upon. Guild members wherever they lived were sworn to brotherhood and in due time Master Hobson was in possession of plans and sketches, and of advice, written and verbal, all concerned with rendering a virtually uninhabitable place habitable. And splendid.

'And when can I expect the work to be finished?' Richard asked.

'Aah,' Master Hobson said, holding to his rule never to make an over-optimistic promise. 'All being well, sometime between Christmas and Easter. Say Easter to be on the safe side, Sir Richard.'

Nobody questioned Sir Richard's assumption of complete control. Even those of Lady Emma's distant relatives who felt a flicker of envy took comfort in the question — Who wanted to live with a pair of idiots and a spoilt child?

Richard had no intention of doing so. His work in Winchester had brought him into contact with a good many 'failed men', clerks of the kind Lady Emma meant when she said they came ten a penny. One of these was a man named Jankyn, a good scholar whose failure was due to a physical cause. He suffered from incapacitating headaches, accompanied by a rain of spots before the eyes. In the ordinary way their onset was unpredictable, but one thing was sure; before an examination or an interview an attack would lay him low for two days. Failure and ill health had soured his temper — just the man to deal with Little Richard! Sir Richard sent for him.

'It is not the easiest post in the world, Master Jankyn,' he said in the easy way which endeared him to underlings. 'The boy is well over five and has never been curbed. I have no doubt that you will know how to deal with him. But I should wish you also to have an eye to my cousin and his wife. They will give you no trouble. They are children too, but amenable. They need a certain amount of overseeing. In effect, you would have three charges.'

Master Jankyn would also have a rewarding post. A bedroom to himself — at Winchester he slept with two other men in a kind of cupboard; there was here a good, well-lighted room, school-room and dining parlour during the day, in the evening, his study; good, regular meals, servants to wait upon him and the princely salary of forty ryals a year. For a man who could only claim that he was a *failed* BA of Cambridge it was a wonderful job and he was duly grateful.

Nobody, Richard thought, could fault his arrangement. The boy who would eventually inherit Moyidan did need a tutor who could instil not only the elements of learning, but manners. And a pair of idiots needed a keeper.

He also brought from Winchester another man whom his sharp eye had noticed; a very good cook; another ill-done-by man who made beautiful things for which the master-cook took all credit.

To him Richard said, 'This is a very primitive kitchen, Matt, but I plan to have a new one. Made to suit *you*. I am not well-informed about ovens and stoves and spits. Hobson's men will take your orders.'

'You mean, sir ... Sir, that I may *design my own oven*? In brick? And hooded?'

'If that is what you wish. Once the work here is done I intend to entertain a good deal. Meanwhile, if you would do your best...'

Do his best! Matt was an artist whose beautiful work had never been recognised, attributed to another. To Sir Richard who had given him his chance, Matt, like Master Jankyn was deeply grateful.

While Lady Emma lived. Richard had made one visit to Knight's Acre. He had heard about the most unfortunate marriage and Griselda was a surprise to him — so neat, clean and almost well-spoken. At first sight he considered that a man in Henry's circumstances could have done much worse for himself. She could cook and everything about the place, including the two children offered evidence of good management.

However, Richard was more of a connoisseur of women than a priest without a parish might be expected to be; mouths were an indication of temperament and about Griselda's there was nothing inviting at all; the thin lips firmly pressed together hinted at a cold nature and possible bad temper, though there was no other sign of ill-humour. Her manner towards the children was firm, but kindly. Richard, eager to ingratiate himself, addressed her as 'madam' and gathered from the look in her eyes that the term of respect pleased her.

He observed — as Tom Robinson had observed from the first — a curious lack of *anything* between Henry and his wife. A stranger, uninformed, would never have guessed that they were married; they never exchanged a meaningful glance, a shortened name, a nick-name, an endearment or a smile. Married for just over two years — and no children.

It was on his first visit that Henry asked, 'By the way, what is John doing?'

Once the property had been divided, John had coaxed Richard to take him to Winchester with him, and Richard had consented, saying that without doubt he could find him some kind of employment in the musical line. Now Richard was obliged to say,

'I don't know. He gave me the slip at Colchester.'

Henry scowled. 'Gave you the slip? How could he do that? He was riding pillion!'

'I know. But we stopped for a meal. He excused himself, left the table and did not return.'

'Did you ask around?'

'Naturally. Nobody seemed to have noticed him.'

'Did you search? Raise the hue-and-cry?'

Here it was again, Richard thought, that elder-brother business which he had always so deeply resented. But he must keep in with Henry who, after that frail looking Moyidan Richard, and a child with most of childhood's ills to face, was heir to Moyidan.

'The hue-and-cry, no! He had stolen nothing. He could hardly be looked upon as a lost child or a horse gone astray. I search, yes, and waited ... Henry, have you ever been to Colchester:'

'No, What has that to do with it?' Henry had never had any particular fondness for John but he had a strong sense of responsibility.

'Colchester is at least ten times the size of Baildon. It is a very busy place, too. John knew where I was. As I say, I waited ... He had his money — and his own ideas.'

'He could have been murdered for his money.'

'Unlikely. He is as big as most men; he wore homespun and carried a lute. He's safe enough, wherever he is — and no doubt doing well. Otherwise we should have heard.'

'Oh well ... I hope you are right. After all,' Henry said, shrugging off responsibility, 'I'd had him from a pup and never gained any real control. You could hardly have been expected ...'

The brothers next met at Lady Emma's funeral and Richard took the opportunity of having a private word with Henry. He had, he said, already looked into sundry matters, including the venery rights. 'From what I read, Uncle James gave you permission to take a deer or two.'

'Me? That was so long ago, I could hardly bring down a hare. Permission was granted to Walter. I always assumed that what was granted to him would not be denied me. Was I wrong? Because if so,' Henry said with a slight grin, 'I took a young buck only yesterday. Clean through the throat.' It was as good a shot as he had ever made — except when he shot his friend Walter, by mistake — and the carcass hung in the larder awaiting dressing. Griselda was probably even at this moment making an umble pie of the entrails, liver, heart, kidneys.

'I just wanted to confirm your right,' Richard said.

Henry said, 'Many thanks!' but he didn't *look* grateful. One day, Richard thought — he would do him a favour which could not be accepted in such lunatic fashion. He went on to say that he planned considerable improvements to Moyidan and Henry did not even bother to ask what they were.

'Old property needs to be kept in repair,' he agreed. 'Thank God, Knight's Acre is new. Even the thatch should be good for another twenty years.'

'If you ever are short of money, you know where to come.'

'I take that kindly,' Henry said with a straight look, 'but as you know, I don't like borrowing.'

It did not strike him as strange that Richard should be in a position to lend; Lady Emma might well have had a secret hoard and left it as well as her bit of land to the nephew who had taken on a pretty thankless task.

'As soon as I have the place habitable,' Richard said, 'you and your wife shall be my first guests.'

And even with that Henry was far less impressed than he should have been.

Nor did he notice that the invitation was long in coming. Winter set in, short days and miry roads. People bent on a long visit might venture forth but it was not the season for making journeys in order to share a meal. Then it was spring, with primroses on every bank and hazel catkins dancing in the wood; and if Richard knew anything at all he'd know that the lambing season was no time for gallivanting.

The invitation came, late in March; brought by a boy, dressed in very fine cloth, buff-coloured. On his breast he wore an oval badge, embroidered with the family emblem. Sir Richard wished Master Tallboys to name a day in the following week when it would be convenient for him and Madam to come to supper and spend the night: and did Master Tallboys wish the wagon sent? The boy's hair, cut level with his ear-lobes and curling slightly inwards, matched the buff of his doublet. He rode a sturdy pony — just the mount which Henry had yearned for when he was young, and would now dearly have loved to afford for Robert, but could not. Quite apart from the initial cost, ponies, though able to fend for themselves in summer, needed hay in winter ... It may have been this thought that made Henry decide that the boy's manner was pert, and dictated his answer. Mistress Tallboys and he would come to supper at Moyidan on Tuesday; they would not stay the night; they did not need the wagon.

Now, for the first time in her life, Griselda faced the age-old feminine problem — what to wear? She was always neat and clean but her wardrobe consisted of the clothes which Sybilla had given her and those she had made herself from the stuff which Sir Godfrey had brought her. Nothing suitable.

Sybilla had had few clothes; what she had owned still lay at the bottom of the clothes chest in the biggest bedroom. They were well-cared for. Griselda, standing in this room had made a promise to the dead lady — I will take care of them all; and she had fulfilled that promise, even to the point of taking these unused garments out now and again, exposing them to the sun and air, returning them, with fresh lavender and rosemary sprigs to deter moths.

Now she stood hesitant. Women often bequeathed their

clothes, she knew that because in the orphanage she and the others had sometimes benefited by such bequests. In this chest there was one silk gown, very beautiful, or so it had seemed to Griselda when Sybilla wore it. Surely the lady would not mind . . . She took out and shook the dove's neck coloured gown and held it against herself. Just the right size. But the stout sensible shoes would not do. She rummaged in the depths of the chest and found a pair of dainty shoes; too short and too narrow, but the pain could be borne for one evening. And what about a head-dress? Delving even deeper she came across things she had never bothered about, moths had no taste for gauze and wire. She did not know that many of these crushed, pitiable things were older than Knight's Acre itself, remnant of Sybilla's other life when appearances must be kept up on a shoestring, and an eye to the latest fashion and nimble fingers and a bit of ingenuity went a long way.

Fully dressed, fully armed, Griselda came to the top of the stairs, just as Henry, hurrying was halfway up. He stopped and reached for the banister rail.

Old Father Ambrose had never mentioned to anybody except Sir Godfrey, his curious experience in the church. Sir Godfrey had never spoken of it. Yet the idea that there was something not quite canny about Knight's Acre had taken hold, part prejudice, and the need to excuse it, part communal consciousness. The place was regarded as haunted, by whom, or why nobody knew but in such matters vagueness simply lent credulity and Henry, recovering said,

'God's teeth! Just for a second I thought you were my mother!'

Natural enough; with the light behind her, in that gown, and in that head-dress.

In a way it was a compliment, however little intended, but under his hard carapace of not caring for anything or anybody any more, Henry was sensitive enough to realise, in a flash, that to mistake your wife for your mother might be hurtful. He amended it to, 'You look very grand.'

At Moyidan everything was very grand indeed. The bleak, high hall of the castle had been ceiled in, the ceiling coffered and painted. The windows were glazed, one with coloured glass, the tiny leaded panes making the family emblem. There were many wall-hangings, all gay and the benches that flanked the vast table were padded with scarlet velvet. Silver glittered on the court cupboards and side tables.

Griselda was awed. Henry only said, 'A bit different from when we used to play here. It must have cost a fortune!' Not quite the response that Richard had desired.

'The improvement of property is always an investment. The boy will be grateful to me, one day.'

At the moment little Richard was anything but grateful. 'Umma used to let me ride in there when it rained,' he said as soon as the workmen moved in.

'What happened to the stairs?'

'They were removed. They were so worn as to be dangerous. The new ones are here.' He opened a door in the screen which now ran across the far end of the hall, and displayed a fine flight of stairs, wide, level and with shallow treads. 'Roofing in the hall gave three extra bed-chambers, which will be needed when I begin to entertain,' Richard said. All were well, even luxuriously furnished.

'Not unlike Beauclaire,' Henry said. Irritating man! Not a word about the care and the taste that had been lavished.

At the foot of the stairs and still on the far side of the screen, Richard pointed to a new door. '*My* kitchen is there.' Some savoury scents were perceptible and Henry realised that he was hungry. In the great hall, however there was no sign of any preparation for a meal.

'This is too large for a small company,' Richard said and opened a door which Henry could not remember; the room beyond he did, changed as it was. It was the main room of the new part of the house, the one in which Lady Emma had entertained. Here the table was set. More silver, a centre-piece, candlesticks, salt bowls and three wine cups. A buff-clad boy stood ready to serve the wine.

'If you will sit here, upon my right, Madam,' Richard said. Griselda sank down thankfully. The shoes were pinching cruelly, and for some reason she felt low-spirited. So much splendour over-awed her, so much space made her ill-at-ease. Even this room which Sir Richard deemed suitable for a small company was far too large. At Knight's Acre she had felt instantly at home; here she was out of place. She lacked the ability to *chatter*, that was it, she thought, pin-pointing a shortcoming. She could remember, during that happy time, before Sybilla became ill, chattering lightly about nothing, being amusing, making pretty gestures. Often in those days the door between the hall and the nursery stood open and although keen wits and a desire to learn had enabled her to catch pronounciation, inflexion, even a certain amount of grammar, the art of conversation had eluded her.

Richard did his best to include her now and again. It was of her that he enquired after the children; but when she had said they were both very well and growing fast, she had said her say, and it was Henry, not usually talkative who added, 'And wicked. At least Joanna is.' He managed to make quite an amusing tale — though he had been anything but amused at the time — of how he had come upon them, yelling with laughter, playing a competitive game; who could get nearest to the target — a patch of mud slapped on the barn door; the missiles eggs, straight from the nest. 'I gave them both a sound good slap. To teach Joanna never to do such a thing again; and to teach Robert not to be so easily led.'

I could have said all that, Griselda reflected; but why should something the very reverse of funny at Knight's Acre, be amusing here?

She eased the shoes off a little, not much, she did not intend to be caught barefoot. Barefoot! The thought occurred to her that if Henry and Sir Richard and she were all suddenly cast out on the roads with *nothing* she'd be the one to survive. Then she gave attention to the food, which was unlike any she had ever seen, far less tasted. In his new kitchen the cook from Winchester had done his best. The new kitchen had a doorway — newly made — which communicated with this room. Through that doorway came dish after dish, mostly contrived to look like something other than it was. Richard explained that what he called the other end of the house was still served from the original kitchen. 'It seemed easier,' he said. 'Richard and Margaret care so little what they eat, elaborate dishes are wasted on them. Children fare best on plain food — and so does Master Jankyn. A dish made with cream or butter provokes nausea with him.'

Abruptly, Griselda, her mouth full of some creamy concoction, felt sick. The ultimate humiliation. She gripped the velvet padded arms of the wide chair and fought back. All right, she thought; now I know! All being well, I shall have a child of my own by . . . by November . . .

'It was a blow,' Henry was saying. 'Less for myself than for Robert. But that is what Johnson said himself, to me, last time we met in Baildon. He asked me how the lambing had gone and I said, badly. He then said that what with men asking higher wages and ponies costing more to keep, he could no longer afford to collect from such an outlying place, and in such small quantity. You see what that means? Hauling the damned stuff to market and selling to miserable little men who pay almost nothing because most of what they buy is maggot riddled or full of burrs.'

A chance for Richard to do Henry a *real* favour.

'No need to let that worry you, Henry. The solution is simple. Get your clip here. Market it with mine . . . with Moyidan's.'

'A good offer,' Henry said with just a spark of what Richard had always wanted from him. Immediately quenched as Henry added, 'And after all, Robert is your brother too.'

Oh how could one deal with this mentally flat-footed fellow and his dumb-seeming wife?

'It'll mean marking my own fleeces, too,' Henry said. 'Robert's are done in red ochre; mine had better be black. I'll see to it.'

Time they were moving Henry thought; at Knight's Acre, as the mornings lightened, they were early astir.

At Knight's Acre, where Tom had been left in charge of the children, the kitchen fire died down to a red glow and Robert leaned sleepily against Joanna's shoulder.

'Time for bed,' Tom said. He liked to retire early, carefully husbanding reserves of strength which lessened all the time.

'Just one last story, Tom,' Joanna said, shifting to make Robert more comfortable.

Tom had a vast store of stories, most of them handed down from generation to generation, muddled and mangled in the process, but still good; most of them with a touch of eeriness about them, capable of sending a pleasurable shiver down the spine when you were indoors, in company, in firelight and candlelight. What he usually lacked was a receptive audience, for living close as they did, he might start to tell a story and be checked halfway through by Master Henry saying not to fill young heads with old rubbish or Griselda saying that it was bed time for children. Now and again both Joanna and Robert would come up to the sheep-fold where Tom spent much time these days and there he would tell tales which sometimes seemed a little less believable in the open daylight. Even so Robert would sometimes turn pale and put his hands over his ears; 'I don't want to hear it! I don't like it.' Joanna had stronger nerves, nothing upset her, but she was considerate and would often halt Tom at the crux of the story which she herself wished to hear. 'Better stop, Tom, if it's what I *think* it is. Robert wouldn't like it.'

The flow of narrative was often interrupted by questions — 'What is a grandmother, Tom?'

'Well, your father's mother or your mother's mother. We'll say an old woman . . .'

Wolf was to them an abstract term, quite familiar because mentioned in connection with greedy eating, but neither child had ever seen one. 'What's a wolf like, Tom?'

'Well, a bit like Wade's dog, only grey and savager.'

That story was the ultimate in horror for Robert. Suppose, just suppose, that he looked across at the other bed one night and saw, not Joanna but something like Wade's dog — frightening enough as it was. Or suppose the dreadful change should come when he and Joanna were alone gathering sticks in the wood.

Joanna's reaction was entirely different. If she'd been that little girl carrying food to an old woman and found something like Wade's dog in the bed, she'd have hit it with her basket, or the poker, and the more it bared its teeth and snarled, the harder she'd hit it.

'You wouldn't turn into a wolf, would you, Joanna?'

'Of course not. How could I? It's just one of Tom's tales. You're safe enough with me, Robert.'

They were deeply devoted to one another but they used no terms of affection. No endearments, except perhaps Sybilla's, lost to memory, had ever reached their ears.

That summer, as Griselda grew heavier and slower, she kept them busy. They were seven years old — a year older than she had been when in the orphanage she had been told to earn her keep. Imperceptibly as her own child grew within her, her attitude towards Joanna and Robert changed. So did her attitude towards Henry, who in her view had behaved badly on two occasions. Once when she broke the news to him and he said, 'Good. Let's hope it's a boy,' and again when, the wool sold, she asked him to bring flannel and linen from Baildon, so that she could begin making baby clothes. Angered that at this of all times, economy must be considered, Henry said, 'What happened to what they wore? Robert and Joanna. I remember Mother stitching away. The clothes must be somewhere in the house.'

They were. Nothing here had ever been lightly discarded; but there were stains on the linen which no amount of washing and bleaching in the sunshine had ever completely removed — or ever would; and the flannel was hard as board. Not what Griselda wanted for her son — she was sure that it would be a boy . . .

One August morning Jem said, 'I've had enough rabbit to last me a year.' Henry promised him roast fowl tomorrow and told Tom to catch and kill a young cockerel first thing in the morning.

Joanna wished to watch because people often said, 'Running about like a hen with its head off', she wanted to see for herself whether a cockerel — not so much unlike a hen, actually would. It was just another old tale; helped by her Tom cornered the rooster, and with one swift stroke severed its head. It did not then get up and run about the yard. Robert had not watched. And he seemed only slightly consoled by Joanna's assurance that the rooster had died instantly.

Griselda said, 'Pluck it.'
Robert looked at the blood smeared on the bright neck feathers.
'I can't,' he said. 'I couldn't touch it.'
'You will when it's cooked,' Griselda said.
'I think not,' Robert said. Curiously, despite his timidity, his willingness to be led, the boy had something, a kind of dignity and a short way with words.
Joanna plucked the bird, nimbly, quickly, separated the edible from the inedible of its insides, tipped the inedible into

the swill bucket and carried it along to the pigs. About the swill pail, the water, Henry had shown some consideration, saying, 'Don't heave anything, Griselda.' She knew it for what it was — care for the child; not for her. In a primitive kind of way she reasoned; Henry had married her in order to get a good housekeeper and a brood animal. Fair enough by her measure, because she had married him to get Knight's Acre. A fair bargain, but bleak . . .

Joanna said, 'Now we have done our duty. We've emptied the swill pail, gathered eggs and sticks and brought water. Shall we *do it* — what we always said — now?'

What they had always said was that they would look into that mysterious, unused part of the house; something not much different from one of Tom's stories about a girl, ill-wished by bad god-mother, who had pricked her finger with a needle and gone to sleep for a hundred years.

'Tom, what is a hundred?'

'Spread your hands,' Tom said; 'thass ten. Do it ten times and there's your hundred.'

Asked about that disused part of the house Henry had said, 'Just some empty rooms, Joanna,' and Griselda had said almost the same thing. 'Rooms we don't need. We have enough to see to. Go give the hall a good dusting.'

Despite these rebuffs the place enquired about held its fascination. It seemed to have no door, for a vigorous rosemary bush had spread upwards and outwards, and a self-sown honeysuckle had grown downwards. But there were windows; two of them, the drawn curtains within sealed to the glass by cobwebs.

'Is somebody asleep in there?'

'Robert, of course not. How could anybody . . .? That is just another of Tom's old tales. But we always said we would *look* in, didn't we: Just to see? I'll go first.' She took off her shoe and hammered a pane which splintered. She reached in and worked, not without difficulty, the latch which held the casement. She clambered in, pushed aside the sun-rotted silk of the curtains and the cobwebs, and leaning out, stretching her hands to Robert, said, 'Up you come. Isn't it *pretty*?'

Apart from flowers and trees their lives so far had held little of beauty and nothing at all of magnificence. Despite the dust and the cobwebs which had collected in five years the silk of the walls and the ceilings, the divan covers and cushions, still shone bright. So much colour excited the children who ran from room to room, and bounched on the divans. They opened the chest that stood by the bed. Tana's outdoor wear in winter had been of fine woollen cloth and fur which moths had ruined but a soft leather pounch, its neck closely drawn, lay intact among the wreckage. Joanna lifted it out and spilled the contents upon the bed which had been her mother's. More and more exciting colours; red stones, and blue and green, and some like the rainbow, and some, strung together, colourless but with a pleasing sheen.

The children who had once shared a cradle and never been apart for more than five minutes at a stretch throughout their lives, often shared a thought; they shared one now though they spoke differing words.

Joanna said, 'Better than pebbles,' and simultaneously Robert said, 'How Many Birds In A Bush?'

'And Five Stones.' Joanna named the other traditional game of poor children. Tom had taught them, with little stones. 'We must get them loose first.'

The experienced Jew who had bought a necklet from this collection had seen that the setting had not been worked west of Damascus. It was too delicate. Eager little fingers made short work of the filigree settings that had been wrought with such care. Joanna's sharp teeth severed the silk thread that held the pearls together. They divided the stones between them and Joanna said, 'You can start, Robert.' It was a simple game, but it held an element of deceit. You kept your main store hidden. Robert rummaged about in his and then presented what looked like a fist strained to the utmost to cover what it contained, 'How Many Birds In A Bush?' he demanded. 'Eight.' With a grin of delight he spread his hand and revealed a single pearl. She solemnly counted seven from her own hoard and paid her debt. Then it was her turn to ask the question.

The new playthings made the old game even more entrancing than usual and they played on until a change in the light reminded them of the time. 'We must go or there'll be questions. We haven't time even to count, but it looks as though you've won.' They hastily pushed the tangled gold and then the pretty things into the pouch and Joanna carefully closed the bedroom curtains. It was hardly necessary to say, 'We shan't tell anybody.' Robert was just about to say, 'This is our secret place, isn't it?' She helped him through the open window, went out herself, drew the curtains, closed the window and reached through the broken pane to latch it. The empty pane showed, but there was ivy on the wall near by. Two long trails, re-directed would conceal the hole. 'It's our very own place, Robert and we can come here whenever we can get away without anybody seeing us.'

CHAPTER TWENTY-THREE

Henry was less casual than he seemed and just before the Michaelmas Hiring Fair he suggested that he should hire a good strong woman for half a year.

Griselda scoffed. Feed and pay a woman for six months just because you were going to be laid up for a few years. She had seen two child-birthings, one a beggar woman by the road side — she'd been up and walking next day; the other a lady on her way home to her mother for the great event, taken short and obliged to use the inn. It had taken her almost a week to recover sufficiently to make the rest of her journey in a litter, but then she'd been one of the soft kind.

'All I need is a sensible woman to be with me at the time. I shall leave plenty of food. A village like Intake must have a midwife.'

A stinging little sentence formed in her mind. *No new clothes for the baby, but a woman hired for half a year; does that make sense?* The words were not spoken, for although she and Henry did not exchange endearments they were resolutely civil.

Tom Robinson did not hear this conversation, but watching Griselda's growing bulk and knowing what lay in wait for her at the end of road he wished — for the first time — that his old granny were still alive. Many of her brews had been horrible but she had one for easing birth pains. He should have taken more notice.

By mid-October Griselda learned that pregnancy was not simply a matter of growing heavier and slower and at the end displaying fortitude. (The beggar woman had shown fortitude; just a few grunts. What the child Griselda, watching, did not know was that this was the twelfth confinement the woman had faced in as many years. The lady, a soft one, had screamed horribly.)

Griselda's ankles swelled first, then her legs. Too late, she admitted that she had been wrong; a woman was needed. But by this time the hiring season was over; everybody was settled in until Christmas, at least. Jem *said* he would ask around Intake, and did indeed do so. He liked a good dinner and could see that Griselda was past it. But Intake was suffering still under a sense of grievance against Knight's Acre.

Tom, mistrusting Jem, went down himself and was treated like a stranger. One of *Them*.

Henry said he would ask about Baildon and if that failed, try Moyidan. He did ask of everybody with whom he came in contact, even the old woman at whose stall he refreshed himself on market days, always as cheaply as possible. She, like everybody else said, 'I'll bear you in mind. If I hear . . .' Not unfriendly, not very promising either. Well, he must try Moyidan; Jill and Eddy had come from there — and Young Shep; all, he now realised in a dissipirited moment, too lightly cast off.

He heaved a sack of flour into the back of the wagon, and turned to confront whoever it was who had said, 'Master Tallboys . . .' in an urgent voice.

It was the saddler at whose shop in Cook's Row, Henry had been a rare, a reluctant and most unprofitable customer.

'Could I have a word with you, Master Tallboys? It has come to my ears that you need a bit of help in the house.'

'That is so.'

'Would you try my niece? She's a good girl, well trained. An orphan, my wife's sister's child. We took her, reared her as our own, but now . . . Well, they no longer hit it off, Master Tallboys. Two women in one house . . . You know : . .'

The secret guilt, the memory of that dreadful moment brought a flush, unevenly disposed to the saddler's sallow face.

'How old?

'Oh, well-grown. Over seventeen. And very skilled. There is

167

nothing in the way of managing a household that Leonora does not know."

Henry knew the shop, obviously prosperous; three apprentices working away in the background; the window full of ready-made leather goods. It struck him as strange that a man with such a business should not be seeking for his niece, not a good marriage, but a job in an outlying place like Knights Acre.

A possible explanation occurred to him — a girl of seventeen, and an apprentice.

'Look,' he said, 'my wife will have a baby in November and is lame. We need help; not trouble.'

'Oh, I assure you, there would be none.' The flushed patches darkened and the pale ones grew paler as the saddler remembered his wife's edict, 'Out of my house . . .' It was her house; the saddler had married above his station and although there was a general rule that a wife's property became that of her husband there were all kinds of tricks, played by careful fathers.

'What wage?'

'Oh, nothing . . .' But that did not sound right, and despite his shattering experience the saddler had not completely lost his head. 'Nothing much. Pin money. Five or six ryals a year.'

'And she could come today?'

'Oh yes.' His wife's fully justified wrath had ended in the ultimatum. By tomorrow!

'Well,' Henry said, still dubious. 'You know where my wagon stands. Bring her along and I'll take a look and decide.' The saddler had just time to think, resentfully — They're all alike; even this one, poor as a church mouse. All tarred with the same brush! Then Henry, with one of those singularly honest looks, said, 'I'd hoped for an older woman. And strong.'

'Leonora is far stronger than she looks,' the saddler said, remembering the clasp of those long, slender arms on the dark, supposedly deserted landing.

The girl's baggage — the neat, leather-covered, bright-nailed chest such as a saddler's niece might be expected to own was in the back of the wagon and the girl herself, well dressed, stood by the horse's head. She had removed the nose bag and unhooked the tether from the railings. It showed sense — but also

168

the assumption that she was hired. Henry felt two conflicting emotions, exasperation and relief. The decision appeared to have been taken for him. The saddler — or whoever had carried the chest for her — had vanished, the market place was emptying, the daylight waning; he could hardly tip out her baggage and leave her standing there. He was further confused by not being able to see much of her; the cloak she wore was bulky, thickly furred, and the hood of it was drawn well forward over her face. What had the man meant by saying that she was stronger than she looked? What did the whole situation mean? And why was he himself not more elated? After all he'd obtained what he had asked for — somebody to help about the house.

'You'd better get in,' he said. 'I'm afraid I don't know your name.'

'Leonora Fitzwilliam.'

The wind was from the east and they drove into it.

'If I'd known I'd have brought a rug.'

'I am well-clad, thank you.' She was; she even had gloves.

At least, he thought, she was a quiet girl. Shy perhaps, though her voice when she replied to his few halting remarks, was clear and assured, and in the one statement that she volunteered — 'I am grateful to you, Master Tallboys, for offering me a place at such short notice,' bitter and mocking. She was consumed with rage, at her aunt, at her uncle, at fate itself. So small a slip to be punished so savagely and the stupid man whining — 'She says that if you're not out of the house by tonight, she'll have me out, too. And then where would the business be? Honey, it's only for a short spell. I'll make other arrangements as soon as I can . . .'

In the kitchen, when she had shed her cloak, Henry understood the remark about being stronger than she looked. She looked anything but strong or workmanlike; very slender, an exceptionally long neck, elegant hands. There was something doe-like about her, in shape and in colouring. Her hair — worn short, just a cap of curls, and her eyes — very large and lustrous, were both chestnut in colour, but muted. Her nose, short but straight and wide nostrilled and a mouth rather too big for her face, added to the doe-like look. She wore a close-fitting dress of cloth so fine that it had the sheen of silk, with some darker velvet about it, and a string of amber beads. She was about the last kind of female creature to be a welcome sight to a woman in the final few weeks of pregnancy — and with swollen legs.

'It remains to be seen,' Griselda said, withholding judgment, 'whether she can cook.'

She could, when she liked. Extravagant of course. Cream, butter, eggs, all the things of which Griselda had been sparing. In the comfortable rooms behind and over the saddler's shop nothing had been stinted; the saddler lived far better than many of his customers, and Leonora's aunt had always, until that shocking evening, visualised her niece taking charge of a solid, prosperous household. She herself had married beneath her, just as her sister, Leonora's mother, had married above; but things levelled out and until that truly shocking evening, the saddler's wife had thought that for Leonora, Master Turnbull's son at least . . .

Exiled to Knight's Acre, anger died down — all her moods were shortlived — Leonora was conscious of one advantage. Freedom. A thing she had never enjoyed before. Even when — as had happened lately — she had been entrusted to do the marketing, the little kitchen maid, or one of the apprentice boys had followed, to carry the basket of purchases. Here she was free, and, the cold wind veered and the weather mild, had all the woods to roam in, with just the children for company. One day, in a sheltered clearing they found mushrooms.

Tom said, 'Here let's take a look at them. We don't want to go poisoning ourselves, do we?' He examined each one and was satisfied. 'They're late, but they're wholesome,' he said. And fried with bacon, very tasty. Leonora and the children gathered hazelnuts, too and a few late ripening blackberries. Of them Tom took a sterner view.

'No good after Michaelmas! Michaelmas Day the Devil fly over and after that they're *his*.'

Leonara said, 'Superstitious nonsense, Tom.'

'Well you wouldn't catch me eating one. Not after Michaelmas.'

Robert, who had eaten several during the gathering, and who greatly feared the Devil, blanched.

Joanna said, in all haste, 'It doesn't matter, Tom, does it, until you're *twelve*.' She fixed him with her cold, ice-blue stare; a *compelling* look. Torn between the beliefs in which he had been reared and his desire not to upset anybody, Tom said, 'Well, so they say.' He sounded dubious and Griselda by the fire took charge, 'Throw them to the fowls.'

'Next day Richard made a visit; just in time for dinner. He brought two men with him, but they rode straight into the wood.

'It is this business about boundaries,' Richard explained. 'So vague as to be misunderstood. There was always some mark, a bank, a line of trees plainly planted, or some stones. They know what to look for.'

Leonora, busy at the hearth, wearing an apron of sacking, hitched high to protect her good dress — one of several — from the spitting and spluttering of the leg of mutton, spiked with rosemary, did not turn her head, but directed her voice over her shoulder. She said, 'I think the Three Pools mark a boundary. They were dug, probably for defence, long ago. They are not natural, the banks are too sharp cut and precipitate.'

Richard's attention was arrested by the clarity and assurance of her voice and by the knowledgeability of the statement, and when, having dished up and divested herself of her apron she took her place at table, he eyed her covertly. Better than beautiful; extraordinarily attractive.

After the mutton there was blackberry pudding.

'I thought,' Griselda said with cold anger, 'that I told you to throw those things to the fowls.'

'It seemed such waste,' Leonora said. 'And now we are all to be saved. Sir, you are a priest and have power to exorcise. Please be so kind as to dismiss the Devil from this inoffensive dish.'

Richard laughed. 'The rite of exorcism requires the permission of the Bishop. By the time that was obtained the dish would be cold. I will show my faith in its inoffensiveness by eating it.'

Nothing actually flirtatious in this exchange of words, and yet there was something — intangible as a scent.

Griselda's temper smouldered. The girl simply didn't know her place! The moment Griselda was on her feet again, Henry could return her to Baildon.

'The children can amuse themselves this afternoon. This table needs a thorough scrubbing.'

This order, inspired by spite, pleased Robert and Joanna because it allowed them to visit the secret place. They quite liked Leonora who in a good mood was companionable. She'd shown them the test for real amber — rubbed between the palms until it was warm it could attract a feather from a handspan's distance. She had a fund of stories, different from Tom's but quite entertaining; she could sing and play the lute. (She had brought the instrument with her, a fact that roused resentment in Griselda, just as the fine clothes, the elegant manners and the ability to make sprightly conversation did.) Leonora in a bad mood was a different creature, silent and sullen, inclined to say, 'Be quiet,' or 'Behave yourselves.'

Leonora had never scrubbed anything; the kitchen behind the shop housed two stout maids and she had only entered it in order to learn to cook, an art her aunt believed should be learned by every girl, and one she herself practised with pleasure.

Griselda sat by the fire, her feet on a stool and watched the unhandy process with malice. 'Don't scrub across. Go with the grain of the wood,' she said. 'Put some weight behind it!'

This on what might well be one of the last sunny afternoons of the season. I'll show her, Leonora thought, expending fury on the table, leaning heavily on her left hand all the while.

By supper time her left wrist was extremely swollen. Henry noticed, asked what was wrong. 'Let me see,' he said. His long brown fingers probed the joint. 'Nothing broken. Just a sprain,' he said. 'Tom, fetch the liniment.'

It was still made to Walter's recipe and was powerful stuff which brought tears to the eyes of the one who applied it, and unless used with great care, took the skin off, being intended primarily for horses who had tough hides. Henry dabbed it on lightly and Tom said, 'A bit of a bandage wouldn't hurt.'

What Griselda felt was not the flare of sexual jealousy which was one aspect of love; she loved neither man. It was the colder feeling of envy for the solicitude being shown.

Henry said, 'Go easy with it for a while. Maybe Tom could scrub the table next time. We're not all that busy just now.' He thought, in a purely selfish and practical way, what a good thing I didn't marry a bird-boned woman!

Early in November there were some foggy days, then a spell of bright, sharp weather. On a Wednesday morning Henry set out for market with three squealing young pigs under a net in the wagon's body. This would be the last time he attended the market before Christmas, the season for which the pigs had been fattened. He had a good many things to buy and his horse needed new shoes. He was not particularly pleased to see the saddler, eager and at the same time, shame-faced. He dealt with the questions briskly. Yes, Leonora had settled down well, and was good with the children. Happy? Well, yes, she seemed happy enough. Henry felt slightly ashamed of himself because he had never taken the girl's happiness into much consideration; nor — fearing to worsen matters — had he intervened when Griselda was unpleasant. 'Anyway,' he said, 'she'll have a bit of excitement today. There's a hunt in the woods near my place and she's taken the children to watch. From a safe distance, of course.'

'She'll like that. She always was one for a bit of a show. I got a little gift for her. For Christmas. With my best wishes, if you'll be so good, Master Tallboys. And tell her ... tell her everything's quietened down nicely here.'

Tom came into Griselda's bedroom, carefully carring a tray which held some dainty slices of chicken breast and a piece of fresh bread.

'Where's that girl? I've been calling and calling ...'

'I thought I heard ... She's gone to watch the hunt.'

'What!' The absolute dismay in Griselda's voice, the look of horror on her face halted Tom as he advanced towards the bed.

'Is it ...?' He knew that it was and for one terrible moment feared that he was going to have one of his falling spells. But his desire to be a source of strength and comfort to her rallied him.

'How far?'

A pang wrenched her, she set her teeth and waited. When she could speak she said, 'Nearly here.'

'Then that look as though you'll have to make do with me. However fast Jem went running ... Horns and hounds sounded well beyond the Three Pools ... Now don't you worry. I know just what to do. I helped my old granny a time or two. You're safe with me.'

Griselda realised that she was better off than she would have been as she had planned to be — in charge herself and giving directions to an ignorant girl. Tom did know — and there were times when, for all her fortitude, she was incapable of issuing an order. And Tom was very comforting and calm. 'Just bear down, my dearie. Don't fight it. Bear down, and yell if you want to.'

This was nothing like the birth she had watched by the roadside, and presently Griselda knew that the lady at the inn hadn't screamed just because she was soft. She was yelling herself and pulling on Tom's horny hands. The afternoon was darkening when Tom said, 'I'll try a good tug . . .' Awkward little bugger, coming into the world feet first! There was pain unbelievable, a moment of blackness and then Tom saying, 'You've got a boy, my dearie. It's over. Take your rest.'

'Is he . . . all right?'

'Couldn't be better.'

What she needed now was wine. His old granny had always said wine was a great heartener. A statement not without self interest, since midwives needed heartening, too. No wine at Knight's Acre, unless . . . Tom was visited by sheer inspiration. That kitchen across the yard . . . Lady Serriff was always well supplied, and nobody had set foot in the place since the coffin was carried out. Worth a look, Tom thought, setting out with a jug. He found a cask full of the sweet red wine which age improved and ripened.

As he fed her the new bread sopped in wine, Griselda said, 'Thank you, Tom. Thank you for everything. You're too good to me.' For a moment the memory of those unvisited bluebells hovered — for Tom tinged with a gentle wistfulness, for Griselda with a new, bitter self-knowledge. Assuming that she could never be fond of any man in *that* way, she'd taken the man with most to offer. And now that she knew how different, how lovable Tom was, it was too late.

Even so the baby's coming might have been a turning point in the marriage. Henry was astonished at the emotions which filled him when he looked upon his son for the first time. Some of the warmth and tenderness might have spilled over on to the woman who had borne the child, but Griselda gave it no chance; even when every allowance was made for the ordeal she had been through, for the natural touchiness of the newly delivered, there was now something so cantankerous, so sharp and hard about her behaviour that it made fondness unthinkable.

It centred first upon Leonora.

'I won't have her near me. She deliberately went off and left me to die. But for Tom I should have died, and the baby with me.'

'She didn't know,' Henry said, making the mistake of trying to reason with an unreasonable woman. '*I* didn't know or I should not have gone to Baildon . . .'

'We none of us *knew*! But I told her several days ago to stay within call if she *must* go out. If that isn't downright disobedience, I don't know what is. Did she ask leave to go?'

'Not exactly. I only knew that she'd promised to take the children to watch the next hunt and I met the first brace of hounds at the end of the lane, so I reckoned . . .'

'You know how you left me, bedridden for the last week. You knew what she'd promised the children. Couldn't you have turned back and warned her not to go galloping off?'

'I suppose I could, but it didn't occur to me.' He had been at fault there, but he'd been thinking of the pigs for sale, the stuff to buy and getting the horse shod, all in one short winter's day.

'I shall be about by Friday,' Griselda said. The swelling in her feet and legs had lessened within an hour of the baby's birth. 'And on Saturday you can take her back to wherever she came from.'

'That I can't do.'

'Why not?'

'Well, for one thing I can't go to market twice in a week. For another I'd more or less agreed to keep her till after Christmas, at the very least.' He had tacitly promised that by accepting the gift. 'And in any case, you mustn't hurry things. You have a good rest.'

'I shouldn't know how to,' Griselda said tartly.

It made you glad to get out of the room.

It was on to Tom that the spare ripple of Henry's emotion spilled over. He actually had tears in his eyes as he wrung Tom's hand and thanked him.

'It was nothing, Master. You saved my life for me. I only thank God I was here and knew what I was about.' And didn't have a weak spell.

'She's talking about getting up on Friday. Should she?'

'No. My old granny always said that where it could be managed — a week in bed.'

'You tell her that, Tom. She might take it from you.'

About the child's name there was no argument; Griselda had no male relatives to be remembered and flattered. The little boy would be Godfrey Tallboys. (And Sir, too, if I have anything to do with it, Henry thought, for once abandoning Walter's standards and those he had considered to be his own.) Over the question of god-parents there was conflict. Sir Richard was an obvious choice, a blood relative, competent in worldly affairs, and celibate. No children of his own to care for.

'And Tom,' Griselda said.

'Tom Robinson!'

'Who has more right? But for Tom there wouldn't be a baby to *be* baptised.'

'I know. But it would look odd. After all, he is only a hired man.'

'I wasn't even hired, and I am the child's mother.' By some curious quirk Griselda had become glib.

'There's a difference,' Henry said. He knew the answer — a wife took her husband's status and by marrying her he had made her a knight's daughter-in-law. But in no circumstances would he have said it — his mother had taught him the elements of courtesy. 'It is the question of looking to the future,' he said, rather lamely. 'God parents should be chosen for the child's benefit. Tom could never . . . advance him in any way.'

The new glib tongue said, 'And who were yours? And how did *they* advance *you*?'

A sharp question. Henry knew that one of his god-fathers had been his Uncle William, Bishop of Bywater who, if he had shown the slightest sign of wishing to be a scholar would have done his best for him. Of his other god-father and his god-mother he could remember nothing.

'Nothing,' he said, 'and that is why I wish him to be better served.'

'So we'll have Tom,' Griselda said. And a woman feeding a

baby must not be crossed. There was always a risk that the milk might turn sour and the baby have colic.

The relatively minor question — for a boy — the choice of god-mother, was easy. Father Benedict, who at Intake would be the 'new priest' just as the man who had taken the Good Bishop's place would be the 'new Bishop' until a whole generation of people with long memories had gone to their graves, had an aunt who kept his house and kept it well.

She was a widow; Mistress Captoft, and although rather young and sprightly to be aunt to a man so little her junior, her status and authority had never been questioned. Nobody now could count, as people had done in old days, on instant attention, in the worst of weather; in the middle of the night. Mistress Captoft answered the knock on the door and almost always said that Father Benedict was at his prayers, or at his studies and could not be disturbed. Sometimes she would ask what ailed the person who needed the priest in such haste and quite often she would say, 'Wait here,' and close the door, presently to open it again and offer a draught; 'Try this.' Her medicaments were frequently effective, but usually so horrible that people thought twice before sending for the priest.

Her manner towards Henry was different; he might work like a hired hand and live little better than a peasant, but he was well-connected, his great-grandmother had built the church, his father had repaired and embellished it. She greeted him with respect, congratulated him upon the birth of a son, and upon learning that Sir Richard of Moyidan was to be one god-father, Tom Robinson the other, enquired tentatively as to the god-mother.

Over that question Henry had realised, for the first time, how thoroughly he had cut himself off from his own kind; he simply didn't know a suitable woman — except Leonora, and to suggest her was useless, dangerous, too, likely to throw Griselda into a fit. What he intended to do was ask Richard who knew many people. He told Mistress Captoft so, and she said brightly, 'If there is the *slightest* difficulty, you can always count upon me, Master Tallboys.' He accepted the offer willingly. She would be on the spot, able to do what god-mothers were supposed to do.

Even that didn't suit Griselda. 'She might have waited to be *asked*.' She had nothing personal against Mistress Captoft, except that she was grand and threatened to usurp the place which had been the lady's and was now by rights, Griselda's. Mistress Captoft appeared to have money; she was always finely clad, had practically re-built the priest's house and made a garden to the side of it, so that Knight's Acre was not now the only source of flowers for the altar.

'Whom would you suggest instead?' Henry asked. It was the first really ill-natured thing he had ever said to her.

On the day before the christening, Richard sent gifts. A quarter of fresh beef, well hung, ready for the spit, the kind of meat which only the very rich ate in winter, a cask of wine, and a good supply of his cook's specialities, all coloured and twisted into fantastic shapes. Watching the gifts being unloaded, Henry thought — very generous! But he wished he had known earlier, before he had killed a young pig or spent money on wine which he could ill-afford. Then, out of the wagon came the family cradle — not quite so splendid as it had been when Lady Emma made it ready for her grandson, but far more impressive than it had been when it was last loaned to Knight's Acre. More than generous, it showed a sensitive thought-fulness. And seeing his son, laid in the ancestral cradle with the family badge above his head, Henry felt again a resurgence of sentiments which he thought he had done with.

The day of the christening dawned bright and clear. Sir Richard arrived early, accompanied by little Richard who was told to go and play with the other children. 'But not anything that will make you dirty,' Griselda reminded them. They approached each other with the cautious inquisitiveness of strange dogs, but were soon playing noisily in the garden.

Henry thanked Richard for all the gifts, but particularly the loan of the cradle.

'It was not in use. The idiots couple enough, God knows, but I am inclined to think that they fired their bolt with little Richard.'

Griselda said that it would be a great convenience to have two cradles, one upstairs and one down. 'But after today this one must go upstairs, the plain one is more suitable for the kitchen.

A sensible, thrifty statement but Richard raised his eyebrows.

'The kitchen? I had imagined a nursery, Madam, with Leonora in charge.'

'That girl! She goes immediately after Christmas. She would not be in my house now but for Henry being so tenderhearted! Even if she stayed, she is the last person in the world to be left in charge of a child — or any other thing.' Griselda bustled into the kitchen where Leonora had been left in charge of the roast.

'What happened there? I thought the girl suitable and settled.'

'They never got on really well. And then there was an unfortunate incident.' He related, briefly, the circumstances of Godfrey's birth. It helped to explain the choice of a labourer as sponsor. 'Sheer mischance. The girl couldn't foresee . . . And she is not utterly useless. She can cook; she's good with the children. And she sets a pretty table.'

The long table in the hall had been polished to a glitter and along its centre, like a spine, ran a bank of green stuff and berries; holly, spindleberry, candleberry and ivy. At intervals candles, their makeshft holders hidden, raised their heads and the pretty trifles from Moyidan were so arranged that when the candles were lighted their shapes and colours would show to advantage.

'And even that didn't suit. Griselda holds that to bring holly indoors before Christmas Eve is to invite bad luck. It was too late to dismantle it.'

Richard changed the subject. 'I have been thinking about Robert. He's my brother, too. I feel I should do something . . . He won't have much money. A little learning is often a good substitute. How would you feel about sending him to Moyidan to share Dick's lessons?' (Little Richard had recently decided that he was now too big for the diminutive.)

'I'd welcome the idea. I have wondered, from time to time what best to do for him.'

On this amicable note the christening day began and it continued well. The baby screamed as the touch of holy water drove out the Devil. Leonora had done nothing to ruin the beef and everyone ate heartily. Mistress Captoft made the slight, but understandable error of congratulating Griselda upon the decoration of the table and was answered rather curtly. Father Benedict addressed a remark in Latin to Sir Richard and was answered in the same tongue — a satisfactory display of learning, proof that the new priest was not one of those who knew only the Latin of the rubric. Tom Robinson produced his godfatherly contribution to the feast, wine so excellent that even Sir Richard remarked on it and asked where it had been obtained.

'I got it where Samson got his foxes, sir.' In rustic talk — I'm not telling you!

To Henry it did not seem remarkable that Tom should produce such good wine. His wage was small, but he had no expenses, apart from his clothes. He did not frequent fairs, or buy from pedlars, gifts for girls.

The candles, lighted not from necessity for the day remained bright, but to give an air of festivity, shed their kind light; on Griselda's dove-grey dress, now retucked and re-seamed so that the darker stripes did not show; on Leonora's glossy hair and string of amber beads — a gift that had been the start of the trouble. The slight bump, darkening to a bruise on Robert's forehead and the even bigger and darker one on Dick's cheek, were not noticeable.

'It gets dark early,' Richard said. 'Before I go, Henry, I'd like a word with you.'

Father Benedict and his aunt were sensitive to the note of dismissal. Griselda lifted the baby and went away to feed him. Tom Robinson said he would bring the horses round. Leonora said, 'I have duties, too . . .'

'Could Griselda be persuaded to change her mind, Henry? About the girl?'

'I doubt it. It took me all my time to persuade her to stay her hand, until after the christening — for the use she could be today and over Christmas, when nobody should be homeless.'

Why? What does it matter to you?

'She took my eye. But I do not wish for scandal. Here she would be under a respectable roof and my visits, however frequent would raise no comment.'

(No shame must come upon this *respectable* house! After all these years of forgetfulness, deliberate and stubborn forgetfulness, Tana's mocking voice echoed.)

Henry was not shocked. Men did, he knew, find vows of celibacy hard to keep. At the same time, in the core of his mind, he thought that any kind of vow should be observed, any promise kept, any debt paid.

'It wouldn't do,' he said slowly. 'Griselda is determined to be rid of her.'

'But you are master here, Henry. Do I scent disapproval? Look at it from my point of view for a moment. They catch us young. You could always count upon Knight's Acre . . . I had nothing; and there are hundreds like me. Nothing to hope for outside the Church. If it demanded an arm or a leg we'd have given it. How much easier to foreswear the love of women? Something we did not know — as we knew our arms and legs. Also, there is more to it. Clerical celibacy is comparatively a recent thing. Our Lord made no such rule. Nor did St. Paul. In times not *so* remote the definition of a Bishop was a man with only one wife . . .'

'It isn't that,' Henry said. 'I'm no judge. Griselda wants the girl out of the house.'

'I can't have her at Moyidan. Nobody would believe she was my aunt! What about the part of the house that is empty? Would you allow me to set her . . .?'

Henry said, 'No!' very loudly. Such instant refusal seemed to call for explanation. 'Even there, Griselda would know. And disapprove. She *is* pious.'

'No more to be said then.' Richard was angered, but he had learned to control his temper. He went quickly to the door where Tom, Leonora and the children and the horse and pony waited.

Dick had refused Joanna's request to have just a short ride. Round from the stable to the front of the house.

'No. I hate you. You hit me.'

'You hit Robert first.'

As he passed Leonora, Richard said something to her and she smiled.

Joanna knew some impolite words which Jem used freely but which were forbidden to her. They were all meaningless and she chose one at random. Going close to Dick she said loudly, 'Bastard!'

Dick recognised it as a term of abuse, freely applied to

animate and inanimate things; even the weather could be a bastard. Nobody had ever called him that before and his interest was roused.

'What *is* a bastard, Uncle Richard?'

'A child born out of wedlock.'

'Why should she say that to me?'

'Hold your tongue. I have thinking to do.'

Quick-thinking too. So little time. He was going to keep Christmas in great style; every bed in the house occupied and day guests coming for dinner; it all took some arranging. He had counted upon Henry's co-operation. Now he must act; because that trap-mouthed woman would do what she said — have Leonora out of the house after Christmas.

Henry also had thinking to do. He had offended Richard who would very likely now withdraw his offer to have Robert schooled. Poor boy, I've ruined your future. And why? For a bit of sentiment that had sneaked in and caught him unprepared. Tana was dead; the whole thing forgotten. Let the rosemary and the other growing stuff obscure the door which had for one evening been the gateway to Heaven; let the roof fall in upon that divan . . . Decay might come, but the place should not be *desecrated*.

It had all been sealed away. Even the memory of Jamil, rampaging about and utterly unapproachable, so that Henry had been obliged to send for Tom Thoroughgood, who came and did clever things with bits of rope, with little leaden weights at their ends and cast enough of them to catch the horse, as in a net.

Five years ago. Why rake the ashes now? Just the casual mention of those empty rooms.

CHAPTER TWENTY-FOUR

There appeared to be no house to rent in Baildon, and only one for sale. It was far too large, but had the advantage of being private, standing at the farthest end of the street called Saltgate, behind a high flint wall. It had its own stables and orchard. Richard knew better than to appear eager, but his impatience showed and the owner, who had recently inherited it and did not wish to live in it, seized the opportunity to make a sharp bargain. He named a sum fully twice the worth of the house and when Richard agreed to it without visibly flinching, proceeded to raise it by a simple stratagem. 'That's for the house, sir. The yard and the orchard come separately.'

'I shall not require *them*.'

'But they go with the house. Can't split 'em, sir.'

Richard knew that he was being fleeced, but he had no time. He still had furniture to find — and a decent, middle-aged woman to act as Leonora's companion and give the establishment an air of respectability.

The house was furnished, and its owner, exploring this goldmine a little further, asked, 'What about furniture, sir?' Richard said he could use some of it, and the man said, 'I'm afraid it's all or nothing, sir.'

The only one of his cronies to whom Richard had confided his plans was Sir Francis Lassiter who fully approved and said he knew just the woman for the post; a widow, a remote relative of his own, very respectable, the soul of discretion. As for the place being far too large, the old roué said, 'All the better. Since I inherited this place I have given marriage my serious consideration — I shall need an heir, after all. But I tire easily and might well be glad to keep another little lamb in another little pen.'

On the third day of Christmas the letter which Sir Richard had promised, arrived for Leonora. She read it with brightness flooding her face. Some of its contents she relayed. Tomorrow Sir Richard was sending the wagon to fetch her and Robert . . .

Henry, assuming that he had irretrievably offended Richard had said nothing of Robert's going to Moyidan. Griselda snatched upon a chance to scold. 'You should have told me. How can I have the boy's clothes ready by tomorrow?'

'I couldn't tell you what I didn't know myself.'

'My new post sounds pleasant,' Leonora said. 'I am to live with an elderly lady, bear her company and see that her servants do not cheat her.'

'Poor soul,' Griselda said. 'She should pray that *she* is never bed-ridden!'

Nobody noticed then, that the two young faces, so curiously alike, had turned sickly green.

Born on the same day they had never known an hour's separation. They'd shared a bed until Griselda married Henry and went to another room. Even after that, when they had a bed each, whenever the night was very cold, or the wind howled dolefully, or thunder rolled, Robert had gone across the room and found shelter and comfort with Joanna. They had worked together — Joanna always taking the heavier work; they had shared their food, each offering the other the preferred little tit-bit. They were one.

Robert — once away from the others, cried. Joanna could have cried, too; the lump in her throat ordered tears, and then, somewhere in her head, rage dried them before they could be shed. She took the positive action of appealing to Henry.

'Why must Robert go? What good will it do? That boy Dick is horrible. He hit Robert, for no reason, that day he was here and would have hit him again, but for me.'

Henry tried to explain; it was for Robert's own good. It was a chance in a thousand. At Moyidan there was a tutor who would see that Dick did not hit Robert, too often or too hard. Here again Henry fell back on tradition — *A boy must learn to stand up for himself*. He had avoided the hurly-burly of the pages' table and sleeping quarters at Beauclaire, but he had contended against other, more demanding things, working with Walter through wind and weather, striving to learn, to match, to excel.

'Dick will be cruel to him. I know he will.'

'Robert is almost a year older than Dick. He'll learn to stick up for himself — all the sooner when you're not there to do it for him.'

'Robert isn't so thick as that boy. Or so rough. Please Henry, *please* don't make him go.'

'That'll do, Joanna.' Henry was out of patience. Griselda was completely without sympathy and at suppertime even kind Tom Robinson said, 'Come on now, eat up. You couldn't look to spend the rest of your lives together, could you?'

In bed together — for the last time; terrible thought! — Robert cried again and Joanna said, 'I shall think about you, every minute.'

'I don't want to go. I want to stay here with you.'

'I shall miss you. I shall be worst off, Robert. You'll have Uncle Richard and this tutor man and Dick . . .'

'I hate him. He hit me.'

'He won't if you hit him back a few times. He'll see that you can stick up for yourself.' She tried to sound confident, though she knew that Robert, so amiable and gentle, would never learn that lesson. Her own helplessness racked her. 'One thing, Robert. Don't cry whatever he does. He'd *like* to make you cry.'

Morning came, inevitable as death, and the wagon came, and with it, on his pony, Dick.

The christening feast had given him a false idea of food at Knight's Acre and he hoped to be asked to stay for dinner. The guests had gone from Moyidan, Uncle Richard with them: dinner there would be left-overs. Master Jankyn was in bed with a head-ache, so Dick was free. And although Joanna had hit him and called him an ugly name, he was fascinated by her. Riding, now before, now beside and now behind the wagon he'd wondered whether to arrange things so that he had a chance to hit her, as she had hit him; or whether to offer her a ride on his pony.

In the dinner he was disappointed. From Joanna he got more than he had bargained for. At the sight of him her feeling of helplessness vanished to be replaced with such an upsurge of power that she was for a moment dizzied. All the stories that Tom had ever told melted into one . . .

'I want to tell you something,' she said, before he could even offer the pony for a short ride. The man who drove the wagon was bringing down Leonora's clothes chest. Robert was fetching his own smaller bundle, and Dick and Joanna were alone in the yard. 'You may *think*,' she said, 'That you can be unkind to Robert. *But you are mistaken*. I shall be watching. All the time and I shall know.'

'How?'

'I shall drink a brew that makes me invisible. And if you are unkind to him, even *once*, I shall turn myself into a wolf and come in the night and tear you to bits.'

Dick had seen only one wolf in his life and that a dead one; caught in a trap, it had died snarling and the cold had fixed the grimace. All suddenly, as she said the last words, this pretty girl looked like that wolf. Shocking to a boy in whose veins ran the blood of the carter who believed that he had spent an afternoon with one of the Little People, a boy who had also listened to fireside tales.

'I swear,' he said. 'I won't lay a finger on him. I swear.'

'I think it will be all right,' Joanna whispered as she parted with half of herself. 'Remember me.'

'Till I die,' Robert said.

She knew that her threat, though it had had an instant and desirable effect, was only a hollow boast. She could not make herself invisible, or turn herself into a wolf. The only true thing was — *I shall know*. She knew with deadly certainty that Robert was bitterly unhappy. As she was herself; everything they had ever done together, like gathering sticks, or eggs, or drawing water was now misery; her misery and five miles away, his, communicating itself with her. Sometimes when the misery struck she would stand still, stiffened, her head at a listening angle and her gaze blank. 'Stop looking like a moon-calf,' Griselda snapped. Do this, do that, run and fetch . . .

'Tom, tell me that story about the wolf again. The one about the old woman the man shot when she was a wolf and she was lame in the morning.'

Tom obligingly repeated this tale — no Robert now to say he didn't like it.'

'*How* did she do it?'

'Magic brews.'

'What were they made of?'

'I don't know. The only brews I ever see were my old granny's.'

'What did *she* use?'

'Herbs and such.'

Tom remembered how the worst of his suffering during the plague had been concerned with the thought of his granny's hideous brews. He'd shrunk away from the lady's harmless ones.

'I never took much heed. Just bits of green and such.'

There was a suitable receptacle to hand — the silver christening cup which Uncle Richard had given Godfrey. It stood alone on the cupboard in the hall, was never used, would not be missed. There was an abundance of green stuff available too, for Leonora's table decoration had been thrown into the yard.

The first dose tasted just like water and had no effect. Perhaps like cream which must be allowed to ripen before it could be made into butter, a brew needed time. It grew nastier, but she sipped it determinedly. Then Griselda missed the cup.

'I only borrowed it,' Joanna said when questioned.

'Where is it now?'

'Under my bed.'

'Fetch it, at once.'

It hadn't worked yet; maybe it was only pretend, but it had been a slight comfort; at least it proved that she was *trying*.

'How dare you?' Griselda demanded. 'How dare you take Godfrey's cup and make such a filthy mess in it?'

It *was* a filthy mess; the clear water had grown murky as the bits of greenstuff and the berries rotted; on the surface bloated berries red, white, pink and black floated, amidst a few bubbles. The last few doses had been very nasty indeed.

None the less, had Griselda said, 'Empty it,' Joanna would have tried to preserve it; but she did not. She took the precious brew and threw it into the yard.

'Now wash it well, inside and out. Then pound up some ashes and polish it. And never, never, touch it again until I tell you to.'

It was now early February and the days, though cold, brought that little lengthening of daylight; preparations for supper could be made without a candle.

'Chop that onion,' Griselda said, and bustled into the larder to fetch the flour, the pig lard and the dried herbs which went to the making of a savoury dumpling. When she returned the onion lay there, unchopped and Joanna was nowhere to be seen. Angrily, Griselda chopped it herself, made the dumpling, lighted a candle and thought that while it cooked she could feed the baby.

The cradle was empty.

She did not immediately fall into panic. Perhaps Godfrey had wakened and cried and Joanna had taken him up to give him a soothing walk up and down the hall.

Not there. Nowhere in the house.

Stoic fortitude, bred by hard circumstance, gave way completely: Griselda ran into the yard screaming. Henry and Tom came running and found her in such a state that time was wasted in the attempt to get an even moderately coherent statement out of her. When they understood, they acted.

'I'll try the wood,' Tom said. 'I know all the paths.'

Henry said, 'She may have gone to Moyidan.'

Running and calling, Henry rounded the church and reached the lane. Darker here, and in the dark a darker shadow. Father Benedict on his good grey mule. (The new priest — or his aunt — had money of their own.)

'Our little girl,' Henry gasped, before Father Benedict could ask what was amiss. Haste and anxiety had not competely overset him. He was the son of a man, the descendant of many men, trained and tempered to a cool head in crisis. 'She has gone astray.'

'Not in this direction, Master Tallboys. All the way from Moyidan where I have been visiting my uncle, I have seen nothing on the road.'

'You are sure?'

'Not so much as a rabbit. What about the village? Children tend . . . Some family, with children may have asked her to stay for supper. If you wish, I will enquire. I will knock on every door.'

The mule, prodded by a kick from its owner's heel, trotted off towards the village. Henry ran back to Knight's Acre, and being on foot, took the shortest way in, through the main door, across the hall. As he opened the door between hall and kitchen, Joanna opened the other, between kitchen and yard and walked in, jaunty as the Devil.

Griselda cried, 'Where is my baby?'

'Safe and warm,' Joanna said. 'But you'll never find him. He'll stay where he is *until Robert is brought home*.'

Infuriated, Henry snatched a stick from the hearth and held it aloft, threatening. 'Where is he? Tell me at once, or I'll beat you.'

'Kill me,' Joanna said. 'And you'll never know.'

Henry had never beaten anybody or anything. Men did beat their wives, their children, their dogs, their working animals, but he had not, and in the midst of all this confusion, stick in hand, he felt ridiculous. What was there here to hit? Compared with Robert, Joanna had always seemed big, sturdy, now she was slight, nothing much but some bird-bones and a pair of ice-blue eyes with defiant fire behind them.

But now he was near enough to *smell*. That fox lair odour which years ago, had clung to his clothes and his hair.

'I know where he is,' Henry said. He was gone before Griselda could ask, 'Where?'

'You are the most wicked . . .' Words of abuse poured from Griselda, but they were not enough. She was beside herself. She snatched up the stick. She knew what a beating was and she applied that knowledge. But she was inflicting pain and hurt on the daughter of a man who under the *khurbash* had prayed God not to let him scream, and of a woman whose forebears, for uncounted generations had regarded resistance to pain as a point of honour. Just as Tana, in the marble quarry had tried to wrench away the overseer's stinging cane, her daughter tried to wrench away the stick, almost succeeded, failed, kicked, dodged behind the table, threw things. And with every act of resistance, every glare from those defiant eyes, Griselda's fury grew.

Only Tom Robinson's arrival saved Joanna.

He ran forward, seized the stick and gasped, 'You could've killed her. Then what'd happen to you, my dearie?'

The kitchen was a shambles. At least two of Griselda's blows had split Joanna's scalp, and head wounds bled freely.

'Master knew where to look,' Tom said. 'Somewhere I'd missed. He sent me back . . . Joanna, dowse your head in the bucket. You and me,' he said, turning to Griselda, 'got a bit of clearing up to do . . .'

The bucket of cold well water stood behind the door. Dizzily Joanna made towards it and knelt, hanging her head forward.

Denied the outlet of violence, Griselda's emotion turned to tears.

'There, there,' Tom said. He put one arm around her and with his hand patted her shoulder. 'He'll be all right. He's well-wrapped . . .'

'Suppose he isn't where Henry ... Oh, my poor baby! That wicked ...'

She began to repeat the words of abuse she had flung at Joanna.

'Now, now,' Tom said, 'You mustn't carry on like that. He'll be all right, my dearie ...'

Henry flung the door open so hastily that Joanna keeled over and the bucket rocked. Cold air and the smell of foxes came into the kitchen.

'Here he is, safe and sound.' Griselda flung herself on the baby, snugly wrapped in his two blankets and sleeping soundly.

'Oh, thank God. Thank God.'

'A mite overcome,' Tom said in an attempt to explain a position which Henry, entering the lighted kitchen had not even observed.

'No wonder!' Henry had had presence of mind not to blurt out the whole truth to Father Benedict, but now that the crisis was over he could admit that it had shaken him. He'd have something to say to Joanna! He turned to close the door, and here she lay, on the floor. Dead? No, breathing, and still bleeding.

'Hold the candle, Tom.'

Among all that hair, water drenched, blood soaked, the wounds were hard to find. One was superficial, one deep.

'I'll make a plaster,' Tom said.

A thick paste of flour and water and salt, spread on a bit of flannel checked the bleeding, but Joanna did not regain consciousness.

'Burnt feathers,' Tom said. There were plenty in the yard where the chickens clucked and pecked all day. But even the stench of burning feathers failed. Joanna remained limp, deathly pale, infinitely pathetic. Not unlike ... Hurriedly Henry thrust that thought aside.

'She'd be better in bed,' he said. 'And she's cold. Griselda ...'

No help from that quarter. While the men had clumsily applied the plaster and waved stinking feathers about, Griselda sat by the fire and placidly fed the baby who had wakened and made the noise which to a mother indicated hunger.

'I'll heat a couple of bricks,' Tom said.

Henry carried her up and placed her, fully dressed as she

was, under the bedcovers. The candle with which he had lighted his way, holding it in his left hand, his right supporting Joanna, thrown across his right shoulder, like an empty sack, had lurched and was burning crookedly. As he straightened it she came to herself. A bit muddled; something about Robert and a wolf and then, less muddled — 'I didn't mean any harm. I would — have looked after — the baby . . .' She murmured a few more words and changed from the position in which Henry had laid her and passed from a swoon, if swoon it was, to natural sleep. He put his hard, work-worn hand to her cheek and felt the warmth of returning life. Let her sleep.

He was hardly downstairs again and in the kitchen when there came the sound of hoofs and a rap on the door. Father Benedict, his breath steaming, his mule's breath steaming on the frosty air.

'All is well, Father. The child was lost for a while; but she is safe home and in bed.'

'I am glad to hear it. I rode all round the village.'

'I am indeed much obliged to you, Father. She had simply lost her way.'

'I do not understand Knight's Acre or its master,' Father Benedict said to his aunt. 'I did him good service. I knocked on every door . . . And he thanked me as though I had been searching for a button.'

'Ah,' said Mistress Captoft who had a taste for gossip. 'If that little girl has disappeared she wouldn't be the first — not from Knight's Acre. The house has a bad name.' As he ate his somewhat belated supper, she entertained him with a patched-up version of what she had gathered from those in the village who had benefited from her medications. She had never mentioned the subject before for tactical reasons. If a foot into Knight's Acre meant a foot upwards she did not care how many scullery boys, drunken archers or even steady — though detested — men like Walter had vanished over the years. But now with a blank between the christening and what she had hoped for, she let herself go. And Ben — she called him that in their intimate moments — said, 'We must keep watch for that child . . . If within a few days nothing is seen or heard of her, we must look into it.'

Henry said, quite mildly, 'There was no need to hit her quite so hard, Griselda.'

'Hard? I didn't hit her nearly hard enough. Putting the baby's life in danger and frightening me out of my wits.'

'You laid her head open to the bone and knocked her senseless.'

'You did that, when you opened the door.'

A false accusation. Joanna's fall might have toppled her over and account for one of the many bruises on her face; it could not account for the wounds on top of her head, or for the bucket of what looked like blood.

Henry did not argue, however. While he put Joanna to bed, Tom had cleared the kitchen while Griselda sat clutching the baby. Even when it had drunk its fill she did not, as usual, lay it back in the cradle; and now she made no move to serve up the dumpling.

'Come on, Tom. If you're not hungry, I am.' Two bouts of acute anxiety in so short a time had left Henry ravenous.

'I'll dish up,' Tom said. Out of doors few men were handier than Henry, making and mending and contriving, indoors he was far less handy than Tom.

Cutting into the savoury-smelling dumpling, Henry said, since Griselda showed no sign of coming to table, 'You going to eat yours there?'

'I'm far too upset to eat. And when I think of what happened while I just went to the larder ... I shall never make that sort of dumpling again.' It was a reaction as natural as Henry's hunger, but it made him impatient.

'Come on, Mistress,' Tom said. 'If you don't eat, you can't feed *him*. I wonder, now . . .' Lighting one candle from another he went into the larder into which, just before the christening, he had carried that cask of Lady Serriff's red wine. It was still there and not yet empty.

'That'll do the trick,' he said, coming back with a jugful. 'Do us all good after such a conflopption.' In many ways Tom's speech, like Griselda's, had been influenced by the lady, but there were some words, acquired in childhood which had no match among those learned later.

Contrasting the behaviour of the two men — greatly to Henry's disadvantage — Griselda accepted the wine, and then, mainly because what Tom had said about feeding the baby was true, but also because Tom had thoughtfully placed a portion of dumpling on the hearth to stay warm for her, she ate it. Then she spoke.

'After this, she goes!'

'Where?'

'I don't care. I only know that I shall never have a minute's peace with her around. She's an orphan, isn't she. Put her in an orphanage.'

'I can't do that. My father owed his life, his freedom to her mother. She is my charge. And part of this place belongs to her. Under my father's will.'

'What part?'

'Nothing much,' Henry said, shying away from the hurt. He intended, when the time came, when he was prosperous, to buy back that part of the house, and the right of way; it would, he thought provide just a small dowry.

'I shall *never*,' Griselda said, 'have her in the house again without somebody to *watch*. And how can I do my work with Godfrey on my hip?'

'I'll make her promise . . .'

'Much good that would be!'

'She was thinking of Robert. Holding us to ransom. And she failed. She won't try that again.' His mind slipped away to his own attempt to hold somebody to ransom — his own mother. Using that same foxhole. The only difference was that he had used himself, and won. Joanna had used the baby and failed. The memory gave him some sympathy with the naughty little girl. And he thought — Funny how things work out, if I hadn't been a naughty boy, well-deserving a beating, I should not have known where to look.

'You'll feel different about it in the morning,' he said.

In the morning Griselda felt no differently and Joanna was banished from the house.

Pale and frail at first, but growing stronger every day, she plodded about with the men, anxious to be useful and prove her worth. And although the brew had failed and the desperate action of stealing the baby had failed, the link between her and Robert had tightened, and she had a sharper awareness of what was happening to him. When she stopped, seemed to listen, and looked as Griselda had once said, 'like a moon calf', what she seemed to hear or to see was more real. Though it was not actually seeing or hearing . . .

Henry and Tom were kinder than Griselda and did not call her sharply to attention; but one cold morning, when she and Tom were building the lambing pens, Tom did say, 'You stand about like that, Joanna, you'll freeze.' Caught off guard she said, 'It's the pony. He's so scared . . .'

In that bitter weather both Henry and Tom made attempts to change Griselda's mind. Separate and private attempts.

Henry said, 'Let her stay in by the fire today, Griselda. The wind is cruel.'

'So it was when she took my baby! I've told you, and I meant it — I will not have her in the house, unless somebody else is here.'

Tom said, 'Can't you find it in your heart to forgive her?'

'So now *you're* siding with her!'

CHAPTER TWENTY-FIVE

Early March, and despite the cold the wild daffodils in Layer Wood were breaking, and in the sheep fold the ewes were dropping their lambs. The shelter which John and Young Shep had called 'our hut' was occupied, day and night. There was no great differences in temperature between the hours of daylight and those of darkness, no great difference in the demands on the shepherd's care but night watches seemed longer and more exacting, so Henry took those.

As soon as the lambing began he had worried about Joanna. Of course, wherever you went you found women and girls working alongside men and boys . . . dressed so much alike that they were almost indistinguishable. But Henry had been reared in another tradition.

One bright morning — red sky in the morning, shepherd's warning — Tom and Joanna came along in the rosy light and Henry said, 'I always knew sheep were witless, Tom. That black-face had a dead lamb, the whiteface in the same pen died, but had a live one. I tried to put the two together but it didn't work.'

'We could trick her maybe. It's an old trick, sometimes it works.' Tom took his knife and skinned the dead lamb, clamped its curly hide over the living one and shoved it in beside the black-face, who, after a cautious sniff or two accepted it. Allowed it to suckle.

Steady to his resolve to do his best for Robert, Henry said, 'Put the red mark on it, Tom.' The little skinned corpse lay there. And Joanna stood there, staring.

Not a sight for a little girl. And Griselda had grown crankier during this lambing time. A man sound asleep was no guard, she said.

Henry, yawning widely said, 'Joanna, I shall be up and about by dinner time. You go and gather some daffodils . . .'

She came out of her trance with a shudder and a stare and said,

'All right, Henry. Sleep well.'

She appeared to enter the wood just behind the church. Mistress Captoft saw her and thought, not for the first time, how deplorable it was to see a little girl of good family dressed like a peasant boy. When Henry realised that Griselda was not going to give in and that Joanna must be out in all weathers, he decided that she must be warmly clad, and suitably clad; he had bought a hooded sheepskin coat, too large, but it was the smallest size he could find; below it Joanna wore a thick woollen bodice, and hose. Over the hose were the woollen leg wrappings that were peasant's winter wear, and her slender feet were shod with heavy shoes that reached above the ankle — a necessity when walking through mud.

At Moyidan the servant who commanded the door which had recently opened to admit the Bishop, took one look and said, 'Go to the back!'

The five-mile trudge had given time for thought and planning.

'I have a message for Sir Richard from his brother, Master Tallboys of Knight's Acre.'

Neither her voice nor her manner was that of a peasant, and from inside the shadow of the hood her ice-blue eyes glittered, unabashed. The servant, however, held to the rule.

'Go to the back and deliver it properly.'

By that time she was inside, slippery as an eel and shouting, 'Uncle Richard!' at the top of her voice.

Inside the smaller dining hall the Bishop said, 'Another nephew, Richard?' Among the clergy the word was often used with a peculiar intonation of sceptical amusement because since paternity could not be admitted an avuncular relationship was claimed. Not that there was any doubt about Dick's being a nephew.

'It sounds more like . . .' Richard was about to say that it sounded more like his young brother; that whining, complaining boy.

The door opened, roughly; a peasant boy darted in. Behind him the servant said, 'I did my best to stop him, sir . . .'

They were then regaled by the sight of a boy making two curtsies, one to each man at the table. The edge of the heavy coat struck the floor and made balancing difficult. But she managed it. Just then she could have managed anything.

'It's Joanna,' she said, and in proof pushed back the hood. Above the no-colour wool her head rose like a flower; the dark-gold curls, flattened by confinement, clinging close to the neat, shapely skull, the profile cameo clear. His Grace of Bywater thought — What a beautiful child; in ten years' time . . .

'And what are you doing here? Disguised as a plough-boy?' Richard asked.

'I wanted to see Robert. May I?'

'Of course you may. How did you get here?'

'I walked.' Her manner was slightly cool — Uncle Richard had not stuck up for Robert as he should have done.

'Have you had your dinner?'

'I was walking.' In as much as he remembered her at all, Richard remembered her as a lively, merry, spirited child. Now, though they were both smiling at her, there was no answering smile.

'Come and eat now,' said the Bishop, making room for her beside him on the bench. Immediately he regretted it. She smelt strongly of sheep, and although His Grace was the shepherd of his flock and on the right occasions carried a crook, that was completely symbolic. The table was littered with what

Henry called kickshaws. Joanna took one, but before biting into it, she said, 'May I see Robert? Please.'

To the next boy who stood waiting Richard gave an order. Joanna then bit into a mutton pasty, shaped to look like a shell. His Grace of Bywater observed that her eye-teeth were very pronounced and sharp. Not entirely unattractive.

The inner door opened and Robert came in. Changed — but she was prepared for that; he looked sullen and cowed — he who had been so merry — and he had been crying not so long ago.

Joanna jumped up from what she did not know was a very favoured place indeed — a seat next a Bishop and on the right hand, and flung her arms around her other half . . .

'Quite touching,' the Bishop said, watching the two young creatures merge, clutch, cling, kiss. 'Are they twins?'

Richard had never said much about Knight's Acre to his new friends, and never taken one of them there. At a distance it was a reliable background — my father's house. Closer to, it had flaws. Henry could be mannerly when he chose, but he did not always choose; Madam did her best but it was not quite good enough.

'Curiously, they are not related at all . . .' While Richard explained, Joanna hissed into Robert's ear, 'Make some excuse to get us alone.'

He understood instantly. He always had.

'Sir, I would like to show Joanna my pony.'

It was the first time that he had ever used the word *my* about that innocent animal and Richard regarded it as a good sign.

'Off you go . . . But you've had your dinner. Joanna had none. Take some food. And tell William to have the wagon ready to take Joanna home.'

In that same hissing whisper Joanna said, 'Take a lot!' Robert obeyed, and she took a lot herself.

In the courtyard and around the stables the after-dinner relaxation lay. The two children slipped away, unobserved. Layer Wood which had sheltered so many fugitives engulfed them. Once within its shelter they sat down on a fallen tree trunk, ate what they had brought and talked. And talked.

Robert spoke of his miseries. Dick had never touched him. So that threat had worked! But he had managed cunningly so that for ink spilt, or ruined quills, for anything blameable on a boy, Robert had been blamed, and beaten. And the pony — 'I was frightened at first, but as soon as I got over that, they did things ... All the serving people are Dick's friends. They played tricks on me — and the pony.'

'I knew,' Joanna said. 'That is why I came to take you away.'

'Where?'

'Our secret place. I'll bring you food. We can play all our old games. It will be pleasant for me too, now that Griselda won't have me in the house.' She explained how that had come about.'

'How brave you are,' Robert said, thinking of venturing into the wood alone, at dusk. The red dawn's promise of bad weather was being kept and dark, sagging clouds were cutting off the daylight. As Robert glanced nervously around the distances between the trees filled with shadows. Moving? Prowling? Watchful? He gave a shiver and Joanna, instantly self-reproachful, realised that he had come out in indoor dress. She wriggled out of the coat and tried to make him put it on.

'No,' he said, 'we'll share.'

'And be on our way.'

Huddled together, their inner arms wrapped around each other, their outer hands holding the sleeves of the jacket, they set off.

Joanna was certain of the way. In the morning she had simply cut through the wood behind the church and reached the lane. Now — because Robert might be missed — she avoided the lane, keeping to a course which she thought was parallel to it. The east wind, sharp with sleet, blew on the jacket that sheltered them both, helping them along. Soon, soon they would come out behind the church, skirt it and be in the Knight's Acre garden. Robert would climb through the window of the secret place and she would go in, pretending that she had forgotten the time, lost her way; that would explain her absence from the dinner table and perhaps gain her an extra large supper portion; most of which she would secrete and save for Robert.

She knew where she was. She had a sense of direction, so innate and strong that she was certain that if her arm were only long enough, she could reach out and touch the church, the priest's house, Knight's Acre. The trouble was that in a wood, with darkness and a blizzard coming on, one could not keep to a direct path. There were thickets of brambles, more fallen trees, a pool, all to be circumvented. Presently she knew that either she had lost her way, or the wind had changed. The sleet was now striking from the left. They skirted another thicket, another pool, almost indiscernible in the gathering darkness, and now the wind blew in their faces.

Joanna did not say 'we are lost'. To do so would frighten Robert and perhaps make him cry. She said, 'I think we should rest a little, when I find a sheltered place.'

'I *am* tired.' He could confess it now that she had suggested rest. 'But, oh! So happy.'

What she needed was a hollow similar to that in which she had hidden the baby, but she had left it too late. Had such a shelter been near at hand the darkness and the driving sleet would have hidden it from her. They almost walked into the next obstacle, a fallen tree. It must serve. Crouched on the side of it away from the wind, they would have some protection.

Robert sank down with a sigh and a shiver and with another pang of self-reproach she thought — his feet! I let him come out in those flimsy shoes! Inside her own ugly footwear — stout, well-greased leather, lined with felt — her feet were dry and warm. She removed his soaked shoes and pushed his cold wet feet into hers, still warm from her body. He was too sleepy to protest.

'We'll play the grunting game,' he said, in a voice that indicated that tonight he would win it. It was one of their old games — who could be asleep first. One would make a little grunting sound which the other, if awake, was in honour bound, forced to answer. Tonight, after one exchange of grunts, Robert slept. A beating in the morning, the excitement of reunion and a long walk had exhausted him.

Joanna intended to stay awake, on guard; for in one of her angry tirades Griselda had spoken of wolves in the wood.

However, on the lee side of the fallen tree it was not uncomfortable; Robert lay with his back to her; her body fitted about him, her arm held him and the sheepskin coat covered them both. Despite all the mistakes she had made, she had done what she set out to do — a good thought upon which to fall asleep.

When she woke it was morning. The blizzard had blown itself out. It was clear, and cold. The sheepskin coat crackled as she moved and sat up and took her bearings. She had been right to halt when she did, for she could tell from the direction of the light that they had been walking due east, away from Knight's Acre.

Robert was sleeping so peacefully that it seemed a shame to wake him, yet. She must re-plan for it had been her intention to smuggle him into the secret place under cover of dusk. Now they must be far more careful, stay in the wood, *just* inside, until they were beyond the back of the church and the priest's house and directly in line with Knight's Acre with only a strip of garden between them and the secret place. She would then help Robert in through the window and go to the sheep fold. Henry would be gone to his bed, and asleep; it would be to Tom that she must explain that hunting for daffodils she had lost her way and been overtaken by darkness and the storm. Tom would have food . . . Joanna's sharp eyes had not failed to notice that these days Griselda took better care of Tom than she did of Henry. Henry could watch through the night with no more than a bit of bread and cheese for company; Tom had stew or broth in a jar, placed inside another, bigger one, lined with hay to keep the inner jar warm. The significance of this behaviour was lost on the child who only thought that Tom was less hardy than Henry, just as she was more hardy than Robert.

She gave Robert a gentle nudge. He went on sleeping. She spoke in his ear. 'Robert! Time to wake up. Time to go.' When he did not respond to that, she shook him and called his name more loudly.

Deeply devoted and attached as they were, they had never used loving words to one another. It was an unknown language which both their mothers had used, but Sybilla had died before it could be communicated and Tana had reserved hers . . . So in this extremity all Joanna could say was 'Robert.' When the name, repeated with increasing force and urgency brought no response, she realised that he had gone, beyond recall.

He was dead. Like old Father Ambrose in the church.

At Knight's Acre she had not been missed until dusk when Henry went to change places with Tom. 'I thought maybe she'd come back to you here.'

'Haven't had sight of her since morning.'

'You'll have to stay here, Tom, while I take a look. She may even be in the house; if so I shan't be long . . .'

She was not in the house and a blizzard was blowing up. Carrying a lantern Henry went to the fox-hole. Not there. He shouted, the sound torn to shreds by the howling wind. He went back to the house, hoping.

'No,' Griselda said in answer to his anxious question. She was sewing and gently rocking the cradle with her foot. Her complete indifference infuriated him.

'God damn it, you might show a little concern!' To that she did not bother to reply.

Fighting his way back to the fold, Henry thought — as once before — of Moyidan. If Joanna had run way, and who could blame her? it was for Moyidan that she would make, and if she had set out for Moyidan in the morning she'd be safe now.

'All right, Tom; off you go.'

It was a bad, busy night. Lambs were supposed to come into the world with their noses pressed close to their forefeet, that way they slid out easily. If for some reason unknown to man, they presented themselves with heads thrown back, feet showing but no nose, then a shepherd had to get busy, pushing and re-arranging. Ewes always knew when they were in trouble and cried for help with voices that sounded almost human. Four called for help that night.

In the morning, all soiled as he was, and gritty eyed for need of sleep, Henry saddled his horse and went to Moyidan. Rich= ard was not there — he had gone to Baildon. Only the door servant knew anything; a girl, looking like a boy, had pushed her way in and been well-received, not only by Sir Richard but by the Bishop . . . Henry assumed that unwanted in the house, unwanted in the sheep fold, Joanna had run way, told a piteous tale and been taken care of.

The story she told would, he realised be slanted to his dis= favour. Unfair, because as far as he could he had always done the best he could for this child — no kin of his. The thought, however did not unduly perturb him; if Joanna were safe, in some place where she stood a chance of being reasonably happy, he would be content. But he needed to be *sure*. He felt that he could not spare the time to go to Bywater, or to search for Richard in Baildon; so he left an urgent message — Would

Sir Richard let him know immediately exactly what had happened to the little girl . . .

He then rode home, and there she was, with Tom in the sheep fold.

He could have shaken her; but she seemed to be in such a poor way; her face deathly white and swollen from crying; it bore scratches, too. She appeared to be calm, though now and again a shudder shook her.

'Tom told me how worried you were, Henry. I am sorry. I went to Moyidan to see Robert.' That much was known; she had been seen. 'Then coming home I lost myself in the wood. There was a storm . . .'

'If you'd only shown a little sense, and waited. I intended to *take* you to visit Robert as soon as he'd had time to settle — and this was over.' He waved his hand around the fold. 'You're a very head-strong, inconsiderate little girl.'

Part of his anger was directed against Richard. God's teeth, couldn't he have sent her home by wagon, or Pillion. She was mired to the knees and her boots were so caked with mud that standing there she seemed anchored to the ground.

'Come on,' he said, reaching down from the saddle. 'The sooner you're in bed the better.'

On the short canter from the fold to the stable he relented; even inside the bulky clothes she seemed so frail. In a kinder voice, he asked, 'Well, and how did you find Robert?'

'He was lonely at first. But not now. In fact one of the last things he said to me was that he was happy.'

'There you are, you see. A lot of fuss and anxiety all about nothing.'

She shuddered again and Henry said, 'God send you haven't taken a chill.'

She had not, though the night in the open had changed her in some indefinable way. Since Robert's going she had been quiet and unhappy; you'd have thought, Henry reflected that having seen him and learned that he was happy at Moyidan, some of her old spirit would have returned. It had not; she still seemed to be quiet and unhappy, though she no longer stopped and stared and listened. It was possible, he thought, that seeing Robert living in comfort had made her compare his lot with her own. He wished very much that there was somewhere where she could go, away from this unnatural life, outdoor work all day and the evenings made wretched by Griselda's unrelenting hostility. But there was nothing he could do, except be as kind to her as he could.

Since she was home he expected no message from Moyidan as to her whereabouts, but on the third morning after the escapade Richard arrived, looking slightly less sleek and composed than usual. He halted his horse by the sheepfold and said, 'Is Robert here?'

'Robert! No Why should he be?'

'He's vanished. Is the girl here?'

'Vanished? How could . . .? Yes, she's here. In the shelter. Joanna!'

This was a moment which she had known was bound to come and she was prepared for it.

Richard, lawyer as well as priest, knew the value of attack.

'Where's Robert?'

'Robert? I don't know.' That was strictly true. She knew where the body lay, but the all-important part, the gentleness and merriment and affection — where were they? She'd knelt and prayed — God, let his time in Purgatory be short; he never did anything bad. He never did anything but I led him into it.

'So far as I can make out you were the last person to see him.'

'I saw him. You said I could.'

Young as she was she had the known feminine way of going off on a side track.

'Yes. I said you could see him and he said he wanted to show you his pony. What happened then?'

'He showed me his pony.'

'And after that?'

'I came home and lost myself in the wood . . .'

Henry said, 'And spent the night there. In a blizzard. I think you could at least . . .'

'I did. As they went out together I told Robert to tell William to get the wagon ready. By the time it was ready they'd both disappeared. Joanna, did Robert say anything to you about running away?

'Not a word.' I was the one who thought of that.

'You say you lost yourself in the wood. Could he have followed you?'

'He didn't follow me. I am sure about that.'

'Could he have gone into the wood by himself?'

'He would never do that. He was frightened of the wood.' Always, even on the fringe of it, gathering sticks or flowers. Now he — or at least his body, lay there alone for ever, under the bracken and leaves she had heaped over it. All her determination could not prevent a shudder. Henry noticed.

'Go and help Tom with the feeding,' Henry said. Once she had gone he asked, 'Have you dragged the moat?'

'The moat?'

'I was thinking ...' Actually he was remembering how nearly Griselda had come to killing Joanna. 'You were away. Suppose that tutor struck an unlucky blow.'

'Most unlikely. He is not at all the kind. When boys need correction he punishes them, in the proper place, with a thin leather strap. And God in Glory, Henry, a corpse is not so easily disposed of.'

No? Walter, with pigs as accomplices, had disposed of more than one; Henry had disposed of Walter's — with some help from Sybilla.

'I will have the moat dragged, of course. He may have *fallen* in.'

'Set up the hue-and-cry, too. I'll set it to work in the Baildon area, you take Bywater.'

'If we must,' Richard said unwillingly. 'It will not *sound* well. Children of that age do not run away from happy homes. And I still think ...' He looked broodingly at Joanna who was distributing hay. 'She showed no surprise or distress.'

'She's not one to make much display of her feelings.'

'All the same, I'd like another word. Call her over.'

Reluctant witnesses must be pressed.

As she scattered the hay Joanna had been thinking about not knowing where Robert's soul was; and how Masses were said for the quick delivery from Purgatory. And she had no money to buy one. Henry would provide — if he knew. But he could only know if she confessed. And if she did ... Griselda had often said that there were places for mad, bad people. Stealing the baby had been bad, and snatching Robert away in his indoor clothes had been mad. Somehow, somehow she must manage to buy a Mass without committing herself to being chained to a post and regularly whipped.

'Now, Joanna,' Richard said. 'You know what the truth is. I want you to swear, on the Cross, to tell the truth.'

'I swear, on the Cross, to tell the truth.'

'Do you know *anything* about Robert that you have not told us.'

Inwardly the wild blood that was her heritage took control. Outwardly she might have been reciting the Credo.

'Yes. I know a great deal. And all your fault. You didn't look after him properly. You let that man beat him for things Dick had done. That man dared not beat Dick because all the servants are his friends and if he beat Dick the man's food came cold to table or some such thing. Then there was the pony. Robert was frightened at first, but it was a nice pony and he liked it. Then Dick would arrange — with servants — that it should be harnessed badly, or hit suddenly before he was properly in the saddle. Robert was always given fat, which made him sick. When Robert complained to you, *you* said he was whining. And that man beat him for tale-bearing. I hate you all, that man, and Dick and you. I hope God will punish you for what you did to Robert. And I shall never call you Uncle again.'

Small, ridiculously clad, a wisp of hay in her wind-chapped hands and sheep's dung clogging her half boots, she flung her challenge to the man on the horse — from time immemorial the symbol of superiority and authority. That her final sentence was the ultimate in bathos only Richard knew. He was in any case not her uncle. It would have been comic, had Henry not been listening, and had Richard not craved Henry's approval.

'I'll try Bywater and the moat,' Richard said, swinging his horse round. 'I'll let you know. As soon as I know anything.'

Henry said, 'Joanna, your stories don't fit. You said that Robert said he was happy.'

'So he was. Happy to see me. Happy to be able to tell all his woes.'

'Poor little boy! If only I had known . . .'

'I tried to tell you. You took no notice . . . If you had believed me, what would you have done?'

'Fetched him home.' That was the hardest blow of all. She wept.

Henry, who had been up all night and about to go to bed, having handed over to Tom, when Richard appeared, said,

'Sweeting *don't*. Boys can't just *disappear*. I'm going to Baildon now. We'll have the criers out in no time.'

Cry his name, his description in every street, along every lane, at every crossroad in the whole world. Robert would never answer . . .

CHAPTER TWENTY-SIX

Richard had been right in assuming that a public search for Robert would draw undesirable attention. A young boy vanished without trace — and not from some humble home. Servants talked, giving Master Jankyn a reputation as a savage flogger of the kind disapproved even by people who believed in a cuff of the ear, or good hammering occasionally. The story became garbled as all stories were, and was confused by the fact that the Moyidan door-keeper said that he knew that a girl was missing, as well as a boy. He'd seen the girl himself and next morning Master Tallboys of Knight's Acre had come asking about her. So some versions mentioned two lost children — done away with the more lurid stories ran, by a wicked uncle who wanted their property.

In the flippant way which made him such good company, Richard said to the Bishop, 'Had I been minded to do away with a boy it would not have been Robert — who, incidentally was my brother, not my nephew, but with Dick who will inherit this place. Not that it would benefit me; it would do my brother Henry some service. He's next in line.'

During the weeks of fruitless search and busy rumour, Richard had often wished that it had been Dick who had vanished without trace.

'Next, that is, after your cousin, the present owner,' said the Bishop, who liked to get things clear. 'I must say, my dear Richard, yours is a very *complicated* family.'

'In more ways than one. And I am the steward — just or unjust as you care to regard it. It is often a thankless office.'

But not unrewarding, His Grace thought, looking about him.

'You have never seen my cousin, or his wife, who — just to make matters more complicated, is my sister. Or their son. One is not inclined to make a display of what is dismal. But if you would care to see . . .'

The Bishop saw two obvious idiots, blank-eyed except when they looked at each other. Both fair and frail-looking, both wearing faded garlands of wild roses — for it was summer now. Neither took the slightest notice of him or of Sir Richard. The boy, their son, did glance up and then returned to gobbling his supper; the man in charge stood up and bowed. Then, in response to a whispered request, he gave, in a quiet voice the kind of report about his remaining pupil which schoolmasters landed with the unteachable must always give. Not good enough to promise anything and not bad enough to decry themselves. Dick could do better if he attended more. Dick was improving, but slowly. Dick would do better in time.

Back in the cosy, intimate atmosphere of the small dining parlour, with fresh wine, Richard said, 'You see what I have to contend with?'

'I do indeed. Breed idiot to idiot and what can one expect but an idiot? The Church has always been against . . . Did they have a dispensation?'

'I cannot say. I was in Winchester at the time.'

At Knight's Acre, too, the wild roses had bloomed and then faded. After them came the big moon-eyed daisies. The shearers came and went, the wool went to Moyidan for sale and Henry conscientiously deposited Robert's share with Master Turnbull. After all the boy had been lost only for three months, it was too soon to despair.

Then it was harvest again; Jem and Henry scything, Joanna and Tom making the sheaves and stocking them.

'Take it easy, Tom,' Henry said. 'She doesn't like to be out-paced.'

Actually he was concerned for Tom, whose attacks of weakness and dizziness came with increasing frequency. Nothing much was made of them, least of all by Tom who usually blamed the weather, the sun was too hot, or the wind too sharp; sometimes he blamed himself, he'd eaten too much, or he'd hurried.

This harvest was hardly under way before he suffered an affliction of which even he could not make light. He stooped to gather an armful of corn, tried to straighten up and gave a yell. Henry put down his scythe and came back across the stubble.

'Jinked your back, Tom?' He knew what to do because it had happened to him several times in his growing days and Walter had put it right in a blink. He took Tom by the shoulders, put his knee into the small of his back and gave a sharp jerk. Tom yelled even more loudly.

'No good, Master,' he gasped. 'It's the Witch's Strike.'

Jem, always ready to waste a minute said, 'Somebody bin ill-wishing you, Tom.'

This sudden, agonising, crippling pain in the back was called Witch's Strike because its onset was so sudden, and so seemingly without cause. The only things to be said of it — small comfort to the sufferer — were that it was never fatal, lasted only a few days and disappeared as suddenly as it came.

'Help Tom into the house, Joanna. Tell Griselda to give him a dab of liniment — not too hard. You'll find it in the stable.'

Fortunately they were working in the field nearest the house.

Griselda was delighted to have a chance to cosset Tom. She installed him on the settle in the hall and wedged him with pillows. He said he was all right so long as he didn't try to straighten out or move. Away from the communal table, she could slip him little tit-bits, presenting them with love and wishing that she could do better.

Apart from the absolutely necessary excursions out of doors, Tom stayed, rigid and bent over, on the settle for three days. Then at a stroke he was restored and out in the field again. A less modest man would have observed with pleasure that he had been missed; things had got a bit behindhand because one girl, however willing and nimble, couldn't sheaf and stook the corn cut by two reapers and from time to time during the three days either Henry or Jem had been obliged to cease scything and make sheaves and stook them. Corn left lying flat tended to sprout, forerunning its season.

'We've got a bit of lee-way to make up,' Tom said.

He had never seen the sea, but like most of his fellow East Anglians he was descended from a sea-faring race who had inherited, with their blood, some ancient terms of speech. Any woman, having clinched an argument would say, 'And that took the wind out of her sails'; any man rebuking a busy-body, would say, 'Now don't you go shoving your oar in.'

So Tom said 'lee-way', and when it was partially made up Joanna said, 'Tom, what did Jem mean by saying somebody had ill-wished you?'

'Oh, just another old tale.'

'I like your tales, Tom. Tell me.'

It was not the ideal situation for the telling of any tale, least of all one concerned with magic rites; they parted to gather up the corn, make the twist of about seven strands which bound for the sheaf, and then met again, stooking the sheaves into a tent-like structure. Just a few words, and another few. But by the end of the morning Joanna had learned what she needed to know about ill-wishing. About the making of what Tom called 'mommets'.

They could be made of anything, mud, tallow, dough. There must be a mockery of baptism — the Cross made the wrong way. Once named they could be subjected to ill-treatment, stuck with pins, set to waste by the fire. One most intriguing thing about this account, so broken and interrupted — 'Go on, Tom, what next?' — was that Tom himself was neither quite a believer nor quite a disbeliever. He said, 'Well, they say ...' and 'My old granny always held ...' He said, 'It's all an old tale, but I remember something funny ...'

As Henry had said she was not one to show her feelings; but they were there. And to Tom's half-reluctant account she added a few imaginative touches of her own. Surely a mock baptism would be more effective if the water was taken from the font. A little cup, hidden in the sleeve.

One by one she made the little figures, named them, mutilated them. Sir Richard Tallboys; Master Jankyn; Dick.

And it all was, as Tom said, just an old story, like the brews that made you invisible, or turned you into a wolf. It just did not work.

Sir Richard was extremely happy, despite a few things that he could have wished otherwise. Leonora was all that, and more than, a man could expect from a mistress. Her moods, her behaviour, were so unpredictable that in possessing her a man possessed a dozen women at least. He never entered that gateway in the grey wall without a sense of keen anticipation; never left it, going the other way, without a sense of satisfaction, and self-congratulation. And even though Sir Francis' poor relation, Mistress Neville, was not exactly what he had expected, perhaps she served his purpose better than a woman he would have chosen himself.

The words 'poor relation' envisaged somebody meek, accustomed to sitting overlooked in corners, sombrely clad, undemanding, grateful for a good home. Mistress Neville was in all ways the reverse of this. She was poorly clad when she arrived, but that was swiftly remedied — at Richard's expense; of gratitude she showed no sign, always acting as though she were doing him and Leonora a favour, which in a manner she was. She was masterful, shrewd and worldly. For a woman in her forties she was not unhandsome; one could only think that the reason she had not married again was that she was penniless — and possibly rather choosy.

She took control from the first. Richard had imagined the two women living quietly together, himself their only visitor.

'But, Sir Richard, that is precisely the way to draw attention to yourself and give rise to gossip. We must entertain frequently. Nothing is less noticed than a straw in a strawstack.' They entertained frequently, and royally. Moyidan supplied meat and various other essentials as well as luxuries such as asparagus and fruit in due season, nevertheless the expenses of the household were staggering.

The furniture and the fittings of the house which Richard had taken over so unwillingly — and at such cost, were, Mistress Neville said entirely unsuitable for the position which she and Leonora must *appear* to occupy. 'No widow of good family and adequate means would live in such squalor,' she said. But he need not bother, she would see to it. That she was herself of good family there could be no dispute and her husband, though he died poor, had been a member of the family whose head was the great Earl of Warwick. Sir Francis called her Aunt Alyson, and again with the air of doing a favour, she proposed that Richard and Leonora should address her similarly. Sir Francis was a very frequent visitor and often stayed overnight — as did other gentlemen though less regularly. 'It will prevent servants' talk.' For of course, they must have servants; three the very minimum.

Towards the world and towards all those they entertained the two women presented a united front. In private a good deal of rivalry smouldered. Who was mistress of this house? Leonora who made its existence necessary, or Aunt Alyson who made it possible? Disputes of that kind usually ended in a victory for Mistress Neville, not because Leonora was incapable of standing up for herself but because she was fundamentally idle.

Unfortunately for Richard this rivalry, took an expensive form. Like any lover, he delighted in giving things to Leonora and did not think it strange that she should want such a number of dresses — most of them with a jewel to match; what was annoying — and eventually alarming — was that Aunt Alyson would support any demand Leonora made, and then, as soon as it was met, begin to throw out broad hints on her own behalf. 'Leonora's new tawny velvet makes everything I own look positively *shabby* by comparison.' Or, even more sinister, 'Leonora's *beautiful* emerald does make one wonder about the wages of *sin*! That *virtue* is its own reward is only too evident.'

Sometimes Richard wondered whether Aunt Alyson was quite as virtuous as she pretended to be. Quite early on she had said, 'Francis, I know you call me *Aunt*. I am in some confusion, when I come to think about it, as to what our exact relationship is.' They had spent a pleasant half hour scrambling about far flung branches of their family trees and reached the conclusion that there was no blood kinship between them at all. And whenever Sir Francis spent the night at the Saltgate House, Mistress Neville would lead him off to her own little parlour with a proprietary air. It was tactful, it was exactly what her position required of her but ...

The setting up of such an establishment had naturally not escaped notice in so small a town.

First of all Master Turnbull was angered to learn that the house in Saltgate had been sold so quickly, so quietly, behind his back one might say. He'd had an eye on it for a long time. A good solid house, big enough to make two, or even three of the sort and size which let so easily; and a big yard and some other ground, a neglected orchard, most suitable as building ground. Peevishly he asked who had acquired it and when told Sir Richard Tallboys, felt an astonishment that he did not betray.

He had been concerned with Sir Godfrey's will — and with Lady Emma's. Neither of them, so far as he could remember conferred upon Sir Richard the kind of wealth that would justify the purchase of a town house by a man already well-housed at Moyidan. It was a thing which justified some looking in to; and the most superficial enquiries revealed that Sir Richard had not sold that remote, not very valuable bit of land bequeathed to him by his aunt. So how?

The next people to be concerned were the saddler and his wife. Mistress Neville, far from pious, regarded attendance at church as a social obligation and one Sunday morning Leonora's real aunt, the saddler's wife saw the viper she had nourished in her bosom, most splendidly clad . . .

'I thought,' she said to her husband, 'that you told me you had found that girl a menial post. In the country.'

'And so I did. With Master Tallboys. Out at Intake.'

'Then I would be glad if you could explain to me how it has come about that she was in church this very morning with more miniver about her than a dog has fleas.'

How could he explain? He knew nothing of it. He could only say, 'I know nothing. It is none of my doing.' How could it possibly be when his wife, being the one who could read and write and reckon overlooked the finances of the business. It had taken him a deal of scheming to buy the ear-bobs as a Christmas present.

'I shall make it my business to find out exactly what is going on,' Leonora's real aunt said.

I, too, the saddler decided in his mind. He was anxious.

Her way was devious and took a little time; his was abrupt; he looked out for Henry's wagon and put the point-blank question which Henry answered shortly, 'I can tell you what I was *told*. She left us to take a post as help and company to an old lady.'

'Well,' said the saddler's wife when she knew what there was to be known. 'What I should like to know is that if the girl had an aunt, named Neville, so well-connected and rich, why she didn't come forward and offer when my poor sister, God rest her, died? *We* had all the trouble and expense of rearing the creature.'

It was a question that she would have liked to put to

Mistress Neville herself, 'but that was the worst of being in business. Mistress Neville was related to Sir Francis Lassiter at Muchanger and so to half a dozen other families, kin to him, and all potential customers. It would not do to offend ... So, on various Sundays and Holy Days for the next eighteen months, the saddler's wife suffered the exasperation of seeing the ingrate come with that peculiar grace of manner, into church; velvet and furs, silk — thick and ribbed, then fine and almost flimsy for high summer; heavy silk again, velvet and fur. Beautiful headdresses always.

At Knight's Acre Joanna gave up the making of mommets. So far as she could see nothing had come either of ill-wishing or well-wishing. The last had been a device of her own. Little images, named Henry, named Tom, lay cradled in sheep's wool and flower petals; if ill-wishing worked, why not well-wishing? But in fact none of it worked. The year 1469 began badly for Henry — the worst lambing on record, and footrot, due to the wet weather, and liver flux, due to nothing certain.

And Tom became weaker and weaker.

Two weak dizzy spells, long-lasting, in one day.

Henry said, 'You stay in bed tomorrow, Tom, and take a good rest. We can manage.'

'I shall be all right tomorrow,' Tom said; but he knew now. Hitherto his funny spells had been something of a mystery, something left over from the plague, now from the way his heart was behaving, he knew what ailed him. And thanks to his old granny he knew a cure.

'You and me,' he said to Joanna, 'we've talked about brews in our time. Mostly old tales, but *some* good. And I need one now. Mostly foxgloves are past flowering, but no matter, it's the leaves do the good. If you'd go gather a good handful...'

The foxglove leaves, eagerly gathered, well pounded and infused, were curative at first, spurring the sluggish heart. Tom was able to help with that late harvesting, half a day here, half a day there, but he knew it would be his last. There was a point past which a dying horse could not be flogged. Or a dying heart. Facing up to death much as he had faced his life, outwardly so bleak and unrewarding, Tom took stock of the situation he would leave behind and was saddened. For some reason beyond his comprehension Griselda and Henry were at odds, even over the child. And Griselda was at odds with Joanna, such a good girl if only Griselda could bring herself to see it. Tom loved Griselda, respected and was grateful to Henry, was fond of Joanna. He wished, with all his heart, that they should be happy.

No field work for him that autumn; he doddered about, doing little jobs about the yard, stopping when the labouring heart seemed to choke his breath and everything went black. He helped in the kitchen, sparing Griselda the most distasteful tasks, skinning pigeons, flaying and de-gutting a hare, but he knew — having earned his keep since he was about four years old — that he no longer earned it and lately, whenever he prayed he added a little piece — God, don't let me be a burden.

One morning, he was skinning pigeons and Griselda was making the dough for the pudding casing that was to enclose them, he said, 'I want you to be happy.'

Taken by surprise she used the voice that she used to others now, but never to Tom.

'What do you mean?'

'More contented, like. Happier. Take Joanna ...' Best to start on the lesser matter. 'I know how much she upset you. But you can't go on bearing a grudge *for ever*.'

'Oh, can't I.'

'Not if you're going to be happy and comfortable. After all, we pray, don't we, to be forgiven, as we forgive.'

'Don't you think I have tried? Tom, I can't. Just to look at her gives a cold grue.'

'Dearie, she's only a child.'

'I know. *What will she be like when she's full-grown.*'

'None the worse for a bit of friendliness now.'

'You talk like a priest,' Griselda said, giving the dough a mauling that promised ill in terms of edibility. Across it she looked at him and saw how greatly he had changed. The weather tan had faded from his face, leaving it the colour of tallow and his lips had a bluish tint. His big hands which had worked about her, gently as a woman's, had softened and paled; dark veins stood out like whipcord.

'There's the master, too.' Tom persisted. 'You're out with him.'

Out indeed!

Henry had compounded all his other faults by never once giving her a chance to repel a sexual approach. Ever since the baby was born all *that* had ceased. Henry got into bed, said, 'Goodnight,' blew out the candle and turned on his side. He was far too much all-of-a-piece to wish to bed with somebody who railed and scolded all day. Griselda, who had always been obliged to set her teeth in order to accept him was now perversely offended. All he'd ever wanted was somebody to keep his house and bear his child.

Her hands motionless on the dough, she said,

'There's no help for the way we are, Tom. I made a mistake, and must live with it. I didn't know it was a mistake, till that day . . .' She glanced at Godfrey, capering about on the hobbyhorse that Tom had made for him. 'Till then all men were alike to me. Too late to do anything about it.'

'I know. But it ain't all loss, my dearie. You got as good a man as ever wore shore-leather; you've got the boy. You've got the house.'

'The house! Oh Tom . . .' Her green eyes filled with tears and she put her floury, dough-patched hands to her face.

He rose and went over to her, put his arms around her, comfortingly, without desire — he was past it. She could hear and feel the heavy, irregular labouring of his heart.

'Make the best of it, honey sweet. Try a little kindness. It'll oil the wheels.' She made no promise, no reply and after a pause he said, 'They'll be wanting their dinners.'

'Mumma cried,' Godfrey informed Henry.

'Don't be so silly,' Griselda said. 'Anybody'd cry, peeling that lot of onions.'

The morning came when the weakness attacked as soon as Tom stood on his feet. The floor dropped away. Heaving himself into bed again Tom thought —— I will *not* lie in bed useless and rotting, like my old Granfer. I will not add to *her* load.

That evening when Joanna looked in to ask how he was — she had offered to carry up his supper but Griselda said *she* could see to Tom — he gave her an exact description of henbane, where to find it, what to do.

'The foxglove worked for a bit; now I need something

stronger. And I wouldn't say anything to Griselda. She took over making the foxglove and it might put her out.'

Of Tom's death Henry said, 'It's a loss. But it's the way he would have chosen for himself.'

Richard's thoughts as he rode into Baildon were as glum as the November afternoon. He had always enjoyed financial juggling, but those who juggled with money, like those who juggled with plates, needed a sound footing, and he had never had that. His was more like a morass, every floundering step took him deeper. He'd made two mistakes — he'd overestimated Moyidan's recuperative power, and underestimated the cost of the Saltgate establishment — now just under two years old.

As he turned in at the gate in the wall, his spirits lifted. He thought — After all, given time . . . and he thought — It is well worth it.

The good smell of roasting venison had penetrated even to the yard. He'd sent in a well-hung haunch, and a hamper of Moyidan's special late-ripening red apples and brown pears and he imagined that Aunt Alyson's hospitable instinct would have been aroused and there would be company for supper. But the stable yard was empty and when he went in he found Leonora alone.

'Aunt Alyson has gone to bed. With a headache.'

She'd never looked lovelier, he thought. She could wear any colour, but always looked best in the various brownish ones which emphasised her fawn-like quality. The dress was new, pale buff velvet, the sleeves lined with cream-coloured lace; with it she wore exactly the right ornament, a necklace of yellow rock crystal and pearls, and the gauzy headdress, cream coloured was held by a band, almost a coronet, that matched. In his pocket he had a ring of the same yellow crystal — a present to celebrate the second anniversary of their real meeting in Layer Wood after the hunt was over and they had reached an understanding.

It was not only the clothes; she was in one of her elusive moods, seeming to melt and slip away from his ardent embrace. And some inner excitement seemed to light her from within. Her eyes shone and her full-lipped mouth, one of the first things he had noticed about her seemed now and then to harbour a smile. Devil take the cost and the danger, he thought; this was a woman in a million. Almost two years and never a dull moment or a regret.

Over the meal — the first they had ever taken alone together he said, 'I have a surprise for you.'

'I have one for you, too, Richard.'

Like a blast of icy air suspicion struck. A baby! That would account for the radiant, excited look.

It was not that he did not wish — as all men did — for living proof of his virility. And he would have welcomed, or at least accepted a child if only he'd been as rich as he seemed, as Leonora believed him to be. Or even had he been successful in his career so that he had influence enough to promote the interests of his 'nephew'.

And how typical of women — even of Leonora, the most exceptional of her kind, to be pleased, to have put on all her finery in order to tell him about the last thing he wished at this moment to hear. Fools, fools, all of them, even the best of them!

She said, 'Bring your wine to the fire, Richard. I have something to tell you.' He saw then that under the excitement, the female complacency, she was nervous, and because he loved her, determined to be kind, pretend to be pleased, not mar her joy by any mention of practical considerations.

The wine in her cup slopped a little; his own was steady.

She said, 'I am going to be married.'

It was an explosion; deafening; reverberating.

'Who?' he asked when he had mastered himself enough to speak.

'Francis Lassiter.'

Another explosion.

'That old man!'

'He is no longer *young*,' she said, steady now that what had to be said *had* been said. 'But not so old either. And he offers marriage, a name, a place in the world.'

'And you . . . you,' he said, filled with fury. 'Where'll you be after a fortnight of his futile fumbling? In bed with the nearest ploughboy!'

It seemed a long time ago since Sir Francis had spoken of settling down, getting himself an heir to Muchanger. And he'd done nothing about it except a bit of posturing flirtation with Mistress Neville — and even that had come to nothing. Roués bought early impotence!

'You wrong me,' Leonora said. 'And him!'

'Have you ever tried him?'

'Of course not. One does not *give* what is of value.'

That simple, cynical statement was not to Richard offensive — simply proof of her worth.

'You are a whore, a born whore,' he said. 'But . . . damn all to hell. If you *must* be married, I'll marry you myself. Vows take a bit of time to cancel out, but it can be done. I'll get myself unfrocked.'

'And that would be ruin for us both. Dear Richard, you may not know this . . .' She looked at him gravely 'In the town there is talk — of money raised by dubious means. I think it is only because you *are* a priest that things are not worse . . .'

And who is to blame, he asked himself. Two rapacious women and a household, costly out of all proportion to its size. Infatuation whirled and showed its reverse face, hatred. And when she stretched out the slender, long fingered hand upon which the yellow crystal would never glimmer — though other rings would, and said, 'Come to bed. It may be for the last time,' he could hardly speak for the nausea which shock and disgust, and dismay had engendered in him.

The entry was dark for nobody was expected to come and go, and Mistress Neville, extravagant in many ways, was sparing over such small items as candles. Richard was fumbling his way to the door when some faint illumination fell downward from the stairs and Mistress Neville said, 'Sir Richard . . .' The light of the candle she held in her hand lit her face in a grotesque way, throwing such shadows that she looked like a gargoyle.

She must have connived, he thought furiously; the skilled deceiver, the paid procuress, open-handed for any bribe.

'How much did *he* pay you?' he asked brutally.

'Nothing. I had no suspicion . . .' Now that she had descended and stood level with him, the light between them, he could see that the change in her face was not an illusion. She was not actually crying *now* but her puffy eyes and swollen nose told of tears shed not long ago. In addition her whole face seemed to have collapsed, from within, just as Leonora's had seemed to be lighted.

'It was a great shock to me,' she said. He believed her, and he understood; for her also Sir Francis and Muchanger would have been a great prize. He did not feel sorry for her; self-pity was the only kind known to him. He thought of her exactions and pretensions and said brutally, 'Then you must be very blind or very stupid. What were you paid for except to watch?'

He made towards the outer door, but she reached out and caught his sleeve.

'What now? Will you keep on the house?'

'Is that likely?'

'Why not? There are other young women.'

'You make me sick! Let go!' But her hold tightened.

'What about me?'

'Go back where you came from.'

'That is impossible. I left in what the family considered to be ungrateful haste. And I cannot go to Muchanger, or to any place where I should be likely to encounter *them*.'

'Then go to the devil!'

'I should prefer the Bishop ...' No need to pull his sleeve now; he stood rigid.

'What do you mean?'

'Clerical gentlemen often employ housekeepers. I am a good manager. I am sure that if you gave me a hearty recommendation ...'

She spoke quietly but the threat rang loud.

'You'd better come to Moyidan.'

'Not,' she said, in her old manner, 'the most *gracious* of invitations. But I accept. One thing more. It would be wise to keep a good face on things. I am disgusted with Leonora — so unfair to you! But we must appear to be on good terms until she is married. Then, if you wish, I will stay and dispose of everything; getting the best price I can.'

'Do that,' he said, and let himself out into the night.

Riding home he had time to think. First of his loss. But he was a man of reason, rather than of emotions; he had loved the false little bitch so far as he was capable of loving anyone, yet he was not heart-broken. Affronted, disgusted, robbed, not broken, or bereft. That was proved by the fact that soon his thoughts centred upon what she had said when he had made her that rash offer of marriage.

'Already there is talk in the town — of money raised by dubious means . . .' Richard did not believe it. The only person who could have the faintest glimmer of knowledge about what he had been up to in the way of raising money 'by dubious means' was that false friend, that Judas, Francis Lassiter who had once, during a particularly tricky piece of juggling, helped, to the extent of writing his name which had all the solidity of Muchanger behind it. And that only for a temporary loan, a bridging operation.

What Leonora knew, Francis had told her; probably using it as an argument; *The time will soon come when Richard will not be able to keep you.* Yes, that would explain much. And not an entirely displeasing thought to wounded vanity.

In reasoning thus, Richard deceived himself. The rumours stemmed from other sources.

Three weeks to the wedding; a fortnight to clear the house and by the time Mistress Neville arrived at Moyidan, she had a perfect excuse for the best prices obtainable being so very low. The sweating sickness had struck Baildon and with the uncertainty of life being thus thrust under their noses people lost interest in acquiring material things.

A life containing many vicissitudes had made her resilient and she had largely recovered from disappointment. She had a home — and she would see to it that it was a comfortable one; she had clothes, beautiful clothes, enough to serve her for the rest of her days. She had her trinkets and she had money. She had saved on the housekeeping bills while appearing to provide lavishly, and on everything she had bought in the early days or sold at the end she had made profit. So she arrived in a cheerful mood which survived even the discovery that she had been relegated to what was known as 'the other side' and would take her meals with the idiots, the tutor and the boy. She'd soon alter that, when she felt more energetic. The fact that she was here at all proved that Richard feared her. But she did not feel disposed to exert herself immediately; there had been the shock, the pre-wedding strain, and then all those bargains to be driven. She needed rest.

On the third day she knew that with all the other things she had brought to Moyidan was the sweating sickness.

This was slightly — not much — less feared than the plague and offered more chance of recovery with careful nursing. But fear made people keep their distance. A devoted spouse, relative or friend could mean the difference between life and death. Also in crowded hovels or tenements where many people lived closely together and contagion was unavoidable, a sufferer could expect attention. Mistress Neville lay alone. Nobody loved her; nobody went near her. She died.

Margaret was more fortunate, and should have recovered. Her husband never left the bedside except on the most urgent errands, and to fetch food and water which nervous servants placed at some distance from the sickroom door. He sat by the bed, holding her hand. When the sweating from which the disease took its name soaked the blankets, he wrapped her in fresh ones. When she was in pain he held her, smoothing back the damp hair and saying, 'Better soon.' But Margaret had never been strong — though she had survived the plague — and she died, too.

There were no other cases, though Master Jankyn was suspicious of himself. He had always been subject to terrible headaches which began with spots before the eyes, moving spots, travelling slowly from left — the side where the worst headache was, to the right. A headache began on the day of Margaret's funeral; it lasted the usual two days; the pain vanished and his appetite returned, but the spots remained. It made reading — his one pleasure — difficult and he was far much too concerned with himself and his affliction to notice, or care that the bereaved husband was eating nothing. Dick noticed and had a characteristic thought — all the more for me.

Moyidan Richard couldn't sleep, either. Any bed was abhorrent to him now; he spent his nights stretched on the cold stone under which his beloved lay; and his days in a futile search for flowers. Margaret had loved flowers.

He outlived her by eight days. Dick was heir to Moyidan.

CHAPTER TWENTY-SEVEN

The invitation to go to the Bishop's Palace at Bywater, to dine and sup and spend the night was somewhat sudden, but quite understandable — and definitely flattering. A Papal Legate, the note explained had just landed at Bywater, after a terrible journey and the Bishop wished to entertain him suitably.

So much, Richard thought, riding out on a frigid February morning, for the Bishop of Winchester's warning that in Suffolk he would find himself relegated to the company of unlettered men.

For some time now His Grace of Bywater and Sir Richard of Moyidan, had, in private, been on Christian name terms while sedulously observing formality in public; the conventional modes of address did nothing to detract from the good fellowship of the occasion. The Papal Legate whose English was adequate, but somewhat inflexible, gladly relapsed into Latin, the language which more than any other lent itself to the witty aside. There was a good deal of merriment and in the morning, the Papal Legate, about to mount his horse to continue his journey to London, where he faced an errand which to put it most mildly, would be difficult, said he was glad that his ship had been blown off course and obliged to put in at Bywater. He only hoped that everywhere in England he would meet such a welcome and such good company.

'Sir Richard,' John Faulkner, Bishop of Bywater said, when the little cavalcade had set off, 'There is a matter I wish to discuss with you.'

He led the way, not back to the comfortable, luxurious place which he had made out of old Bishop William's dismal place, but along a passage to some part of the building which Richard had never seen before; the series of rather bleak rooms where business was done; men making lists, men doing sums; the backwater to which Richard had once thought himself doomed for life. In the farthest room, comfortably but austerely furnished, the Bishop seated himself behind a wide table on which papers and parchments lay in neat piles. He had shed all his geniality and was no longer the hunting, drinking and feasting companion of the last few years. Richard sensed the change and did not, as he would otherwise have done, take a seat until invited by a gesture to do so. The Bishop pulled one of the small piles towards him and said,

'I have received a letter from a man who calls himself a lawyer. His name is Turnbull. Is he known to you?'

'Very slightly. He *is* a lawyer. He drew my father's will. And that of my aunt.'

'Is there any reason why he should bring unfounded allegations against you?'

'None that I know of, Your Grace.'

'Then I find myself in a most difficult position.'

Richard thought — Leonora! But the liaison had ended in November and this was February; it was not a thing about which either Sir Francis or his wife was likely to speak, and Mistress Neville was in her grave. And how was Turnbull concerned?

'Perhaps you would care to examine these.' The Bishop handed over three papers. Two of them represented Master Turnbull's unpaid work for two years — his hobby. The other was a covering letter, couched in the most humble and respectful terms. Master Turnbull begged permission to draw His Grace's attention to certain irregularities which had come to his notice regarding the administration of the Manor of Moyidan. Since the perpetrator of the malpractices was a man in Holy Orders, Master Turnbull thought it fitting to refer his findings to His Grace. He enclosed a copy of the transactions which a preliminary investigation, necessarily superficial had revealed to him and begged leave to point out that the present heir to the estate was a child of tender years.

With one of those sour twists of humour which judges allowed themselves, His Grace said, 'If this is the result of his *preliminary* investigations one rather dreads to think what thorough ones would reveal.'

Taken as a whole it was damning and as he read Richard paled a little; but he did not lack courage — he was Sir Godfrey's son, Sybilla's son: he was also a trained lawyer, well versed in the art of disputation and the even subtler one of picking a case to pieces.

'He was right to say *superficial*, my lord. Much of this is superficially true, lifted out of context. Take this — "That he did waste his ward's substance upon the restoring and embellishing a derelict building to make for himself a grand dwelling." It was not a derelict building; all it needed was to be made comfortable, and that I did — for the benefit of others — eventually. And the term *ward* is completely misleading. Neither my poor dim-wit cousin, or his son was ever committed to my guardianship ... Or take this — "That on divers occasions he did commit forgery." Is it *forgery* to write your own name, Richard Tallboys, when dealing with the affairs of an idiot who never learned even to spell his own name, identical with your own?'

The Bishop listened — not without admiration. But his first casual perusal of Master Turnbull's accusations had revealed what he thought to be the real object — a challenge to the Church. Act and thus expose a scandal; do nothing and provoke one even worse. The open enemies of the Church — the Lollards, had been driven by persecution and the bad odour adhering to their followers, underground, but something remained, critical, obstinate among the middle sort of people, like this man Turnbull. Laymen with some education, a danger to everybody.

Richard Tallboys was clever; but John Faulkner, Bishop of Bywater was clever too and presently he said, almost in his old, amiable way, 'Very well, Richard, we need not chase every word. But this I must ask. Was the buying of a house in Baildon, with money raised by a mortgage on Moyidan, a profitable investment?'

'No. At least, not yet. It could prove to be.'

'It is in your name?'

'Yes. One of my worse ventures. In fact an act of charity. To put a roof over the heads of two women. One is now married to Sir Francis Lassiter of Muchanger; the other, the older, is dead. The house is now for sale.'

'In your name? What else is indisputably your property?'

'The piece of outlying land, difficult of access, a remote sheep-run, willed to me by my aunt in a return for a promise to care for them all. Which I have done. And intend to do. This homespun lawyer, counting pence, bandying words ...'

'How old is the boy?'

'Dick? Nine. Nine next month. And despite whatever Turnbull may have to say about my management, by the time he is of age, he will have much to thank me for.'

'No, my dear fellow. Not you. The Church. This is what we must do. And if this Master Turnbull had no malice towards you, only against the Church, this will make him gnash his teeth. Listen ...'

Despite the more friendly manner it was plain that the

Bishop was sitting in judgment and had indeed reached his verdict before even discussing the matter; his plan was already so well-thought out. The last bit of hope and confidence drained out of Richard as he listened. The man whom he had regarded as friend bore heavily on the charges over which he himself had chosen to skip lightly — the word 'embezzlement' was several times repeated. 'There may be some more esoteric term for it. There may be mitigating circumstances. And of explanation, I am sure, no lack. But to the ordinary man it is embezzlement. You appear to have milked this estate for purposes of your own.'

'It may seem so, Your Grace, but I assure you that given time ...'

'The *one* thing we cannot afford. All this reflects upon Holy Church and requires swift action.'

Having outlined his plan which would leave Richard penniless, and almost demolished his self-esteem — not quite, Richard was still too proud to ask mercy, His Grace relented. He remembered the hours he had spent in Richard's company, the splendid hospitality he had received from him. Richard might retain his Thoroughgood horse, one servant and a horse for him; he could choose a bed with all its appurtenances, so that wherever he lodged he would sleep snug, a little silver to uphold his prestige ... Richard, reduced as he was, could not resist a quip.

'That is generous, my lord. All, except the servant, saleable or pawnable!'

'It will not come to that. I have a very good friend who holds high office in the Treasury. I shall commend you to him in the warmest possible terms.' He allowed himself to smile. 'With your aptitude for financial juggling, who knows, you may end as Chancellor.'

'Is this a sudden decision?' Henry asked.

'Not really. I soon reached the conclusion that I had sacrificed my career for very little substance. Aunt Emma's property was so near worthless. On the other hand I could not very well ask the Church to take charge of Richard and Margaret without the danger of exposing their lunacy. So I was tied ...'

'And the boy? Where does he go?'

'Oh, he stays at Moyidan, with his tutor. The Bishop proposes to use the Castle quite often and will keep some staff there. Dick will hardly notice the difference. Except when there are a few monks about.'

'Monks?' Richard explained.

Actually it was one of the Bishop's more cunning touches. In the present climate of opinion, with so much criticism of the Church about, especially in East Anglia, it might not look *completely* well for Moyidan to be used merely as His Grace's country residence; so he had visited the Abbot of Baildon and offered some rooms to be set aside for the use of monks who had been sick and needed convalescence in clean country air, or for ones who were to be rusticated for some offence. And that, when Master Turnbull learned of it would make him gnash his teeth even more, for the ordinary layman's resentment he bore secular Church was as nothing to the resentment he bore towards the religious houses, regarded as being full of fat, idle, lecherous fellows.

Having explained about monks Richard proceeded to the real reason for his visit.

'I want you to store some stuff for me, Henry. A few things at Moyidan are mine. The Commissioners will arrive any day now, noting down every salt spoon. I should not care to have confusion; once anything of mine was entered on their lists, I should never get it off again.'

Unsuspecting, Henry said, 'Send it along. It can go in the barn.'

Richard's few things proved to be almost a wagonful of bales, wrapped in canvas, neatly corded. The man who drove the wagon was one whom Richard had called from Winchester and now chose to take with him to London, a most welcome move.

'Sir Richard said, sir, not to unload. He'll be bringing a few personal things later.' The man trudged back to Moyidan and the wagon, snug under a piece of sailcloth, stood in the yard.

It was not stealing as Richard saw it. *Nobody* was being robbed. And although he had not actually paid out of his own pocket for these wall hangings, bed hangings and other luxurious bits and pieces, he had used his taste and judgment in choosing them, and spent valuable time in acquiring them. He should — in a just world — have enjoyed them for many years; until Dick reached his majority. His plans had been wrecked — but most wrecks washed up a bit of salvage.

Some days later Richard on his Thoroughgood horse, the servant on the ordinary one, arrived, bringing smaller bales. They were tucked under the sailcloth. The horse which had drawn the wagon and which in the interval had stood in the stable, eating its head off, was hitched between the shafts, the horse the servant rode was tied to the wagon tail, and Richard once again, moved out of Henry's life. As John had done. As Robert had done.

In explaining the new arrangement Richard had said that Dick would hardly notice the difference. That was untrue. Fond of his fare to the point of being actually greedy, Dick soon noticed that his food, hitherto plain but plentiful was now becoming meagre. While Uncle Richard had been in control, entertaining, living in style, there had often been oddments, things left over, eagerly consumed. None of that now. Somebody in the Bishop's office had reckoned with parsimonious exactitude what was needed to keep a boy, an inactive man and three servants. The clever cook had been taken into the Bishop's household, the one who had hitherto cooked for this side of the house had found another post, a new man ruled the kitchen and helped with the cleaning of the house as well, for although the Bishop intended to use Moyidan chiefly as a summer residence, and a place from which to hunt in autumn, dust and cobwebs must not be allowed to gather, nor beds allowed to get damp. When, in the early days of the new regime, Master Jankyn who also liked his food, ventured a complaint, Wat answered him curtly and said it was impossible to do two jobs with only one pair of hands. Since Master Jankyn did not carry the complaint further, grumbling to one of the Bishop's men that food was bad and Wat was rude, the tutor ceased to count.

Master Jankyn in fact dare not call much attention to himself. The spots before his eyes — particularly the left one — grew worse rather than better, and rubbing his eyes, which he did constantly, though knowing the uselessness of it, had inflamed the lids. He was so conscious of his affliction that he felt it might be noticeable to everyone and who wanted to employ a tutor with poor sight? So whenever the commissionary men came — bright young clerks, especially chosen because they had country backgrounds — Master Jankyn was careful to stay out of their way, engrossed in reading or writing, with the spots dancing between him and the page.

Dick's friend Jacky had been kept on but he no longer spent his whole time in the stable; he worked in the garden, too. The third servant whose name was Joseph acted as yardman, helped in the house, helped in the garden, and should by all ordinary standards have occupied the lowest place in the hierarchy of the kitchen. But he was soon in the ascendant. He had a vile temper, a foul tongue, a vast amount of general knowledge and as much cunning as Wat and Jacky put together.

Moyidan was being used as a larder for Bywater. 'Robbing you right and left my boy,' Joseph told Dick. 'And nothing you can do about it. A minor can't go to law on his own account; only through his parent or guardian and the bloody Bish ain't going to take hisself to court is he?'

When summer came with its gifts, green peas, asparagus, strawberries, raspberries, the Bishop came too, with the clever cook, serving men and a horde of guests.

Dick was introduced — not without some ceremony which should have elated but actually humiliated him. He was growing rapidly now and his clothes no longer fitted well. In addition to being greedy, he was very vain. Sleeves that now did not reach his wristbones made his hands look clumsy; trunkhose too tight made a bow dangerous exercise. But there he was, heir to Moyidan, a well-grown, well-fed boy.

'Come and gone like a lot of locusts,' Joseph said when this invasion was over. Jacky and Wat and Dick, who now spent more and more time with the servants — he had even managed to ingratiate himself with Joseph — didn't know exactly what locusts were. Joseph explained. Devourers who passed over and left nothing behind. 'Only these is worse because they don't really *go*. I reckon the regular buggers know every bloody fowl by name.' They almost did; the fat capon with the black tail was missed when Joseph had wrung its neck, Wat had cooked it, and the three servants and Dick had enjoyed a secret feast.

Autumn came and the 'grease season' when the deer were sleek and fat. The Bishop and his friends came for hunting and momentarily everybody ate well though Joseph was critical. 'Ignorant sods,' he said. 'Killed a couple of does that could have bred in the spring! This go on, Dick boy and you'll end up in a poor way. Keep taking out of the well and put nothing in and one day there's nowt to *take*.'

Weather grew cooler and appetites sharpened. One day a sow farrowed and produced four piglets. Joseph saw his chance. He removed one, wrapped it warmly and placed it under his bed. The locusts were always gone by nightfall, so every evening this special little pig was carried out to the sty, his siblings were pulled away and he took his fill. Thus privileged he soon grew fat.

'Piglets 3,' the locusts wrote at their next visit. They would make a dish for Christmas; each roasted whole, restored by the clever cook's art to semblance of life, and holding a red apple in its mouth.

Handicapped as he was, Master Jankyn still adhered to the outer forms of professional conduct. 'Show me your exercise before we sup.' A page of scribble or a page of figures, with the moving spots intervening. After supper, he intended to read, his left hand cupped over his left eye, until the spots, as though aware of this ruse, began to invade the right. He really could not waste his eyesight by closely scrutinising what this unpromising pupil had to show. 'It is not well done. Repeat the exercise tomorrow.' Dick now had several pages, all of which had been submitted several times and would be again, since his master either couldn't see, or had ceased to care.

Supper was thin, onion-flavoured broth and dark bread. The fire was growing low and Master Jankyn knew without looking that the wood which should be piled on the hearth would not be there.

'When you go to the kitchen . . .' not 'if' for Dick spent every evening in the kitchen where the company was more to his taste and the fire good, 'tell Wat I need logs.' The likelihood of their coming was remote and as a precaution Master Jankyn had brought down a blanket from his bed. Wrapped in it he covered his left eye and read until the spots transferred themselves. His right eye often benefited from a short rest so he closed both his eyes and waited, musing as he often did over the injustice of a world where a man of considerable learning and honest reputation should be reduced to such a pass. He was not aware of falling asleep, but he must have done because he dreamed. A beautiful dream of fresh roast pork; he could taste it and smell it. And when he was awake, he could still smell it, the most appetising scent in the world. After a minute he realised that he had not been asleep and dreaming. The scent was real and it was coming from the kitchen. He took up his candle and went into the little lobby which separated the schoolroom from the kitchen, and off which the stairs serving this part of the house led. Also in the lobby was the door to the parlour where the idiots had lived.

He had never entered the kitchen, regarding it as beneath his dignity to do so: blinking and peering he stepped in now. A different world, very bright; there was a huge fire and three candles. Before the fire a sucking pig turned slowly on the spit. Fat and juices fell into a dripping pan set to catch them.

Dick and the three servants sat on stools near the fireside end of the table, and they were drinking ale. The ale allowance at Moyidan had lately been as meagre as everything else, but for some days — ever since the date of the piglet's death had been decided, the men had saved theirs — and Dick's and Master Jankyn's. The first time ale had failed to appear on the school-room table Master Jankyn said, 'You have forgotten the ale, Wat,' and Wat had replied, 'There ain't none.' Now there were two large jugs.

The tutor's entrance was not immediately noticed.

Wat said, 'Wind it up, bor.'

Dick rose and wound up the spit which worked on a wheel and a weighted string.

'Time thass run out, he'll be done,' Jacky said.

'Better drink up then! Come fill the cup. Death and dam-nation to all locusts and all bloody bishes.'

'If they could on'y see us now!'

'Sod all. Thass the boy's pig, reared on his place,' Joseph said. 'He had his rights he'd hev sucking pig whenever he fancied.'

'Thass right,' the others agreed.

'And if the bloody bish walked in this minute I'd tell him so to his face.' As Joseph said that he looked towards the inner door — the only one by which anybody was likely to walk in. 'Look who's here! What d'you want?'

'I have come to join you.'

'The devil you hev! We'd wanted you, we'd hev arst you. Sling your hook,' Wat said.

Joseph then spoke in such a low voice that Master Jankyn could not catch the words. Joseph was the quickest witted of them all — he had planned this affair — and there was reason in what he said — if the tutor shared the feast he couldn't very well report it. On the other hand his company was not welcome.

Dick had the last word. As roughly and disrespectfully as the others, he said, 'You can hev some if you promise not to tell. *And to ask about my shoes.*'

Short sleeves and tight hose were not actually painful, outgrown shoes cramped the toes. Dick had himself tried to draw the attention of the Bishop's men to his need for new shoes, but they had pushed him aside. It was not their business. Dick had then urged Master Jankyn to write to the Bishop, but he had not yet done so.

Swallowing his dignity and his pride, Master Jankyn said,

'I promise,' advanced to the table and pulled up a stool, stared hungrily at the pig, and thirstily at the ale jug. Jacky, the best natured of the four, reached for a mug and filled it.

Wat rose, plunged a knife into the carcase and hit bone.

'Thass done,' he said.

Here there were no niceties of serving. The sizzling meat was lowered into the pan and the pan set on the table and they set about the meat with their knives. They had bread which from time to time they dipped into the greasy gravy.

At first there was little talk; then, when the edge of appetite blunted, there was a good deal and a lot of laughter. Much of the talk and many of the jokes — he supposed they must be jokes to rouse such merriment — were beyond the tutor's comprehension. He was not a Suffolk man and, keeping himself to himself, had never learned the dialect. Also they all talked with their mouths full and grew tipsier as the second jug went round. Master Jankyn had never before eaten in such uncivilised company; and he had never enjoyed a meal more.

Throughout its course he had only one uncomfortable thought and that provoked by the reflection that his pupil was completely indistinguishable from the servants. Master Jankyn had resigned himself to the fact that Dick would always be a poor scholar and do him little credit so far as learning was concerned; but he *had* insisted upon a certain standard of manners, and of speech . . . He blamed himself for allowing the boy to consort so much with servants, but he had been glad to be rid of his company — who could read with a boy fidgeting about? Tomorrow he would deal with this problem — how exactly he did not know, but sufficient unto the day was the evil thereof. Food and ale had made him comfortably soporific. It was time for bed. The travelling spots had increased in size, speed and scope. Master Jankyn rubbed both eyes furiously.

'I think I will retire now.'

They had all except himself who had come late to the drinking and Dick — given small portions of ale because he was young — reached that stage of tipsiness where good humour tipped over to bad. Left alone they would probably have squabbled among themselves over some triviality, a drunken quarrel, easily patched up. As it was here was the alien, the one who did not belong; a ready target, saying 'retire' when ordinary people said 'go to bed'. And by merely mentioning time reminding them that the feast was over.

'You ain't emptied your mug,' Wat said. 'Wasting good ale! Come on, down with it!'

He lifted the mug and held it to Master Jankyn's mouth, forcing the rim between his lips.

It was a mistake, the tutor realised, to have come. He had lowered himself, because he was meat hungry. But he had courage of a sort and gulped down the unwanted draught, lest it should spill on his clothes.

Dick, seeing his master thus reduced said, 'And don't forget what you promised, *sir*!'

'I will write to His Grace at the first opportunity.'

Dick at least knew that asking and writing could mean the same thing. The others did not.

'There you are,' Wat said, 'breaking his word as soon as he got a bellyful!'

They all entertained the illiterate man's distrust of the literate man.

'Break one promise, break both,' Jacky said. 'Poor little bastard with no shoes to his feet!'

It was the one word which sent Dick's temper flaring.

'Don't you call me bastard or I'll crack your skull.'

'Let's see you do it, bastard yourself!' They fell into a grapple, relatively harmless, though both had bruises and hacked shins next day. Wat looked at the almost but not quite stripped skeleton of the little pig, bedded in congealed fat — pork dripping best of all, frilled round the edges and with the gravy set solid beneath it, and thought that he must think of a hiding place for it, because the locusts did not come at regular times. They were tricky and could well be here tomorrow.

The coolest if not the most sober mind in the kitchen was Joseph's. He knew that the pig had been stolen, so to speak; and what Jacky had said about broken promises had meaning. They could be accused.

He said, 'This way, Master. I'll light your way.'

What with the noise and the spots Master Jankyn was grateful for the small civility and the guidance. Joseph opened the door which gave upon the moat, the door through which kitchen refuse was thrown. It took only a slight push; the bit of stone pavement between house and water was here very narrow. Master Jankyn went to his death surrounded by such bits of the little pig as Wat had judged to be uneatable.

Nobody missed Master Jankyn. Except for seeing that it had its allotted ration of food the schoolroom was no concern of the Bishop's men and the tutor had always avoided them. Nobody had pangs of conscience or sought to apportion blame; they'd all been a bit merry and there'd been an accident. Dick was glad to have done with lessons and moved in with the servants happy about everything except his shoes. When he mentioned them Wat said, 'Give 'em here. I know a way out of that!' He took a sharp knife and cut away the upper at the toe part of the shoe, leaving the sole like a platform upon which Dick's toes lay comfortably.

After some days Master Jankyn's body, swollen and buoyant with gases rose to the surface. It was an unpleasant sight, but no one who saw it was squeamish. Wat suggested hauling the corpse out, weighting it well with stones and returning it to the water. But Jacky remembered the dredging of the moat in the hunt for Robert. 'Do we do that and he was ever found there'd be trouble. Better tell the priest and make out it was accident.'

'He couldn't see very well,' Dick said, and told about the same exercises being handed in again and again.

Father Thomas remembered how of late Master Jankyn had always come to the altar, looking as though he had been crying; he made no demur about burial. Nor did he feel under any obligation to report the sad accident. Since Moyidan had been taken over by the Church Father Thomas had carefully avoided anything that might give the impression that he was interfering. For that reason he ignored Dick's request that *he* should write to the Bishop concerning shoes. That would be interfering indeed!

After Christmas the cold weather came and Dick's unprotected toes developed chilblains. He thought Wat and Joseph, even Jacky very lacking in sympathy; they had not spent their early years as pampered little boys. Everybody had chilblains some time or another; they all knew of an infallible cure — a good thrashing with nettles — but not one of them had actually tried it, and Dick did not feel disposed to. *Some* people, they reminded him, went barefoot all the year round. If he wanted new shoes he should ask the locusts when next they came.

'But I did! And nothing happened.'

'Try again, bor.'

He had a feeling of being let down, of seeing, for the first time, something false in their friendliness. In genial moments they were happy enough to point out that all Moyidan was his, that he was being cheated, done out of his rights, poor little bastard, poor little sod. But when he suggested that on the locusts' next visit they should all line up with him and back his request . . . 'They took no notice of me, maybe because I am young. They brushed me aside; but they couldn't brush four . . .' Joseph said, 'Use your wits. We did that the first thing they'd ask is where's that teacher man and afore you could blink, you'd hev another. Maybe worse.'

It was plain to Dick that if he were ever going to be properly clothed again, he must depend upon himself.

The locusts, although similar in appearance and behaviour, were not always the same and the pair whom Dick accosted were not the ones to whom he had entrusted his former, and unanswered plea. They were surprised to find themselves confronted by a raw-boned peasant boy, clad in garments, far too small for him, obviously handed down to him by some charitable person. His manner surprised them, too; it accorded so ill with his appearance. Arrogant?

'I want you to carry a message from me, to the Bishop. I sent one before but it was never delivered. I am in great need of clothes, particularly shoes. Tell him that as soon as you get back.'

How ignorant he was. They saw their master but rarely, and then only from a distance. Whatever they collected from Moyidan was turned over to the head of the kitchen staff, their meticulous accounts went to some secretary. The world was full of boys who needed clothing; this one must be mad!

No answer. No clothing. No shoes. Plainly verbal messages were ignored. Faint and far away, from the grave, came Master Jankyn's voice. 'You must learn to write, boy. The word spoken lasts as long as the breath that bore it. The written word lasts as long as the paper or parchment.'

The schoolroom was deserted now. No one had kindled a fire on its hearth or dusted the table. But it was not disused. In a corner, snug in straw lay another purloined piglet. Joseph did not mind harbouring one under his bed in the earliest days of its life, but little pigs growing stronger, did as he said, 'tend to root about a bit'. Also a little pig, fattening in a satisfactory way grew heavier to haul upstairs and downstairs. So the schoolroom was the obvious place.

The little pig, associating the opening of the door with the prospect of feeding, ran to welcome Dick with squeals. He silenced it with a kick.

The ink bottle, left unstopped had either dried out or frozen and Dick spat into it and stirred vigorously, and with the uneven mixture thus produced he wrote, wishing, *wishing* that he had paid more attention. Something of what had apparently drifted unobserved, because uncared for over his head, came to help now.

My Lawd Bishop of Bywater, I have sent messages by yor servats but they were not headed i nead noo close shoose most. My Toes is frosen this is not rite or fare if yoo new wot yor servats wil not tel yoo yoo wood ackt.

On the whole, looking it over, he was not ill-pleased with his effort. It said what he needed to say. He signed it with his proper name, scorning the diminutive, for it was all his now. And that he could write well. Richard Tallboys. Master Jankyn had once made him write it twenty times. With a little less skill, but no decline of confidence, he added — 'of moidan'.

Nothing came of this great effort.

CHAPTER TWENTY-EIGHT

By the time he was three little Godfrey Tallboys was suffering the boredom of the overfussed, over-protected child. He was a strong, active boy, full of curiosity and he must never be for more than a minute out of Mumma's sight. If he played in the yard it must be within view of the kitchen door. He mustn't go near the sty — pigs might bite him; he was forbidden to go into the stable — horses kicked; there was a cat in the barn, but he was not allowed to play with it — cats scratched and had fleas. If he got a speck of mud on his hands or his clothes he was immediately washed and changed.

He had two outings. Griselda went often to church, holding his hand all the way; in church he must be very quiet. He preferred the stick-gathering errands to the edge of the wood, where with both hands busy, Griselda could not hold him; but even there she never took her eye off him. 'Don't wander away, dearie.' 'Show me what you have in your hand.'

On the fringe of his life were other people who because they came and went, occupying a different world most of the time, were interesting. There was Farder who gave him rides on his knee, with pretend falls that made him squeal with delight and say, 'More!' or held him under the arms and swung him round until he was pleasantly dizzy. Such games almost always ended with 'Don't'. 'Don't, you make him so wild that there's no doing anything with him.'

There was somebody called Janna who must be watched from a distance. Godfrey was not allowed to go near her, for some reason that he could not understand; she seemed unlikely to bite or kick or scratch. Once, when she sat, as she often did, very quietly, making fascinating patterns with a piece of string between her fingers, he went close to watch. Mumma said, in a voice that threatened another wash — though he had just had one, 'Come here, Godfrey.' Mumma then said to Janna, 'It's a pity you can't find something more useful to do than playing Cat's Cradle.' Farder said, 'For God's sake. She's done a full day's work today.'

Perhaps Farder was interested in what could be done with ten fingers and a piece of string, for he said he'd like to see how it was done. Janna went and stood on one side of Farder and gave directions. Godfrey went to the other, but Farder was soon in a tangle, at which they both laughed, and Godfrey joined in. 'Now me! Now me!' His tangle was even worse, and they all laughed again. Mumma did not even smile. She had on what her son called her sewing face.

That expression was the outcome of sharp observation.

Nowadays when Griselda sewed she scowled and pressed her lips together. At no time was her poverty more sharply brought home to her than when she was trying to make certain that Godfrey was as well clad as any little boy for miles around — and with nothing to do it on. When he was a baby he would wear clothes which Robert and Joanna had worn, shrunken and stained as they were. By the time they were the size Godfrey now was, they had begun to *wear* their clothes, so that mended, patched and outgrown, they had been not discarded, but put to other uses; kitchen clothes, cleaning cloths.

And despite all the hard work, a profitable year in yard and in field, Henry still had no money to spare for non-essentials; so Griselda cut up and worked angrily upon what remained of Sybilla's clothes. Even the dove-grey silk.

Interest in her own appearance had ceased with Tom's death. Griselda no longer bothered to do her hair in a becoming style. She had neither the impetus nor the time to spare. It was washed — her standard of cleanliness had not lowered — straightly combed back and done in a little tight knob at the nape of her neck. She never even noticed that its colour was fading from the bright colour of new straw to that of old straw and that the little light knob was gradually, but steadily becoming smaller.

One thing which made her angry with Henry was his stupid

behaviour over what he called Robert's money. It was still being meticulously, conscientiously put away.

'But he's dead,' Griselda said.

'Of that we have had no proof. Not a shred.' So every lamb dropped by an ochre-marked ewe was promptly marked with ochre. Fleeces or the sale of an animal 'on the hoof' as the slaughterhouse was called, religiously reckoned.

Joanna who was well aware that although the money being set aside for Robert was not very much, it could make all the difference, one day said, 'Henry, I am sure that Robert *is* dead.'

'How could you know, sweeting?'

'Because ... because while he was alive I always knew what was happening to him. Now there is nothing.'

It was not the kind of statement that Henry was prepared to regard as evidence.

Dick's letter brought no response because it had never reached His grace of Bywater who employed men to sift the important from the unimportant, and who were in any case unlikely to pass on a complaint about 'yor servats'. By February Dick was desperate and bethought himself of his Uncle Henry. Somebody must do something!

With Tom dead, despite all the well-wishing, and Henry just as overworked and worried, and the evil-doers, Richard particularly, seeming to flourish, Joanna had abandoned dabbling in spells, deciding that they were what Tom had always said — just old tales. However, when Dick arrived one bleak February morning, neither he nor his pony looked quite as they had done on their earlier visits. The pony was on the Moyidan list, but fodder as well as food was rationed there; and Jacky said, rightly, that nowadays he had more to do than groom ponies. Dick had never sufficiently adjusted himself to his new way of life to undertake the work himself, so the animal had been neglected. As for Dick ... Velvet was beautiful material for gentle wear, given rough treatment it was less resistant than homespun and Dick, despite plain and sometimes scanty feeding — interspersed by illicit feasts — had grown so enormously that his sleeves now ended just below his elbows; his feet were wrapped in sacking.

Surprised as he was by the boy's appearance, Henry was

kind as Dick had somehow expected that he would be. Griselda was horrid. 'What now? Another pauper?'

It was a difficult meal. As soon as Dick started on his tale, Henry, aware of Jem's presence said, 'We'll talk about it later, boy.' Griselda banged the pots and pans about as she always did when she was displeased and Joanna sat watching, her fingers linked to prop her chin. Outside a thin sleety rain began to fall.

Henry said, 'All right, Jem, go on with the baling. There's nothing much more to be done on such a day. Now, Dick, let's hear the whole of it.'

Joanna listened. Of the three most hateful and blameworthy people, the three who had made Robert so unhappy and had been ill-wished with the whole of her violent nature, only Richard had seemed to escape. Master Jankyn who had beaten Robert without cause had stumbled into the Moyidan moat and drowned; Dick, who had been to blame for most of those beatings was here, saying, 'Look!' and unwinding the sacking wrappings exposing his toes, with their broken, festering chilblains. Good. Oh, good!

Margaret as a person had never meant anything to Henry, but he was sensible to the fact that her son was his kin and that injustice had been done. He must take some action, what exactly he could not immediately decide. What he could do at once was something practical about these chilblains. A good soak in warm water, an application of goose grease.

Griselda had whisked Godfrey away as soon as the meal had ended; Dick looked so dirty, was likely to be lousy, far from fit to associate with her son. Henry found a bucket and from the pot on the fire tipped in hot water, then cold. 'Put your feet in there, Dick. Joanna, look in the larder and see if there's any goose grease.'

Joanna sat still, her eyes sparkling. After a perceptible pause she said, 'If I do, it's because *you* asked me to, Henry. Not for *him*! I wish his toes would rot clean away and drop off.'

Dick, whose whole tone had been whining, began to blubber.

'Cry baby!' Joanna said with infinite contempt.

'That'll do. Fetch what I want. Come on, Dick, pull yourself together. Nobody ever died of chilblains yet.'

Joanna, working as she did had enough experience of small cuts and abrasions to know that salt could sting where the skin was broken, so she poured a lot of salt into the soft, viscous grease and stirred it well. The result was most gratifying. Henry privately thought that his nephew was a poor-spirited fellow, but that was no excuse for the way he had been treated.

'There you are,' he said, when he had wrapped Dick's feet in clean linen, and shod them in his own church-going shoes. 'And tomorrow I'll go down to Bywater and try to set things straight.'

The Bishop knew of Henry's existence, had indeed seen him, but always at a distance, Henry at work in the fields, the Bishop on his way to the hunt. Richard had often spoken of his brother with a mixture of affection and mockery; Henry, who had refused to go to Beauclaire, Henry, who had refused the position and the legacy which had thus come to himself; Henry, who had chosen a yokel's life, and married a servant. He made his brother sound mildly eccentric. Not enough so to be interesting.

It was a surprise to be confronted by a man of considerable dignity and presence whose manners and speech were at odds with his humble dress, and who seemed perfectly at ease in these palatial surroundings. The palace had undergone changes but to Henry it was still the place where he and Richard had romped and quarrelled and always been slightly hungry.

Henry wasted no words. His Grace listened, genuinely shocked.

'I take it that you have proof of all this, Master Tallboys?' The question was a mere formality; this was not the kind of man to concoct or exaggerate a tale.

'I only know what the boy told me, Your Grace. I have seen his clothes, and his feet. He must have been practically barefoot for months.'

'I am appalled,' the Bishop said, and began to make excuses to this fellow who followed the plough and had married a serving wench. 'Of course, I am not always here; I have in fact only just returned from an absence of some duration. I left the boy in good hands. Your brother himself appointed Master Jankyn and I thought it right to retain him. Two of my staff make regular visits to Moyidan. Why did nobody see fit to inform me — or in my absence, the chaplain whom I leave in charge?'

'That, my lord, I cannot answer. The boy says that he has sent messages, both by word and in writing.'

'Not one of which ever reached me, I assure you. I was not even informed of the tutor's death.'

'Well, you know now. The question is, what happens next?'

Smoothly the cunning, experienced mind went to work. Here, unless promptly checked was material for another scandalous story about the avarice, the callousness of the Church. Fodder for Master Turnbull and his ilk, should they ever hear a whisper of it. Another tutor — who might go mad or deaf; an unreliable breed, all failed men. Keeping the house serviced for the benefit of a boy and his master? Or the grand gesture, which would shed the responsibility and silence all criticism?

'I often think a little wine lubricates difficult discussions, Master Tallboys. You will take a cup?'

'I thank you,' Henry said, oblivious to the honour being done him.

Over the wine, which came promptly, the Bishop said,

'You are the boy's natural uncle?'

'Yes. His mother was my sister.'

'Would you be prepared to take charge of him?'

That needed thinking over. Although he had never loved Griselda, and now occasionally hated her, Henry was still considerate. Establish Dick and a tutor and that would add to Griselda's burden; bring in a woman to help and there would be conflict; Griselda had quarrelled with Ursula, with Leonora and towards Joanna her hostility was rock hard.

'Only on my own terms,' this extraordinary fellow said, giving His Grace a straight look from eyes very blue and candid.

'And they are?'

'No nonsense. He said he *wrote* you a letter. If he could do that — more, I admit, than I could do myself, he has enough of learning. On the other hand, when he comes into his inheritance, some sound practical knowledge might be to his good. I *know* that. I learn as I go. When I employed a shepherd I considered him an idle fellow. Since I have had charge of a flock — smaller — I know otherwise.'

'You would be willing to take and train him?'

'I could at least see that he was fed, and had shoes on his feet.'

That stung and the Bishop said, 'Master Tallboys, there is one aspect of this whole affair which you do not know about. I admit that there has been negligence. But I will take you into my confidence and tell you *why* Moyidan has been so meagrely run ...'

He spoke — and it was for the first time openly, for he was a man who preferred not to let his left hand know what the right was doing — about Richard's depredations; about how long it would take for Moyidan to recuperate. 'That bit of outlying land, the one thing that was definitely his own was virtually unsaleable to any outsider; there is no access, except through Moyidan. I managed, since the whole manor was being taken over into a kind of guardianship, to buy and incorporate it. That and the house in Baildon which he had brought in his own name, but with money illicitly raised from mortgages on Moyidan, were all that Sir Richard owned, even in the most tenuous way ... In a most difficult situation I did the best I could. You understand? I *liked* your brother.'

'So did I,' Henry said; shocked in his turn by these unexpected revelations. 'We never spent an hour together without quarrelling. But I liked him. I apologise for the mess he left. I thank you for dealing with it so — discreetly.' Had the Bishop not been so discreet Henry knew that he himself would have been committed, pledging Knight's Acre and the hard-won fields in order to save the Tallboys name.

'Naturally,' the Bishop said, 'there would be an allowance. For clothes and keep.'

'Clothes, yes, my Lord. He'll earn his keep.'

It was not the up-turn in fortune which Dick had expected as soon as attention was drawn to his plight. True he now had clothes and sound footwear but he had to *work*. Uncle Henry was kind enough until he saw signs of slackness or carelessness, then he could be nasty. Aunt Griselda was nasty all the time and Joanna was horrid. Dick made overtures. 'You can have a ride on my pony if you like.'

'I wouldn't ride your pony if I was walking all the way from Baildon in the rain!'

'Why not?'

'The way you treated Robert!'

'Me? I never did nothing to Robert.'

'You saw to it that that man did. I hate the sight of you. I don't want to talk to you.'

The servants at Moyidan had failed him over the appeal for new shoes, but they had been company and had given lip-service at least to his ownership of Moyidan. Here he had no company and of his inheritance no mention was ever made. He missed even those secret feasts. The food here was bad. The only fowls ever seen on this table were old hens, past laying, that had to be boiled to tastelessness before they could be eaten. Birds fit for roasting, sucking pigs, even eggs were destined for market. Godfrey occasionally had little treats; Godfrey was indeed treated much as Dick had been in Umma's day.

Ever since his grandmother's death Dick had gravitated towards servants and felt at home in their company but here even Jem was unfriendly, turning a deaf ear to Dick's blunt hints that he might ask him home to supper with him.

Nor was this new, bleak way of life, free as it might have been expected to be, of correction concerning speech and manners. Henry could be as strict as Master Jankyn, often saying to Dick what had been said to him — it was just as easy to say *my* as *moy*, *old* as *owd*. Griselda was equally strict about table manners and washing. 'Don't think,' she said once, 'that you are coming to church with those dirty ears. What would people behind us think? If you can't wash yourself I'll do them for you.' A positive threat of discomfort.

Dick was far from being as miserable as Robert had been at Moyidan but he was miserable enough until he discovered the significance of those days when Uncle Henry and Joanna came down in the morning more tidily clad than usual and then drove off in the wagon.

It was now April, and he had been at Knight's Acre for almost two months and he had seen it happen twice. On the third time he asked,

'Where're you off to?'

'Market,' Henry said. Since he did not regard going to market as an outing it did not occur to him to ask Dick to accompany them. Joanna had been going ever since she was banned from the house.

'Can I come?'

Joanna said, 'No!' in a ferocious tone.

243

'Not in the wagon,' Henry said, 'we've a full load. But you could ride your pony. Go and make yourself tidy.'

Dick scampered off to don the better of the two outfits which the tailor at Nettleton had made for him — allowing for growth. Joanna said bleakly, 'Now my day is ruined. Completely and absolutely *ruined*.'

'You're carrying this a bit far, honey. Maybe he was a bit cruel and thoughtless, boys often are. But he's young and pretty stupid.'

'You don't know half of what Robert told me *before he died*.'

It shot out in anger. For a second her anger was transferred to herself and she used in her mind all the words that were forbidden.

'What did you say?' Henry asked.

She had made an instant recovery. 'I told you that I *knew* Robert was dead, didn't I? I should have said what Robert told me the last time I saw him ... Dick had been vile. And if *he* is coming to our booth today, I'd sooner stay here and work with Jem.'

'Don't be so *silly*,' Henry said. 'Who'd take the eggs to the inn? or buy the red flannel?' Griselda had been insistent upon red flannel. Red guarded against small-pox.*

'Is he coming to our booth?'

'No. I'll give him a farthing and tell him to spend it elsewhere. Come on, get in.'

'You promise?'

'I promise, sweeting.'

He was unaware that he had slipped into the habit of using towards Joanna, terms which were the right of the sweetheart or the wife. Griselda had not at first invited, or latterly deserved any terms of affection, and almost every day, by some show of willingness, or hardihood, or a glint of humour, the child endeared herself to him. He sometimes worried about her future and wished he could do more for her. His youthful dreams of prosperity were receding now. This year had begun badly with the worst lambing season he had yet known and towards the end of March there had been winds so fierce that in places the topsoil, with wheat and barley grains already rooted and sprouting, had been whisked away.

The drive into Baildon, with nothing to do but sit and ride,

* An old superstition, now partly justified by modern science.

gave them an opportunity for talk. Often Joanna regaled Henry with tales — either those she had heard from Tom or ones she had made up and in return Henry raked his memory for anecdotes told him by Walter or things he remembered from his own past. She loved to hear about Beauclaire and all its glories and his Aunt Alyson who was so beautiful. He found that he remembered more than he realised. He spoke without sentiment, however, and when he said, 'It's ruined now. The war put an end to it,' the regret in his voice was for Joanna, not for the place; had Beauclaire still existed he would, by hook or by crook have persuaded his Aunt Alyson to take Joanna into her household.

When they reached the market Henry tied his horse to the church railings and indicated an empty space near by for Dick's pony.

'Don't forget what you promised,' Joanna said.

Henry took out the farthing. 'Get yourself something to eat. There's plenty of choice. You'll hear the the church bell at mid-day and again at Nones. We shall be here, ready to start back then.'

Joanna realised with a sigh of relief that the little ritual which was the high-light of her life was not to be spoilt by the presence of the horrible boy.

Dick had never before been into Baildon and the market entranced him, such a noise and a bustle, so many things to see. Not only the people and the stalls, but the entertainers; a man juggling six plates; a man with a dog which danced, and answered questions, one bark for yes and two for no; a man who appeared to swallow a knife; a man so seemingly boneless that he could wrap his legs around his neck and roll about like a ball. Unfortunately each entertainer had an attendant who moved among the watchers, cap in hand. A failure to contribute led to rough speech, 'Get outa the way, then.' 'Don't stand there blocking the view.' He was pushed and jostled; the ragged little girl collecting for the knife swallower actually spat at him and he spat back at her.

He turned his attention to find something to eat. He had never actually *bought* anything in his life and had no idea of the value of money. He decided against pies, sausages, brawn, slices of cold pease pudding, for although Knight's Acre was poor by his standards, dull and flavourless, it was plentiful enough and he wasn't hungry in quite that way. He craved something really tasty; and presently found it; a comparatively small stall, covered with a white cloth and set out with things he had not seen since delicacies from Uncle Richard's table had sometimes been passed on to the schoolroom. Sweetmeats. He took his time making his choice. Had he looked hungry or ragged the woman behind the spread board would have ordered him off; but by Baildon standards he was well-dressed. A likely customer. So she waited and presently Dick pointed to the three things of his choice and tendered his farthing.

'Trying to be funny?' the woman asked, quite amiably. 'Come on, out with it! You know everything here is a penny — except them,' she pointed to the little squares of marzipan. 'Them's twopence!'

'This is all I have,' said the indisputable heir to Moyidan.

'Be off with you then,' she said, seeing from his expression of real disappointment that what he said was true.

As Dick moved away, disconsolate, the woman said to her neighbour who sold new pots and mended old ones, 'Did you see that? A farthing: For fourpennorth of stuff! Must be a idiot though he didn't look it.'

When he had satisfied himself that no other stall offered sweetmeats, Dick decided to buy a pie. Behind this stall a girl of about his own age was temporarily in charge and when, having made his choice, though the pies varied little in size, he pointed and again held out his farthing, youth responded to youth.

'That all you got? Pies is a ha-penny. You could hev a sausage.'

'I wanted a pie.'

The little girl took a quick glance to see whether her mother was in the offing. She was not. 'All right, then,' she said. 'Hev a pie. But don't tell nobody or I'll get my ears boxed.'

Not at that pie-stall, but another, Henry and Joanna kept their tryst; sharing something *very* special. Eating together at leisure and alone. They sometimes took food to the field or the lambing pen, but such mouthfuls were always hasty. Here, the day's business done, there was a kind of cosiness, for the pie-stall not only stood near the church wall — one of the reasons Henry had chosen it since it was so near the rails where the wagon was, but this pie-seller, a matriarch of seventy, liked a bit of sail-cloth between her and the wind, and over a charcoal brazier she kept pies and sausages in an iron pan. By now she knew them, and knew that they always had the farthing thing, a sausage poised on a wedge of bread.

'Did you get all you were told to?' Henry asked. To forget one of Griselda's errands would provoke a tirade that would last until the next market day — and beyond.

'Yes. And all wrong. As usual. The flannel is *red* but the weight will be wrong, too light or too heavy. As for the thread . . .' She laughed a little and took a bite of her food. It was perfectly true, Henry knew; every shopping expedition ended with a scolding; but it was not the kind of talk to encourage. So he said nothing and Joanna dismissed Griselda and gave herself to the joy of standing with Henry in this little enclosed space, a buttress of the church wall on one side, the stall on the other; isolated, in the market but not part of it; almost like being in a tiny house of their own.

Dick, circling the market inevitably arrived again at the sweetmeat stall. It was almost bare now for the woman who kept it knew almost to the last bit of sticky gingerbread what she could sell in a day. The marzipan which needed real sugar and was cheap at twopence a small square, was all gone, God be thanked, so had the saffron cakes. So she could turn away and enjoy another little gossip with the tinker. Dick's hand shot out and closed on the nearest piece of gingerbread. Nobody noticed and it tasted all the better for not costing him anything.

The disastrous year went on. Rain in April was good; but in showers, not in the steady downpour which rotted the seeds so painfully and carefully planted to replace those which the wind had uprooted. Wet weather, too long continued, made the sheep-run soggy and the sheep developed footrot. Henry remembered, bitterly, that Walter had said at the beginning that Knight's Acre, lying between the wood and the river was not suitable for sheep. The men of Intake had recognised this truth generations ago and on their holdings kept only a sheep or two, tethered and moved about every day and in exceptional conditions taken indoors.

May brought a few dry sunny days, but towards the end of the month the rain came again. Good for the hay, Henry told himself in despair, for it would plainly be a poor harvest the fields were patchy looking. Even June was wet and the shearing was done in the rain, by disgruntled men whose leader and spokesman said that a day and a half's work wasn't worth the trudge. That was unpleasant news, linking in as it did with the wool-merchant's decision that such a small crop of wool was not worth collecting. About that Richard had been helpful but Richard had now been gone for more than a year and last summer Henry had sold his wool — and Robert's — on that bad, casual market. And must do the same this year.

Intending not to work here again, the shearers were slipshod, making more nicks in the hides than usual so that Henry was kept busy with the tar-stick and not troubling to keep the black marked fleeces and the ochre-marked ones in separate piles, that duty fell to Joanna. The gang's woman attendant this year was a stringy, middle-aged woman with a brown face and very red hair; she seemed faintly familiar though at first Henry could not place her. Her manner was markedly hostile, even when Henry handed over the food which, as the employer he was bound to provide. It was good food, too; fresh pork and newly baked bread. She took it without a word, but her manner said — *Thank you for nothing!*

His memory worked. 'I've seen you before. You married Young Shep, didn't you?'

Hostility deepened. 'Worst day's work I ever did.'

Henry had thought Young Shep an idler, then changed his mind but that remark and the fact that she was back in this rough way of life indicated that as a husband and a provider Young Shep had been a disappointment.

'Why was that?'

'Due to that young brother of yours! We hadn't been married more'n a year when he came along, all fancy clothes and fancy talk about music and where he'd bin and where he was going. Turned Shep's head. He up and left.'

This was the first word that Henry had heard about John since he'd given Richard the slip, seven years earlier and he was anxious to hear more.

'Do you ever hear anything of your husband?'

'I used to at first. He'd send money. So he should — I'd got a baby to keep. But money don't make up for being left and made a laughing stock of. And I ain't even had money for a long time now.'

Greatly against his will Henry felt the nag of responsibility. It was John, his brother, who had robbed this woman of her husband. He wished that he could afford a generous gesture, give her some money and say, 'Buy something for the child.' But it was impossible. All he could do was to say, 'I am sorry.' She did not answer, except with a look which said very plainly — *So you damn well should be!*

Afterwards, thinking it over, Henry reflected that if for some time Young Shep had sent money home the pair of strolling musicians had not been doing badly. That the money had ceased to arrive did not necessarily indicate that they had ceased to prosper. Young Shep might have thought that the child's dependent days were over. Henry hoped that was the explanation. John had been idle, defiant, sly, but nobody liked to think of a brother fallen on evil days. Soon, however, Henry was too busy to have much time for thought.

Fleeces cut in the rain and heaped together while still damp quickly deteriorated, felted together and lost weight. So Henry made primitive racks upon which the wool, well squeezed, was hung out. When the sun shone the racks were carried out of the barn to the yard; when rain threatened or fell, they were hastily carried back under cover. It was a constant anxiety. So was the hay. It could, it must be cut whatever the weather, but it was hard work. When hay was ripe and stood straight the scythe went through it sweetly, each swishing stroke cutting a wide swathe. In weather like this, the hay beaten down by the rain it was often a sickle job, slow, done by the handful, the left hand holding the grass upright, the right hand wielding the smaller tool. Nor was the cutting all. Pile damp hay into the ordinary haycocks and it went mouldy before you could blink. It must be left as it fell and regularly tossed; on the rare, sunny day, turned about as often as three times.

'When are we going to market again, Uncle Henry?'

'That depends upon the weather. As soon as the wool is dry. And the hay in.'

'*I* could go,' Dick said, 'and do Aunt Griselda's errands.'

'Yes, I suppose you could.' Dick's services could be dispensed with. Utterly unlike his Uncle John in appearance and in character, Dick resembled him closely in his attitude towards work. Henry had always been obliged to goad John into activity and it was the same with Dick.

Dick had several most enjoyable days in the market. He was shrewd enough to perform any errand entrusted to him scrupulously and to keep the money apart. He had his farthing to spend and he always spent it at the pie-stall where the coin bought him a ha-penny pie while the friendly girl was in charge, as he always made certain that she was before approaching. Once, taking his priced-down pie he gave her a length of red ribbon for her hair. She was pleased, even though at the back of her mind she wondered how a boy who had only a farthing to spend, could have bought such a gay and expensive thing. Her mother, coming back from a very necessary errand in the churchyard where the mounded heaps of the dead provided a little privacy for the relief of bladders and bowels, wondered, too. 'Who give you that?'

'A boy.'

'And heven't I towd you time and again, not to hev nothing to do with boys?' The box on the ears was duly delivered.

Of that Dick knew nothing. What he did know was that a similar offering, blue this time, was completely rejected by Joanna whose goodwill he still craved.

'Go hang yourself with it!' she said. And Uncle Henry asked, 'How did you come by it, Dick?'

'I spent my farthing on it.' Moving between schoolroom and kitchen at Moyidan the boy had become a glib, convincing liar. Around Baildon market place he had become a slick thief.

CHAPTER TWENTY-NINE

In early July when the sun shone it had power. The wool was at last saleable. Henry mounded the wagon high, loaded bales on to the other horse, even called Dick's pony into service. Joanna, who weighed light and did not take up much room, was to drive the wagon; Henry, leading the horse would walk. So they made an early start.

Overnight there had been a squabble. Griselda said that now that the time for selling the wool had come, something must be done about Godfrey's clothes. Those she had contrived for him were now outgrown or washed and worn into shreds. She needed this and that. Henry said, 'I'll see how the wool sells.'

'Do you realise,' she asked, becoming shrill, 'that apart from a bit of red flannel your son has never had anything *new* in his life? For myself I ask nothing. I never did. I never shall . . .'

She was infuriated to think that some of the wool money was set aside for the benefit of a dead boy. Robert *must* be dead or there would have been news of him long before this. She was also infuriated by the fact that out of the money entrusted to Henry for Dick's clothing the stupid fellow had not squeezed out something for his *own* son . . . All the stored-up anger poring out, the voice as grating as an ill-tuned saw until Henry who usually bore her tirades with patience, said, 'Be quiet! Can't you see that I'm doing the best I can for you all?'

'And a fine best it is! Best for everybody except your own.' She grew almost tipsy with the delight of denunciation. 'Work yourself into the grave,' she said, 'work me into the grave. And for what? Ask yourself *that*.'

It was a cogent question and one that had now and again occurred to Henry himself. The struggle did sometimes seem to be hopeless. What he had to sell seemed to loose value, what he must buy seemed to increase in prices. And there were taxes, more exorbitant with every assessment. Old sheep with foot rot, lambs dead with navel trouble, despite all his care. And for what? He knew the answer to that; simple; to go my own way.

He always had, and though the way he had chosen was hard and unrewarding, he had managed so far to hold his own. And honestly.

The Baildon market was less happy-go-lucky than it seemed to be. It was in fact, strictly ruled. There were inspectors of weights and measures, any offender was liable to a spell in the stocks, arms and legs thrust through holes, head exposed and likely to be pelted with sticks and stones, and filth. There was also the market overseer who saw to it that no stall encroached upon its neighbour. His authority straight down from the time when the market had been the province of the monks in the Abbey. There was also the constable whose power was derived from an even older time. Long before abbeys. Thieves, people who caused a disturbance, or made an obstruction on a public highway must be dealt with by the constable — the caretaker.

Both men were there to protect the public, and the public was markedly ungrateful. Even the testing of weights and measures and the tasting for the quality of ale, all designed for the public's protection, was not popular. And although everybody hated thieves few were ever handed over in the proper fashion. For one thing the punishments were so ferocious, for another the whole thing took so long. It was seldom sufficient to say — 'This boy stole from me; I caught him in the act.' You had to produce at least one witness, invariably unwilling because it meant a waste of time. So the market people had devised their own system, completely illegal since it involved taking the law into their own hands.

They kept one another informed. The whisper would go round — 'Look out for such-and-such a person; he or she is a thief, or a cheat, or a passer of bad coins.' Thus everyone was on the alert and punishment was prompt since almost everybody carried a stout stick.

There had for some time now been a dubious character around the market, a biggish boy with black hair and tidy clothes. He had two methods. Turn your back for a second and he had whipped something away; or have a crowd near your booth and he would join it, as though waiting to be served, due to his clothes he looked a likely customer, then when you were serving a customer, he'd slip away — and something had gone with him. This had happened twice to the man who sold ribbon and tape and such things.

This morning there was a new stall on the market — new at least to Richard. It was filled with small trinkets; the man who owned it had come to Baildon for the Midsummer Fair and done rather poor trade, so he had stayed on for a bit.

Dick was not actually caught in the act; he stood staring at the pretty, gaudy things trying to decide what to take as an offering for the friendly little girl who had already let him have a ha'penny pie for a farthing. There were beads of all colours, ornaments for hair and for hats, thimbles that looked like silver, rings that looked like gold. He decided upon beads, red ones to match the ribbon he had given her. The stall-holder who, being an outsider, had not been warned by the whisper, saw nothing suspicious, but the ribbon-seller said, 'Thass him!' and somebody else said 'Clubs!'

Such punishments, slam! slam! were administered with the minumum of noise and fuss because the constable resented such usurpation of his legal office; and most offenders had the sense not to yell, since to draw attention was to invite official punishemnt later. Dick yelled lustily and the market overseer and the constable came running. Within two seconds all the people who had been hammering Dick were back behind their stalls, their sticks concealed, only the trinket seller who had now guessed what it was all about, and Dick, bearing marks of punishment, still stood there.

'Whass all this about?' the constable enquired.

The trinket seller was a quick-witted man.

'Lazy little sod,' he said, giving Dick a warning glance which was not understood. 'Fine thing, I must say, if a man can't give his own son a wallop or two to teach him not to go forgetting.'

Through the blood and tears streaking down his face, Dick said, 'I ain't his son.'

Nobody heeded that. Stepson perhaps; adopted; or an apprentice. Satisfied that no law had been broken, no disturbance caused the two men strolled away.

'You're a thick-headed young fool,' the trinket-seller said. 'But for me you'd be on your way to the Bridewell.'

'My name is Richard Tallboys,' Dick sobbed.

This piece of information quickly went the rounds. Tallboys was a well-known and honoured name. Henry was not popular, too stand-offish, and too close-spending, but he was respected. And if this snivelling little sneak thief were his son, he was also the grandson of Sir Godfrey, the good knight in whom the neighbourhood had taken a vicarious pride, and who had come back from the dead! Oh, what a disgrace! Shame enough for any decent family to have a thief among its members; but a Tallboys!

But these were people not ruled by sentiment. Alongside the story on its rounds, ran a certainty. If Master Tallboys knew what his son had been up to he'd give compensation, good honest man that he was. All the stallholders would have been shamed to have a son caught stealing, but a bit of sharp practice was quite another thing. Almost everybody except the seller of pots and pans, suddenly remembered missing something lately, and multiplied its value by ten at least.

Henry was at that moment closeted with Master Turnbull, handing over Robert's share of the wool money. An act of faith, the lawyer thought, making a meticulous entry and mildly regretting that the sum had decreased again.

'And you still have no news of the boy?'

'None. I heard of the other young one — John — only the other day. And that after seven years. And my father; as you may remember, was gone even longer.' Master Turnbull supposed that his family history accounted for Henry's stubborn refusal to accept that Robert was dead. Though there *was* a difference between a full grown man, a boy in his teens and a child! However, it was none of his business.

Henry crossed the sunny market place, making for the pie-stall where Joanna would be waiting. He was not a self-conscious man and did not notice the stares. Today, he decided, Joanna should have a pie, a twopenny one if she liked, and also a glass of the sweet cider which the old woman added to her wares in summer. Not that the wool price justified extravagance, but Joanna's exertions did. He only wished that he could buy her something really expensive and pretty and useful.

She was waiting, as he expected her to be, for his business with Master Turnbull had delayed him. But surely, he thought, as he approached, a little waiting could not account for her expression of acute distress. She never, even in the finest summer acquired much sun tan; in this almost sunless season she had not tanned at all; so now she looked very pale, blanched, her very lips white. He saw her before she saw him, he was taller. When she did see him, threading his way through the crowd, she ran and seized his arm in a frenzied grip.

'It's awful, Henry! But don't pay! Don't pay. They can't make you. Even *she* says you can't.' She jerked her head towards the pie-seller who was not looking very cheerful.

Everybody knew where Master Tallboys took his dinner,

and the pie-woman had been deputed to speak for all. And she rather liked Henry; not a good spender, but regular; he didn't come every week, but whenever he came — and she knew because she could see his wagon, what he had to spend was spent with her; and he was always civil. So she broke the news to him without taking any pleasure in the task, and without claiming, as she could easily have done, that Dick had robbed her.

Henry was furious. Furious with Dick; greedy little bastard! Hadn't he always had his farthing, exactly the amount that Henry spent on himself: Furious, too with the exaggerated claim for compensation. If the little swine had come to every market and eaten himself silly each time he couldn't possibly have consumed what he was said to have consumed. And if only he'd been rich! Rich enough to throw money in front of these money-grubbing liars and watch them grovel for it! A silly way to think for a man who had in his purse only the price — disappointing at that — of his own share of the wool; which must last until after harvest.

He said to the pie-woman. 'They shall all be paid. Now we want two twopenny pies and two mugs of your good cider.' He and Joanna then retreated to their little nook and he said, 'Cheer up, sweetheart. Don't let it spoil your appetite.'

'But how can you? Pay I mean? I told you not to. And it's a lot of money.'

'I know how to get it,' Henry said. *'I'm going to sell his pony!'*

For a second they looked at each other with eyes which despite their differing colouring, were exactly alike, dancing with mischief and with malice. The expression made Henry look *young*.

'What a wonderful idea,' Joanna said, biting happily into her pie.

Henry thought — Practical, too! It would punish Dick; it would restrict his movements; and it would be saving. For when Henry had undertaken to supply Dick with his keep he had not taken the pony into consideration. A pony could share the sheep-run in summer; in winter it needed hay, and soon it would need to be shod.

Dick had taken refuge in the wagon. Henry dragged him out, made sure that he was not hurt, bruised and battered but with no wound in any way comparable to the one Griselda had inflicted on Joanna because several sticks aimed at the same target clashed and defeated one another's purpose.

'Now you walk,' Henry said, remembering how, long ago, he and Richard had quarrelled in the wagon bringing them from Beauclaire to Knight's Acre and Walter had told them to get out and walk.

For those who had gone to market an eventful day; and not less so for Griselda who had stayed at home.

About clothes for the child whom she now regarded as far more Tom's than Henry's, Henry had been evasive, promising nothing, saying I must see how the wool sells. An evasive and unpromising answer. So Griselda sought about in her mind for some other way, and presently was visited by much the kind of inspiration as had touched Henry when he thought of selling the pony.

Those empty rooms on the other side of the house!

She had been into Tana's pavilion on various occasions, but once the two babies were weaned she had no reason to go there, and with Lady Serriff dead that part of the house was of no importance. Knight's Acre was quite big enough to manage single-handed. Now, all of a sudden, some memory stirred. A lot of silk! Griselda had not asked Henry for silk — only for good linen and some sound homespun.

She entered as the children had done, hauling Godfrey in after her. The place smelt of dust and neglect and of something which she did not recognise though it reminded her sharply of the loft at the Swan. Bats found their way in through the pane Joanna had broken.

'I don't like it here, Mumma.'

'We shall not be long,' Griselda said. She was amazed to think that she had not thought of this treasure-house before. Silk everywhere! Godfrey could be silk-clad for the rest of his life — even in winter, for a tunic and hood made double and stuffed with sheep's wool and quilted would keep out the coldest winds.

Then, staring, she thought silver! Enormous, four branched candlesticks, several wine cups, and a bowl; all black with tarnish, but that was proof that they were silver.

'I don't like it here, Mumma.'

She hushed him with an impatience unusual in her dealings with him. She thought — Oh Tom, if only I'd used my sense! You could have had wine and manchet bread . . . All the luxuries in the world.

Then she thought that if she had been stupid, Henry had been even more so. He should have remembered.

She investigated further, entered the inner room, opened the chest. She had never owned a trinket in her life, but she had seen precious stones. The image of Our Lady in the Convent chapel had worn a crown of them, and now and again travellers of a better sort had lodged at The Swan because it was handy. God in Heaven! Here she and Henry had been all these years, working their fingers to the bone, counting pennies, with wealth unimaginable waiting just across the yard.

'Can we go *now*?' Godfrey demanded with all the imperiousness of a spoilt child. There was nobody to notice the resemblance but very often his manner towards his mother closely matched that of Dick's to Lady Emma.

'Yes. We can go now. You hold this.' She whipped off her apron and into it piled the emeralds, sapphires, diamonds and pearls, rubies and the tangled mass of gold setting out of which they had been broken. About them she twisted the apron as she would have twisted the cloth about a bag pudding. 'Hold it tight,' she said, and lifted him out of the window. The silver things she dropped out, one by one on to the soft soil and then clambered out herself.

She spent the rest of her afternoon polishing the silver things. She'd have something to show and even more to say to Henry when he came home!

Joanna and Henry walked into the kitchen together, bringing their frugal purchases. Through the west facing window of the kitchen the lowering sun sent its rays, winking upon the glittering silver and waking the fiery colours in the stones, precious things brought from the world's farthest end, now spread out on a well-scrubbed kitchen table.

At the sight they both stopped as though the floor had dropped just before their feet. Then Joanna ran forward and spread her hands over the coloured stones with which she and Robert had played five-stones and How Many Birds In A Bush.

The silver things, the tangled mass of gold she ignored. Only the stones mattered.

'They are ours,' she cried. And then, realising that she alone was left, 'Mine. They are mine.'

Henry said, 'She is right. They belonged to her mother...'

The shoes which Dick wore on Sundays and market days were not yet softened by use; soon he had a blister on his heel and began to limp. The old woman pedlar overtook him easily and then slowed her stride, glad of company on what she always thought of as the nasty bit of road. She was not much frightened of being robbed, though all her wordly wealth was contained in the pack she carried. Her father had been in this trade and he had made for himself a very cunning box. Opened out, and held forward on her solid bosom it made a splendid tray for display; folded up, it was compact and easily carried on her back; it had a secret drawer in which gold coins, well wadded with sheep's wool so that they did not rattle, lay hidden. As often as she could she changed the small currency of her earnings into gold, reserving just enough to meet her day-by-day expenses. So she reckoned that the most she could lose was her stock and a few pence. She fell into step with the limping, snivelling boy because they were nearing the point where Layer Wood ran alongside the road, and some very funny tales were told of that wood.

She had been in the market that day and recognised him instantly as the boy who had received a well-deserved hiding. She had no sympathy with thieves and her amiable manner towards him was entirely false.

'Did they hurt you bad?'

'They nearly killed me.'

'What made you do it? Take stuff I mean.'

'I was hungry.'

'Don't your father give you enough to eat.'

'I ain't got no father...'

He had no friend, either. No friend in all the world except the little girl for whom he had intended the red beads. At the thought of his friendless state the snivelling changed to real crying for a while. This old woman seemed interested at least and into her ears he poured out the story of his woes and his wrongs, not failing to mention that really Moyidan belonged to him; the Bishop had taken Moyidan and kept him without shoes; his Uncle Henry made him work like a labourer and only today had sold his pony and made him walk home.

A lurid story, the old woman knew, was as good as stock. Everybody liked a story and women at kitchen doors, unwilling to buy, would stand and listen and decide that after all they could do with a reel of thread. So she clicked her tongue sympathetically and now and again said, 'You poor boy!' while her mind took note of every detail and improvised embellishments. And didn't this tale of cheating and ill-treatment link up with another? Two children deliberately lost in this very wood and left to die? By a wicked uncle?

'You hungry now?'

Dick said, 'Yes.' And that was true. A swollen jaw and a tooth loose on that side where a stick had reached its mark was no hindrance to eating; misery had never lessened his appetite. So presently, to her highly coloured tale the old woman could add with some truth, 'I was that sorry for him, I give him my own bite of supper and he ett like a starving dog.' In fact she had shared her bit of supper — bread and cheese with a careful eye to her own interest.

'Your Grace,' said the young clerk, about the only one who would ever get anywhere, being the only one with a spark of spirit, 'when the Moyidan boy was found to be without shoes, you complained, if I may say so, quite rightly, that you had not been informed.'

'That is so.'

'Would Your Grace welcome more information about the same boy? A singular story is going around.'

'Tell me.'

The Bishop listened with some consternation, but even more disappointment. He remembered the impression that Henry Tallboys had made upon him and how he had thought — as Master Turnbull thought from time to time — how unlike his brother Richard; so honest and forthright and short-spoken. Even now His Grace found it rather hard to believe that Henry Tallboys over-worked, underfed and regularly beat his nephew. Had sold his pony and left him to walk home from Baildon in shoes so ill-fitting that the boy could hardly hobble.

And so hungry that a pedlar woman had felt obliged to give him her own meagre supper.

'Where did you get this tale, Jonathan?'

'Your Grace, from the inn on the waterfront. The landlady there is second cousin to my mother — and she is growing old. I feel it my duty to look in upon her from time to time.'

'Most admirable,' the Bishop said. Deplorable, too, because if Jonathan, a bright boy, played his cards rightly, the Church would lose and the Welcome To Mariners would gain.

'You were right to inform me. I will look into the matter myself.'

Henry and Jem were scything, Joanna and Dick working behind them. At the sight of a mounted man Henry came towards the edge of the field and when his visitor was recognisable, looked pleased. With that incongruous grace of his, he bowed, spoke words of greeting, laid his hand on the horse's bridle and led the way to the front of the house, steadied the stirrup.

'It was in my mind to come to see you, my lord, but once harvest starts . . .' He threw open the door and stood aside.

A very poor place, His Grace thought, looking around the hall of Knight's Acre for the first time and accepting the only comfortable seat, its cushions now much the worse for wear.

'About the boy?' It seemed incredible, but it was just possible that living in such near isolation, Master Tallboys did not know what tales were being told of him.

'No, the girl . . . I wish I could offer you wine. All I have is ale.' And that only because there was an understood agreement that hired men, at harvest time, should have ale.

'Ale would be very acceptable,' the Bishop said graciously. Henry fetched it himself. Not good ale; very thin and sour.

'You wish to speak to me about young Richard,' Henry asked.

'Some story regarding him, his welfare, has reached my notice.'

'Rightly so. He behaved very badly and had he not been soundly thrashed in the market, I should have thrashed him myself. But it was taken out of my hands; the people he had stolen from beat him much harder than I could have brought myself to do; they then claimed extortionate compensation, which I managed to meet by selling his pony. So he will not trouble Baildon market any more.'

Short and to the point.

'As it was reported to me, he stole because he was hungry. When I heard that I felt inclined to blame myself for accepting your offer not to charge for his board . . .'

'Greedy,' Henry said. 'All boys are. He has eaten alongside me ever since he came here, and in the market he had to spend exactly what I spend on myself. Would you care, my lord to see him and assure yourself that he is well nourished? I'd like you to see Joanna, too. *Her* future is what I am concerned about.'

He went out and gave a clear piercing whistle.

His Grace remembered thinking, years ago, at Moyidan, that given ten years this girl would be beautiful and he did not retract his opinion now though all the childish beauty had gone and she was angular, the youthful curves not yet replaced by those of budding maturity. All arms and legs, eyes and mouth. But her hair was the colour of a well-kept saddle, her eyes the colour of aquamarines and her profile, if anything, more clear cut than ever. The boy looked well-fed enough; indeed beside the girl he looked thick and sullen. The marks of the beating he had received in the market had vanished and he bore no resemblance at all to the ill-fed, ill-treated boy of the story which the pedlar woman had hawked around with her wares.

'All right,' Henry said, dismissing them. 'It's hardly worth going back to the field before dinner.'

As soon as they had gone, he went to the court cupboard, with its solitary silver cup and reached up to its top for something hidden behind the carved pediment. A bundle wrapped in a piece of old cloth.

'I wanted your advice about these, my lord.' Out on the table tumbled a wealth of jewels and a tangled mass of gold.

'Great God in Heaven! Where did they come from?'

'They belong to the girl. They were her mother's.' Whatever it had been which had forbidden Henry to speak, or even think of Tana, which had made him ignore that part of the house, and which had prevented him from ever regarding Joanna as Tana's daughter, had now lost power. He was able to say in a natural manner, 'I suppose you know the story? No? Well, my father went to Spain, to fight against the Moors. He was captured and was enslaved for almost nine years. A Spanish lady — Lady Serriff — contrived his escape, and he brought her back with him to England. She was pregnant and Joanna was born some months later. The lady had an unruly horse which eventually threw her and she died. It did not occur to anyone to go through what she left and these were discovered only a few weeks ago.'

'What a story!' From the tumbled, flashing heap of colour one thing stood out, a ruby of exceptional size and darkness. He picked it up and held it against the light. What a thumb ring it would make! 'Who broke the stones from their settings?'

'The children. Joanna and my youngest brother — the little boy who was lost. They found things and regarded them as playthings, prettier than pebbles, so they pried them loose ... What I wanted to ask Your Grace was advice upon how to deal with them.'

Extraordinary man! A small fortune within reach of his hand, and drinking this poor ale.

'These represent a small fortune, Master Tallboys.'

'So I hoped, for the child's sake. My father once, through my aunt, Lady Astallon of Beauclaire, disposed of a few similar things. I have no such outlet. I have no knowledge. I do however remember another thing. When my sister — that boy's mother — was younger, my parents wished her to go to Lamarsh, but they would only accept girls with money behind them. I have been wondering — you are the only person I know who could advise upon such matters — if you, my lord would help me, both about the disposal of the trinkets and about getting the girl accepted there.'

The Bishop frowned. All this for Lamarsh; so rich already! The old breach between the secular clergy and the religious houses opened and yawned in this ill-furnished hall where an honest man sat, asking advice.

In theory all the religious houses; the abbeys and the convents were ruled by the Bishop of the diocese, subject to regular visitations; always excepting such places as that decayed house at Clevely where a few old women rotted under a rotting roof, the blind propped up by the lame, the lame guided the blind. He had never visited Clevely, but he knew Lamarsh. Its financial arrangements solidly founded by a former Abbess — ah yes! Another member of this very curious family? Now it was full of women, the widows and spinsters whom every war threw up, more boarders, with little pet dogs in their sleeves or in their laps. They defied all discipline and by their bad, indeed loose, behaviour, they brought convents into disrepute.

'That,' His Grace said, after cogitations which had lasted only a few seconds, though wide in scope. 'I should not advise.'

Not only the waste of a small fortune, but a waste of a girl who was going to be beautiful.

'Then what would you suggest, my lord?'

'Placing her with a family of repute, with daughters of its own. Somewhere where she could learn all the . . .' he hesitated for a second, 'accomplishments necessary for a gentlewoman. All this does not make her a *great* heiress, but properly handled it could make a not inconsiderable dowry. How old is she?'

'Eleven years and some months.'

Six or seven years then for the handling.

'So long as she's safe,' Henry said. 'And happy . . .'

'If you care to leave this to me. Offhand I cannot name a family such as I envisage. But I have no doubt . . . I am shortly going to London. A tiresome conference. I could, at the same time dispose of all this and make arrangements . . .' In these troubled times dozens of men, not actually poor, and some with power, would welcome ready money, and what it could earn in seven years. His Grace's eye looked again at the tangle of gold and saw what he was almost sure was the setting from which the big ruby had been pried. He thought — Any competent goldsmith . . . Like Lady Astallon he considered that the middleman was worthy of his hire. *This* would be his!

Henry bundled the whole treasure into a cloth and handed it over; glad to be rid of it. He had been obliged to take it and hide it in a place which neither Griselda nor Joanna knew about — or could reach, for the discovery had brought their simmering hostility to a head and *he* acknowledging Joanna's claim, refuting Griselda's strident, 'Findings keepings!' had fallen into even deeper disfavour. A bad father!

'Oh,' he now said, remembering, 'there was more. Some silver things.' He stooped and opened the enclosed part of the cupboard. Candlesticks, four-branched, fit for any altar; cups; a bowl. Gathering tarnish again for since Griselda's claim to ownership had been denied she had not bothered and Joanna had had no time.

'Of considerable value,' the Bishop said. 'I cannot well take them with me, but I will send.' He had come alone because if what he found at Knight's Acre should correspond in any way with the rumour, the fewer people who knew about it, the better. Always, everywhere, there were eyes watching, tongues wagging and ill-informed minds all too ready to think the worst.

Henry felt as though a load had been lifted from his shoulders. What he had always wanted for Joanna now seemed likely to come about. Safe and happy — that was his wish for her. Thus relieved, he remembered his manners. 'If you would care to eat with us, Your Grace ...' It was only rabbit, but rabbit in harvest time was as good meat as one could wish for. Henry had derived from his mother not only his manners, his way of speech, but something deeper, not an ignoring of class distinction but the capacity to over-ride it. Sybilla, poorly dressed, ill-provided for, had never failed to preside graciously over her table, even when that table was in the kitchen, and one she had just scrubbed with her own hands.

'I thank you. But I have guests awaiting me at Moyidan.'

Outside the house, between the roses, again overgrown because Griselda had lost interest, the two men took civil leave of one another. The Bishop mounted, and remembering his waiting guests, set off at a swift trot. Henry turned back into his house.

Just beyond the church where the track turned into the lane, something hurtled out of hiding and in the most reckless manner grabbed the horse's bridle and swung on it. His Grace was almost unseated. Recovering himself he said, 'What the Devil ...' and then recognised the boy.

'What do you think you're about? You could have caused a serious accident! What do you want?'

Dick said, 'I sent you messages. I writ you a letter. And you took Moyidan and sent me here. I hate it here. And it ain't right that I should be.'

The Bishop said, 'So far as I can see you have no cause for complaint. Let go of my horse. You make him restive.'

'Then you'd ride off! You gotta listen to me.' And uncouth, ill-spoken boy! 'Umma always said Moyidan belonged to me. I was a *rich* boy and I'd be a rich man. Here I work like a labourer — but unpaid. I have horrible food and Griselda grudges every mouthful I chaw. Something oughta be done about me. Umma'd turn in her grave . . .'

'Who was Umma?'

'My grandmother. Lady Emma. She always said . . .'

'She would certainly turn in her grave could she know how wicked, how *ungrateful* you are.'

'What hev I got to be grateful about?'

It was curious — the boy did not look like a Tallboys, but he had something, quite indefinable that linked him with Richard who at his lowest moment would make a jest about the un-pawnability of a servant, and with Henry who had just tipped out — and handed over a collection of jewels, as though they were hazel nuts; what exactly this quality was . . . there was no word.

'You should be grateful,' His Grace said sternly, 'that your property is in safe hands, being properly admin . . . looked after, until you attain your majority. You should be grateful to your uncle.'

'He sold my pony!'

'Quite rightly. You had stolen in the market.'

'Because I was so poor. If I had my rights I wouldn't have to steal, would I? I'd be at Moyidan, with all I wanted. And servants. Like when Umma was alive.'

'Your grandmother is dead. Your father and mother also. You have a good home . . .' Strange to have come here this morning in order to scold the uncle and now to be scolding the nephew. 'Many boys in your position — especially trouble-some boys such as you are — find themselves in orphanages, or schools.'

'If they're *poor*,' Dick said stubbornly. 'I'm rich. Moyidan is mine . . .'

His Grace thought quickly. The boy was obviously not starved or ill-treated as rumour held; he was a liar. But liars could be dangerous. Doubly so when mingling with the lies there was an element of truth. As in this case.

With a change of manner he said, 'If you are not happy here some other arrangement must be made. Would you like to come with me to London?'

'What for?' Suspicious as a peasant.

'To enjoy yourself and see something of the world.'

What an absurd situation, he Bishop of Bywater, actually coaxing this young oaf who still kept firm hold on the bridle.

'I druther go to Moyidan, if I could hev proper food and shoes when I wanted. I don't know about London only what Joseph said — all right if you was rich, like living on a muck-heap if you was poor. And I *ain't* poor. Moyidan . . .'

'I think you would enjoy London.'

'Would I hev my pony back?'

For the animal *as* an animal Dick had been little concerned, but it had been a possession, something poor little boys didn't have.

'Naturally. You would need one in order to ride to London.'

'All right, then. I'll go.'

Alongside the faint warning bell about the danger of lies mixed with some truth, the word 'school' had run in the Bishop's mind.

There was one, already famous. It was called The King's College of Our Lady of Eton beside Windsor. It had been founded by Henry VI some twenty years earlier for the benefit of twenty-five indigent boys; now it housed over seventy — and not all indigent, for even the rich and the noble were beginning to see some value in learning. Places there were eagerly sought but the Bishop had no doubt that with his contacts and his influence he could contrive for this boy to be squeezed in. It would look well; what more could the Church do for an orphan who had fallen into its hands than administer his property to the best advantage and send him to the best school in England?

And there the blabbermouth boy could go about saying, 'Moyidan,' and nobody would even know where the place was.

It was slightly ironic that the Bishop of Bywater who, if he had ever indulged in amorous ventures had done so with the utmost discretion, should appear seeking at the same time a place at Eton for a loutish boy and a place in a good household for a girl. The boy, when he became of age would inherit a flourishing estate; the girl — said to be pretty — had a considerable dowry, in ready money, money that could be invested now and begin to earn.

His reputation was not damaged. Obviously he was clever, a

good manager. A great ruby of exceptional size and quality shone on his thumb . . .

CHAPTER THIRTY

Joanna had watched Dick's departure with mixed feelings. It was pleasant to think that she would never have to sit at table with him again. But he had left somewhat grandly, mounted on a new pony, bigger than the other. When he arrived, almost barefoot, when he had been beaten in the market and lost his pony she had almost thought . . . almost . . . that ill-wishing was not entirely futile. Now, seeing him ride off, all cock-a-hoop, she had a feeling of defeat. There was no one to tell her and that extra sense which she had possessed where Robert was concerned did not operate where Dick was concerned — that Dick's ultimate destination was the reverse of joyful. Tutors far more strict and more powerful than Master Jankyn had ever been; dozens of rules, and to break one meant a real beating; no ponies allowed and food intended for pauper boys, every half year lagging a little behind what was absolutely necessary because the Bursar always reckoned backwards; so much meal, so much bread, so much fat coarse meat had sufficed so many boys for the last half year; it would serve for this; time enough to think about the extra mouths next year.

At Knight's Acre it was a bad and troublesome harvest. Far too much rain. A *sickle harvest*, a vast amount of labour and small reward.

One day, coming in because the rain made work impossible, sharing an old sack to protect them from the downpour, Joanna said, 'Henry, if those things of mine are so valuable, this wouldn't matter so much. We could give her half, to stop her mouth and buy things for ourselves. A cow *with* a calf and some more of the black-faced sheep. They do better. Don't they?'

They did, with their longer legs and lighter fleeces.

'Honey, I don't know what the things were worth. I expect to hear any day. But whatever it amounts to it must belong to you, not spent on Knight's Acre.'

'Why not? It is my home.'

And what a home, Henry thought. Griselda, hostile and spiteful ever since the baby episode, had become ten times more so since the finding of the treasure and Joanna's claim, and his backing it.

You couldn't say that she had gone mad — she had sense enough never to mention the subject in front of Jem at midday; sense enough to provide food then. It was the evenings that were horrible. Rave, rant, scold, denounce and deride. Sometimes it seemed as though she was talking to herself — as indeed she might well have been. Henry and Joanna had learnt to take refuge in silence and anybody looking through the window, seeing the trap-like mouth open and shut, open and shut, would have been justified in thinking that Griselda was addressing two dumb mutes. Anything could start her off; nothing ... On and on, and much of it so unfounded as to sound insane. She'd linked, somehow, the finding of the treasure with Dick's going to London. 'Riding off like a lord and your own son dressed in bits and pieces. No doubt you'll do the same for *her* one day. Here am I working my fingers to the bone —' That was one of her favourite expressions, for all the tasks in which she had once taken pride and pleasure now seemed to be heavy impositions — 'and what do I get? I *found* the things after all.'

So, when Joanna made the remark about Knight's Acre being her home, Henry said, 'Not much of one, lately, I'm afraid. Still let's hope ...' He left it there, having heard nothing from the Bishop.

'It suits me,' Joanna said. She seized his hand and swung on it, taking a few hopping steps. 'Outdoors, that is,' she added in the voice she used when referring, however indirectly, to Griselda.

Henry gave her a sideways glance. True enough; she seemed happy, seemed to have forgotten Robert. And even indoors, with Griselda at her worst, she would occasionally catch his eye and flash him a glance of wry amusement; or make an almost imperceptible movement of the shoulders. He'd miss her, indoors and out if the plan came to anything. And for the first time he wondered how she would take to a new way of life, so utterly different from the one she now led. Easily, he assured himself; children were very adaptable.

'Up! Up the Maiden,' Jem cried, heaving the last sheaf of this prolonged harvest on to the wagon. 'Oughta hev a bitta ribbon on her. For luck.' He said it every year. He was inclined to think that Henry's disregard for such old customs was responsible for the way in which things seemed to go against him. Not that anybody could help the weather of course; a bad season hit the careful and the neglectful alike. But look at the way he'd got married, no jollifications, nobody to wish him luck, drink his health or throw an old shoe; and how had that turned out?

Joanna had been prepared for this moment and with glee whipped out a length of blue ribbon. 'Dick left it behind,' she said. 'I found it when I had to clean his room.'

'That should work miracles,' Henry said dryly. 'It cost enough.'

She began to scramble into the wagon which was not loaded high; then she dropped back and stood rigid and staring in exactly the way she had done soon after Robert's departure to Moyidan.

'There's a man coming. Henry, don't see him. Don't talk to him. Send him away. It will do us no good!'

He turned to look. This, the last field to be cleared, was called Far Field, the one farthest from the house and very slightly higher than the others. He had a clear view of the track which led from the house between the sheepfold and the church and the priest's house, where it curved to join the lane. Nothing moved on it. Nor was there anyone on the narrow footpath beyond the sheepfold, the path which since the common had been enclosed had linked the village to the church.

'There's nobody there,' Henry said. But even as he spoke a mounted man came out of the lane, rounded the church and the priest's house and came towards Knight's Acre.

'Please, Henry. Please. Don't listen. I know it is bad. I always knew . . .'

'Don't be silly. Of course I must see the man. Up you get. Tie the pretty bow on and wish next harvest better luck.'

He lifted her into the wagon. Her bright brown hair brushed his face and revived something which he had no time to recognise.

His Grace of Bywater was still in London, but he had

269

written a lengthy letter to one of his secretaries at Bywater and directed him to go immediately and convey the gist of it to Master Tallboys.

Richard's fate was easily disposed of — a place for him had been found at Eton, the best school in England.

Joanna's could be enlarged upon. Her small fortune had not yet been entirely converted into currency — such things took time. Also time-consuming had been the Bishop's meticulous search for a completely suitable home for her; but one had been found in the household of Sir Barnabas Grey in Hertfordshire. Sir Barnabas was a knight of the highest possible reputation, extremely well-connected, a remote relative of the Queen's first husband. He had two daughters, one aged twelve, the other nine, and his lady who was extremely accomplished was educating her own daughters and was willing for Joanna to join the household. About monetary arrangements the Bishop thought it only necessary to say that a satisfactory arrangement had been reached. Sir Barnabas was scrupulously honest and would invest wisely what was available now and what was to come when the rest of the goods were sold. He would use the income from it in return for treating Joanna as his own — even to the point of finding her a suitable husband when the time came.

'Would you like me to repeat, Master Tallboys?'

'Thank you, no. I think I have it.'

'His Grace also wished me to tell you that a suitable escort will be arranged if we are notified.'

It was exactly what he had wanted for her. A suitable home, suitable company, in due time a suitable marriage — all the things which he could not provide. He should have felt elated, but he did not.

'It is always the same,' Griselda said, slapping the only-just-belated meal on to the table. 'As soon as the food is ready somebody comes and you talk and talk. What did the fellow want?'

'Nothing that concerns you.'

Such a downright snub was unusual. Henry's tone of voice, the expression on his face convinced Joanna that she had been right. The man had brought bad news. What? There were

curious limits to her flashes of knowing and seeing and although she had seen the man, before he rounded the corner,
and known that the news was bad, she could only guess at its
nature. She wanted to say — 'Never mind, Henry, we shall
manage.' Such a statement would merely provoke Griselda
who had a tendency to pick on one word and overwork it and
was likely now to say — *manage*. How do we manage? We
manage by scrimping and scraping and working harder than
labourers; but we *manage* to provide well for other people,
never for our own . . .

Jem had not stayed for dinner. It was an unwritten rule that
as soon as the last sheaf was carried the rest of the day was
given over to merry-making, eating, drinking, singing, dancing.
There was none of that at Knight's Acre, but if he hurried
down to the village, with any luck, he'd find somebody cele-
brating the end of harvest properly. And everybody welcome.

Henry quickly finished his meal and stood up. Joanna bolted
her last mouthful and stood, too. With the last field cleared,
gleaning could begin; and she and Henry would be alone. He'd
tell her what the man had said, and she'd do her best to make
light of it. Though it was bad! She knew by the way he stood in
the yard, irresolute. Quite unlike him!

He said, 'We'll take a holiday. We'll go blackberrying.'

She had never known him waste an hour. She thought,
'This is supposed to be a treat for me; because the bad news
concerns me.' Then she knew. The pretty pebbles *were* only
pebbles, not the jewels Henry had thought them.

'We'll need a basket. I'll get one.'

She ran back into the house.

'What *now?*' Griselda asked as though this were the
twentieth interruption.

'I want a basket. For blackberries.'

There were two on the larder floor. One was broken; she
took the other.

'Not that one,' Griselda said.

'The other has a hole.'

'Use a dock leaf.'

Joanna changed baskets and ran. Godfrey's wistful stare followed her. He longed to be free to join in all the exciting things
that Farder and Janna did outside the house, and more and

more often lately he'd said, 'Can't I come, too?' Sometimes he sensed that Farder would have taken him, but Mumma always said, 'No,' and gave some silly reason. Once not long ago Farder had said, 'Not today, my boy. But you're big enough now to help with the gleaning.'

'When?'

'I'll tell you.'

Mumma had been angry — not with Godfrey, but with everything else, he knew by the way she banged things about and muttered. (Indeed Henry's promise to take Godfrey to the field with him was the result of a realisation that the boy couldn't spend his life tied to his mother's apron strings. And Griselda had simultaneously realised it. Then what would she have left?)

Joanna, now that she knew what the trouble was, and how trivial compared with what it might have been — something about taxes! — decided not to open the subject but to let Henry tell her. She set herself to cheer his mood, as she had often done after a bad market day. She was not very successful because Henry was preoccupied with the problem of how to make the proposition sound attractive and then wondering why it must be made to sound so. Surely any girl . . . Surely just to get away, out of reach of Griselda's tongue . . .

It was the third week in September; under the trees it was cool, but in the clearings, where blackberry bushes grew the sun was warm and the air was scented by the ripe fruit. Joanna's chatter moved from the superstition about blackberries being cursed after Michaelmas to such beliefs in general. 'Like tying a ribbon on The Maiden', she said. 'You don't believe in such things, do you, Henry?'

'Not much. I may be wrong. I spent most of my time with Walter, you see; and he wasn't superstitious. I remember what he once said about salt and it being unlucky to spill it. He said it was concocted to make people careful.'

'Well,' she said, 'we shall see if Dick's blue ribbon and the good wish bring a better harvest next year.'

Dear child, you won't be here to see; you'll have forgotten such things.

He began to look around for a fallen tree on which to sit. Light talk could go on across a blackberry bush but it did not seem a suitable way to conduct a serious conversation. Presently he saw what he wanted and said, 'Let's sit down. Sweetheart, I've got something to tell you.'

She waited, but he looked so bothered and took so long to get started that she said,

'I'll tell *you*. Those jewels weren't worth anything.'

'On the contrary, they were worth a great deal of money. It is being handled for your welfare. Listen . . .'

She sat quite still, her hands, work-roughened, blackberry-stained, yet elegant, clasped together. Her crystal blue gaze fixed on his face discomfited him by its intentness and some of the sentences he had prepared forsook him. When he had blundered his way to the end she asked, in a thoughtful way,

'This money is mine? It really belongs to me?'

'Oh, beyond any shadow of doubt.'

'Then I should have some say in how it is spent. And that won't be on learning to embroider, or play the lute!' Something, amusement? derision? flashed in her eyes.

'Darling, it is for your good.'

'How do you know? I should hate it. Wasting time on such nonsense. I told you what we would do with the money.'

'You're too young to have any say. Too young to understand that the way you live . . .'

'And what is wrong with the way I live?'

'Everything. It may seem all right to you now but . . . It's the future we must think of. It always has bothered me, Joanna. I'd always hoped to be able . . .' Oh, why pursue that thought of failure? 'This is exactly what I hoped for you, and by sheer lucky chance . . . It is a wonderful opportunity and you must take advantage of it.'

'Must? Who says so?'

'I do sweeting. You must trust me to decide what is best for you.'

'Is it best for me? First I have nothing — more than once Griselda has called me a pauper, but I tried to earn what I ate — more than Dick ever did — and I am happy. Then *she* must go prying and suddenly I am rich. So *because* I am rich I must go away and live with strangers and break my heart. That is nonsense. Unless . . .'

Suddenly, with the widening of the pupils of her eyes, they darkened and she said in a less reasonable voice,

'Is it because of *her*; would she be nicer to you; would you be happier with me away? I know I did a silly thing. Two silly things. And both times you were kind and that angered her. Is *that* why you wish to be rid of me?'

'No. Griselda has nothing to do with this — except that she stumbled upon the jewels that made the whole thing possible. And I don't want to be *rid of you*. That is wrong. I shall miss you, your help with the work, your company. But it is for your good.' He flung off all of Walter's egalitarianism and spoke of her mother having been a lady and therefore it was only right and proper that she should be reared to be a lady too.

Convinced?

It seemed so, as he talked, dredging up things he had forgotten, the ladies' bower at Beauclaire; ladies bright as butterflies, doing their stitching, making their music.

Again she seemed to be listening.

She sat planning desperate things. Refuse to go. Be forcibly handled. Get there. Refuse to eat. Who would care? Run away. Where to? No welcome back here at Knight's Acre. Cast on to the scant charity of the roads and market places and every step taking her farther from Henry.

She said, 'You really *mean* this?'

'Yes, sweeting. For your good.'

'I see.' She did, in one blinding, emotion-intoxicated flash. She jumped up, skipped lightly over the tree trunk and began to run in the wrong direction, into the wood, towards the Three Pools.

She was light and nimble; he, though lean and hard, was more accustomed to plodding than running. She outdistanced him easily.

Neither of them could know that this was an inexact re-enactment of a scene in Spain played out between the mother of one of them and the father of them both. Tana had flung herself over a rotting balcony into a great river, sullied by the refuse of a great city. Joanna flung herself into a quiet pool, where the last of the water-lilies, yellow, pretty but stinking, floated on their pads above a surface green with duckweed. Sir Godfrey had been able to swim after a fashion, past the swollen carcase of a dead dog and a lot of kitchen rubbish; his son could only wallow through sucking mud towards the place where the lily pads were disturbed and some bubbles rising.

Dead?

Dead. And I killed her.

But in fact he had never really forgotten anything that Walter had ever told him, and one of Walter's most spectacular stories had concerned the bringing back to life of a man seemingly drowned dead. *He laid him over his knee,* Walter said, *and gave him a good bang. And that brought the water out. Then he put mouth to mouth and breathed in. That got the air back.*

He did it all, just as though Walter were standing behind him, giving directions. It worked. Not immediately; there was time enough for pity. So young, so frail: and for remorse — my fault! Then she gasped, once, twice.

Her first conscious act was to twist aside and vomit up the water that had reached not her lungs but her stomach. Henry held her as she retched.

'Better now?'

'Yes.'

'A fine fright you gave me. God! I thought you were dead.'

'I wanted to be. Rather than go away. Oh, Henry . . .'

As swiftly as she had turned from him, she turned towards him, her mouth smelling of muddy water, of blackberries and bile, pressed against his. Against his mouth, his eyes, his hair. She murmured endearments between the kisses. Things she could never have heard.

His seemingly uneventful life had held terrible moments but this was the worst. So stark, so shaming. Utterly shaming. A child, of eleven! It was unthinkable. But there it was.

He mastered himself, and her. He pulled himself free of her hands and stood up and said in a voice so hoarse that it growled, 'Come on. We're both soaked.'

Ignore it. Forget it. He began to walk back along the path and although she could outrun him his long loping stride gave him an advantage so that she had to take a running step now and then in order to stay level.

'Are you angry with me, Henry?'

'Yes, I am. Who wouldn't be? Such a daft thing to do.'

'The only thing. I couldn't live away from you, darling. And if you are angry I don't want to live.' He heard the threat and countered it.

'Walk ahead of me.'

As she passed him to obey she gave him a look, not shame-faced, not apologetic. Incredibly, a look of triumph, explained by her next words which she spoke without turning.

'*If* you were so angry, why did you pull me out?'

'Step out,' he said. 'We shall both catch our death of cold.'

'You love me, too, or you wouldn't have bothered. And I shall love you for ever and for ever, with all my heart and my soul and my strength.'

'Rubbish. If you were even mildly fond of me — or grateful — you'd do what I say.'

'Go away? And die of grief?'

'You don't know what you're talking about. Step out.'

They always knew, damn them, he thought. Tana had known that he loved her even as he was denouncing her. Griselda had known that he did not love her even as he was getting her with child.

The leaf-lined basket full of berries waited by the tree trunk. Neither noticed it.

Henry, hitherto not over-troubled by imagination, now considered the future with dismay. There had always been casual physical contact between them, as innocent on his part as on hers. She'd swing on his hand and say, 'What a lovely morning.' Between the church and the end of the pie-stall they'd stood close together with their sausages, and often, in the wagon she'd lean against him or snuggle close. No more of that! But how would he manage?

He could see where he'd made this error this afternoon. He should have said, 'Yes, with you away, things will improve between Griselda and me.' She'd have gone then, and within a week forgotten him and been happy as a lark. Not that he doubted the sincerity of her fondness for him. Since Robert's going who else had there been? Poor child.

A child of eleven, he thought, with another wave of self-disgust. He was far too ignorant of the world to know that races differed in the age of reaching maturity. Half Joanna's blood was that of a tribe where girls were nubile at eleven, often married before they were twelve. Tana had been only just over twelve when she gave her heart, once and for ever to Sir Godfrey.

While Henry walked in miserable self-abasement, Joanna went lightly, too happy and elated to be aware of the chilly touch of the drenched linen smock. Ordinarily she was susceptible to cold. She viewed the future with joy. Henry might be angry now because she had given him a fright, but he'd come round. She'd make him come round. She knew exactly what she wanted, and what it would be like when attained. She was even capable of distinguishing between the love she had felt for Robert and what she felt for Henry — so different that it was silly to use the same word! And there would be added zest in deceiving Griselda!

Griselda!

Joanna stopped dead and turned, her hand to her mouth.

'Holy Mother! We forgot the blackberries! Shall I run back?'

'No. We've got to get home and into dry clothes.'

She gave him one of her merry, companionable looks. 'Well then, the Devil can have them without bothering to fly over. And Griselda will have enough to scold about — the state we are in! What shall we tell her?'

'Accident.'

'Yes. I over-reached for water-lilies and fell in. You pulled me out.'

The deceiving of Griselda had begun, the logical outcome of those half-amused glances, a lifted shoulder, the change of voice when she was referred to, either as Griselda or the more significant *she*. All, up to this moment innocent enough, the natural allegiance of two people suffering the same affliction. Now, suddenly, it had a deeper significance, smacking of connivance. Ugly and dangerous.

They had now reached the fringe of the wood, more frequented, more threaded with tracks, for even Sir Richard had not thought of withholding from the Intake men the right of appanage, a right which allowed them to drive their pigs, in autumn to eat the acorns which the oak-trees dropped. Nor had any ban been laid upon the gathering of hazel nuts and blackberries. So there were several beaten paths and Henry said, 'All right, that's settled! Take the shortest way. To the yard . . .'

CHAPTER THIRTY-ONE

The yard was flooded with the mellow, pre-sunset light against which, emerging from the shade they both squinted their eyes and squinting, saw in the entry, between the end of the house and the ruin of what had been Walter's cottage, a black, moving mass, at first sight neither human nor animal.

Henry said, 'What the Devil?' and lengthened his stride. The mass resolved itself: two men and a donkey. All three skeletonally thin and in the last stages of exhaustion.

Beggars.

One man sat astride the donkey, sagging forward. The other man, on his feet, was engaged in the almost impossible task of supporting his fellow with one hand and with the other urging the animal to take its few last steps. Both men wore rags which fluttered in the little breeze; the one on his feet wore shoes, badly broken; the one on the donkey was barefoot.

Beggars.

The man on the donkey coughed, sagging lower and spitting. The other steadied him and said, 'Bear up, Nick. We're *home*!' With his free hand he flailed the donkey.

John and Young Shep! No time to think. Henry knew enough about animals to see that the donkey was about to fall. He leapt forward and caught Young Shep just as it did so.

John said, 'Henry! Thank God! He can't walk . . .' Then he coughed too, a cough less shattering, less prolonged, but bad enough. Recovering from it, he said with a pitiable imitation of his old jauntiness, 'I'm afraid we're in rather a poor way.'

'Let's get in,' Henry said. Young Shep, though reduced to skin and bone was an awkward burden. Unyielding, all arms and legs, quite different from old Father Ambrose who once lifted, had accommodated himself. By the feel of Young Shep Henry thought he might be dead, and as he staggered around the end of the house and towards the kitchen door he reflected that it might be just as well. John circled round, getting in the way, saying, 'We're home, Nick! We did it. We're home!'

Joanna followed; interested, but wary. She did not recognise either man.

Griselda was giving Godfrey one of his special little meals, a treat to make up for his lack of freedom. It was not exactly surreptitious, even she, at her worst, could not persuade herself that Henry would grudge his own child a couple of coddled eggs! But it was private, something between herself and her son. It could be made into quite a performance — hunting the eggs, letting him choose between white shell or brown, letting him crack the shells. She never shared these little repasts; she no longer cared what she ate. Just enough to keep alive, and she knew from experience that she could keep alive on very little. She no longer took any care over supper; dinner yes, or there would be complaints from Jem. More often than not, nowadays Henry and Joanna fetched the loaf, the bit of hard cheese, or cold bacon. And it delighted Griselda to say, 'He's had his supper.' In equal measure it annoyed her when Godfrey persisted in standing by his father and accepting, with obvious relish, something from his platter. 'That's right,' she would say. 'Make him sick. I told you, he's had his supper.'

Once Henry had said, 'But he's hungry. Anybody who can eat this must be sharp set.' And once he had said, 'At his age I could have eaten an old woman on a horse, harness and all.'

Now Godfrey, spoon poised, turned his head in a listening attitude. 'Farder,' he said, his face lighting up.

The door was flung open and Henry staggered in.

Just for once Griselda was rendered speechless. Henry and Joanna, all muddied and slimed with green, and two strangers; one dead; the other mustering a kind of smile on his death's head face and saying, 'Ah, Griselda! Still here.'

As Henry had done, she recognised John by his voice. Dumbfounded at first by surprise she was now rendered speechless by rage. Her mouth opened and shut without sound. Two more paupers! Joanna, Dick, Robert — worse than a pauper because, alive or dead he was a drain on the frail resources of Knight's Acre. And now this!

Henry lowered the dead-looking man into the chair which had been Tom's — specially provided for him as he grew more feeble. Seated, he began to cough, and John coughed too. Then Griselda recognised the lung-rot. It had been endemic in the orphanage, a slow killer for which there was no cure. And the nuns had believed that it was spread by coughing, sufferers had been ordered to turn their heads away when they coughed.

Still without speaking, she seized Godfrey by the hand and hustled him towards the door of the hall. He protested.

'I wanted to *see*. And I hadn't finished my supper.' She pushed him through the doorway, turned back, snatched up the bowl and the spoon, went into the hall and slammed the door behind her.

Here she could speak. 'Now mark my words. You are *never* to go near those men. Never!'

'Why not?'

'They have a sickness on them and if you go near them you will catch it and die.' Godfrey had never seen a dead person — only dead animals and birds. The thought that *people* could die was appalling. He stared at her wide-eyed and with something of the repulsion that attached itself to those who gave unwelcome information.

'Like rabbits?' he asked in a stricken voice.

'Yes. Just like that.'

He pushed the bowl away. 'I don't want any more.'

'Don't be silly. If you don't eat you will be sick, too.'

'And die?'

'Yes. People who don't eat do die.' Oh, why hadn't that pair died before they got here? Reluctantly Godfrey took up his spoon and began to eat, but with less than his normal gusto. As he ate Griselda repeated her warning, never, never to go near those men. She thought — God alone knows what else they have brought with them; other illnesses probably; lice almost certainly. And how could life be so organised as to avoid all contact?

The black pot used for broth stood on the hearth. It was seldom empty. Lumps of meat or stringy fowls were boiled in it, taken out and eaten. To the liquor onions, dried peas and beans were added, bones were returned to it. From time to time bones and other solids were scooped out and the process begun again. When the broth was often set like glue.

Henry lifted the pot and hung it on the hook over the dying fire. Without being told to Joanna added dry sticks, one by one until the fire revived. She put four bowls and four spoons on the table. John knelt by Young Shep and said, over and over again, 'We did it, Nick. We got here. I told you. Get some food inside you and you'll feel better.'

Henry said, 'Joanna, go and get out of those wet clothes.'

'What about you?'

'I'm all right.'

John turned on his knees. 'A little wine would help.'

'There's not a drop in the house.' As he went to fetch bread, Henry thought sourly that if John had been content to leave his share of the flock in the field, and buckled down to hard work, things might have been different here.

Young Shep had another coughing spell, and John held him, pressed to his mouth a piece of old linen, already horribly stained.

Henry's knowledge of the disease was less intimate than Griselda's, but he had seen people coughing and spitting in the market. To spit red, as people said, was a sure sign that the end was not far off.

'Lung-rot,' Henry said.

'It is *not!*' For a man in so weak, emaciated a state John spoke with astonishing vehemence. 'He caught a cold. In Italy — it can be very cold there, in winter — and it settled on his chest. I caught it, too, but more mildly.' He coughed. 'You can't sing or make music with a chest cold. So we began to go hungry — the very worst thing. A little good food and a rest will set him right. Won't it, Nick?'

Joanna came back. She had cleaned herself a bit, though green duckweed still clung to her damp hair. She had on the clothes she wore to church or market and she carried Henry's winter coat, a rough sheepskin.

'It'll warm you,' she said. Henry, that independent, strong-minded man, entertained for a moment an extraordinary thought. Nobody, since Mother died, has ever given my comfort or welfare any consideration. Even in the early days of their marriage Griselda had done her duty, but as a duty, no more. He thought — I have been nothing but a provider; the workhorse of the place. And things would be worse now; more to provide for. And so unfair. John could say, with justification, that this was his home. It was not Young Shep's!

The black pot bubbled. Joanna swung the hook so that the base of the pot was no longer over the fire. 'I'll do it,' she said, seizing the ladle, 'you cut the bread, Henry.' Having filled the bowls she lighted a candle.

John left his broth to cool while he fed little bits of sopped bread and spoonfuls of broth to Young Shep, encouraging him, as a fond mother would a child. It was ridiculous, Henry thought — two grown men! But it was touching too. Abruptly, Henry remembered a day when John had shovelled muck in order to spare Young Shep the distasteful job.

Something in Young Shep revived. He spoke for the first time. 'I never thought . . . we'd do it . . . Johnny boy.'

'I knew we could — because we must. And we did. There now, you sit back and rest.'

He came to the table and began on his own broth, cooling, slightly scummed with congealing fat. Between spoonfuls and great chunks of bread — he was plainly starving — he talked, bragging, bringing into this candle-lighted kitchen in a remote corner of England a tale of far places, of palaces, success and acclaim beyond any comprehension. His playing of the lute, the songs Nick made — even when translated — had been recognised, applauded. One great lord had commended them to another . . . They'd had a wonderful life, until . . .

'We were in Padua,' he said, 'and bound for Venice. The Doge had expressed a wish that we should sing and play before him. We had a new — a wonderful song all about an old custom they have. They call Venice the Bride of the Sea, you know and every year . . .' Coughing interrupted him.

'Better not talk,' Henry said. 'It'll keep.'

Yes, it would keep, the long sad story of the chest cold which would not budge; the attempt to earn a living and look after a sick man; falling sick himself; the decision to try to reach home; begging a way across Europe — and even the charitable feared the cough; the final act of despair — the sale of the lute and Nick's silver pipe to buy a passage from Calais to Bywater and the acquisition of the old donkey which had been abandoned as worthless.

'Yes,' John said, 'and Nick should be abed. Even if we could have paid, innkeepers don't like customers who cough. I can't remember where or when we last slept in a bed.'

'Shall I get it ready?' Joanna asked. Henry was about to say yes when the door opened and there was Griselda. She had taken a decision and nothing would move her. She had no fear for herself — had she been likely to catch the lung-sickness she'd have taken it long ago in the orphanage, but she had the child to consider.

Addressing Henry, ignoring everyone else she said,

'I'm not having them here. Let that be understood!'

'It's *my* house. And John's *home*,' Henry said. Young Shep had a coughing spell and she raised her voice. 'Listen to that! It may be your house, Henry Tallboys, but it's mine too. Hard earned if ever anything was and I will not have them under my roof. If they must stay, let them go in the barn.'

She was not aware of speaking and acting very much as the landlady of The Swan had done, all those years before. And it did not occur to her to explain the reason for banning them. Fear and fury, mingling with long cherished resentment had intoxicated her. The light of the one candle on the table, the fire dying down again to a glimmer, did not give light enough to show the crazy determination in her eyes.

Henry said, 'The barn isn't suitable.' It was in fact a ramshackle building, hastily built from odds and ends of timber, a thing he meant to replace; one day; when he had money and time.

'Go make that bed, honey,' he said to Joanna.

'Don't you dare,' Griselda said. She stopped by the hearth and thrust a dry twig into the embers; it blazed and holding it high she said, 'I'll set fire to the bed first. I'll fire the whole place. If I'm to have no say, I'll burn it down.'

Joanna watched. What would Henry do?

Henry went towards his wife and took hold of the wrist of the hand that held the burning twig. In a flash she transferred it to her other hand and jabbed it at him. Had his hair been dry it would have flared, but it was damp. He seized her other hand, threw the stick towards the hearth, took Griselda by the scruff of her neck and propelled her into the hall. But it was — and he knew it — only a temporary victory. There would be tomorrow . . . and tomorrow. Fire always accessible to her.

The smoke that the blazing brand had given off had set both the coughs going. Mastering his attack, John said, 'Actually a barn would be welcome, Henry.' Across his ravaged face there flitted the ghost of his old cheeky smile. 'I take it you married her.'

'Never mind that now.' Henry looked at Young Shep, his long limp limbs asprawl in the chair. 'It'd be easier if I could get him on my back and he'd put his arms round my neck and hold on.'

Young Shep had not spoken since he'd said, 'I never thought we'd do it, Johnny boy,' and now John answered for him, as a mother would do for a child. 'Oh, Nick'll hold on, won't you, Nick? Just one more effort, my dear, then you can rest and get better.'

Young Shep still said nothing, but his sunken, over-bright eyes looked at John with adoration, and he nodded.

Well, Henry thought, love comes in all shapes and sizes. He slipped off the cumbersome coat and went towards the chair.

Joanna said, 'Henry!'

'Well?'

'Wouldn't the rooms across the yard be better?'

'Of course! Why didn't I think?'

'But the door is blocked . . .' She was already busy with the lantern, lighting its candle from the one on the table. 'I'll help,' she said. 'You chop the rosemary and I'll pull away the other stuff.'

Outside Henry found a hatchet and together they went around the end of the pavilion to the door of the pavilion which had figured so largely in both their lives — old lives, over and done with, like a cast snake-skin.

The rosemary, overgrown as it was, offered little resistance and as Henry hacked at it and Joanna ripped down the honey-suckle trails, he had time to think. He thought of John's reply to Young Shep's one remark. 'I knew we could — because we must.' That was the voice of the survivor — of all survivors; and he was one. Because he must he could; because he could he must . . .

He could and must disregard utterly what had happened by the pool that afternoon. Any man worthy of the name should be able to rule himself. He must, because he could, now assume responsibility for supporting two sick men — one perhaps not for long. John, not yet spitting red, might linger for years.

'That'll do,' he said. 'Stand clear.' He put his shoulder to the door which briefly resisted and then slowly creaked open. It was impossible not to remember that night when, entering in anger, he had found Paradise, but he thought of it, and of the morning that followed in a distant kind of way, just one more thing that he had survived — like Walter's death, and Sybilla's, and his joyless marriage which had this evening revealed itself for what it was.

Joanna was remembering, too. Those few happy times when she and Robert, entering by the window had played pebble games with jewels; and the plan she had made to hide him here, and of what had come of that. All past now; not exactly forgotten, but pushed aside. *Lived through.* That was the answer. It wouldn't do, she realised, to make any open display of her love. It simply made Henry uncomfortable and therefore angry. He was married to Griselda, who, by her behaviour this evening had surely forfeited any claim to consideration. Griselda had threatened her with places where mad people were confined, chained, whipped. And surely any woman who threatened to set her own house on fire was mad. And bad.

Rounding the house again, Joanna said, 'Shall we go gleaning tomorrow? If we do I think Godfrey should come. You did promise ...'

'So I did.'

With instinctive feminine wisdom Joanna knew better than to swing on his hand, clutch his arm or press against him. She said, conversationally, 'I want to hear more of John's stories, when his cough is better. Don't you?'

'Yes. But there'll be time for that. The thing is now to get them both to bed.'

Back in the kitchen, Henry went straight to what had always been regarded as Tom's chair, stooped to a level at which Young Shep, urged by John, helped by John, could clamber on to his back. Upon shoulders, braced to take the load ...

NORAH LOFTS

KNIGHT'S ACRE

Sir Godfrey Tallboys was a knight-errant, famous for his success at tourneys, but far from wealthy. In an attempt to make his fortune he left his wife Sybilla and travelled to Spain to fight a minor crusade against the moors.

But treachery lurked in that far distant land and soon Sir Godfrey became a prisoner, a helpless slave in a hostile country. Back in quiet Suffolk he was reported dead. And so it fell to Sybilla to fend for the whole family. The modest house of Knight's Acre became the scene of much hardship and poverty, and only someone with Sybilla's determination could triumph at last. But Sybilla, resigned to growing old before her time, was to find that life still held many surprises for her . . .

CORONET BOOKS

NORAH LOFTS

CROWN OF ALOES \

Through her marriage with Ferdinand of Aragon, Isabella of Castile united their neighbouring countries to form the kingdom of Spain. It is through Isabella's own eyes that we experience the towering events of her day. The harsh world of European politics with its brilliant intrigue, magnificent personalities, danger and excitement is contrasted with the poverty of the peasants, the cruelty of the Inquisition and the massive discomforts of everyday life in fifteenth-century Europe.

But through it all we discover the fascinating character of Isabella herself – a queen with the mind of a statesman, the courage of a soldier and the tender feelings of a passionate woman.

CORONET BOOKS

HISTORICAL ROMANCE FROM CORONET

NORAH LOFTS

☐	15111 0	The King's Pleasure	75p
☐	16950 8	A Rose for Virtue	50p
☐	16216 3	Lovers All Untrue	50p
☐	19352 2	Crown of Aloes	50p
☐	17826 4	Charlotte	50p
☐	18403 5	Nethergate	50p
☐	20764 7	Knight's Acre	60p

JUDITH SAXTON

☐	20650 0	The Bright Day Is Done	70p

ANYA SETON

☐	15701 1	Katharine	£1·25p
☐	15700 3	The Turquoise	80p
☐	02713 4	Avalon	80p
☐	01951 4	The Winthrop Woman	£1·00
☐	02469 0	Dragonwyck	80p
☐	17857 4	Green Darkness	£1·00

All these books are available at your local bookshop or newsagent, or can be ordered direct from the publisher. Just tick the titles you want and fill in the form below.

Prices and availability subject to change without notice.

CORONET BOOKS, P.O. Box 11, Falmouth, Cornwall.

Please send cheque or postal order, and allow the following for postage and packing:

U.K. — One book 19p plus 9p per copy for each additional book ordered, up to a maximum of 73p.

B.F.P.O. and EIRE — 19p for the first book plus 9p per copy for the next 6 books, thereafter 3p per book.

OTHER OVERSEAS CUSTOMERS — 20p for the first book and 10p per copy for each additional book.

Name ....

Address ....

....